MARVEL

MYTHS

AND LEGENDS

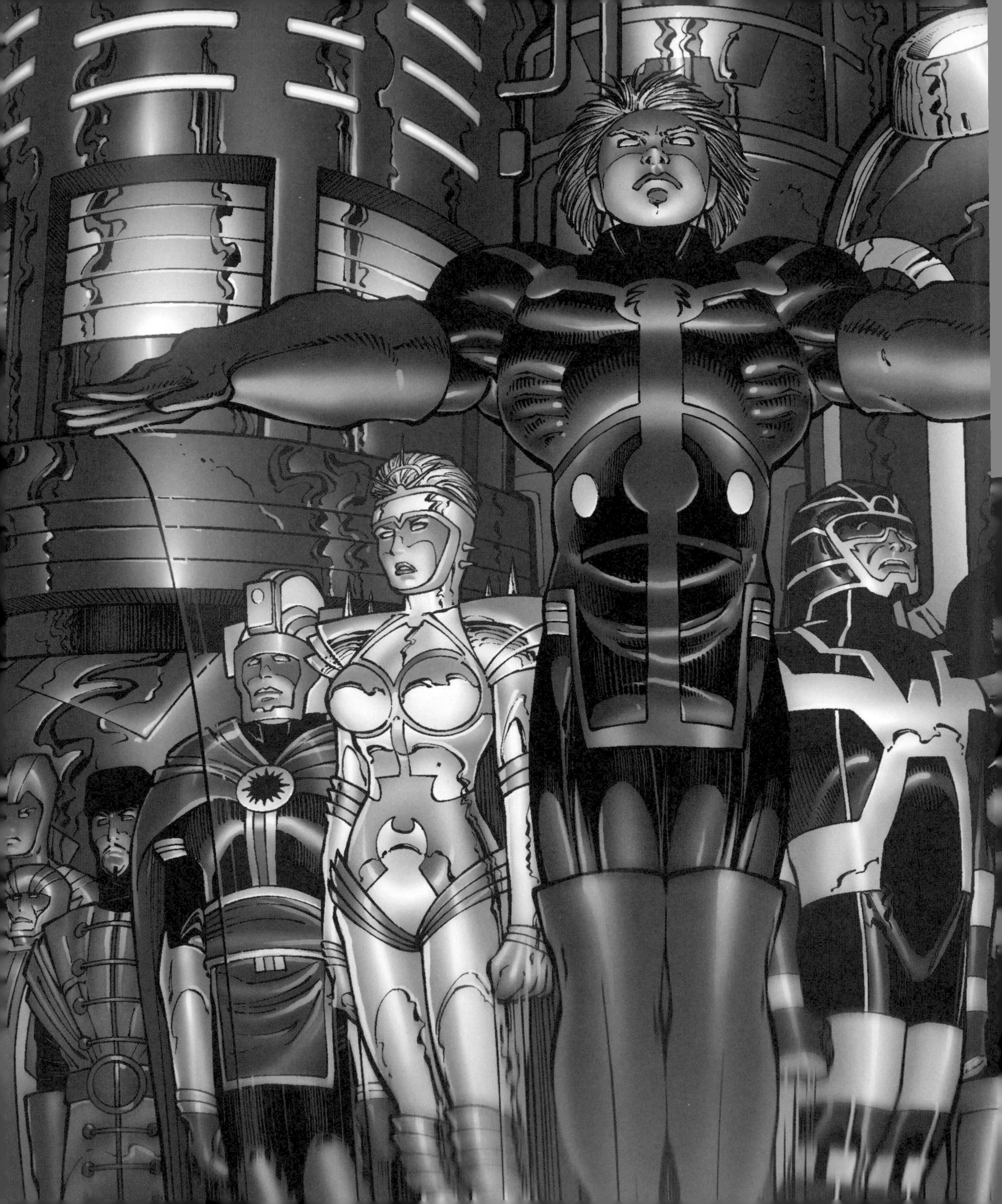

MARVEL

MYTHS

AND LEGENDS

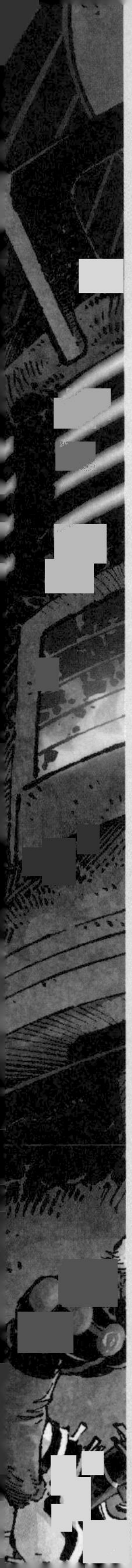

CONTENTS

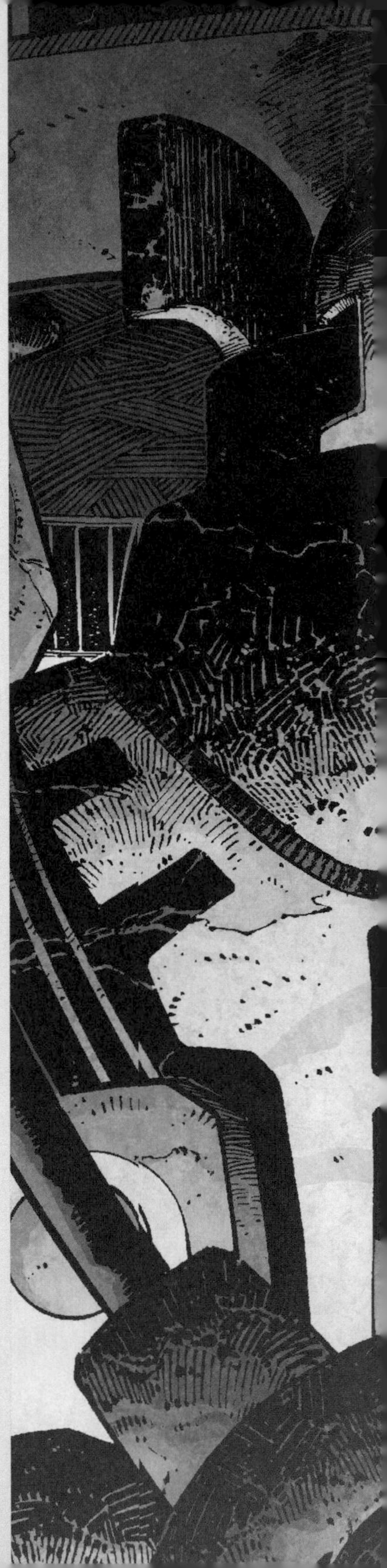

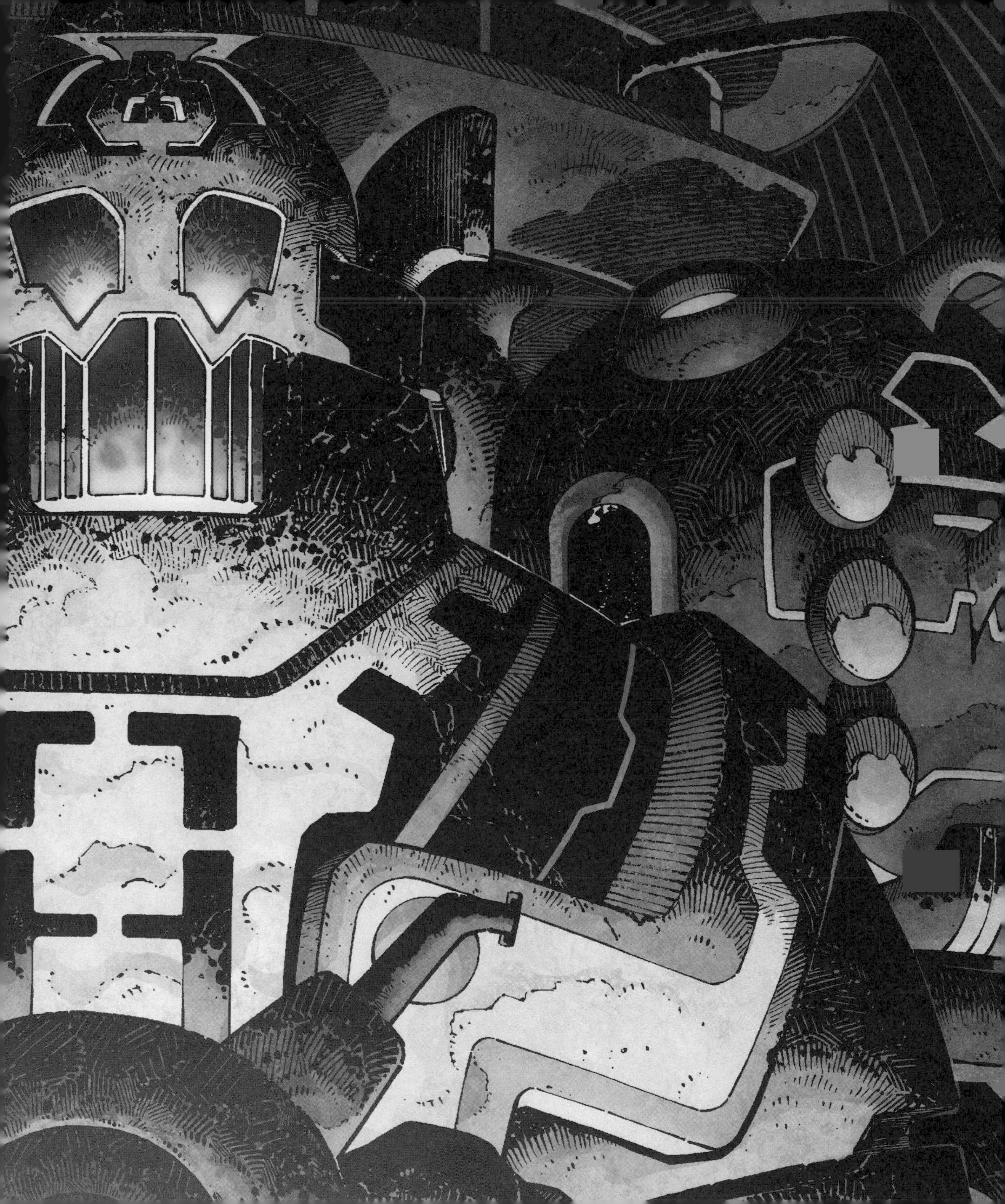

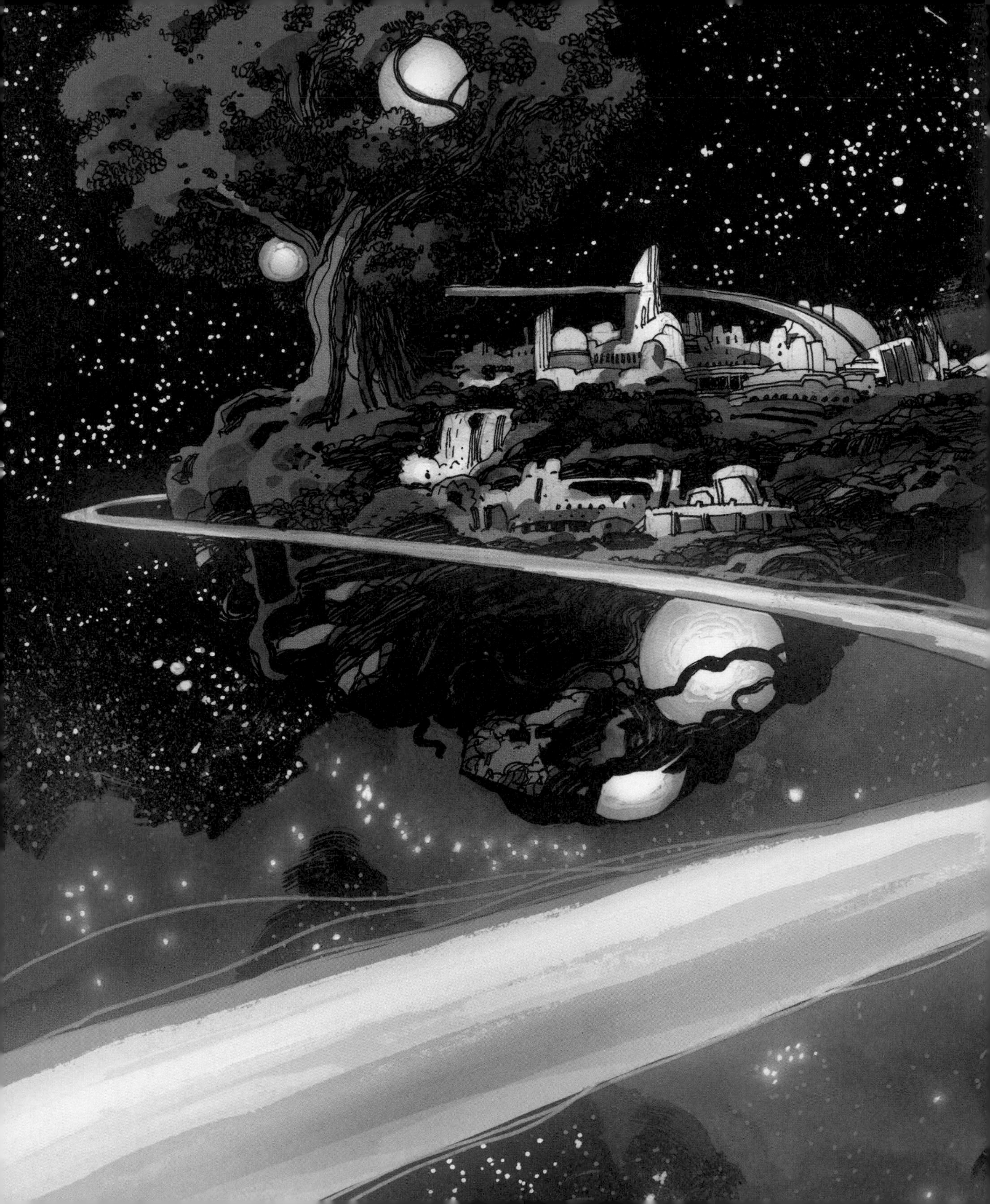

INTRODUCTION

All myths are stories. They tell of wondrous beings in fabled lands bestride with gods and goddesses. Myths are borrowed, retold, and refreshed. They are stories of beginnings that shape the way people understand themselves and their world—and resonate over millennia.

Marvel Myths and Legends lifts the veil on the mysterious realms of the Marvel Universe, recalling the long-ago sagas and legendary events that ultimately gave birth to the modern age of Super Heroes. A compendium of individual stories, this book chronicles the exploits of numerous elder gods, divine pantheons, and otherworldly mages. Featuring familiar heroes such as Thor, Doctor Strange, Black Panther, and the Avengers, these epic tales weave together to form an illuminated tapestry that spans the entire history of the Marvel Universe. From the birth of Earth-Mother Gaea at the dawn of time to the awakening of the Dark Celestials in the present day, these stories expose a history that has unfolded, largely in secret, over billions of years. *Marvel Myths and Legends* explores the mythic folklore and the tumultuous, time-lost events that underpin and enrich one of today's most beloved fictional universes.

The Marvel Age of Comics began with the launch of *Fantastic Four* #1 in 1961. It was clear from the outset that there was something different about this new line of comics. Pioneering creators Stan Lee, Jack Kirby, and Steve Ditko never talked down to their readers, trusting a more sophisticated approach to storytelling would be appreciated. Crucially, as the line grew in size, it became apparent that the new characters all shared the same universe. Spider-Man encountered the Fantastic Four who battled the Hulk who clashed with Thor.

Early Marvel writers and artists laid the foundations for a modern-day mythos. Of course, the comics were not created in a vacuum, and Lee and his creative partners drew some of their inspiration from the deep well of classical myths and legends. Their reworking of Thor as a Super Hero was perhaps the clearest example of this. However, what began as a simple conceit, soon developed into something far grander. Fueled by Lee and Kirby's interest in the Norse Edda—and their conviction that those sagas had universal appeal—the *Thor* comic broadened in scope to encompass the entire Asgardian pantheon. Soon, other ancient gods like the Olympians were brought into the fold and, similarly, the mystical beliefs and philosophies of East Asia were used to expand the cosmology of Doctor Strange. But the Marvel team didn't merely take from the past, they augmented it, reshaping their source material into something spectacularly original.

In the 1970s, Kirby added another beam to the mythical framework of the Marvel Universe. Reflecting the then-popular theory that aliens had visited Earth in ancient times, he created the star-spanning Celestials and their genetically-engineered offspring, the angelic Eternals and the devilish Deviants. Authors Roy Thomas, Mark Gruenwald, and Neil Gaiman helped integrate these concepts into the wider Marvel Universe. Significantly, Thomas, a former English/history teacher, wove numerous classical references into the Marvel canon. Among his many contributions, he entwined the history of the heroic Black Knight more closely with Arthurian legend and, in homage to the Himalayan utopia of Shangri-La, he conceived the heavenly city of K'un-Lun as a home for the Immortal Iron Fist.

Recent Marvel writers have tread a similar path, with Ta-Nehisi Coates referencing African deities in his exploration of Black Panther's Wakanda and Jason Aaron imagining a team of stone-age Avengers who operated a million years ago. And, just as the legends of old evolved over time, Marvel mythology has been granted a new lease of life in the Marvel Cinematic Universe, with blockbuster movies such as *Thor, Black Panther, Doctor Strange,* and *The Eternals* remaking the myths for a wider audience.

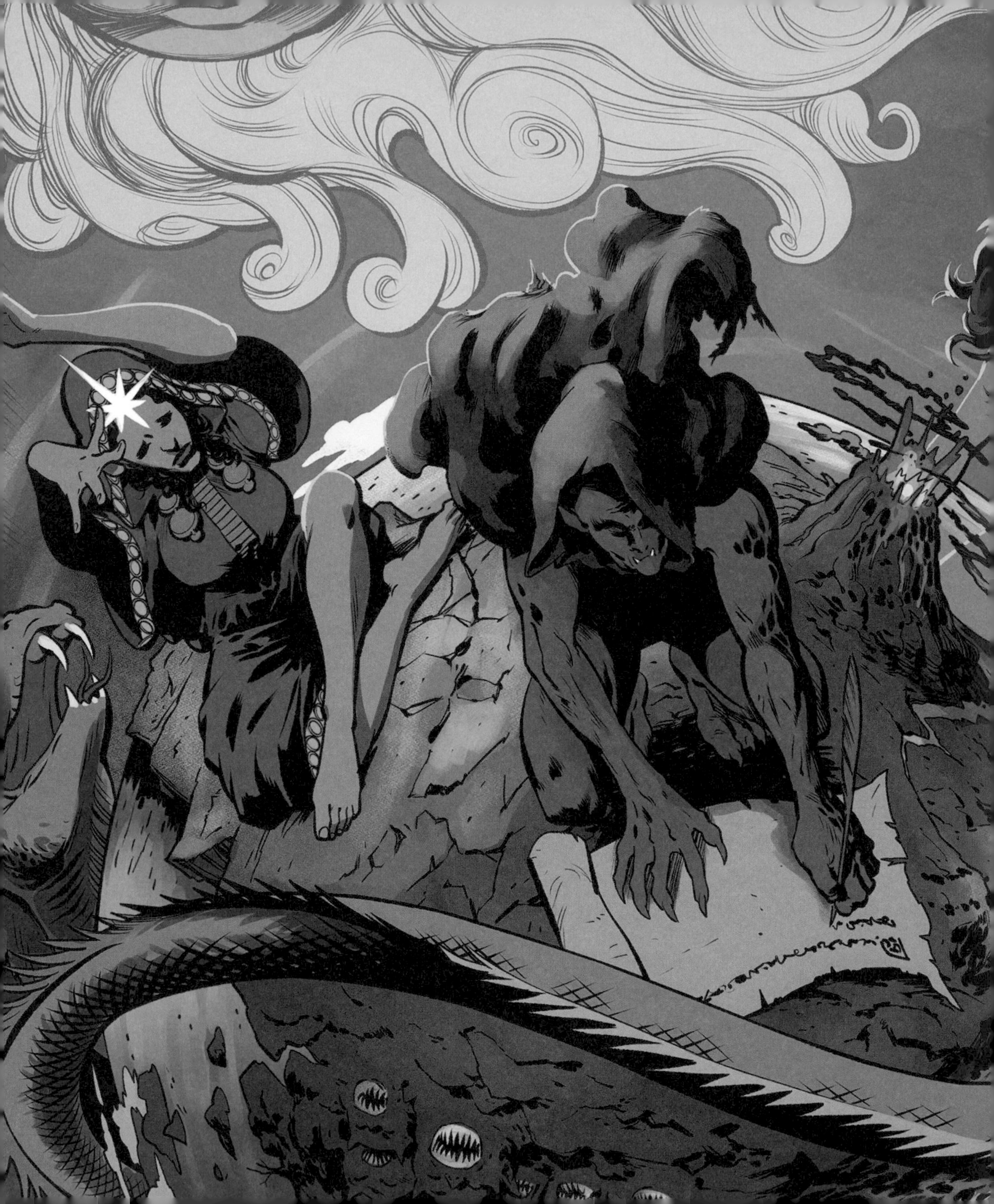

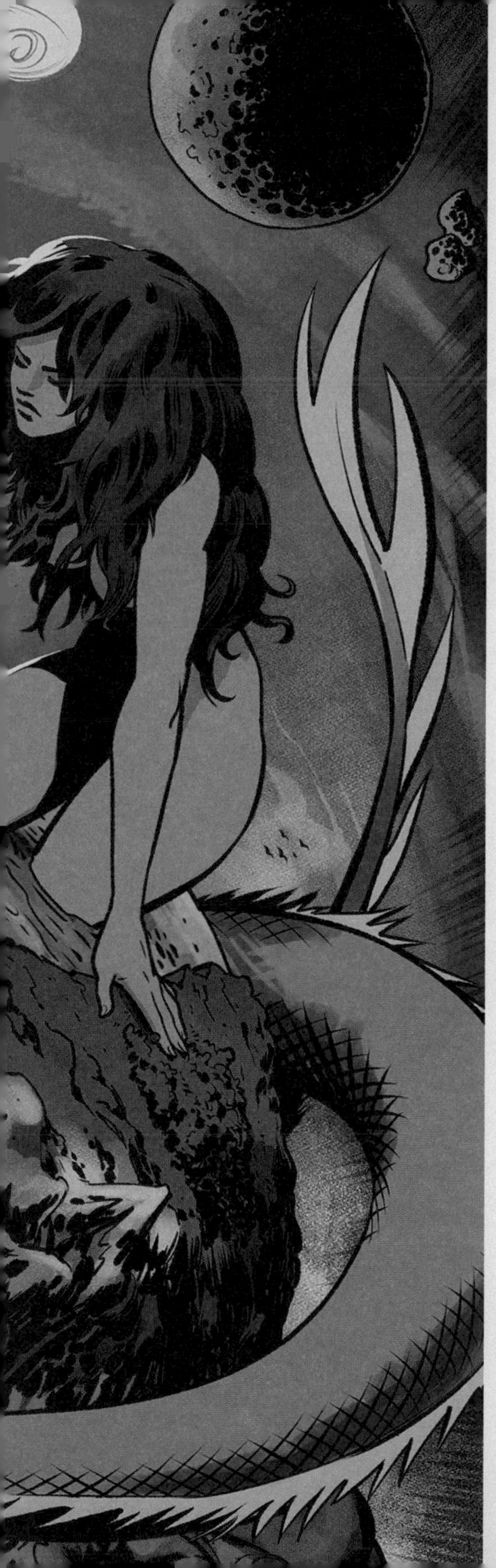

FIRST MYTHS

From the beginning, Earth was a breeding ground for beings with enormous powers and equally enormous appetites and desires. Elder gods, degenerate demons, and mighty heroes all proliferated thanks to the Earth's unique biosphere, infused as it was with cosmic energies and the essence of a dead Celestial. First there was Earth-Mother Gaea, who nurtured the planet's emergent life-forms. Then came Atum, who slew the demons. Ultimately, Odin and the Prehistoric Avengers emerged as the world's first coalition of superpowered individuals.

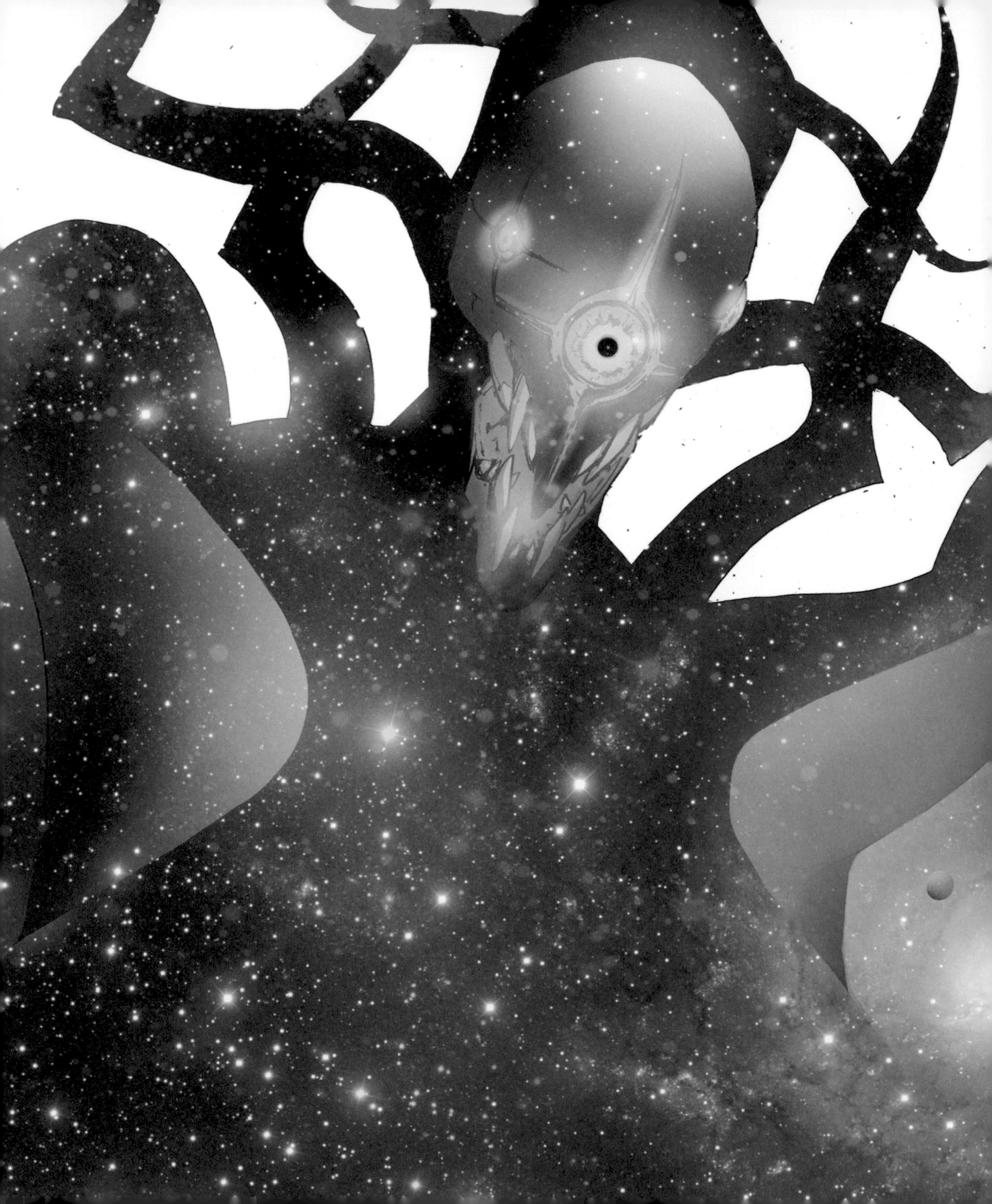

Birth Pangs

In a time before time, the First Firmament created the Celestials and set in motion an unimaginable series of events that would shake the cosmos and make Earth unique among the stars.

The First Firmament was the first universe ever to exist. Self-aware, it knew all there was to know about the nature of its own reality. Most of all, it knew that it was alone. To assuage its loneliness, it created offspring—cosmic entities designed to entertain and enthrall. Some of these beings, known as Aspirants, worshiped the First Firmament unconditionally and prayed that their universe would remain unchanged forever. Others, called Celestials, were compelled to continually discover more about their own nature—to grow and evolve, and to transform the universe as they themselves changed.

Inevitably, open conflict erupted between these two factions. Celestials attacked Aspirants, and the First Firmament was convulsed by all-out war. The battle raged for eons, on such a scale that the First Firmament itself was shattered into countless fragments when the warring parties finally detonated their ultimate weapons. The splintered remains of the Celestials and Aspirants became universes in their own right, forming a new Multiverse that was the next iteration of reality, the Second Cosmos. No longer in thrall to the First Firmament, the Celestials were free to explore this virgin cosmos as giant space gods, visiting planet after planet and experimenting upon any indigenous species they encountered.

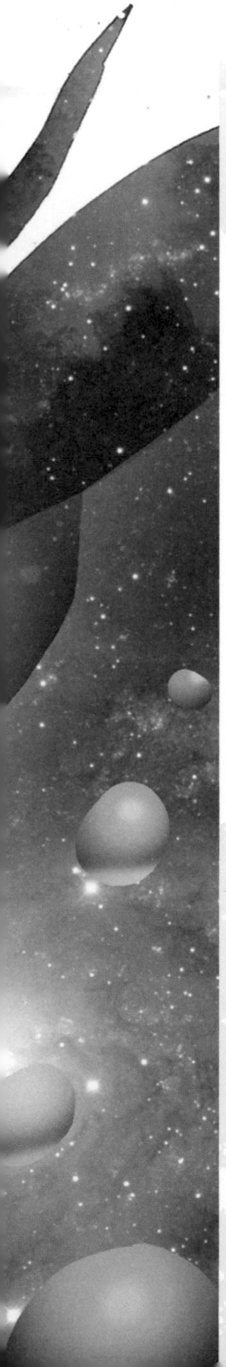

In the beginning...
To escape a profound sense of loneliness, the sentient universe of the First Firmament created life. Its children fell into conflict, however, and shattered the very fabric of reality.
The Ultimates 2 #6, Jun. 2017

Billions of years later, the planet Earth emerged from a maelstrom of space debris and roiling gases, forming around a bright yellow star that would one day be known as Sol. While the planet was still fresh and new, it was visited by the Celestial Progenitor. The space god was dying, and his arrival was merely happenstance, a cosmic fluke that would have a profound influence on the fate of the Earth and its inhabitants. Somewhere in the vastness of space, the Progenitor had been infected by a swarm of cosmic locusts called the Horde. Consumed from within by these monstrous parasites, the Progenitor had crashed to Earth in a fit of anguish and all-consuming insanity. As the Celestial's life force ebbed away, his blood and decaying flesh seeped into the very fiber of the planet itself. This forever altered the Earth, making it unique among the stars as a potent breeding ground for superhuman beings and events. The Progenitor's essence added to a primordial soup that would give birth to countless myths and legends—and ultimately give rise to the modern age of Super Heroes.

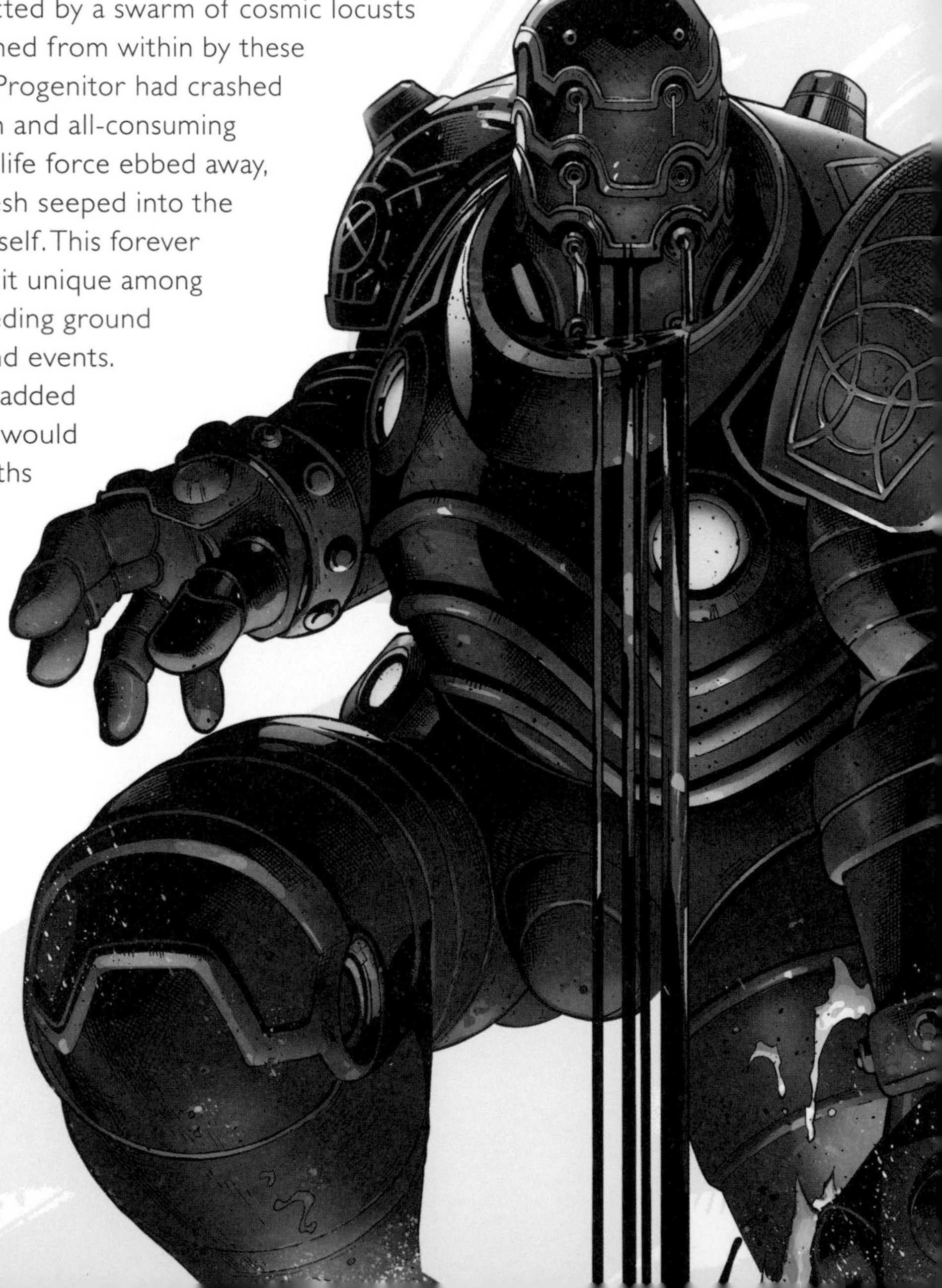

Death throes
Infected by cosmic locusts, the Celestial Progenitor fell to Earth and breathed his last—his blood and bone infusing the planet's rich biosphere with the potential for superhuman development.
Avengers #5, Sep. 2018

Seeds of Life and Death

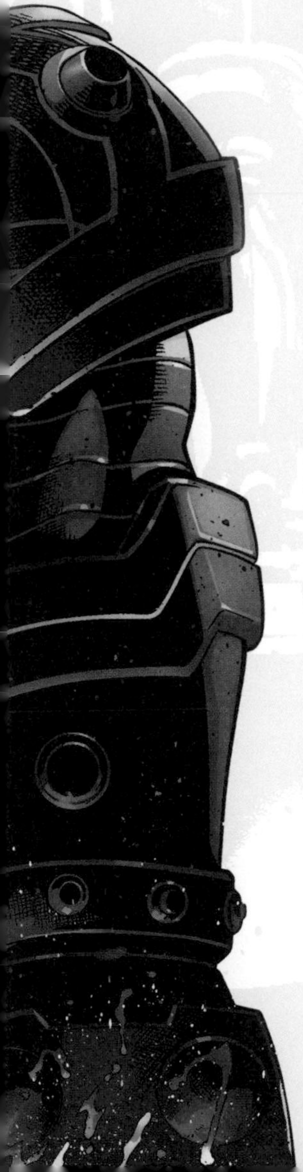

Born from the planet's very essence, the Elder Gods emerged as Earth's first living creatures—primal beings whose passions and rivalries lit up the heavens.

While Earth's soil was being altered by the decomposing body of the Celestial Progenitor, the heavens were undergoing a similar transformation. As the planet slowly cooled and took on its final form, the skies above it crackled with power and the potential for life. This energy exploded into sentience to become the Demiurge, the living consciousness of Earth's fertile biosphere. In a huge burst of creativity, the Demiurge showered the Earth with sparks of its own life force. This energized the primeval mud, bringing forth Earth's first life-forms—the Elder Gods. These entities were ethereal in nature, as much abstract concepts as corporeal beings, and they proliferated in number.

Some of the Elder Gods were benevolent and nurturing while others were selfish and hostile. Earth-Mother Gaea devoted herself to protecting the organic life beginning to evolve in Earth's oceans, while sinister Chthon sought to pervert nature with dark magic. The serpentine Set plotted global domination, in stark contract to the mystical Oshtur, who promoted concepts of harmony and universal justice. Over time, Set discovered that he could increase his own power by feasting on the life energies of his rivals, and so it was that the concept of death entered the world. Set devoured many of his enemies, becoming Earth's first murderer in the process.

Following Set's heinous example, many Elder Gods degenerated into life-stealing demons, constantly vying for power and supremacy. Gaea was among the few who held out against the violent madness, a madness she recognized instinctively as evil. She feared that the battling demons would wipe out all life on Earth and she meditated on how best to save the world she loved. Her yearning called forth the Demiurge and together they conceived a child who would become a powerful new force for good.

Shortly after her union with the Demiurge, Gaea retreated into Earth's cooling depths to give birth. Blazing with the power of a thousand suns, the golden Atum emerged from within his mother. He was Earth's first true god, the first of many who would protect the planet and its life-forms. Atum slew the demons, but at great personal cost. As he defeated each of his foes in turn, his body absorbed their demonic forms, becoming hideously misshapen. Over time, he became the monstrous Demogorge, the God-Eater.

"...my purpose is to destroy your degenerate forms." The Demogorge

When his task was complete, the Demogorge released the energies he had absorbed, seeding the skies with "godstuff." Transformed back into Atum, Earth's protector then flew into the sun to slumber for untold millennia.

Atum's actions changed the Earth for all time. When humankind took its initial faltering steps, its embryonic consciousness tapped into the "godstuff" left behind by Atum, creating many different godly pantheons. The Asgardians, the Orishas, and a host of others were born and sustained by the faith of early humanity. Empowered by the energies bequeathed by Atum, Earth's gods were given form by the will of humankind.

Golden child
Born from a union between Earth-Mother Gaea and the Demiurge, Atum possessed the power of a thousand suns. As Earth's first true god, his legend burned brightly for eons.
Thor Annual #10, Oct. 1982

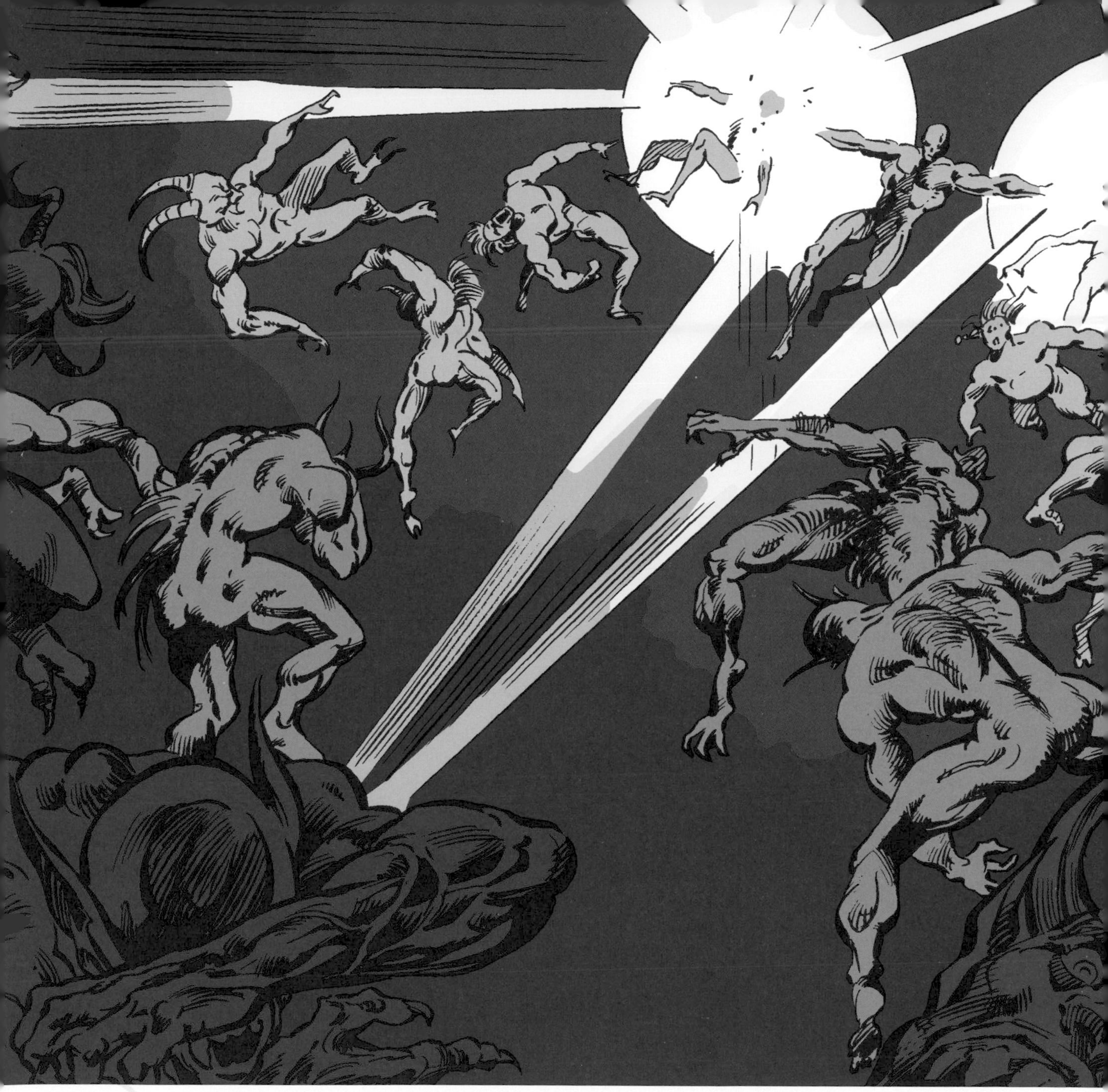

Demonic devastation

As he slew Earth's first generation of demons, Atum absorbed their appalling power and was transformed into the demonic Demogorge.

Thor Annual #10, Oct. 1982

First Champions

In the distant past, a band of heroic individuals pooled their strength to protect nascent humanity—their righteous call-to-arms echoing down through the ages.

One million years ago, a second Celestial reached the shores of Earth. Zgreb had come searching for the Progenitor, but like his missing comrade he, too, was felled by the Horde. The parasitic creatures had been dormant deep beneath the surface of the planet and, as Zgreb landed, they awakened to his presence. Acting like a living contagion, they infected the Celestial's giant body, driving him hopelessly mad. In his delirium, Zgreb began to tear apart the planet in a vain attempt to find his lost companion. Humankind's primitive forebears looked on with incomprehension, unaware they faced extinction even before they had a chance to make their mark on the universe. There were other witnesses, however, who recognized the significance of these events and were unwilling to go down without a fight.

An assemblage of mighty beings watched Zgreb's senseless rampage. Brought together by Odin Borson, the recently anointed king of the Asgardian pantheon, the team was a unique collection of gods, monsters, and cavemen, some of whom had been blessed—perhaps cursed—with the incalculable power of the stars. They called themselves the Avengers, and they had already saved Earth more times than Odin cared to count.

"All accounted for... And assembled." The prehistoric Black Panther

Agamotto, son of Oshtur and the world's first Sorcerer Supreme, was the group's quiet voice of reason. The first Black Panther provided the team with animal cunning and stealth, while the hulking Starbrand was the embodiment of raw strength. Iron Fist was a martial artist hailing from the mystical realm of K'un-Lun, and the Phoenix was the first human vessel to contain

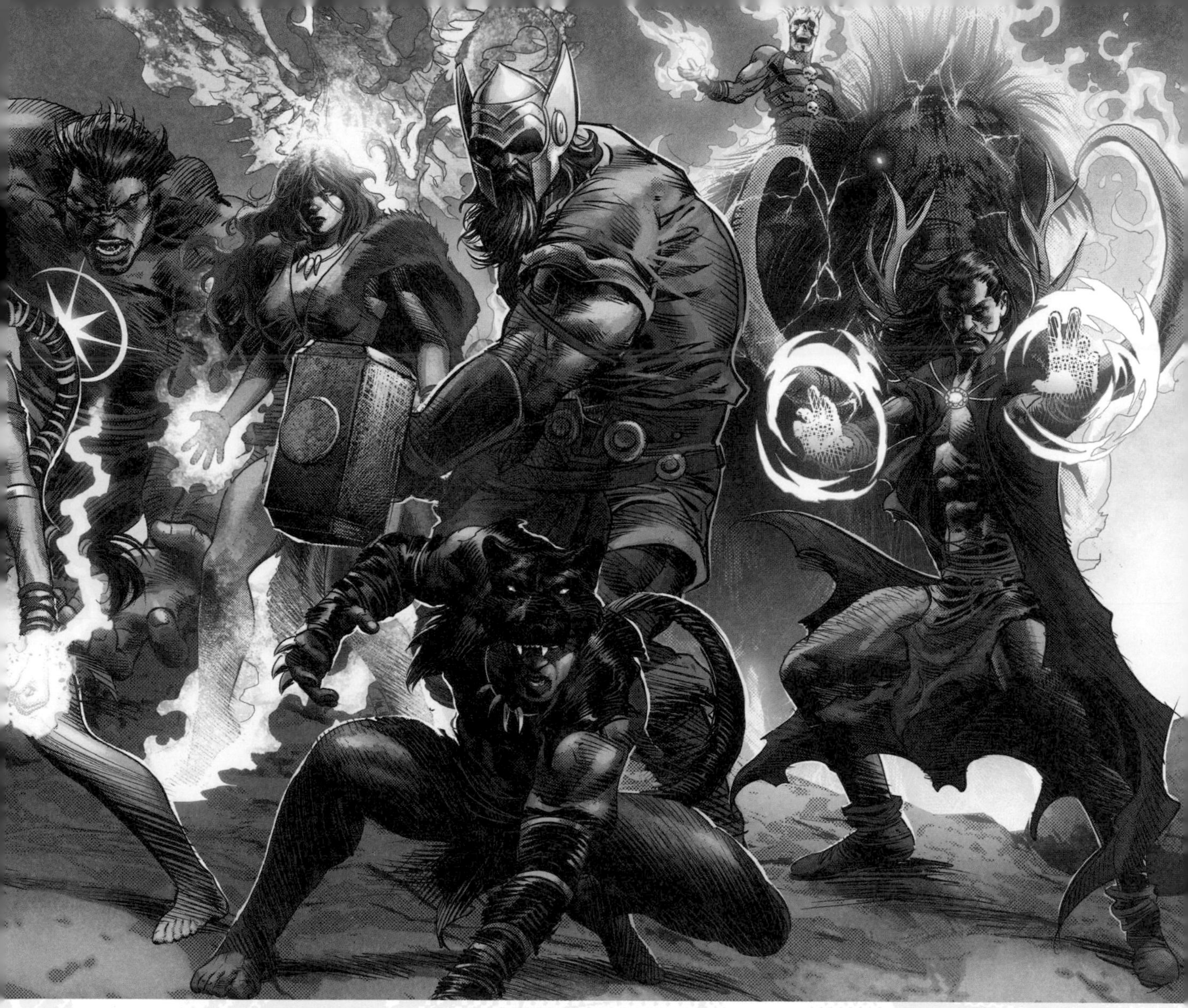

the unimaginable power of the cosmic Phoenix Force. Finally, there was Ghost Rider, a boy who had gained infernal abilities but lost his soul in a devilish pact with a demon, and who now charged into battle astride a fiery mammoth. In Odin's own words they were "a ragged assortment" but they were they were Earth's only hope. Suggesting they might leave the corpse of Zgreb pinned to the moon as a warning to others who would dare threaten humanity, Odin led his team against the deranged Celestial.

Primeval power
Odin Borson gathered together the Prehistoric Avengers—Iron Fist, Starbrand, Phoenix, Black Panther, Ghost Rider, and Agamotto—to protect and preserve planet Earth in ancient times.
Marvel Legacy #1, Nov. 2017

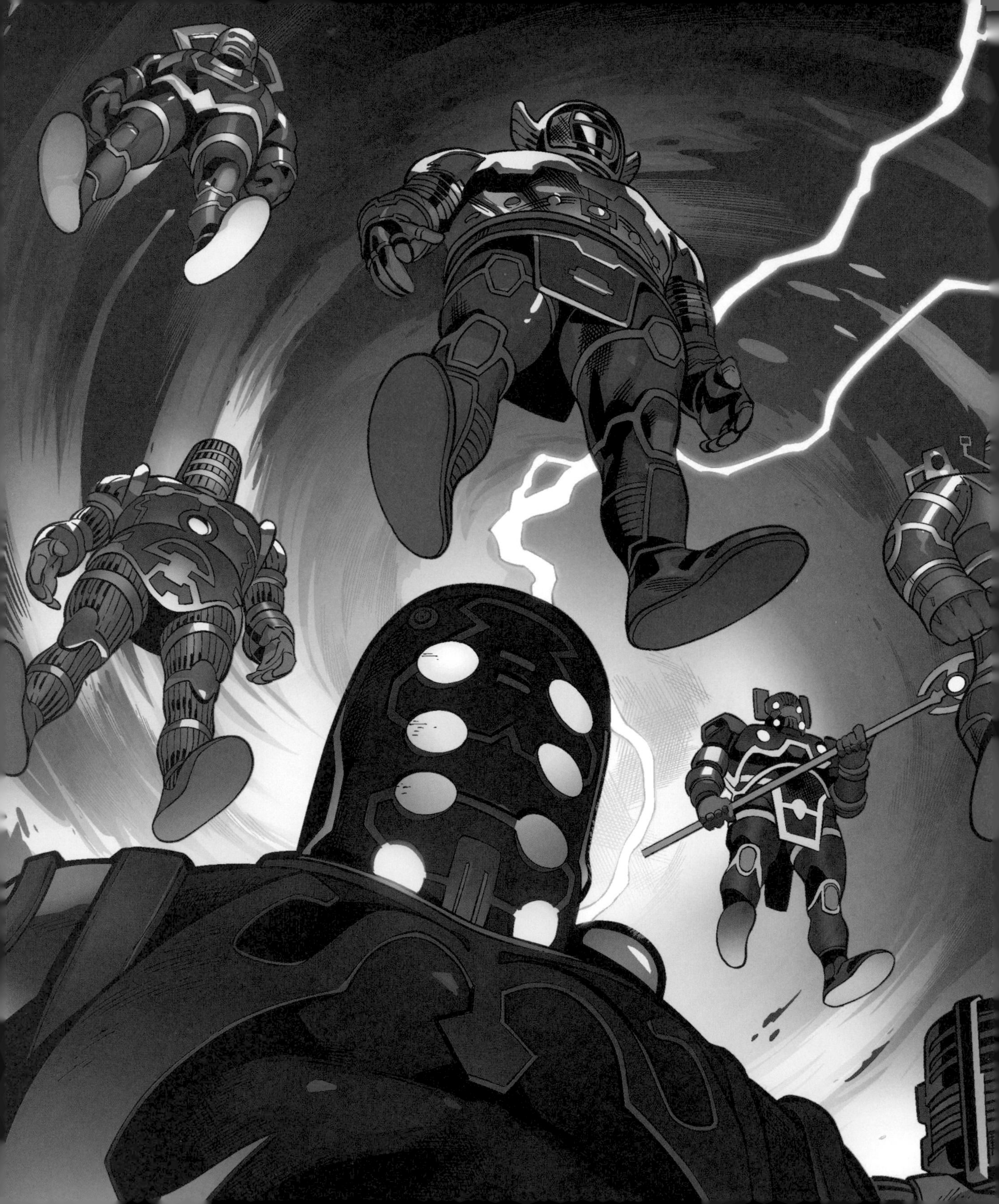

Zgreb fought back, but was ultimately felled by a blow from Mjölnir—Odin's recently forged mystical hammer—that had, until now, proved to be somewhat unwieldy. Anxious to celebrate their victory, the Avengers buried the Celestial's body deep within the bowels of the Earth. They hoped they had seen the last of his kind.

They hoped in vain, however. A short while later the First Host arrived—ten Celestials descending from the heavens to plant their mighty feet upon the Earth. Fearing the space gods sought to avenge Zgreb's death, Odin marshaled Earth's Mightiest Heroes once more. On the eve of battle, the Asgardian raised a toast to his fellow warriors. "Here's to endings! And to good deaths for us all!" he intoned. Then the Avengers faced their towering foes without fear; faced them with fire and fury and the righteousness of their cause.

In the end it was all for nothing, and the Celestials batted away the heroes as if they were no more than bothersome insects. The First Host had not arrived on some personal vendetta, but on a mission of far greater importance, and the machinations of gods and godlings were beneath their notice. As he knelt at the feet of the Celestials, the defeated Odin finally realized how insignificant his power was in comparison with that of the space gods.

"I will fight until the final twilight." Odin

However, Odin and his fellow champions had set an example that would endure for eons. Despite insurmountable odds, they had banded together to defend the Earth. While the details of their existence would not be revealed for centuries, many other heroic teams followed in their footsteps. The legacy of the Prehistoric Avengers lived on, and their myth was reflected in modern times when other superpowered individuals set aside their differences to form a new team of Avengers.

Heavenly visitation
A million years ago, the First Host of Celestials arrived on Earth. Their visitation would give birth to countless myths and legends—and alter the planet's destiny forever.
Avengers #3, Aug. 2018

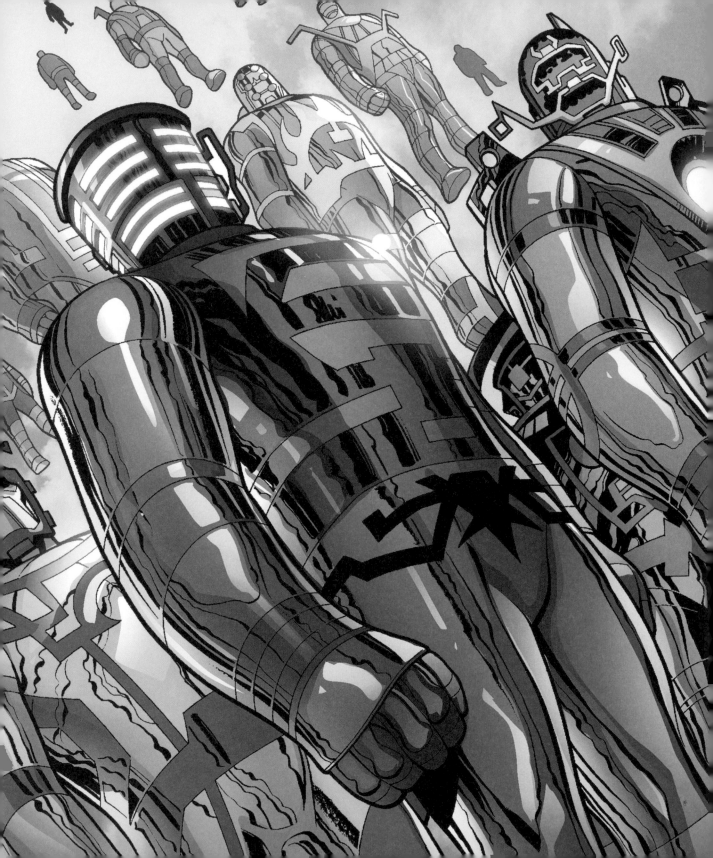

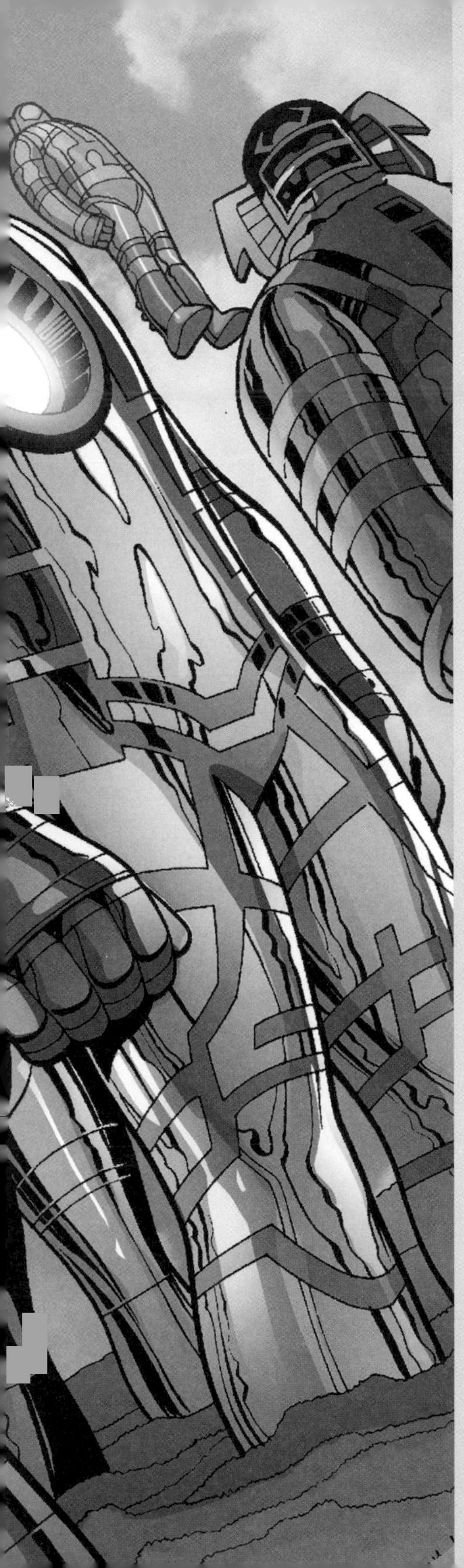

SPACE GODS DESCEND

The spacefaring Celestials visited Earth in ancient times and experimented on primitive protohumans, creating two offshoots of humanity: the godlike Eternals and the monstrous Deviants. The Eternals built, while the Deviants destroyed. Humankind's encounters with these mighty beings spawned innumerable myths and legendary tales. In modern times, the Celestials returned to assess and pass judgment on the success of their genetics experiment. It fell to a third generation Eternal, known as Ikaris, to rally his fellow Eternals, including fierce Thena and swift Makkari, to defend humanity.

Coming of the Celestials

The Celestials arrived from outer space to shape Earth's destiny. They created two evolutionary offshoots of humanity—one in the image of gods, the other more akin to devils.

The First Host of Celestials arrived some time after the death of Zgreb. It is uncertain whether the space gods were aware that one of their number had recently perished on Earth or that the Progenitor's cosmic DNA had already enriched the planet's biosphere. What is known is that they were drawn to the Earth because of its potential for superhuman life. As on countless other worlds, over countless millennia, the Celestials were on a mission to further the evolutionary process, and Earth provided a unique opportunity for experimentation.

Disembarking from a spacecraft so large that it blotted out the sun, the First Host marched across the fertile plains of Africa. There were ten towering Celestials, each tasked with a particular function. Gammenon the Gatherer was assigned to collect some protohumans to serve as test subjects. He scooped up a handful of anthropoids and took them back to the hovering mother ship. There the specimens were placed in "incuba-tubes" to keep them docile, and Gammenon stepped back to allow Ziran the Tester to begin his work. Wishing to study the genetic adaptability of the protohumans, Ziran took some of the test subjects and altered their DNA, creating the malformed Deviants, an evolutionary offshoot of humanity that was cursed with an unstable genome.

Panic stricken
The extraterrestrial Celestials made planetfall in ancient Africa, causing wild stampedes in their relentless search for early humans on which to experiment.
Eternals #1, Aug. 2006

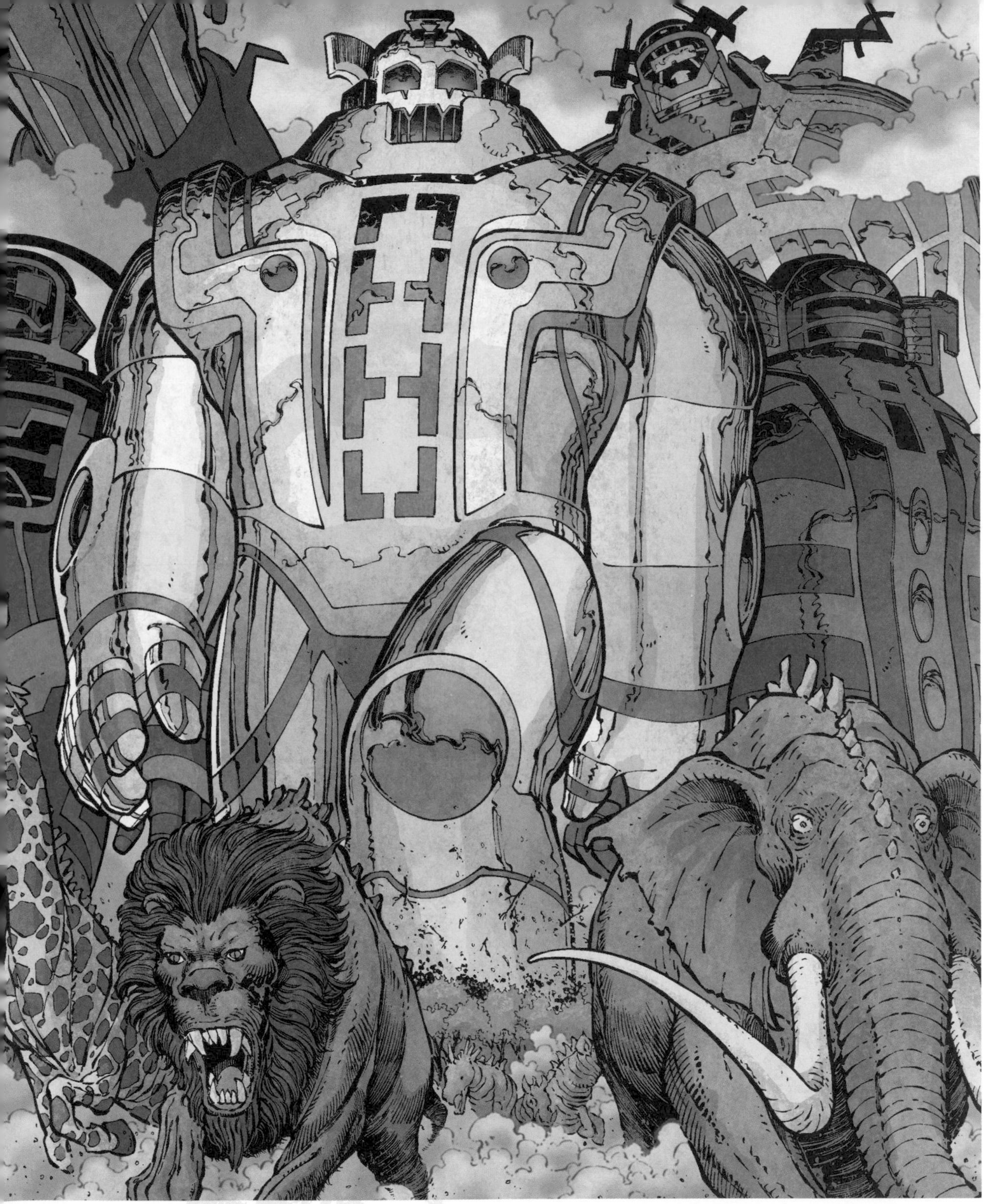

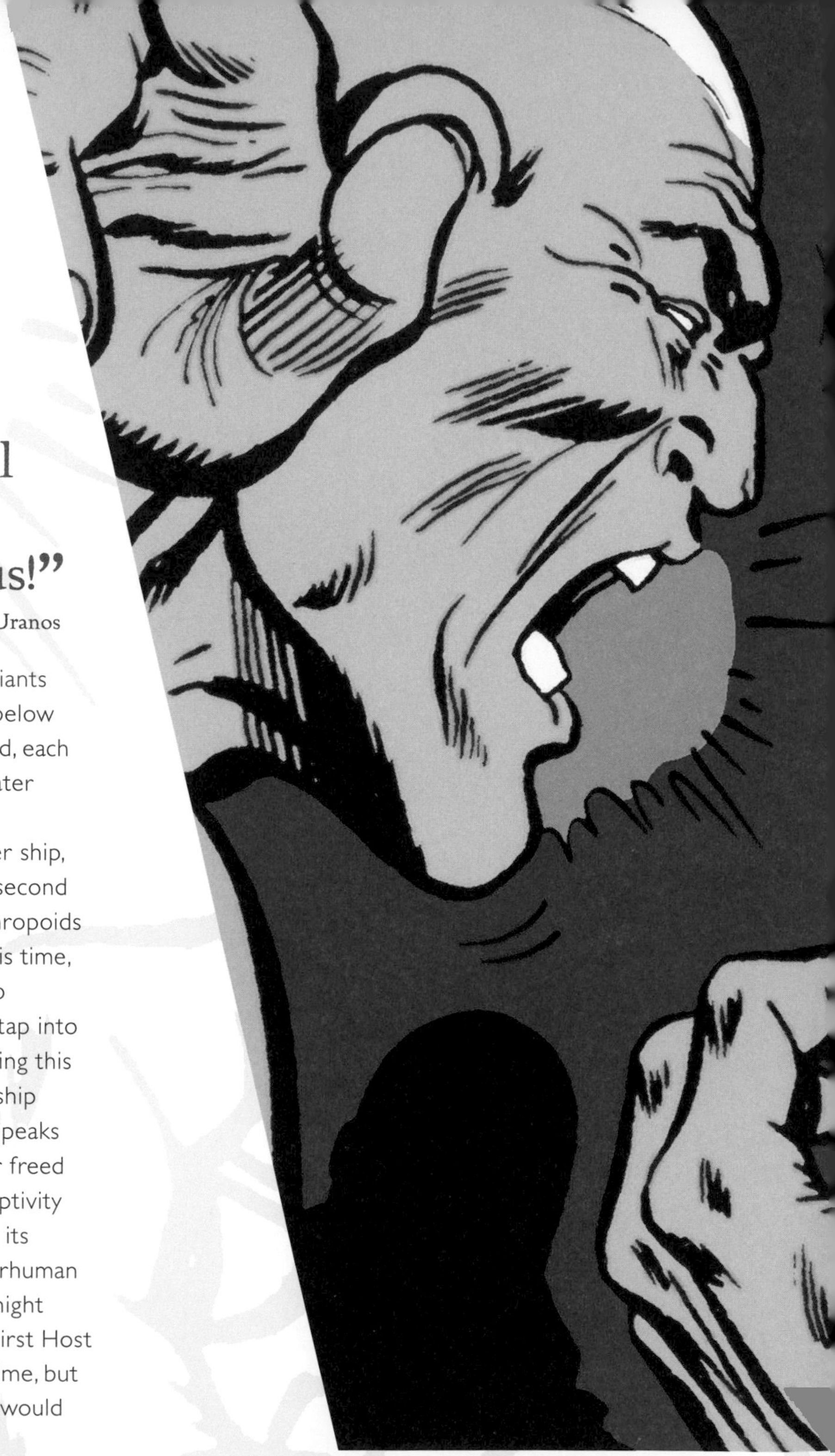

“Now only war will decide the great issue that divides us!”

Uranos

Released back into the wild, the Deviants instinctively sought sanctuary deep below ground and, as they went on to breed, each successive generation produced greater and greater monstrosities.

Meanwhile, on the Celestial mother ship, Nezzar the Calculator undertook a second experiment. Once again, several anthropoids had their genetic codes rewritten. This time, however, they were transformed into Eternals—godlike beings who could tap into the energies of the cosmos itself. Using this power, the Eternals left the mother ship to make their home among the high peaks of the world. Finally, Oneg the Prober freed the last of the protohumans from captivity unaltered, intrigued to see how, with its latent capacity for mutation and superhuman development, ordinary humankind might compete with its sister species. The First Host remained on Earth for only a short time, but amazingly, the effects of its visitation would be felt for centuries to come.

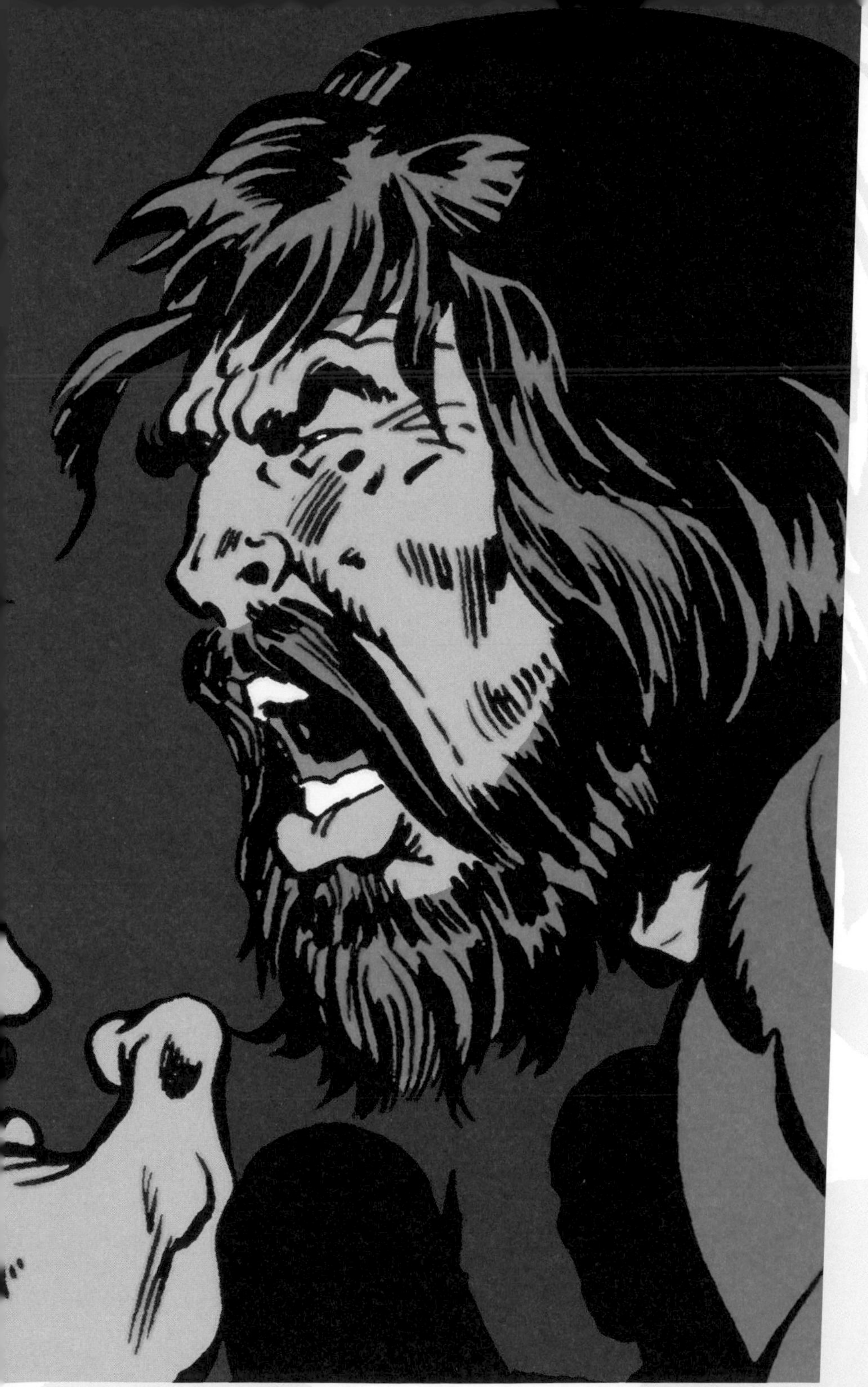

Eternal conflict
Brothers Kronos and Uranos argued how best to use their formidable powers, ultimately sparking a brutal civil war among the Eternals.
What If? #24, Dec. 1980

After wandering the globe in search of a suitable home, the first Eternals built the city of Titanos in the protective environs of the polar mountains. It was an architectural wonder, full of soaring structures and wide-open boulevards. Kronos—foremost among the Eternals—hoped the tranquility of Titanos would encourage his people to devote their time to the arts of philosophy and meditation. There were others, however, who

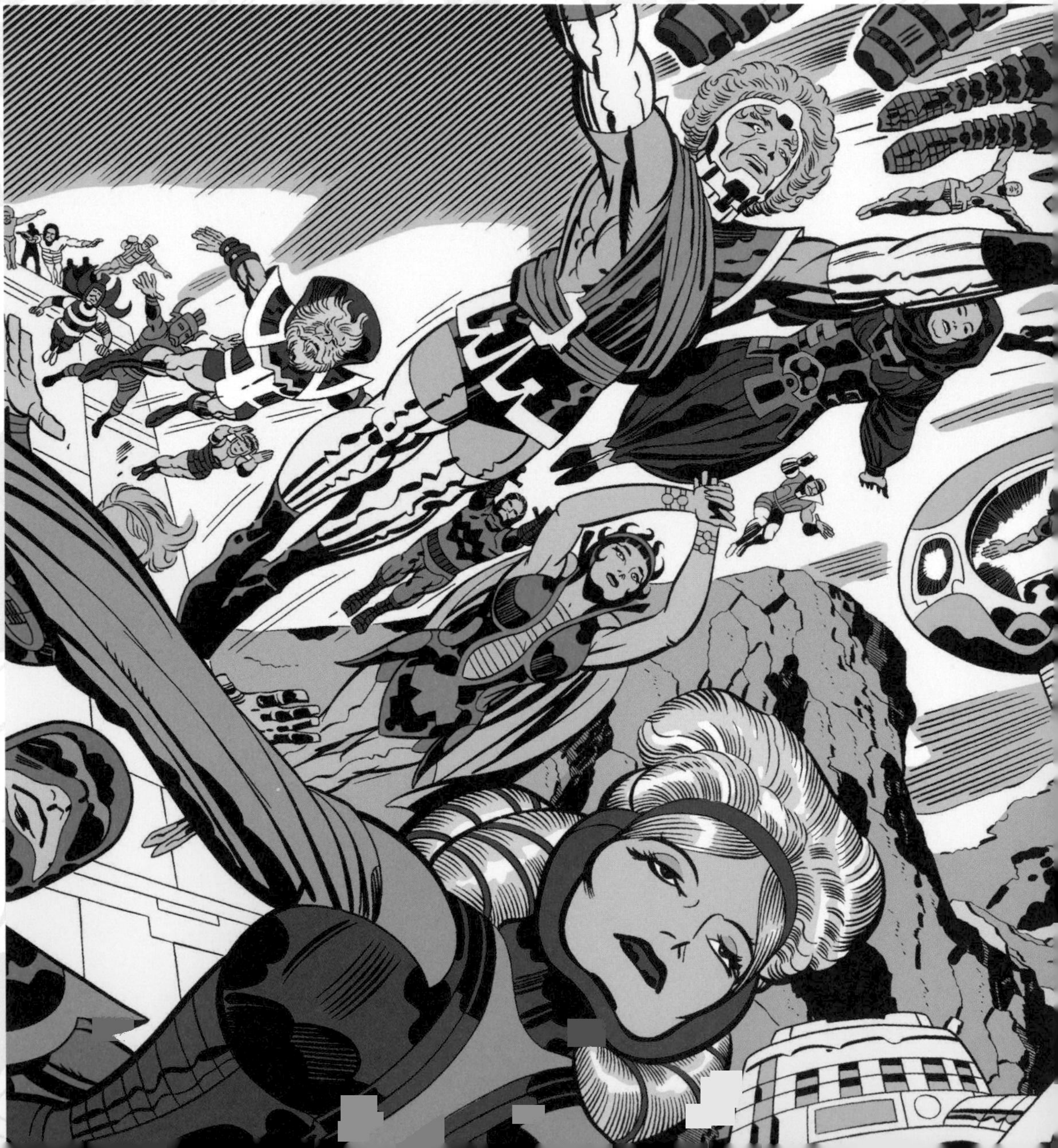

argued that the Eternals should use their formidable gifts—enhanced strength, the power of flight, and the ability to transmute matter—to tame the world and make it their own. One such voice belonged to Kronos' own brother, Uranos. "It is our lot to conquer… to advance on the weaker world around us and subdue it," he argued. Kronos met Uranos' belligerent cry for conflict with equal hostility and civil war broke out among the Eternals.

The battle was so intense that proud Titanos was rocked to its foundations and fell into ruin. In the end, Kronos and his followers defeated Uranos and the rebels. After much deliberation from the victors, Uranos and his fellow ideologues were banished into outer space, eventually settling on Saturn's moon, Titan.

Now finally free to contemplate the secrets of life, Kronos dedicated his days to scientific study. Unfortunately, an experiment involving cosmic radiation resulted in an explosion of unprecedented magnitude. Kronos was vaporized and his consciousness swept into outer space where it merged with the very fabric of the universe. On Earth, the explosion irradiated the Eternals with cosmic particles, enhancing their already superior genetic makeup and making them truly immortal. Kronos' eldest sons, Zuras and Alars, were among those invigorated by the particle bombardment.

Sky gods
The Eternals instinctively flocked to the high peaks of the world. They first settled in the polar mountains, eventually finding a permanent home in the sheltered regions of Ancient Greece.
Eternals #11, May 1977

Seeking answers to what had befallen them, the brothers investigated their father's demolished laboratory. There, before finally fading away, Kronos' disembodied essence told his heirs of his reckless experiment. With his departing words, Kronos cautioned that the future of the Eternals now lay in the hands of Zuras and Alars.

The brothers convened a council to discuss matters. As was customary, the gathered Eternals opened proceedings with a ritualistic circle of flight. However, as they took to the open skies, they found themselves drawn together, fused into a single entity that resembled a giant, pulsating brain. This was the Uni-Mind, a bizarre side-effect of the particle bombardment. Fused within the Uni-Mind, each individual Eternal was one small part of a much greater consciousness and they were able to communicate with each other instantaneously.

"From this day forth we are Eternals." Zuras

While sharing the form of the Uni-Mind, the Eternals determined that Zuras should succeed his father as ruler. To avoid disunity, Alars relocated to Titan where he renamed himself "Mentor" and founded an extraterrestrial branch of the Eternals that would ultimately give birth to Thanos, an abominable, despotic individual who possessed a latent Deviant gene.

Ruling as Prime Eternal, Zuras ordered the immediate construction of expansive new cities around the globe. The capital of Olympia soon nestled among the mountainous regions of Ancient Greece, and it was joined by Polaria in the Ural Mountains in western Russia, and Oceania in the Pacific Ocean.

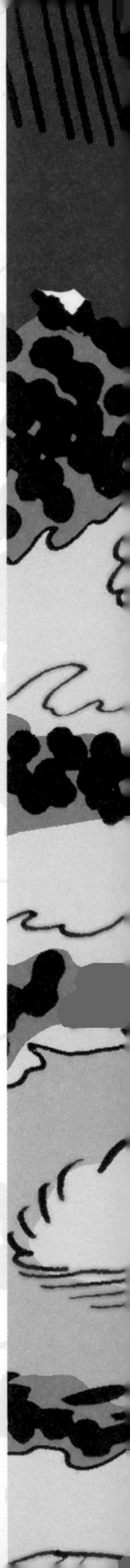

One mind
Irradiated with cosmic particles, the Eternals were able to fuse their beings into a single gestalt entity of infinite wisdom: the awe-inspiring Uni-Mind.
What If? #25, Feb. 1981

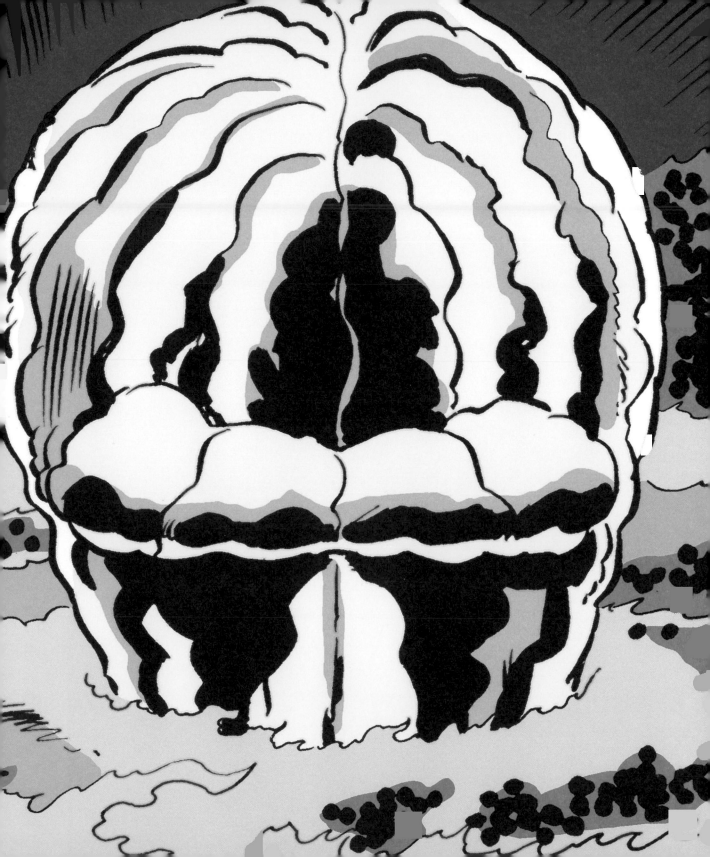

As the centuries rolled by, a fresh generation of Eternals came to the fore, including Zuras' headstrong daughter, Thena, the fleet-footed Makkari, and the telepathic, hedonistic Sersi.

While the Eternals devoted themselves to the study of science and the arts, the Deviants plotted global domination. Although genetically unstable, they were remarkably intelligent. The Deviants developed advanced technology centuries before their human cousins and used it to build and maintain vast underground cities. Growing ever bolder—and ever stronger—they emerged from their infernal caverns and swarmed across the surface of the world. With a capital based on the island of Lemuria in the Pacific Ocean, the Deviants ruled as kings.

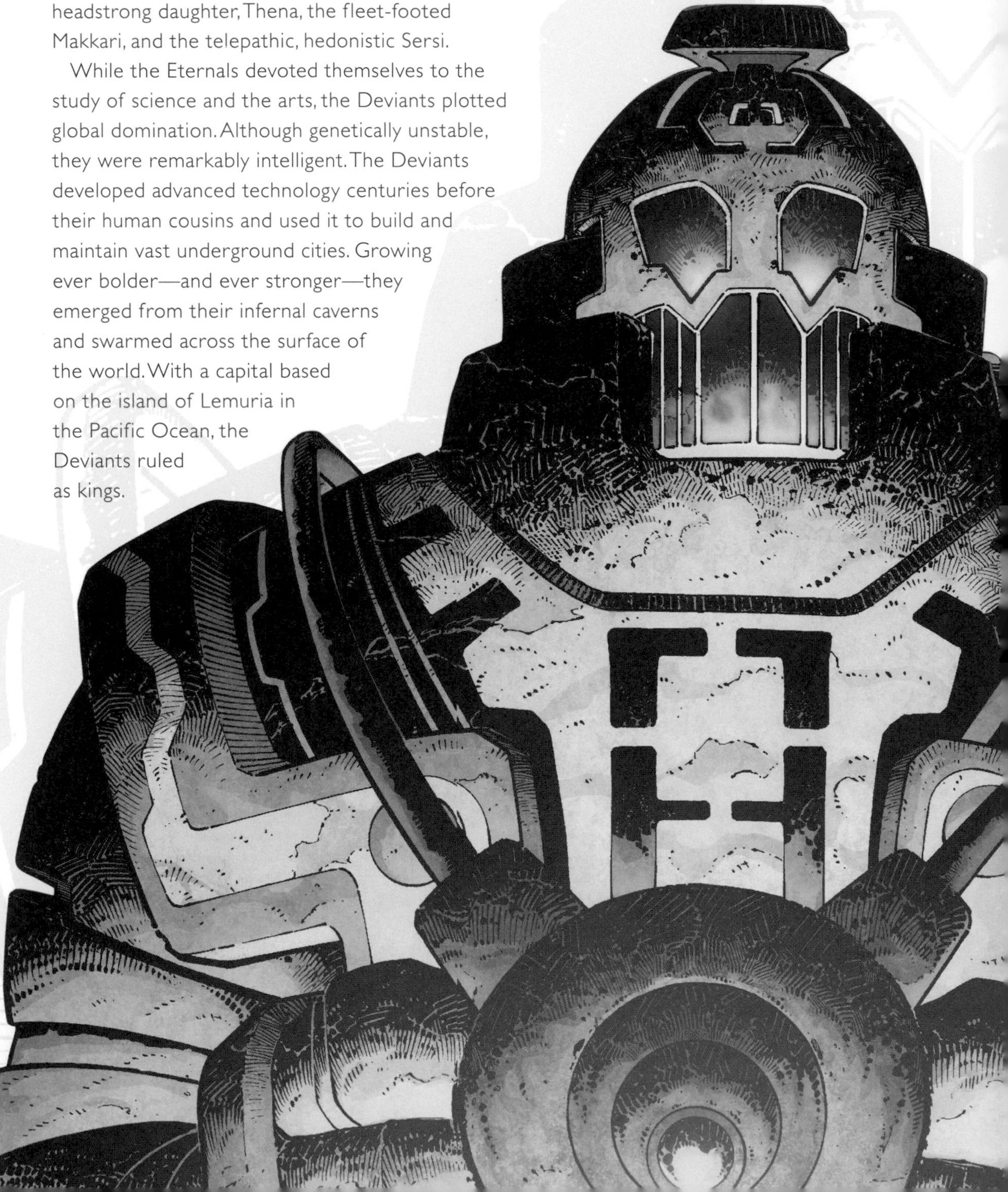

They enslaved much of early humanity and encouraged the rest to battle each other in endless proxy wars. Millions of human women and men lived as slaves and, with each lash of the whip, a racial memory was reinforced, the repellent, pitiless Deviants becoming associated with pain and suffering. This would inspire many parables about a hellish afterlife.

The Deviant Empire reached its zenith in 18,000 BCE. The elite thought they were unassailable, that the Deviants were destined to rule for all time. They were wrong. When the Second Celestial Host appeared in the skies above Lemuria, the Deviants finally appreciated their insignificance.

"The Deviants brought every human beneath their heel." Ikaris

The space gods had returned to evaluate the progress of their genetics experiment, but the Deviants feared the worst. Panicked at the mere sight of the immense Celestial mother ship, they struck at their creators with a sustained bombardment. The Celestials retaliated with a single bomb. The resulting explosion was so powerful that Lemuria was swept away by blistering firestorms and a huge tidal wave. Some Deviants survived the destruction, escaping back below ground. Their descendants would remember the sinking of Lemuria as the Great Cataclysm.

While the Deviants cowered in their subterranean refuges, the floodwaters rose so high that entire landmasses became submerged. Many humans feared it was the end of the world.

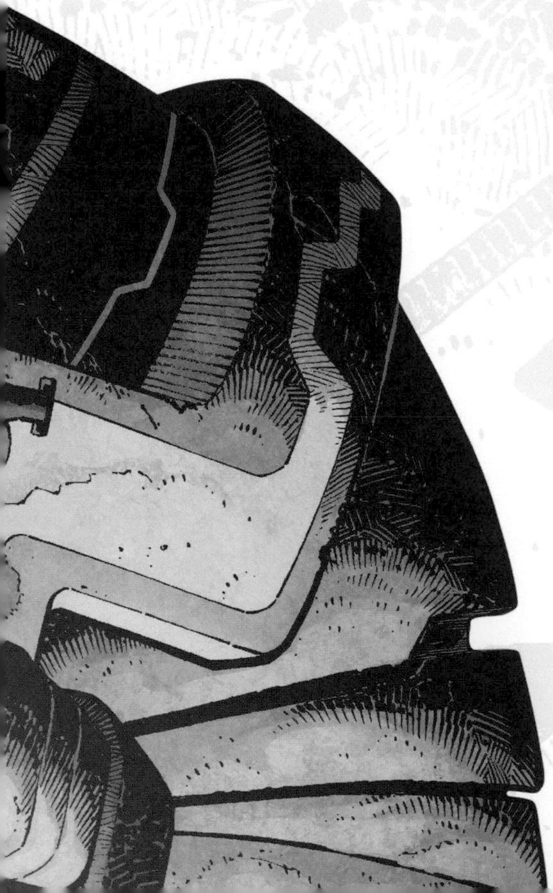

Cataclysmic encounter
The mere sight of the returning Celestials caused mass panic among the Deviants, sparking the apocalyptic events of the Great Cataclysm.
Eternals #1, Aug. 2006

It was only thanks to an intervention from a mysterious Eternal that a wooden ark containing a cargo of people and animals was able to reach dry land. Like some great bird, the Eternal flew ahead of the vessel, guiding it out of the deluge and toward safety.

The Great Cataclysm taught Zuras a valuable lesson. He now realized that the Eternals' unique perspective and enhanced abilities meant they had an obligation to safeguard the world and prepare it for the inevitable return of the Celestials. Frequently, this meant the Eternals had to emerge from their hidden cities to engage with ordinary humans or to thwart the plans of the ever-conniving Deviants.

"Are we never to spend our days in peaceful pursuits?"

Zuras

These encounters formed the basis of modern-day myths and legends. With no other frame of reference, primitive humanity mistook the Eternals for gods and considered their seemingly miraculous abilities as evidence of the divine. To add to the confusion, Olympia had been built close to the extra-dimensional nexus that connected Earth to the realm of the true Olympian gods. Thus, the peoples of Ancient Greece and Rome frequently confused the Eternals with the Olympian pantheon.

Mass destruction
Deviant Warlord Kro took charge of a vast arsenal of weapons of mass destruction, including an enormous, tank-like bomb.
Eternals #13, Jul. 1977

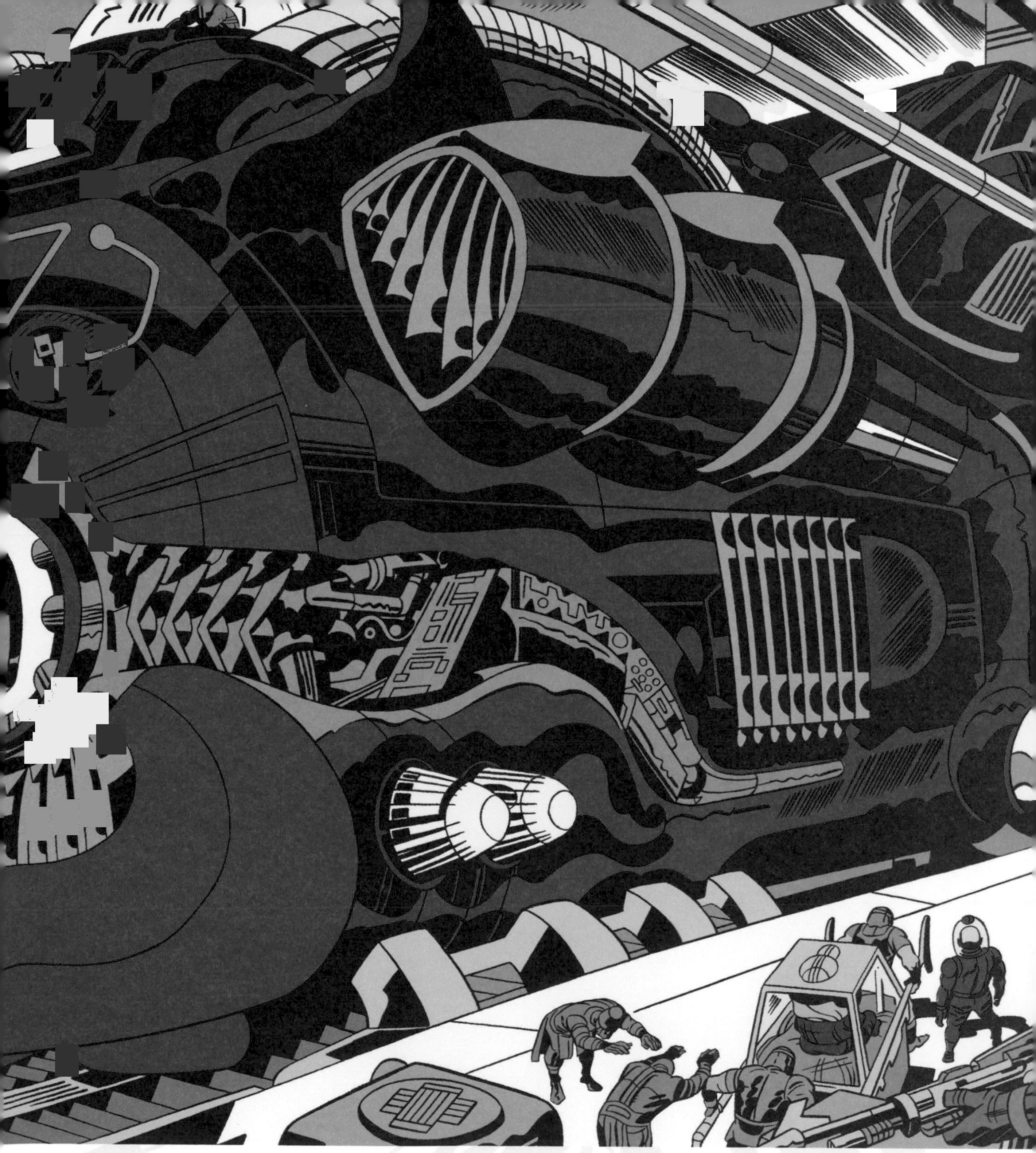

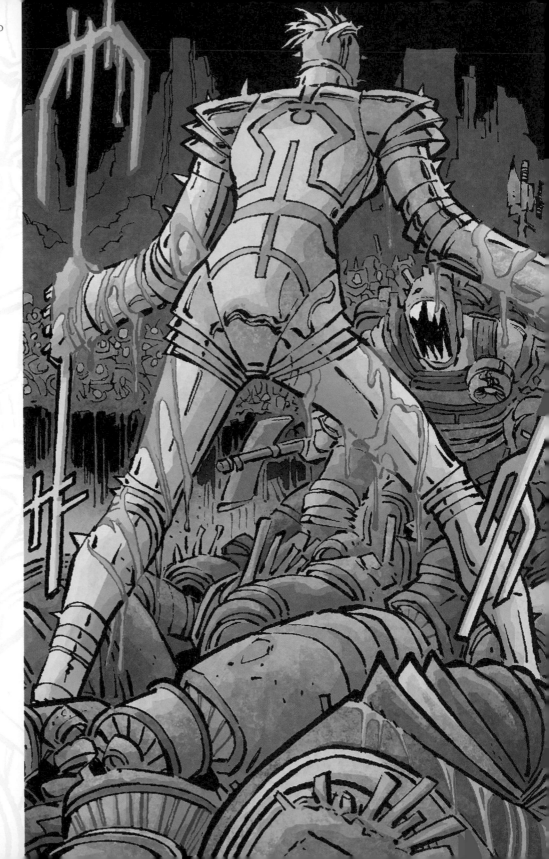

Warrior woman
On several missions to safeguard humanity, Thena, the daughter of Prime Eternal Zuras, battled the Deviants with an intense ferocity and an uncommon sense of purpose. *Eternals* #4, Nov. 2006

Much to his everlasting annoyance, Zuras was even mistaken for Zeus himself on more than one occasion. Of all the Eternals, it was Virako's polar clan who were the most remote, both in terms of geography and personal inclination. They preferred to remain in the cold climes that reflected their aloof nature, but even they ventured forth when it was necessary. In fact, it had been Virako's young son who had saved the ark during the floods of the Great Cataclysm.

Centuries later, Virako's son was once again sent out into the wider world. He was dispatched to ancient Crete to root out a horned Deviant lurking in a labyrinth of tunnels; his adventure was remembered down the ages as the Legend of the Minotaur. While in Crete, the Eternal's icy heart melted, and he fell in love with a human woman. They married and had a son together. The child possessed no extraordinary powers of his own and, to make up for this, his father fashioned a mechanical set of wings for him. The youngster was overjoyed at the prospect of finally taking to the skies beside his father, but he was warned never to use the wings on his own. Unfortunately, the young boy did not listen and his first solo flight ended in disaster and death. The Eternal buried his son and then took the child's name as his own, calling himself Ikaris for the first time.

The newly named Ikaris had feared he might revert to the cold ways of the Polar Eternals and, over the long centuries to come, harden his heart against his loss. By calling himself Ikaris he would always honor, and could never forget, his firstborn child. Zuras' plan of engagement proved successful and, when the Third Host arrived circa 1000 CE, the Eternals were on hand to cooperate with the Celestials. The Polar Eternal Ajak assumed the identity of the Incan god Tecumotzin and had the local human population prepare for the visiting space gods. While the Deviants had lashed out at their unfathomable creators, the Eternals would take a far more cautious and conciliatory approach.

Judgment Day

The Celestials returned to pass final judgment
on Earth. Would humanity be allowed to progress
to the next evolutionary level or be condemned
as a failed genetics experiment?

After gathering data on the development of Earth's three
intelligent species, the Celestials of the Third Host departed
Earth, leaving behind tantalizing clues to their visitation. Preserved in
the archaeological record left behind by the Incans and the Aztecs
were crudely carved images of the huge space gods. In modern times,
scientists speculated that this was proof that human civilization had
been guided by an extraterrestrial hand. Archaeologist Doctor Daniel
Damian was a leading proponent of this theory and he spent decades
searching for the so-called Lost City of the Space Gods. He finally
found it deep in the Peruvian Andes. Alongside his daughter, Margo,
and an assistant called Ike Harris, the doctor followed in the footsteps
of the ancients and was vindicated by what he found. As they picked
their way through the ancient ruins, the trio unearthed icons depicting
the Celestials aboard their star craft and stone tablets inscribed with
what appeared to be maps of the Milky Way galaxy.

Further revelations were to come. Harris knew far too much about
the space gods to be a junior archaeologist and he finally revealed
his true identity. He was Ikaris of the Polar Eternals, on a mission for
Prime Eternal Zuras. He told his astonished companions that they
shared their world with two sister species: the Eternals and the
Deviants. By way of further explanation, he recounted the history
of Celestial Hosts and announced that Zuras had now detected
a spaceship heading directly toward Earth. This was the Fourth Host,
noted Ikaris, and it was his task to trigger a homing beacon that
would safely guide the space gods back to their ancient landing site.

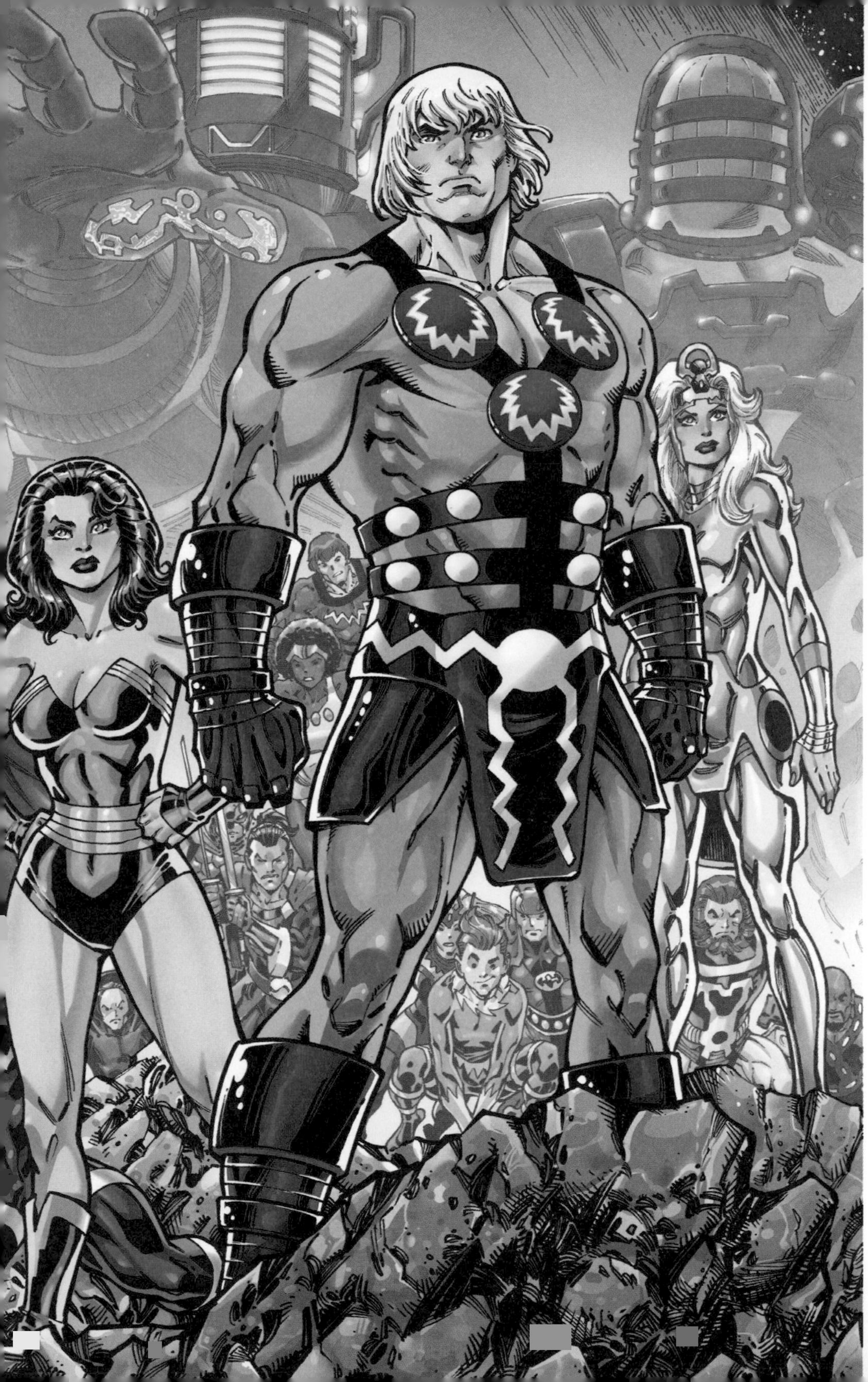

Eternal forces
Supported by Ajak, Makkari, Sersi, and Thena, the Polar Eternal Ikaris revealed the existence of his kind in preparation for turbulent times ahead.
Eternals: Secrets from the Marvel Universe #1, Feb. 2020

After activating the beacon, Ikaris entered what he called a "resurrection crypt" to meet with an old friend. Ajak had slumbered for a thousand years—held in stasis since the departure of the Third Host—and he awoke with the vigor of a man eager to make up for lost time. Alongside him were numerous Inca technicians, who also sprang into action, serving as a high-tech ground crew for the inbound Celestials. Doctor Damian and Margo looked on in awe as the first Celestial slowly descended from his heavenly spaceship. The monumental figure came to rest upon two giant pylons, silent and seemingly unmoved by the buzz of activity around him.

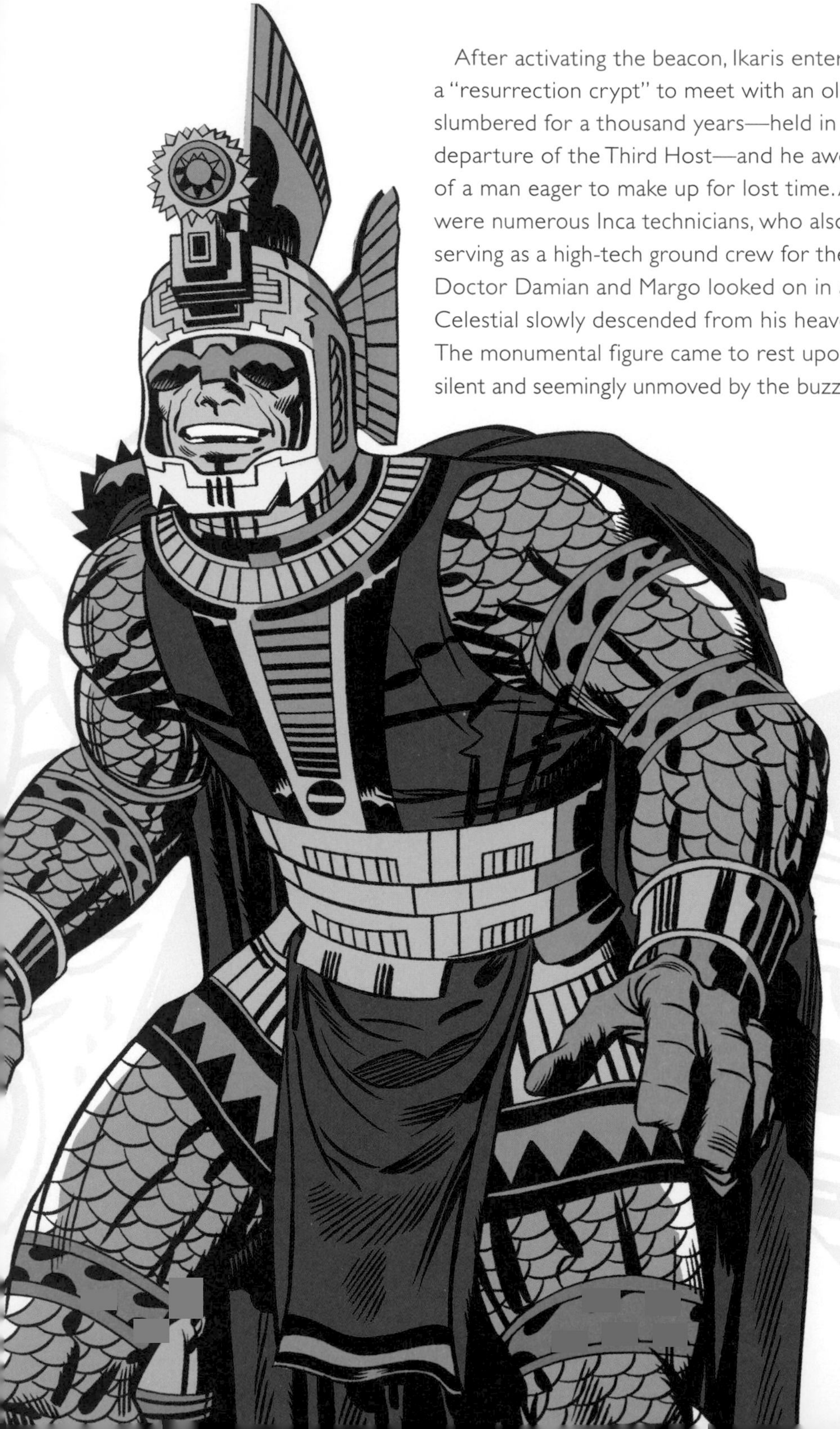

Ready and waiting
Ajak the Eternal awoke from many centuries of suspended animation to greet the returning Celestials and resume his work as chief liaison to the space gods.
Eternals #2, Aug. 1976

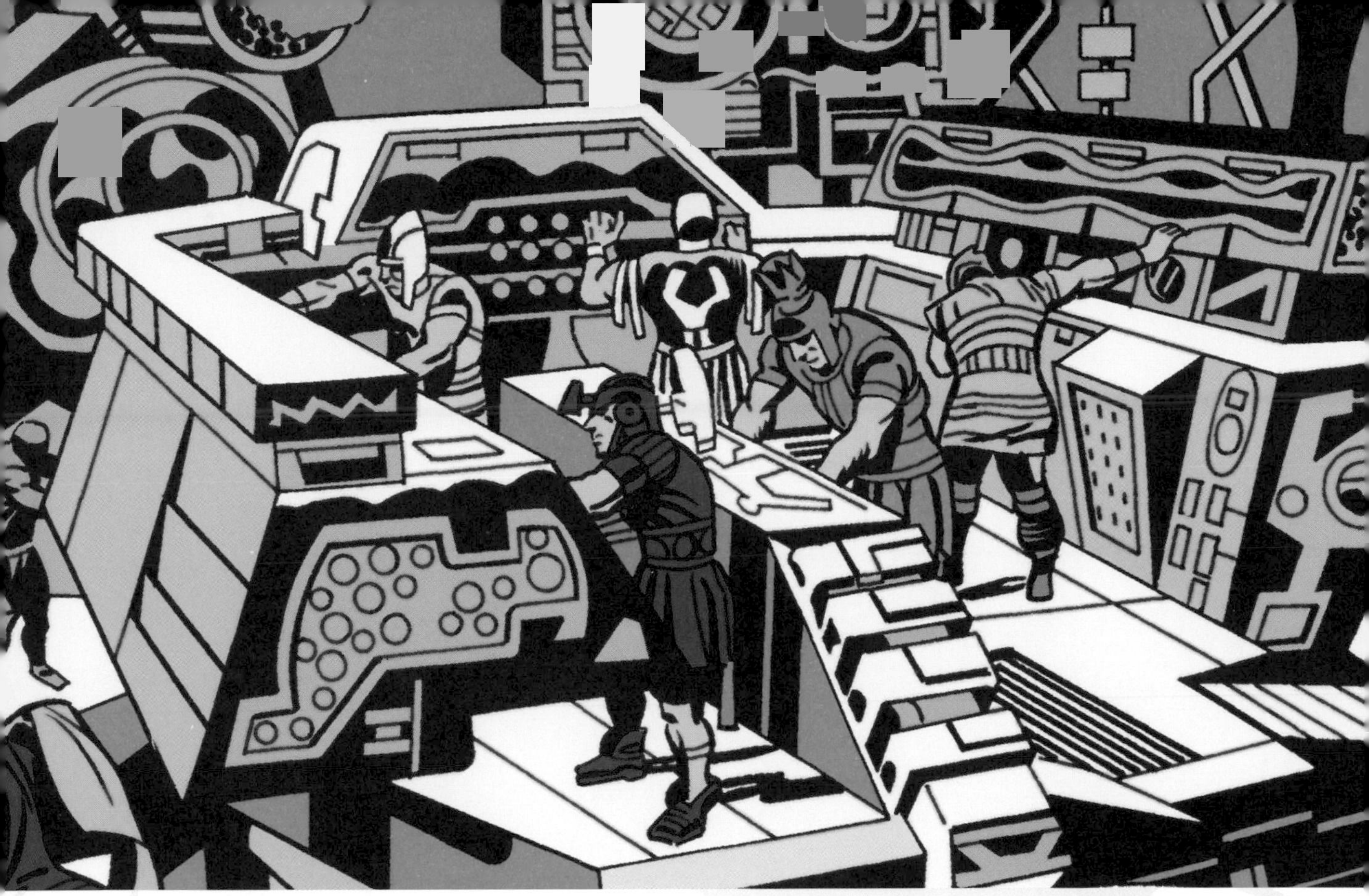

Recognizing the Celestial as Arishem the Judge, Ajak finally understood the purpose of the Fourth Host. It was the time of Final Judgment. Arishem would assess whether or not humanity—and its two sister species—were worthy of continued existence. He would spend the next 50 years in quiet contemplation and only then would he make his pronouncement; when the inhabitants of Earth would learn whether they would live or die.

The Eternals were not the only ones who were aware of the Celestials' return. The Deviants had also detected the imminent arrival of the Fourth Host. Since the time of the Great Cataclysm, the Deviants had operated largely in secret, rarely emerging from their new subterranean capital known colloquially as the City of Toads. Now, though, Deviant Warlord Kro led a raiding party to the Lost City of the Space Gods in a reckless bid to turn back the Fourth Host. A short scuffle with Ikaris ensued, but it proved to be an exercise in futility.

Ground crew
Retrieved from hibernation, a ground crew of ancient Incans prepared for the inbound arrival of the Celestials and their massive spacecraft.
Eternals #2, Aug. 1976

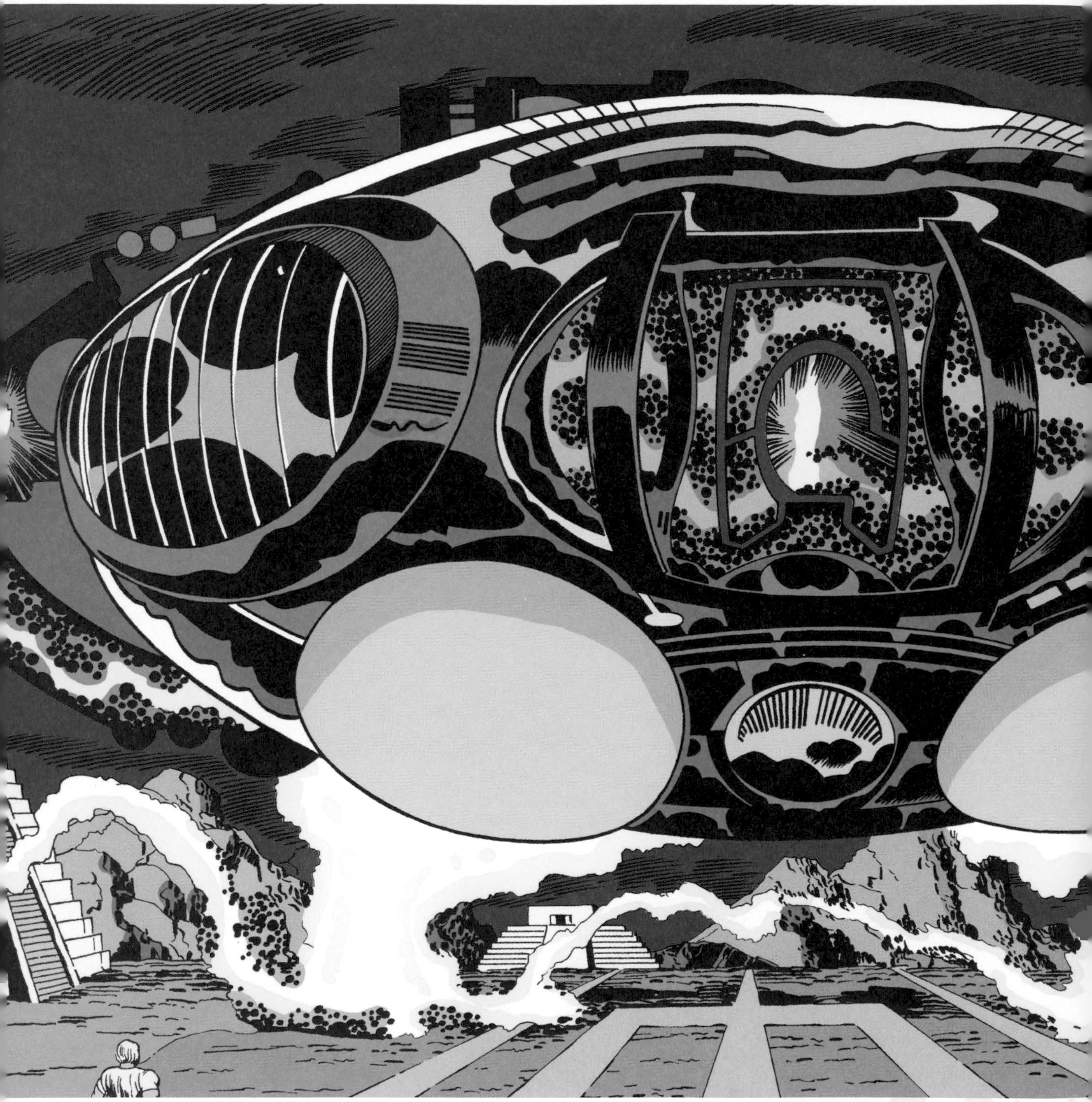

Kro had arrived far too late to sabotage the space gods' arrival. In his impotent rage, Kro screamed at the Celestials in their hovering starship, denouncing them for their past brutal treatment of his people. His words were bitter and angry, but also defiant. He pledged never to bend his knee before his immense, enigmatic creators and warned that the Deviants also possessed powerful weapons.

"And so it begins— a new age of the space gods on Earth!" Ajak

As if to make a mockery of Kro's words, the Celestials unleashed a wave of cosmic energy that drove the Deviants from the Lost City of the Space Gods. Kro bristled at the ignominy of defeat and he swiftly devised a scheme to get even. The Deviants would not take on the Celestials directly, rather they would trick someone else into fighting on their behalf. Remembering how humanity had previously mistaken his kind for hellish demons, Kro disguised himself as the devil and attacked New York City with a small army of Deviants, each soldier armed with an advanced weapon that belched out choking flames.

Sky fall
Amid a storm of cosmic energy, a Celestial spaceship alighted on Earth. After a thousand-year absence, the space gods had returned!
Eternals #2, Aug. 1976

The plan was to incite mass panic and prompt an overreaction from the human authorities. Kro hoped that they would mistake him for an agent of the intimidating space gods and would retaliate with a devastating nuclear strike on the Celestials' growing base in the Andes.

"If you find reason in war, Kro, —then I say—to battle!" Ikaris

As Kro's plan was set in motion, events in the Andes were also coming to a head. More Celestials had descended from their mother ship and had begun updating the compound. Ajak observed that the space gods were preparing to erect a shield around the landing zone and, as only the mighty Celestials would be able to move through the opaque barrier, he suggested it was time for Ikaris to take the humans back to civilization. Doctor Damian refused to leave. As an archaeologist, he could not turn his back on the opportunity of a lifetime. Ajak warned that it would be 50 years before the barrier was lifted, and that the aged Damian would likely spend his last days imprisoned in the Andes. The doctor was unperturbed; he had spent a lifetime researching the space gods and would happily take his last breath while studying his subjects up close and in person. Margo was alarmed at the prospect of leaving her father behind, but Ikaris quickly realized the scientist's mind was set.

Judge and jury
Viewed from many miles away, the gigantic Celestial Arishem stood in silent judgment, contemplating the fate of the hapless inhabitants of planet Earth.
Eternals #3, Sep. 1976

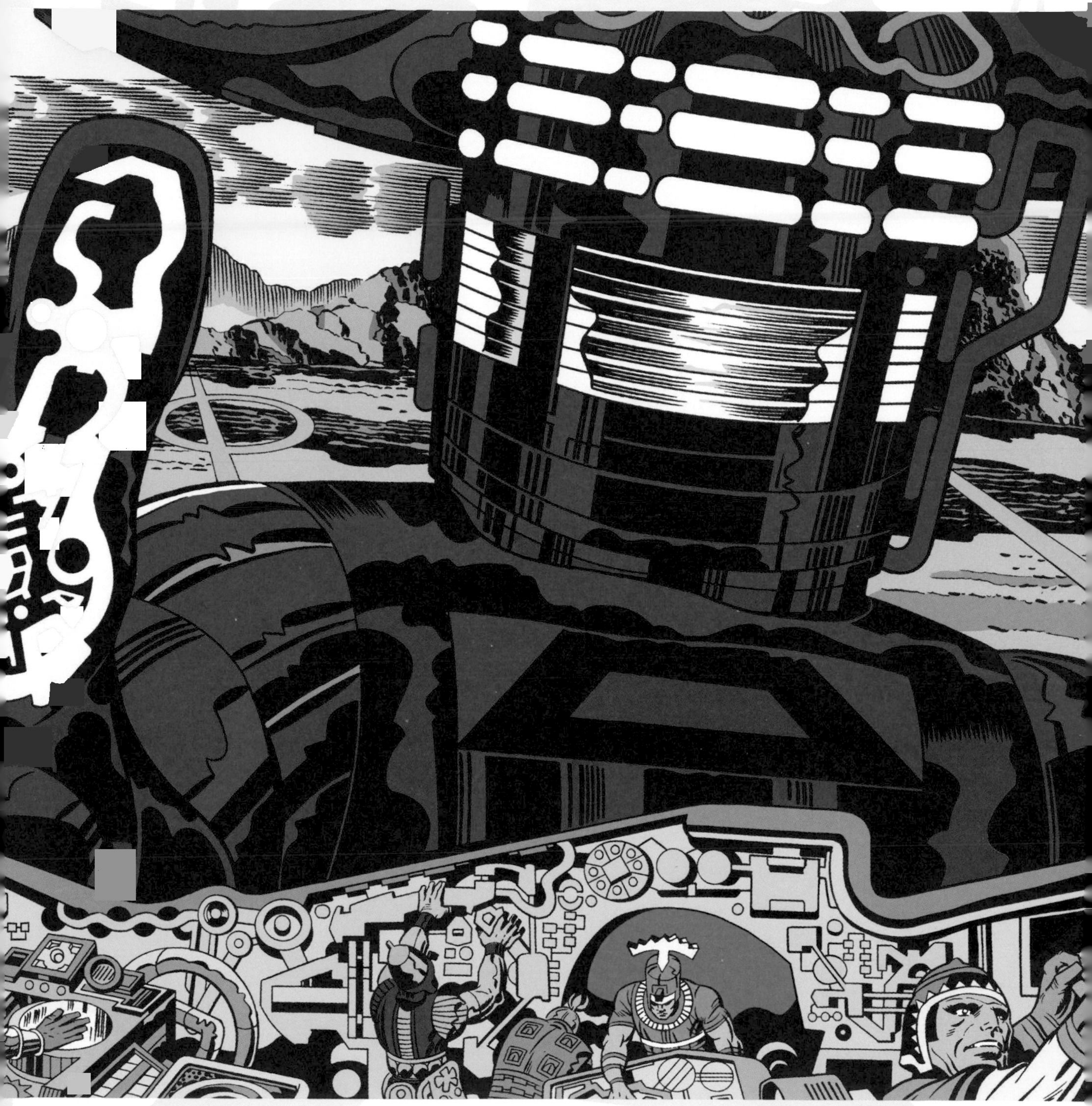

Ikaris forced Margo into the expedition team's small airplane and the pair escaped the mountain stronghold barely moments before the barrier finally solidified.

On learning of Kro's assault on New York, Ikaris left the distraught Margo in the care of Sersi, an Eternal who had made her home amid the bustle of midtown Manhattan. Margo was perplexed by Sersi's insouciant attitude and astounded to learn that the Eternal's outlandish escapades in ancient times had been recorded by the Greek poet Homer. Ikaris flew from Sersi's apartment into a raging battle. Kro's minions had already overwhelmed the police and were on the verge of victory. At the mere sight of the monsters in their midst, the usually urbane citizens of New York panicked, fleeing from the supposed devils just as their superstitious ancestors had in the past.

"The devil remains your fear— and my weapon!" Warlord Kro

Ikaris subdued numerous Deviants but he was hopelessly outnumbered and was felled by a paralyzing Brain Mine. Learning that Ikaris was out of action, Sersi feared the worst and reluctantly joined the fight. She fought off a band of Deviant warriors and then contacted her kin in distant Olympia. Alerted to the situation, Zuras dispatched his warrior daughter, Thena, and the pilot Makkari to the war zone. "Go then—both of you! Vent your aggression upon the Deviants," came the command.

Deviant defiance
Dismissed as inconsequential by the Celestials, the Deviant Warlord Kro raged against the indignity, vowing he would have his revenge on the unfathomable space gods.
Eternals #2, Aug. 1976

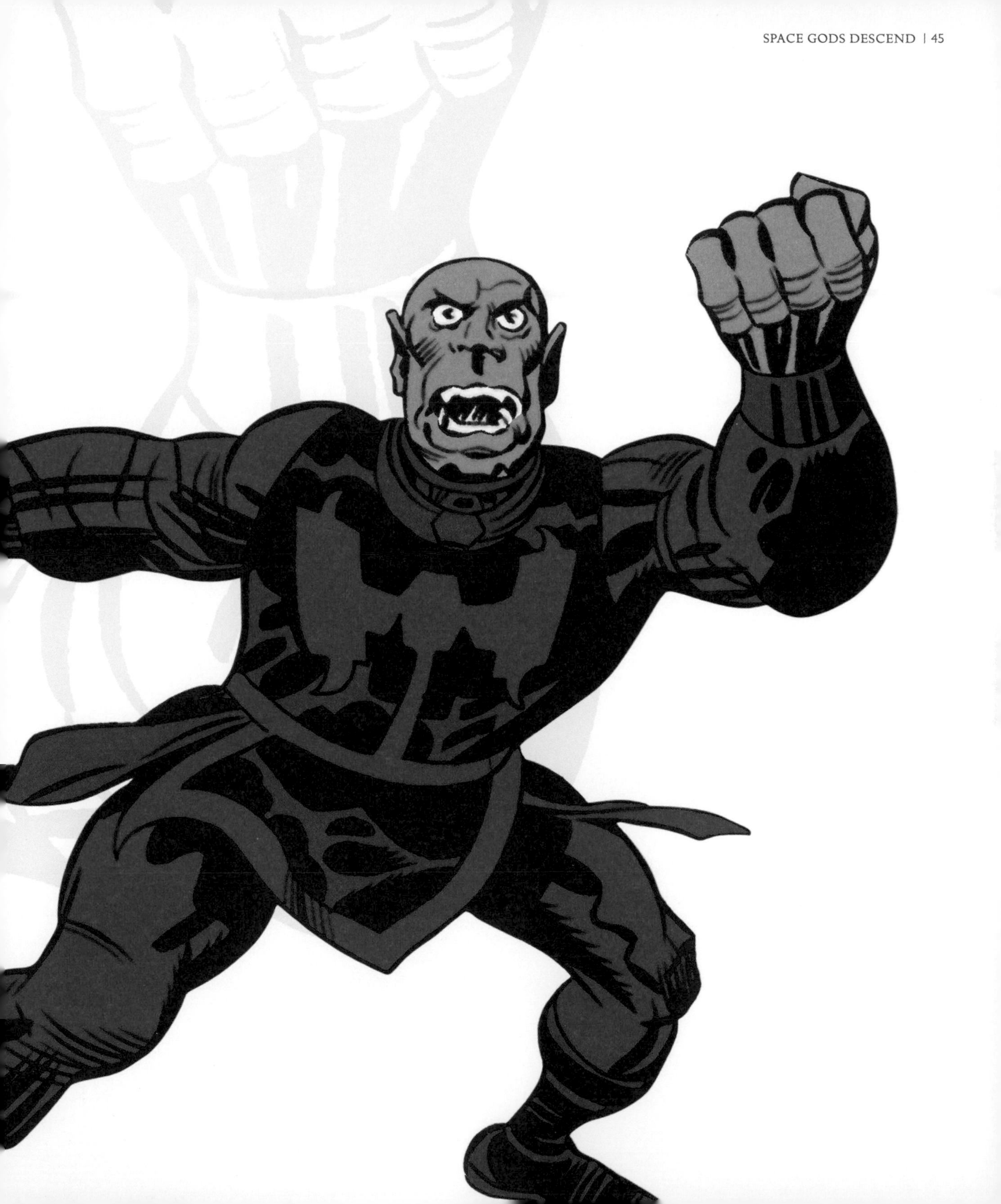

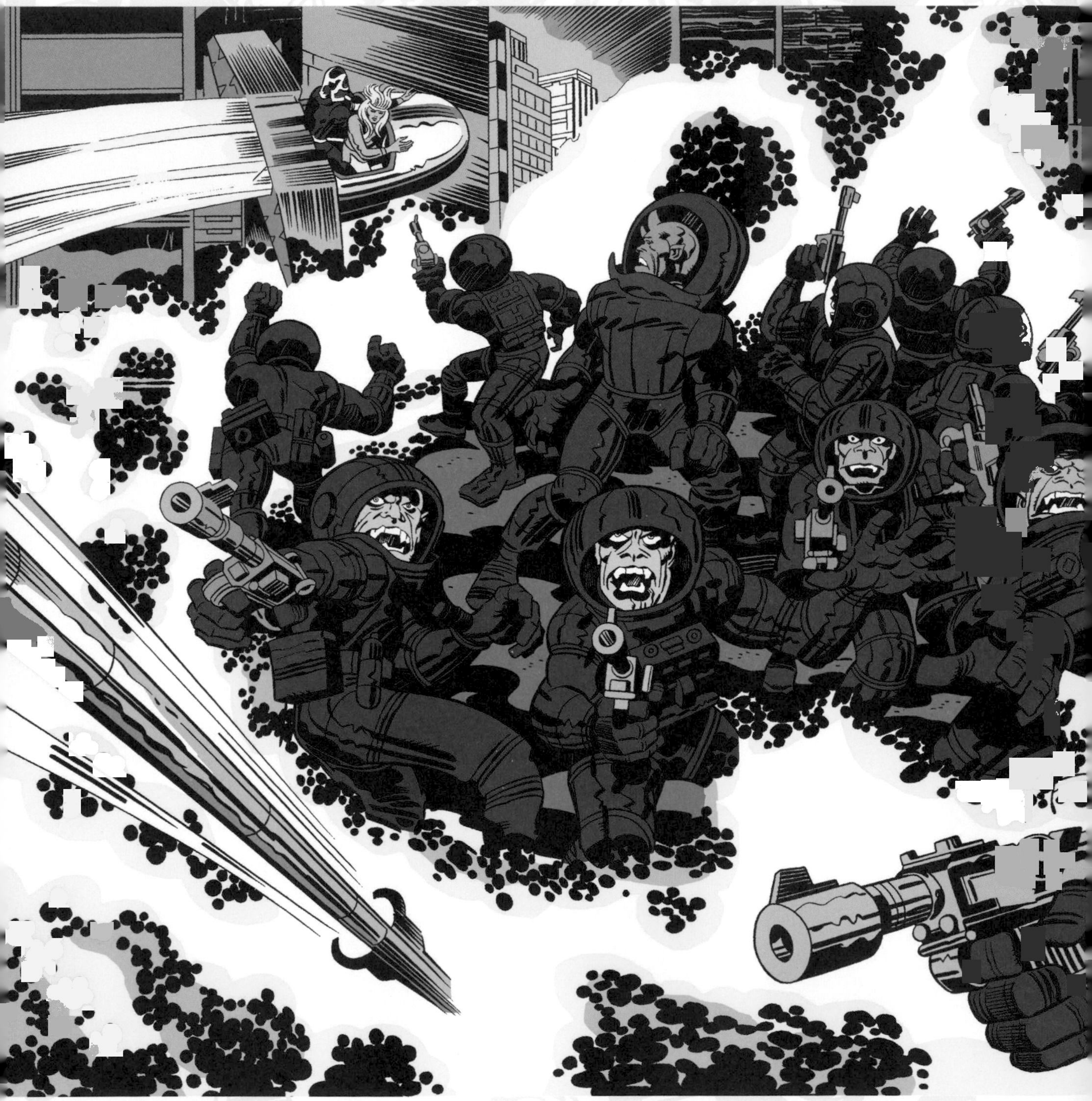

Thena and Makkari followed Zuras' orders enthusiastically, striking at the Deviant army with seeming impunity. Riding a jet-powered chariot and armed with high-tech crossbows and energy lances, they made easy work of the enemy. With defeat in sight, Kro soon bowed to the inevitable and surrendered. Having known Thena in the past, he used his familiarity to ingratiate himself with the victors. He proposed a formal truce, arguing that all three species should set down their weapons until a common response to the Celestials could be found. Although suspicious, Thena agreed to Kro's terms. Ikaris was revived and returned to his fellow Eternals.

"You savages will regret this attack on the humans!" Thena

The battle for New York was over, but the battle for Earth had barely begun. The whole world had watched events unfold in the city and now humanity was aware that it shared the planet with two sister species. Weeks after the cessation of hostilities—and still under the terms of the truce—Ikaris and his fellow Eternals attended a lecture at a New York City college of anthropology. They answered questions about their long lives and amazing abilities. While some students were entranced by the stories they heard, others were skeptical, declaring the whole affair an elaborate hoax. Kro was also present at the event and he continued to mock his human hosts with scare stories of devils and demons. The lecture ultimately ended in chaos and confusion. Nevertheless, it was clear from this incident that the world had entered a new era. How the disparate species of humanity responded to each other, and how they reacted to the arrival of the Celestials, would have profound implications for the future of life on Earth.

Hell on Earth
Warlord Kro led his forces in an attack on New York City where the devilish army met its match in the form of Eternals Thena and Makkari.
Eternals #6, Dec. 1976

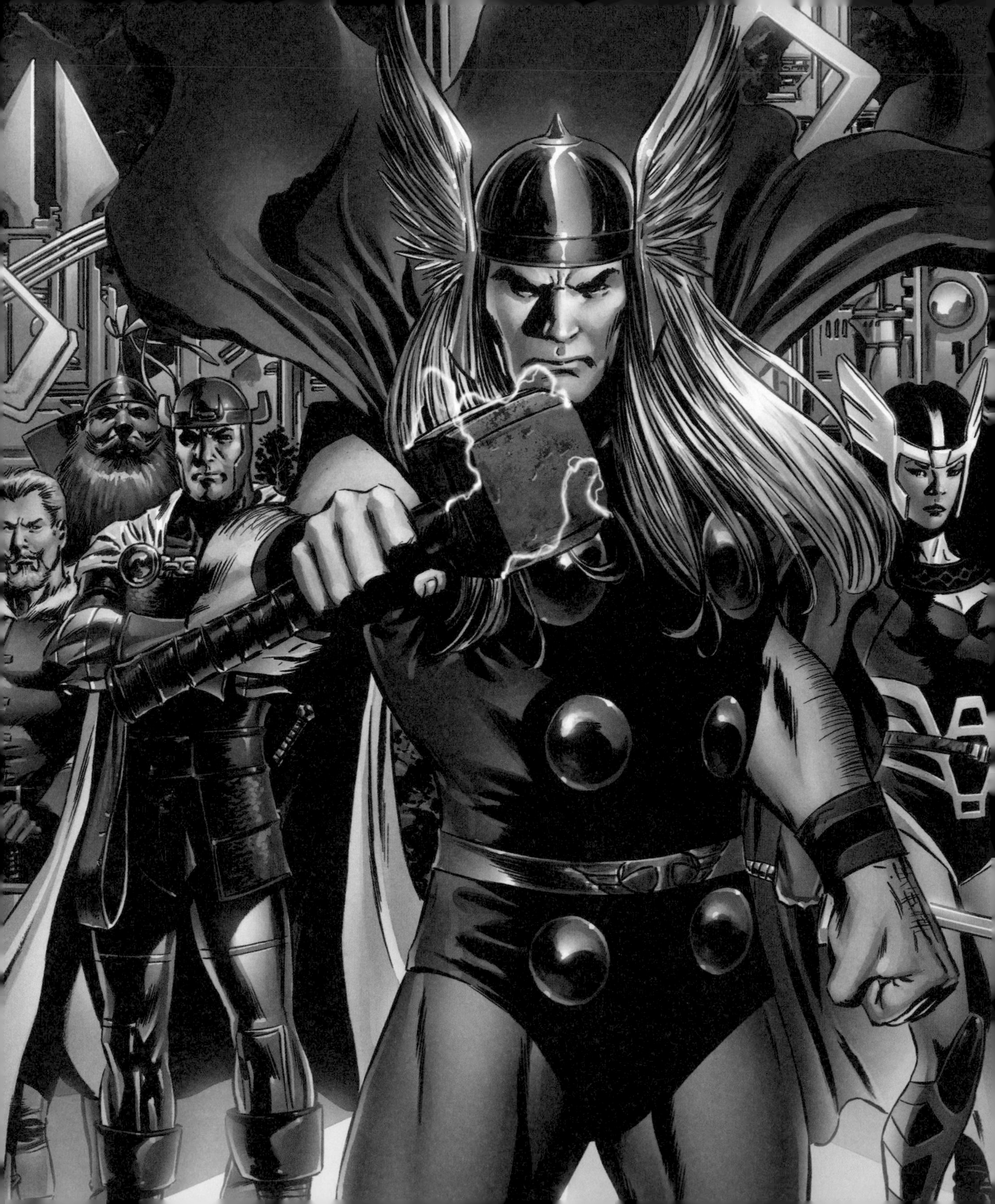

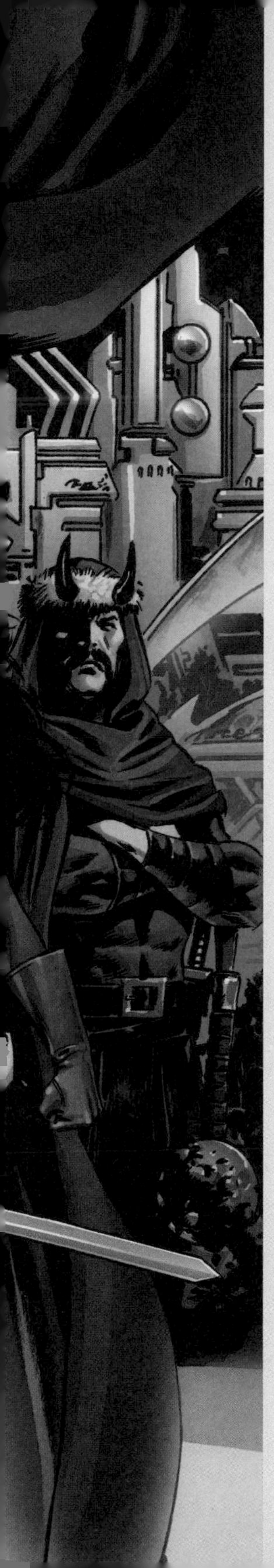

PANTHEONS RISE

The gods of Earth were given form and substance by the thoughts of mortals. As nascent humanity took its first steps, its hopes and fears conjured into being numerous divine pantheons. The Olympian gods shaped the ancient civilizations of Greece and Rome, while Bast of the Orisha inspired the African Bashenga to create the Black Panther Cult. As faith declined, so did the power of the pantheons. In response, Odin—All-Father of Asgard—dispatched his son, Thor, to Earth to continue the fight for justice in a new age of Super Heroes.

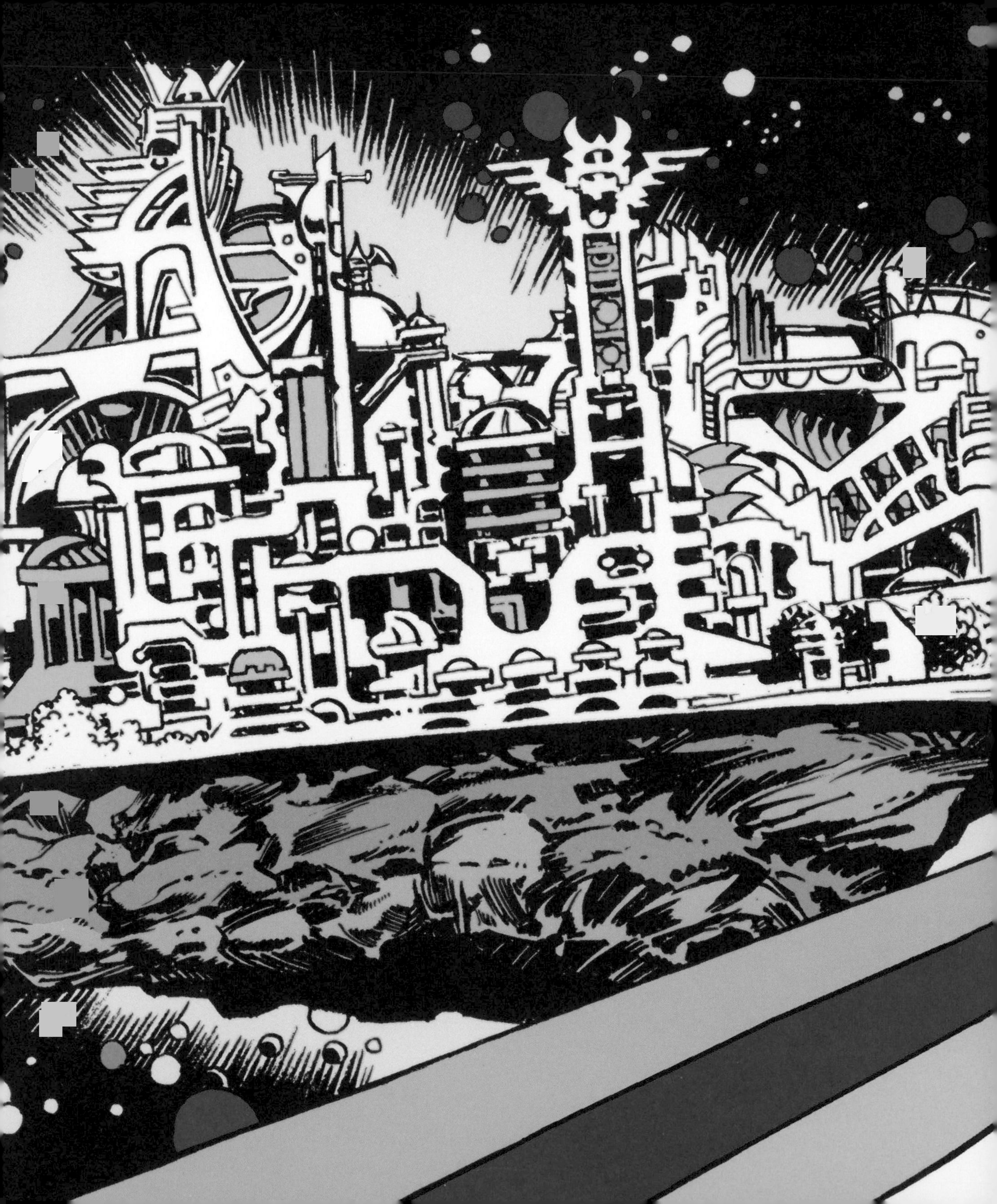

The Asgardians: Death and Rebirth

The gods of Asgard were trapped in a seemingly endless cycle of death and rebirth. All-Father Odin was determined to break the chains of Ragnarok, however, and forge a new destiny for his people.

The Aesir was one of the earliest godly pantheons to emerge in the wake of Atum's purge of the demonic Elder Gods. Led by the indomitable Bor, its members were a hardy race of clansmen and women, and they staked a claim to the world's northern lands, embracing the snow and ice. Unfortunately, their territory was increasingly impinged upon by the worshipers of other deities, and so the Aesir used the branches of the mystical World Tree Yggdrasil to escape to an otherworldly realm they named Asgard.

Odin ultimately succeeded Bor as All-Father of Asgard and, to his dismay, learned that his people were locked in a 2,000-year cycle of death and resurrection. At the twilight of each era, the Asgardians were wiped away by the catastrophic events of Ragnarok, only to then find themselves reborn in slightly different forms, and cursed to repeat the cycle all over again. Proud Odin fumed that his people were constrained by these iniquitous shackles of fate, and he put in motion a centuries-long plan that he hoped would allow the gods of Asgard to finally become masters of their own destiny.

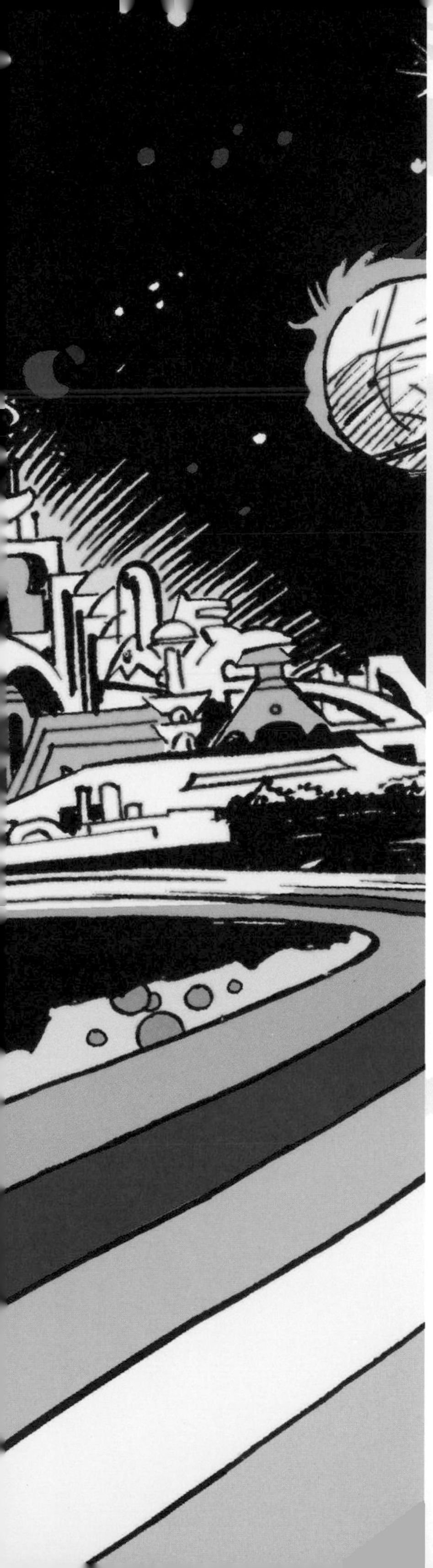

Over the rainbow
After establishing their home in Asgard, the Aesir explored the Ten Realms via the rainbow-like Bifrost Bridge—a kaleidoscopic conduit to anywhere in the universe.
Thor Annual #5, Sep. 1976

As part of his stratagem, he traveled to the mortal plane to father a child with Earth-Mother Gaea, who met her godly suitor in the guise of the goddess Jord. Deep within the Earth itself, and with magical sprites and nymphs on hand to assist with the delivery, Gaea gave birth to Thor. Of course, thanks to the inescapable workings of Ragnarok there had been other versions of Thor in the past, but this incarnation was different. Because of his unique heritage, he was as much a son of Earth as he was a son of Asgard. He was a god whose strength was enhanced by a direct link to the mortal realm. In years to come, Thor would develop an abiding affinity for Earth—or Midgard as the Asgardians referred to it—and discover that his power was far greater because of this unprecedented connection.

Back in Asgard, the baby Thor was given into the care of Odin's wife, Freyja, who raised him as if he were her own child. Like many of his fellow Asgardians, Thor grew up to be headstrong and reckless, living for the day and caring not what tomorrow would bring. He enjoyed fighting and carousing with his fellow warriors and was proud to be worshiped by mortals, particularly the hearty Norsemen of Scandinavia. After Thor saved the young goddess Sif from the clutches of the death-goddess Hela, Odin rewarded his son for his heroism, bestowing on him the Uru-forged war hammer known as Mjölnir.

Fathers and sons
Son of warrior-king Bor, Odin fought at his father's side, but when it came to his own heir, Odin wanted to free Thor from senseless conflict.
Thor #7, May 2008

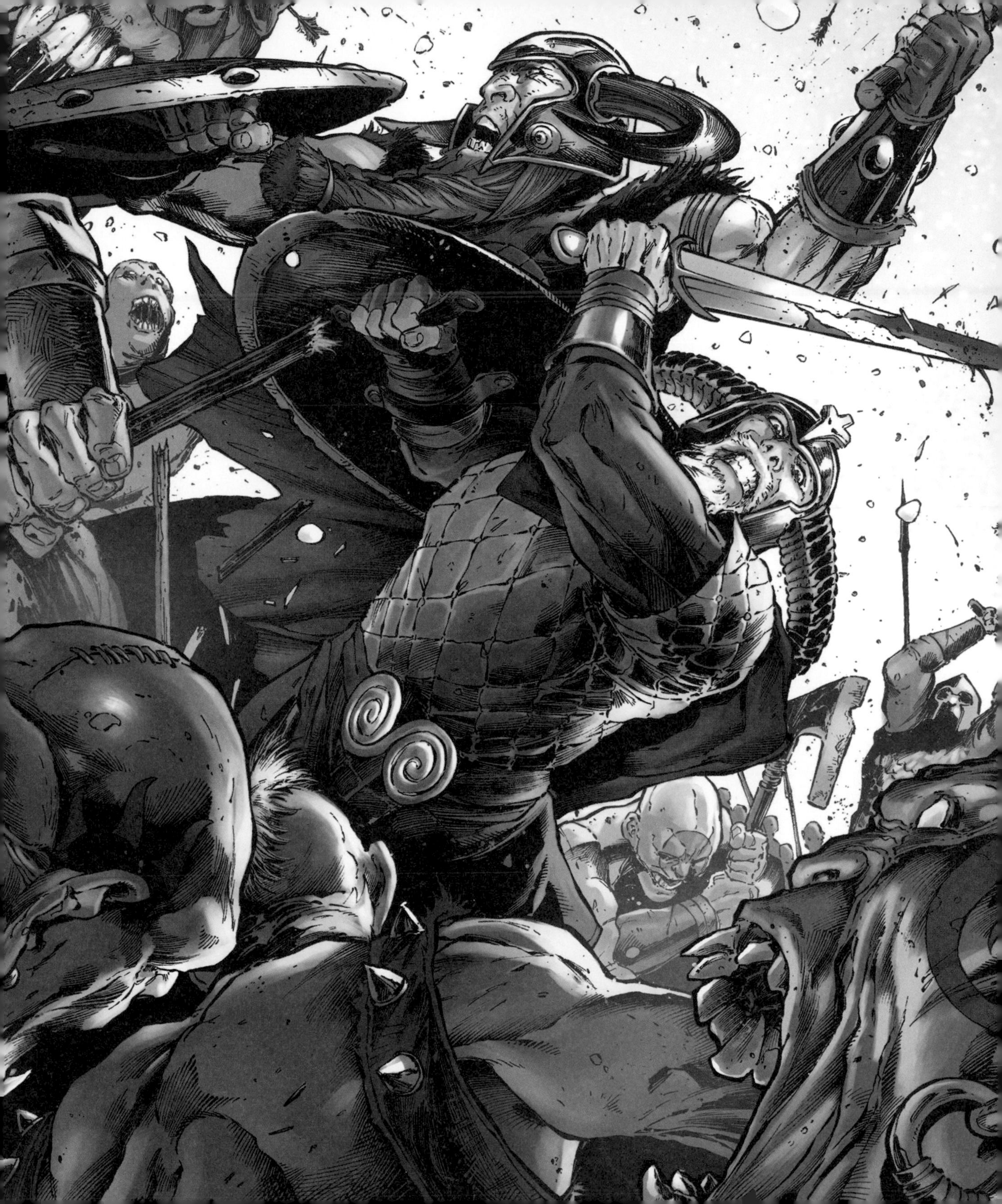

Odin himself had wielded the mystically charged weapon in the distant past, using it to defend Earth from existential threats, and he hoped his son would be similarly inclined. If anything, the gift of Mjölnir only served to make Thor even more arrogant. The young god continued to indulge in petty squabbles and pointless battles. When a confrontation with a band of Storm Giants fractured a hard-won truce, Odin's patience with his son's willful behavior finally ran out. Judging him unfit to inherit the throne of Asgard, the All-Father exiled Thor to Earth.

"I seek an heir whose power surpasses Asgard." Odin

As part of his punishment, the God of Thunder was transformed into a frail, disabled mortal. Left with no memory of his previous life, Thor believed he had always been "Don Blake"—an American doctor with a gift for surgery and a passion for helping others. After years of service, Blake took a vacation to Norway. There, he became embroiled in an invasion by stone-like aliens called Kronans. Pursued by these extraterrestrials, Blake dropped his walking cane and was forced to seek sanctuary inside a cave. In the gloomy interior, he discovered what looked to be a gnarled wooden stick.

When the good doctor unintentionally struck a boulder with the stick, a miraculous event occurred. The seemingly innocuous piece of wood was transformed into Mjölnir and Blake's slight form was replaced with the towering physique of Thor, God of Thunder. A glance at the inscription on the side of Mjölnir gave the confused Blake/Thor something of an explanation: "Whosoever holds this hammer, if he be worthy, shall possess the power of Thor." Blake used his new godlike powers to defeat the Kronans and went on to other adventures, appearing to many as just another Super Hero.

Family values
Odin sought to prepare Thor for his role as king, while Freyja wanted to ensure her son grew up to know there was more to life than duty.
Thor #301, Nov. 1980

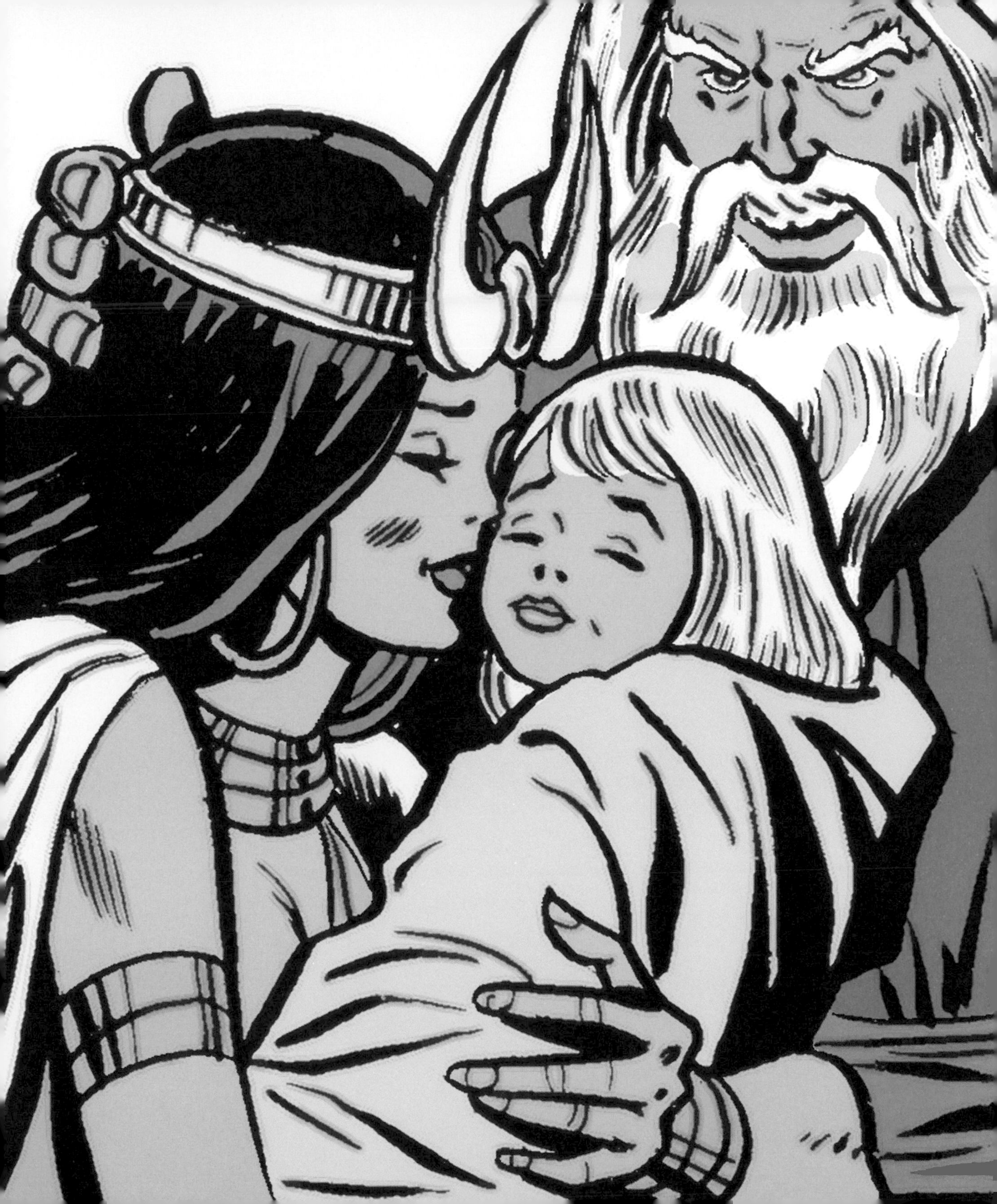

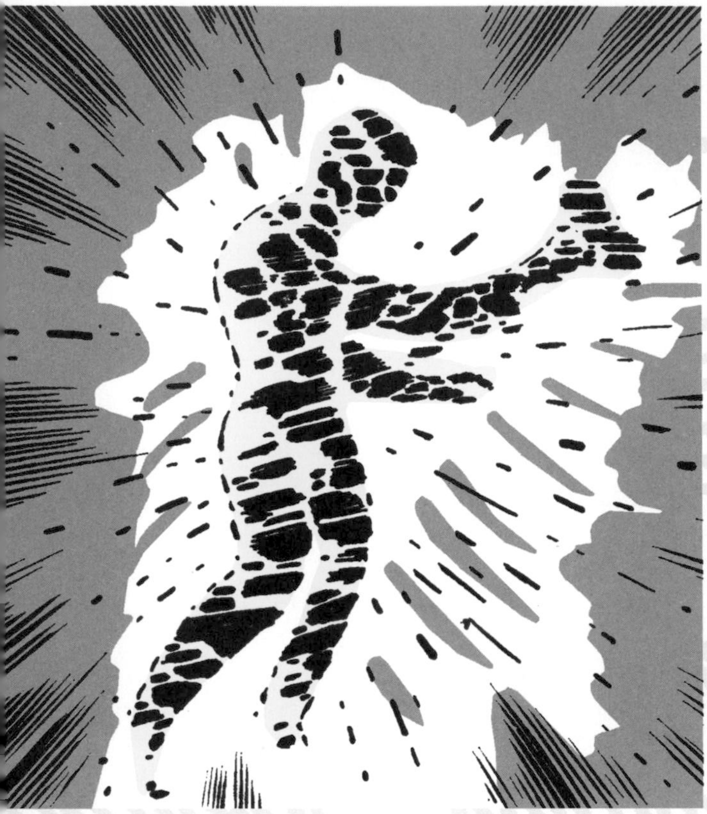

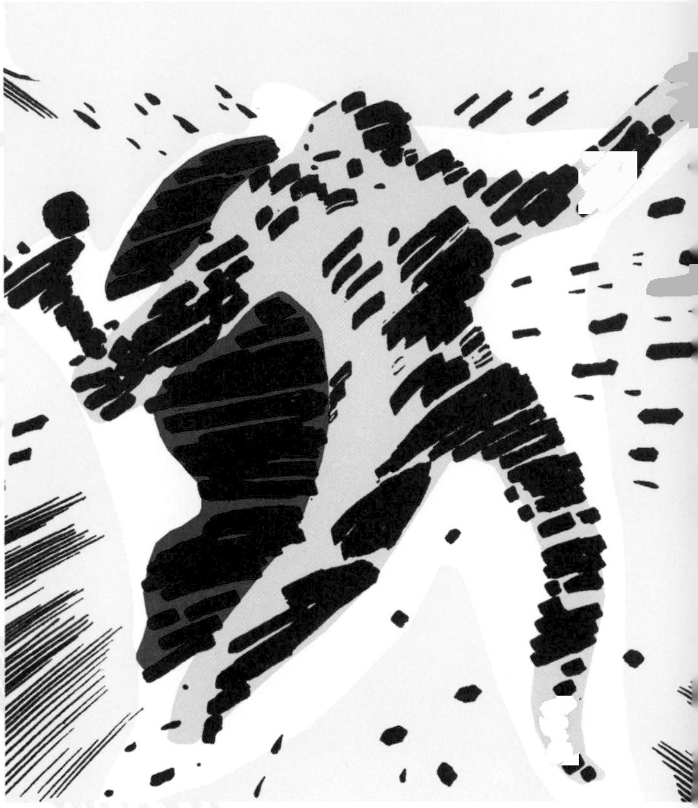

Of course, Thor was much more than an ordinary costumed crime fighter. Eventually, his old memories returned, and he split his time between Asgard and Earth, often drawn back to the mortal realm because of his love for Don Blake's colleague, a nurse named Jane Foster. Reconciled with his son, Odin confessed he had banished Thor to Earth to teach him humility. As Blake, Thor had been forced to put the needs of others before himself. In Odin's words: "Thou didst treat the sick and the afflicted! Thou didst walk amongst the weak and give them strength." In finding the hammer in the cave, Blake had simply recovered his lost heritage—and all according to Odin's grand plan. The All-Father had taught Thor a valuable lesson, but he had also strengthened his son's bond with Earth in preparation for struggles yet to come.

While still a callow youth, Thor shared many adventures—perhaps better characterized as misadventures—with his adoptive brother, Loki. Sired by the Frost Giant Laufey, Loki was adopted by Odin after victory in battle. Uncharitably considered by some to be no more than a war trophy, Loki was unlike any other Frost Giant. He was short of stature, physically weak, and something of a misfit. Over the years, he grew increasingly jealous of the fawning attention heaped upon Thor. Eagerly embracing his role as the God of Mischief, and employing magic as his primary tool, Loki often plotted to humiliate his brother. What started out as mere pranks, however, became more serious over time. When the God of Thunder began his Super Hero exploits on Earth, Loki frequently manipulated others into doing his malicious deeds for him.

Hammer of god
After being reunited with mystic mallet Mjölnir, the God of Thunder was reborn, embarking on a new career as an earthbound Super Hero. *Journey into Mystery #83*, Aug. 1962

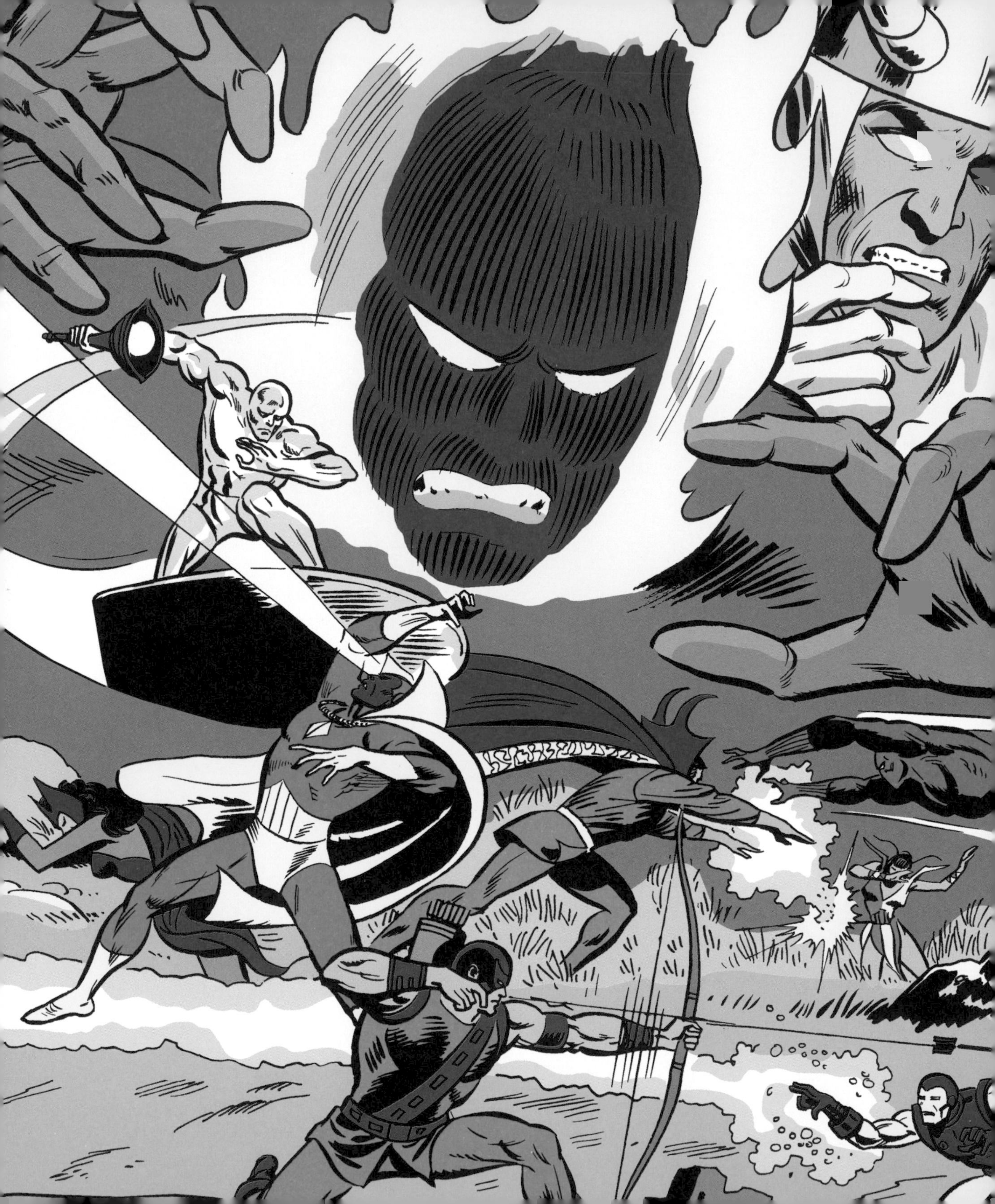

The team of Cobra and Mr. Hyde, Zarrko the Tomorrow Man, the Absorbing Man, and a host of other Super Villains, was empowered by the God of Mischief and set against his hated sibling. It was all seemingly in vain, however, and Thor inevitably shrugged off such attacks. To Loki's endless regret, a plan to use the Hulk as a pawn against his brother inadvertently led to the formation of the world's greatest Super Hero team, with the gamma-spawned monster eventually joining forces with Thor, Iron Man, Wasp, and Ant-Man as a founding member of the mighty Avengers.

During a particularly intense confrontation with Thor, Loki was accidentally blinded by a lightning strike. In his weakened and confused state, he fell from a mountaintop to his apparent death. In reality, though, he was plucked from the mortal realm by the Dread Dormammu, ruler of the otherworldly Dark Dimension. Sometime earlier, Dormammu had attempted to conquer Earth but had been defeated by Doctor Strange, the world's foremost mystic, and made to promise he would abandon all thoughts of invasion. Dormammu now proposed an alliance with Loki and outlined a scheme that would allow him to swallow up Earth without breaking the terms of his oath.

"Will you aid me, Prince of Evil?" Dormammu

The Lord of the Dark Dimension had learned that an ancient mystical artifact known as the Evil Eye had been shattered into six parts, each buried around the globe. When brought back together, the Evil Eye would possess enough power to bring the entire Earth into the Dark Dimension. Dormammu would, at last, have his prize, and he would have obtained it without going back on his word.

Shock and awe
The Dread Dormammu tricked the Super Hero group the Defenders into doing his bidding, but found his plans thwarted by the Avengers.
Avengers #117, Nov. 1973

With Loki sightless and Dormammu bound by his oath, the two villains decided to rely on the God of Mischief's tried-and-true tactics, and fool hapless intermediaries into acting on their behalf.

Employing his magical skills, Loki sent a telepathic communication to Doctor Strange purporting to be from the heroic Black Knight, whose soul was currently trapped in limbo. For some time, Doctor Strange had been searching to find a way to reunite the Black Knight's essence with his inert body, which had been turned to stone by the Asgardian Enchantress, and the fake message finally gave him a glimmer of hope. It suggested that the Evil Eye was the key to restoring the Black Knight to full health, and Doctor Strange and his allies in the superteam the Defenders were soon racing around the world in search of the artifact's constituent parts.

"What a fool I have been!" Loki

Witnessing Dormammu's maniacal joy at the mere thought of victory, Loki grew increasingly apprehensive. He feared that once the Evil Eye had been retrieved, his diabolical partner would turn on him. To hedge his bets, the God of Mischief appeared before the Avengers, concocting a story that the Defenders intended to use the Evil Eye for their own nefarious purposes. Soon the two teams of Super Heroes were battling each other for possession of the arcane artifact. Dormammu was enraged at this surprise turn of events, but the Avengers-Defenders war nevertheless provided him with a unique opportunity. Once all the parts were unearthed, Dormammu dispatched a demonic acolyte to retrieve the reconstituted Evil Eye. He then made good on his vow and transported Earth into the Dark Dimension. The Avengers and Defenders fought valiantly to contain the ensuing madness, but it was Loki who ultimately saved the day. He snatched the Evil Eye from Dormammu, causing the Dread Lord's fiery essence to be sucked into the artifact. Caught in the mystical blowback, Loki's sight was restored, but at the cost of his sanity.

Strength test
On opposite sides during the Avengers-Defenders war, the Hulk and Thor traded powerful blows in equal measure.
Defenders #10, Nov. 1973

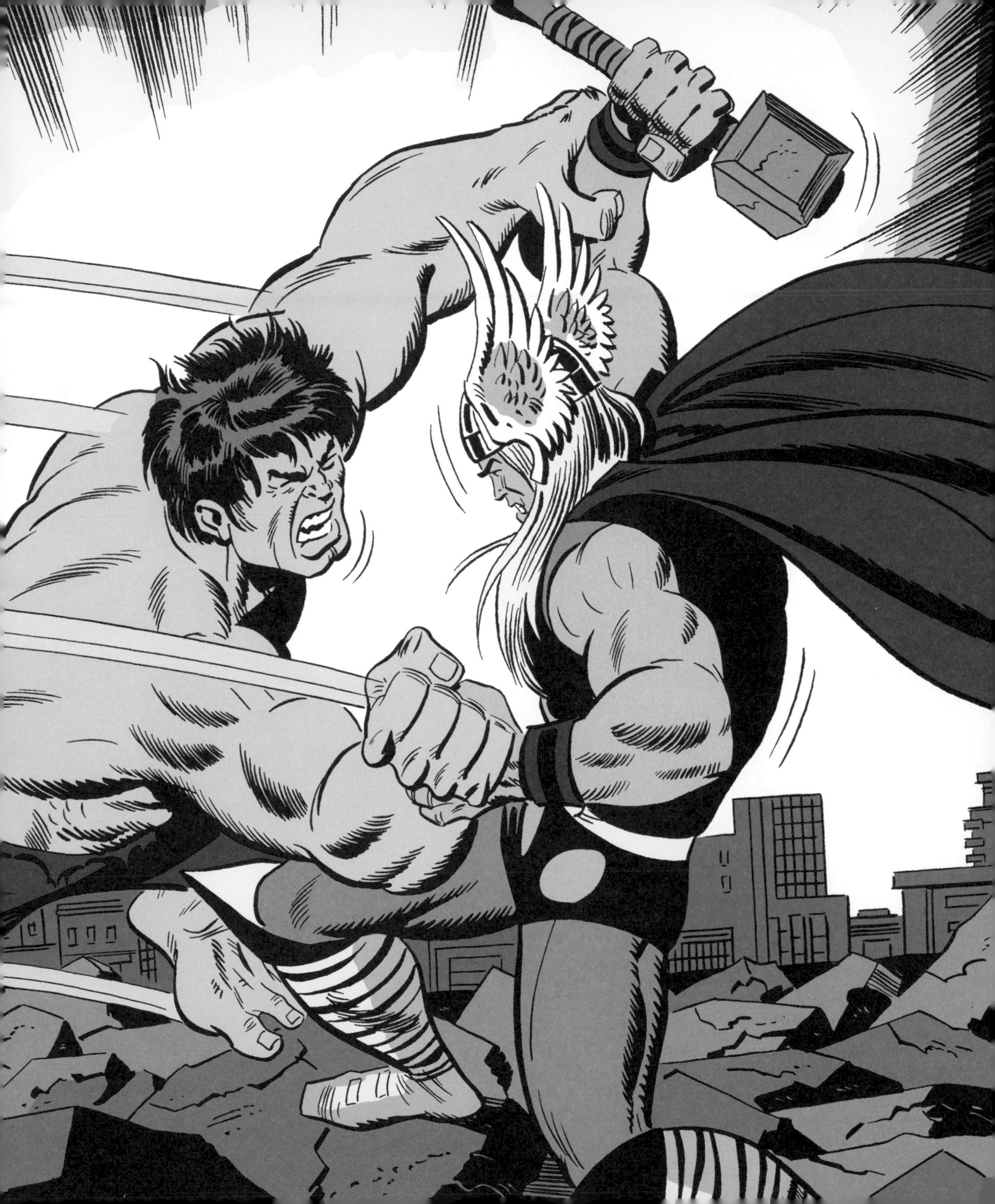

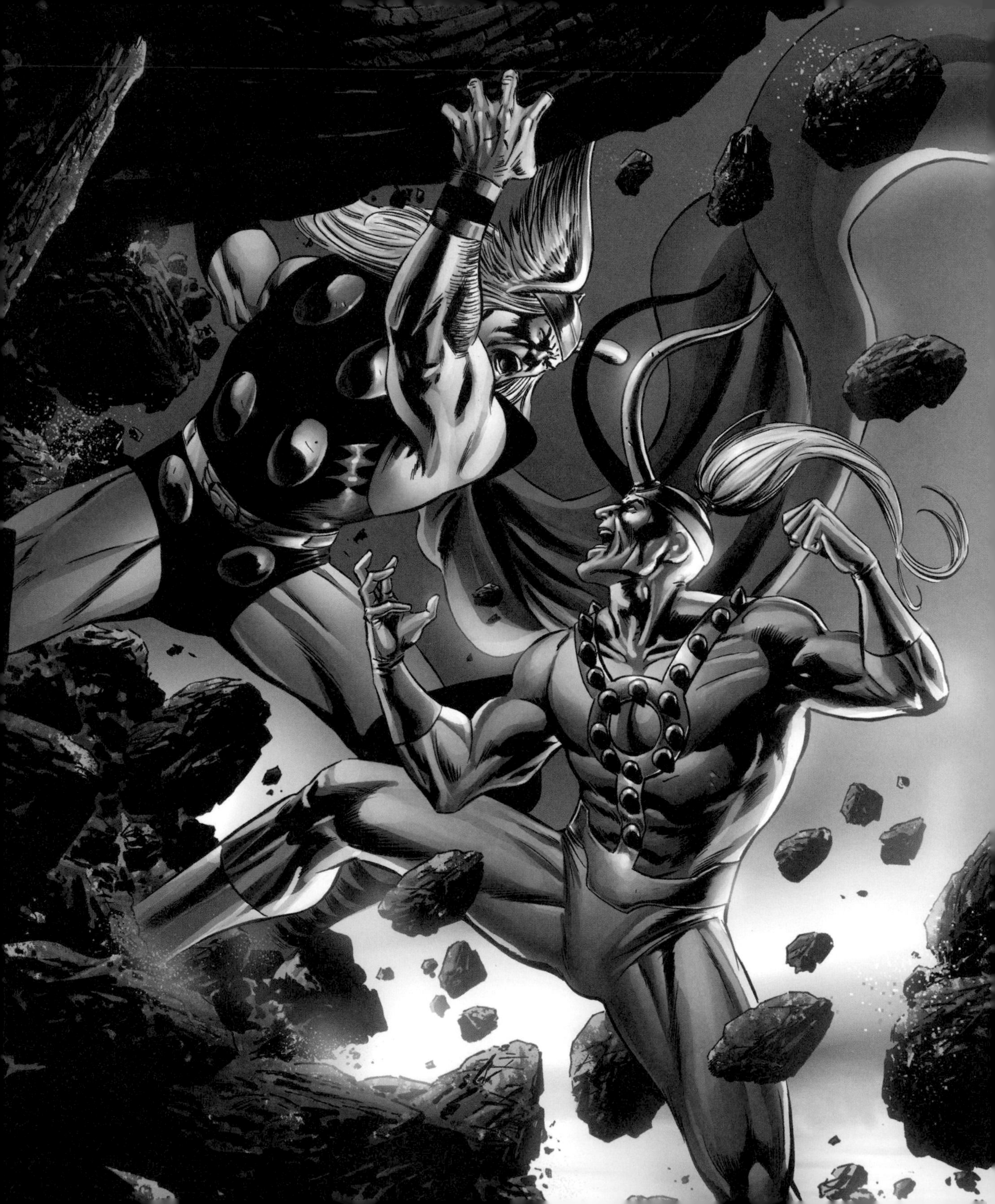

The God of Mischief eventually recovered his wits and, as fate's wheel rolled on, he continued his feud with Thor. Finally, after Odin passed away and a reluctant Thor sat upon the throne of Asgard, the day of Ragnarok arrived. Seemingly more hostile than ever, Loki fulfilled his preordained role and unchained the savage Fenris Wolf. Then, entering into an alliance with the infernal demon Surtur, he used the mold from which Mjölnir had been struck to forge a set of mighty hammers. These he bestowed on his newfound allies—the monstrous trolls Ulik and Geirrodur among them—and then he unleashed his forces upon Asgard.

Mjölnir was broken into three pieces during the first clash of arms and, fearing the worst, Thor escaped to Earth to assemble allies of his own. With Captain America and Iron Man at his side, the God of Thunder returned to the battle, only to discover he was too late. Loki and his savage accomplices had overwhelmed the Asgard's defenses and were now busily picking over the city's carcass. The trio of Avengers did what they could for the survivors and then lived up to their name by seeking out Loki and his fiendish lieutenants. Captain America subdued Fenris, while Iron Man and Thor took to the skies to directly confront Loki.

After trading countless blows with his adoptive brother, Loki recognized imminent defeat and chose retreat over capture. Thor, too, bowed to the inevitable. The signs of Ragnarok were all around and, not wishing to see his compatriots crushed in destiny's maw, he teleported the Avengers back to Earth, then gathered up the rest of the Asgardians and prepared to make a final stand in Vanaheim.

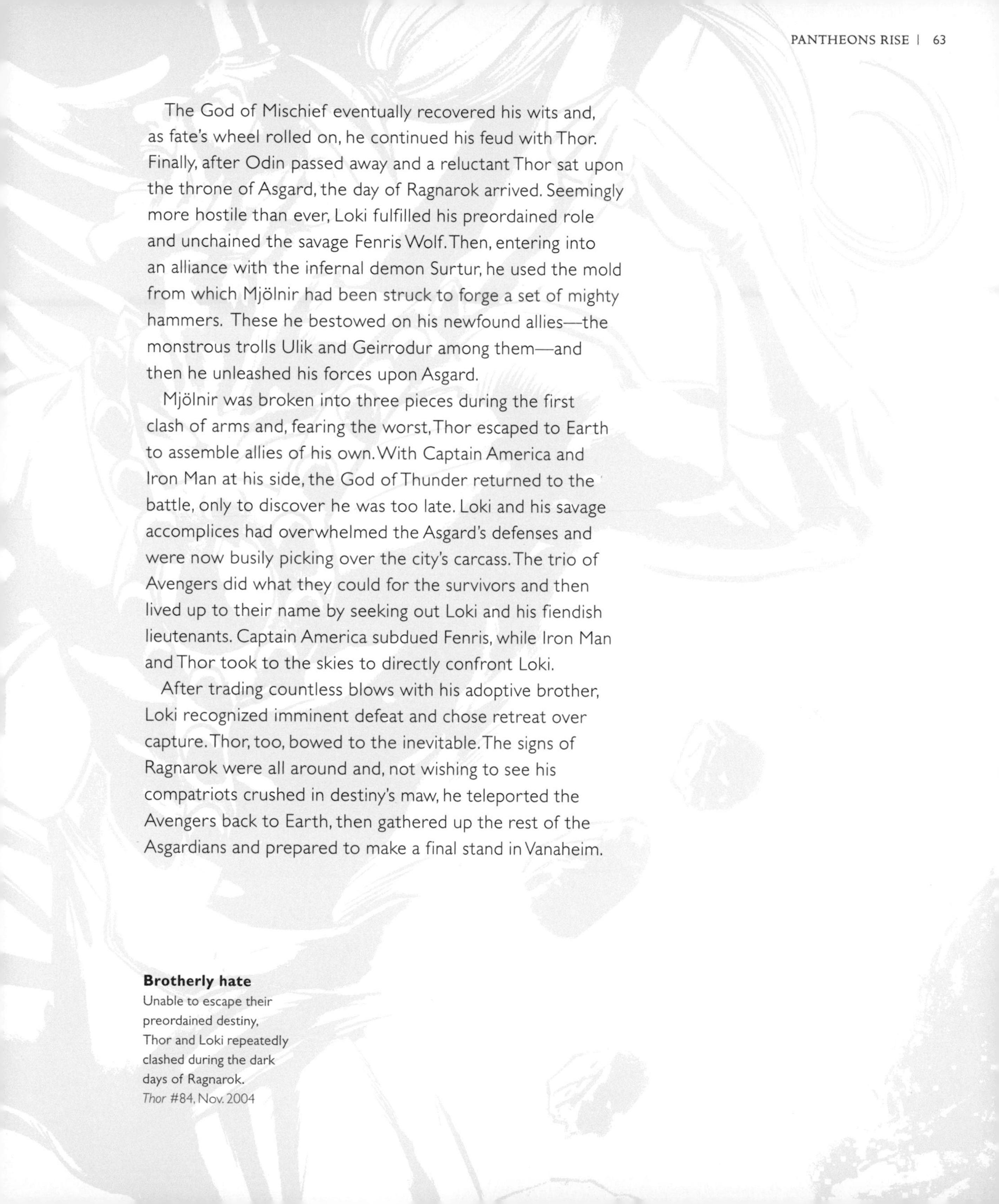

Brotherly hate
Unable to escape their preordained destiny, Thor and Loki repeatedly clashed during the dark days of Ragnarok.
Thor #84, Nov. 2004

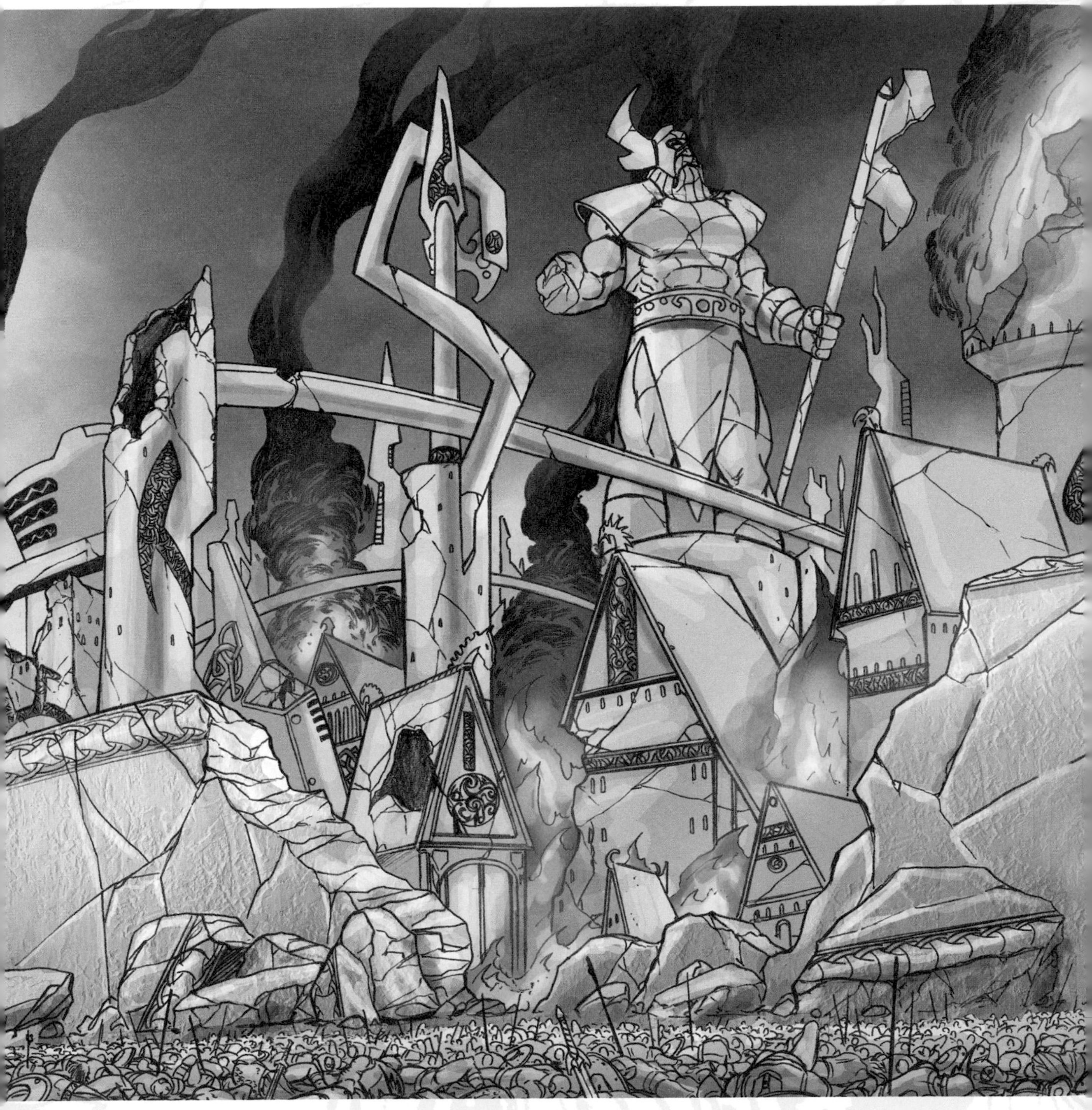

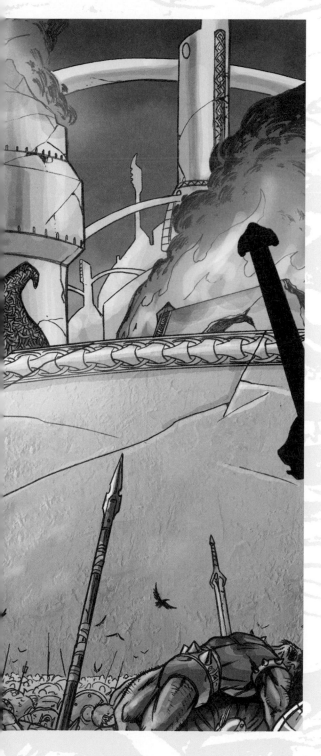

Bone-tired and battle-weary, the God of Thunder searched restlessly for some way to forestall Ragnarok. In his quest, he traveled to the World Tree Yggdrasil. As his father had done centuries earlier, Thor plucked out his own eye, offering up the orb as a sacrifice in exchange for arcane knowledge. Wisdom was not quickly forthcoming, however, and Thor was forced to tear out his second eye and hang himself from Yggdrasil's branches in order to receive the visions he so dearly craved.

Thor died and entered a region of Hel. There, tapping into the runic magic of his people, he finally perceived Ragnarok to be a cycle and not a singular event. What's more, he learned something that even Odin had not known. Ragnarok was not some random act of fate, but a deliberate occurrence, orchestrated by a band of self-styled "gods to the gods" called Those Who Sit Above in Shadow. Each Ragnarok produced vast quantities of mystical energy that Those Who Sit Above in Shadow consumed to maintain their strength and clandestine authority.

Eventually returning to the land of the living, Thor was determined to free the Asgardians from the grip of the godlike parasites that had been feasting endlessly upon their trials and tribulations. His human side gave him a uniquely mortal perspective and he realized that the only way the Asgardians could ever hope to escape the cycle was to surrender to their fate one last time. And so, as prophesized, doom came for the Norse pantheon. Thor looked on helplessly as his fellow Asgardians succumbed to the rampaging armies of Surtur.

Asgard aflame
As the day of Ragnarok finally dawned, venal Loki unleashed his forces upon the Golden Realm, leaving Asgard's capital in ruins.
Thor #81, Aug. 2004

With Surtur's forces triumphant, Ragnarok was complete—the Twilight of the Gods had fallen. Then, to prevent the cycle's continuation, Thor destroyed the tapestry of the Three Fates. The Asgardian gods had died, but they would be reborn, and this time they would be free. This had been Odin's plan all along. He had pushed and cajoled his son for centuries, making him embrace his Earthly side, so that the God of Thunder would know what it meant to be mortal and would have the courage and imagination to acknowledge that endings are often beginnings.

"I am a god with a man's heart." Thor (Odinson)

His task complete, Thor decided to join his fellow Asgardians beyond the veil of death, to "breathe deep the slumber of the gods... For a while, at least." The Asgardians were eventually reincarnated on Earth. After some literal soul-searching, Thor gathered together his people and helped build a new capital city in the unlikeliest of places—the skies above the sleepy town of Broxton, Oklahoma in the United States. The unique locale came with unique challenges. The authorities were intimidated by the power of the Asgardians, fearing that a dangerously unpredictable threat had suddenly materialized in the heartland of the US.

Fire and fury
Lady Sif marshaled Asgard's remaining warriors in a desperate attempt to defeat the fire giant Surtur and armies of Muspelheim.
Thor #85, Dec. 2004

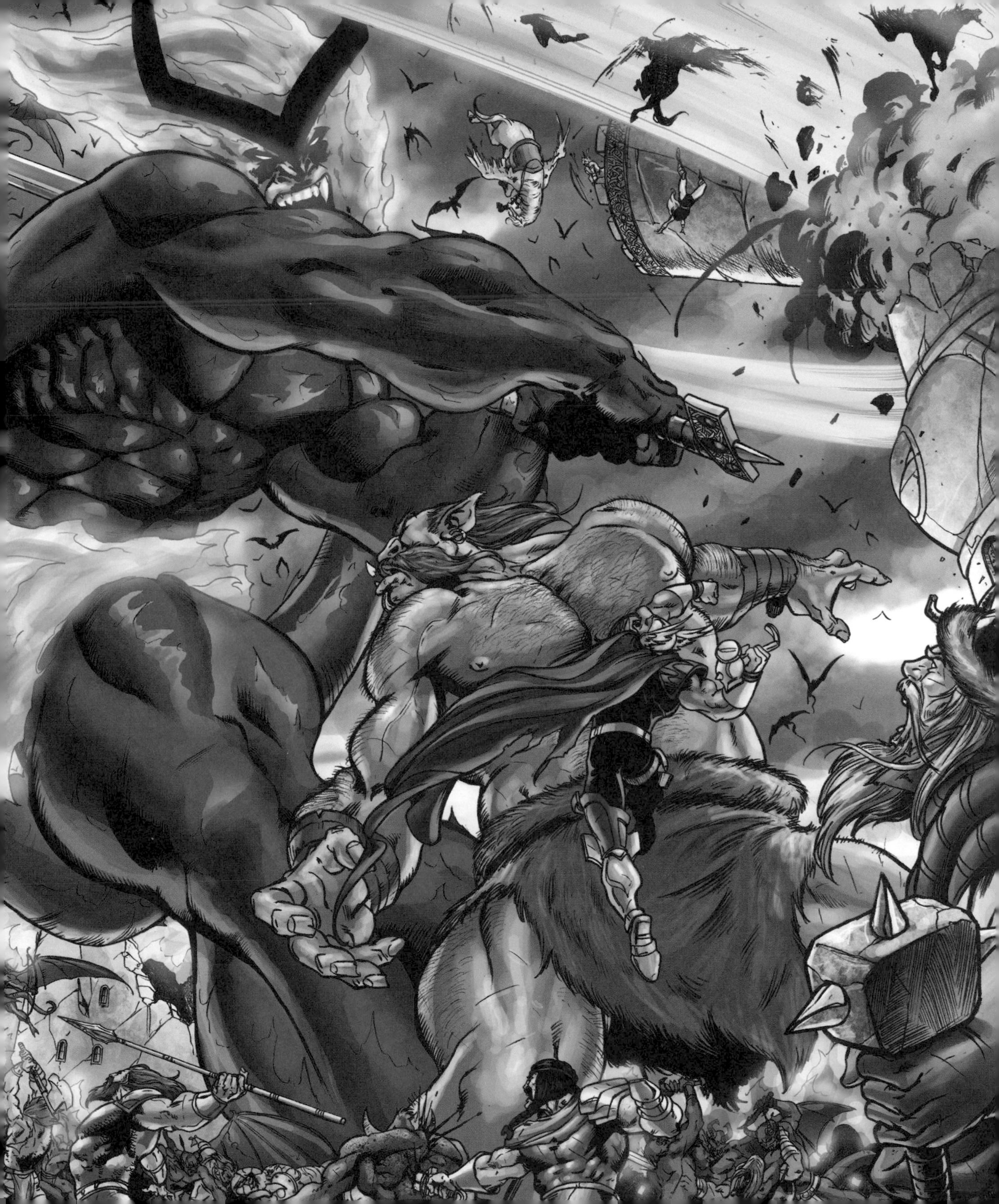

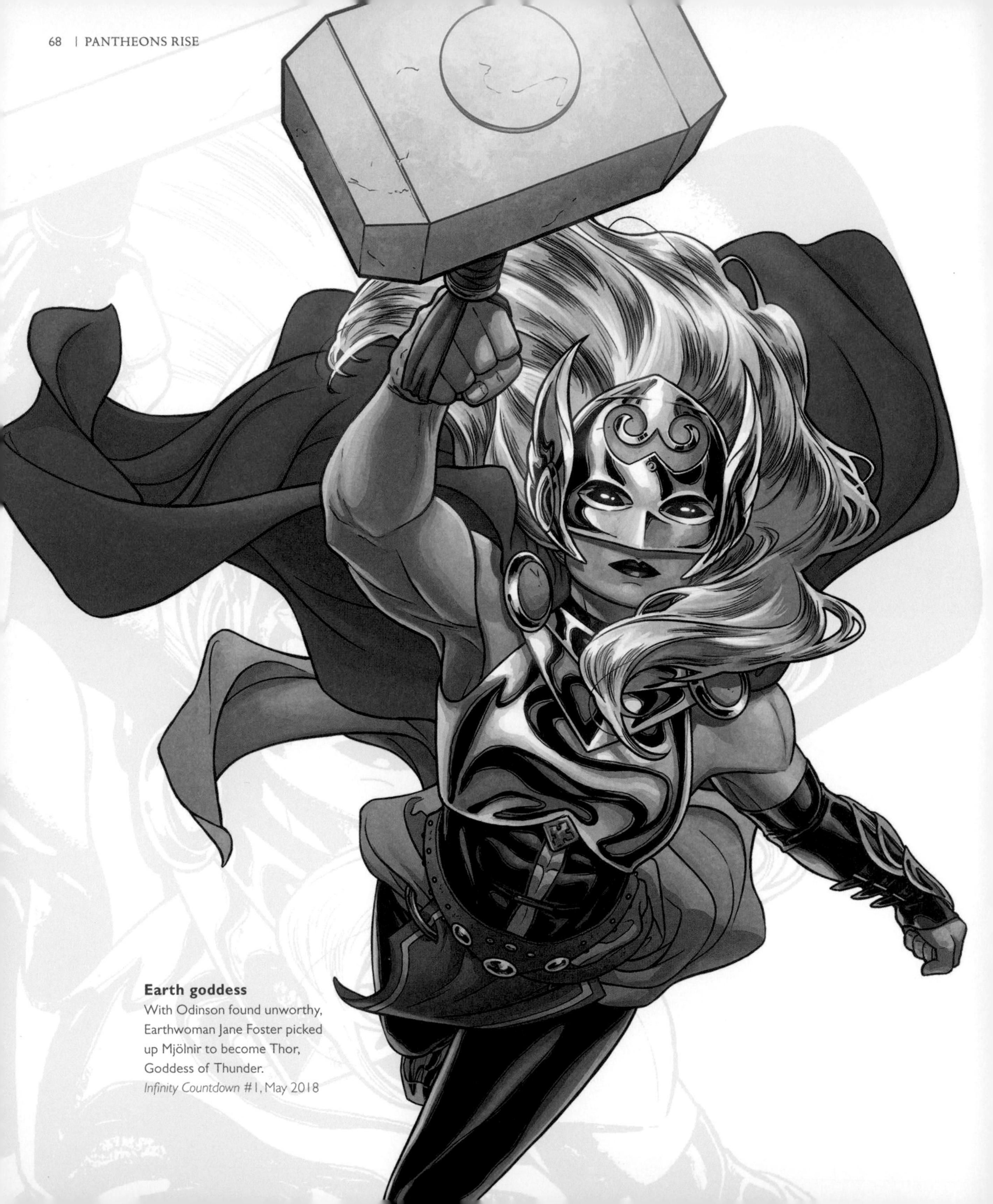

Earth goddess
With Odinson found unworthy, Earthwoman Jane Foster picked up Mjölnir to become Thor, Goddess of Thunder.
Infinity Countdown #1, May 2018

Although a compromise was found—Asgard being granted the status of a foreign embassy with full diplomatic immunity for its inhabitants— tensions remained high. The new city was ultimately destroyed by the Machiavellian Norman Osborn and his team of Dark Avengers. Under the rule of All-Mother Freyja, the city was rebuilt and renamed Asgardia. Transported off-world, it settled in orbit around the planet Saturn.

It seemed the certainties of the past were gone forever. Increasingly, Thor had misgivings about his role in the universe and the wider role played by his fellow Asgardians. He came to see the Norse pantheon as vain and arrogant, undeserving of worship. Plagued by these doubts, he himself became unworthy, no longer capable of lifting Mjölnir or commanding the power of Thor. He was the God of Thunder no more, now he was merely the Odinson.

"Mortals... would all be better off without us." Odinson (The Unworthy)

Left unattended, Mjölnir called out telepathically to Jane Foster, now a successful doctor in her own right. Upon lifting the hammer, she was transformed into Thor, Goddess of Thunder. Every bit as valiant as her predecessor, the new Thor went on to meet numerous threats and serve as a steadfast member of the Avengers. Unfortunately, her powers and newfound sense of purpose came at great personal cost. Foster was undergoing chemotherapy as treatment for cancer and, when she transformed into Thor, the life-preserving drugs were purged from her system. Changing back to Jane wiped away any benefits received from her treatment, leaving her perilously ill as her cancer continued to grow.

When the Dark Elf Malekith launched an all-out war, Jane was forced to neglect her health and come repeatedly to the defense of the Ten Realms of Asgard. In response, Odinson and Doctor Strange staged an intervention, informing the new Thor that just one more transformation would result in her death. Reluctantly, Jane Foster agreed to put down her hammer and focus her energies on beating her cancer. However, when Malekith unleashed the deadly Mangog upon Asgardia, Jane took up Mjölnir once more and flew to the city's aid. She bound the hideous creature to her hammer with an unbreakable chain and hurled Mangog and Mjölnir into the blazing heart of the sun.

As Mjölnir melted away, Thor reverted to her Jane Foster persona and finally succumbed to her grave illness. Death wasn't the end for Jane, however, and Odinson channeled the power of the God Tempest, the Mother of Thunder—an elemental force that had been released from within the destroyed Mjölnir—to revive her.

Although Jane had successfully stopped Mangog's murderous rampage, Asgardia's flight controls had been damaged and the city plummeted into the sun, prompting All-Mother Freyja to evacuate her people to Midgard. Also returned to Earth, and with her cancer finally in remission, Jane gifted Odinson a small splinter of Mjölnir that she had managed to save. Whether he was worthy or not, she encouraged him to take back the mantle of Thor. And not a moment too soon. The War of the Realms was going badly. Malekith had already crushed nine of the kingdoms and the conqueror now had Midgard in his sights. What Thor Odinson did next would mean life or death for the mortals he so admired. Malekith's Dark Elves moved in darkness, using the Black Bifrost to slip unseen from realm to realm. They attacked without warning, capturing Thor and imprisoning him in Jotunheim, the barren wasteland of the barbaric Frost Giants.

World War Ten
When the Dark Elf Malekith declared war on the Ten Realms, Odinson formed a coalition of heroes and gods to turn back the invaders.
War of the Realms #1, Jun. 2019

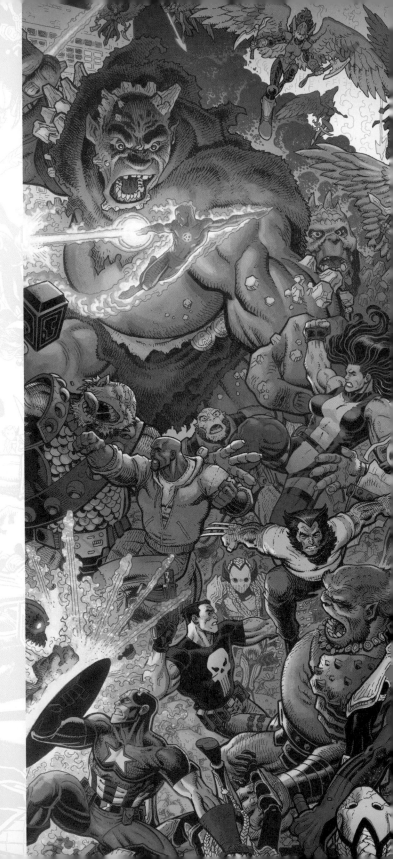

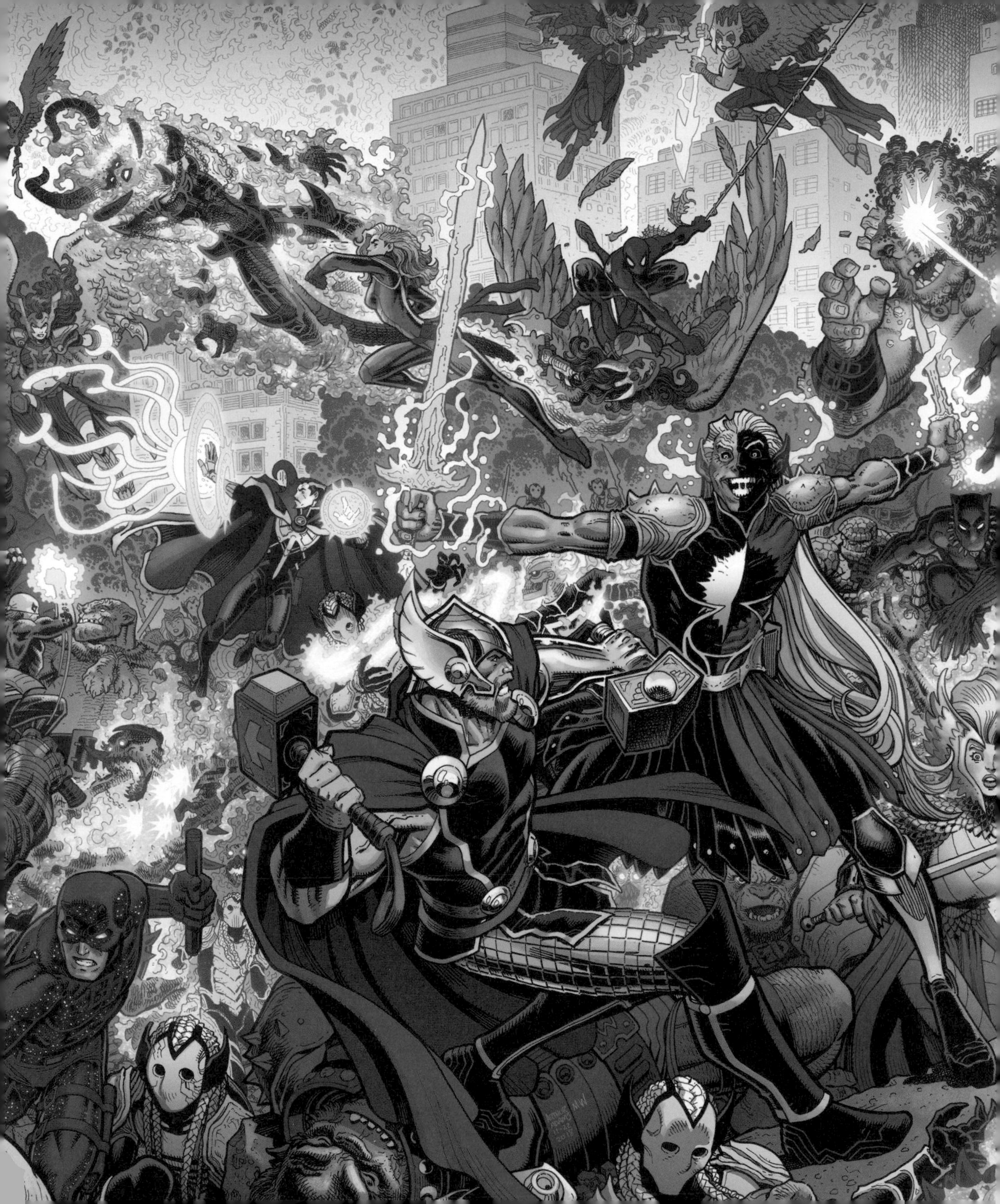

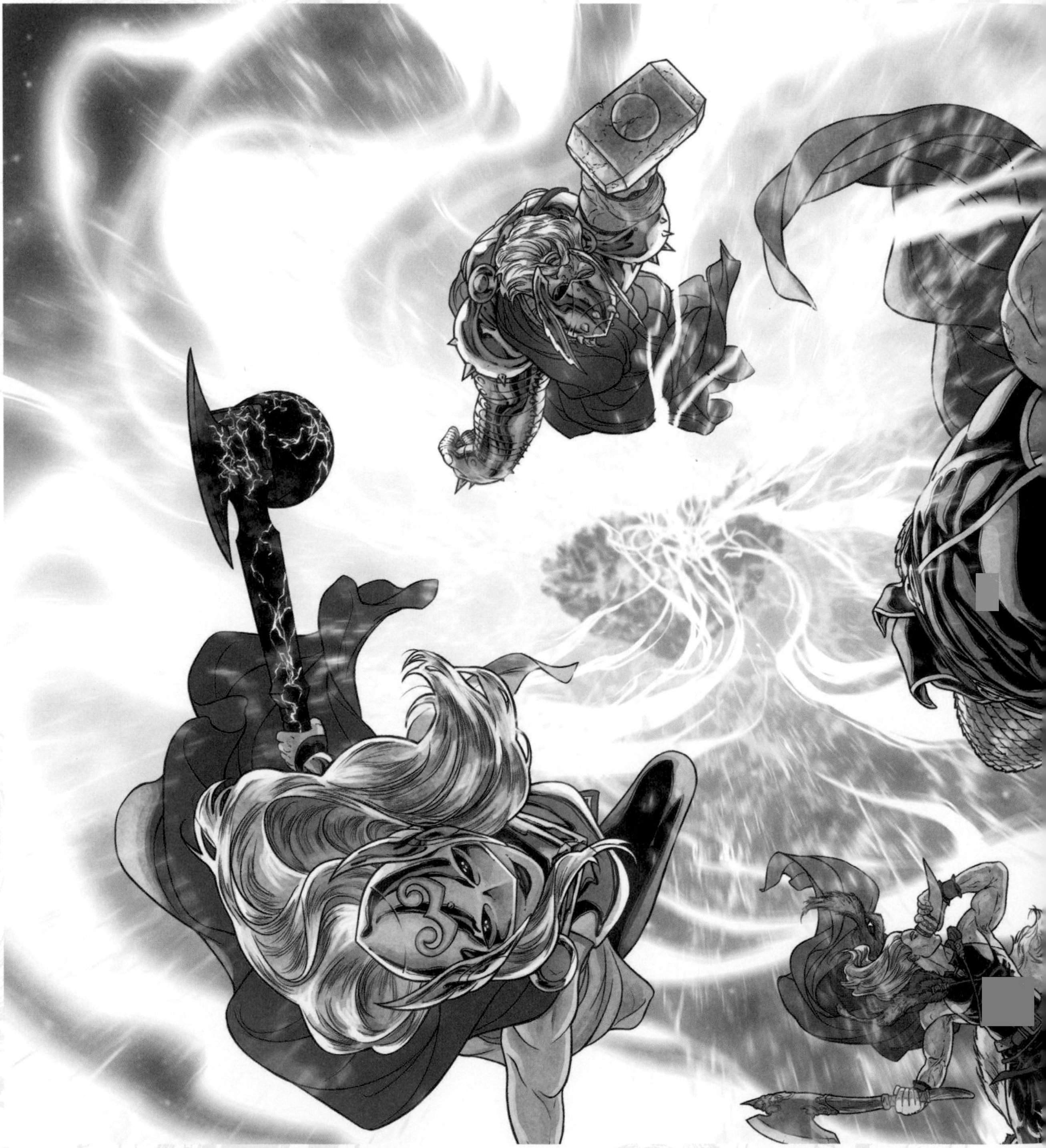

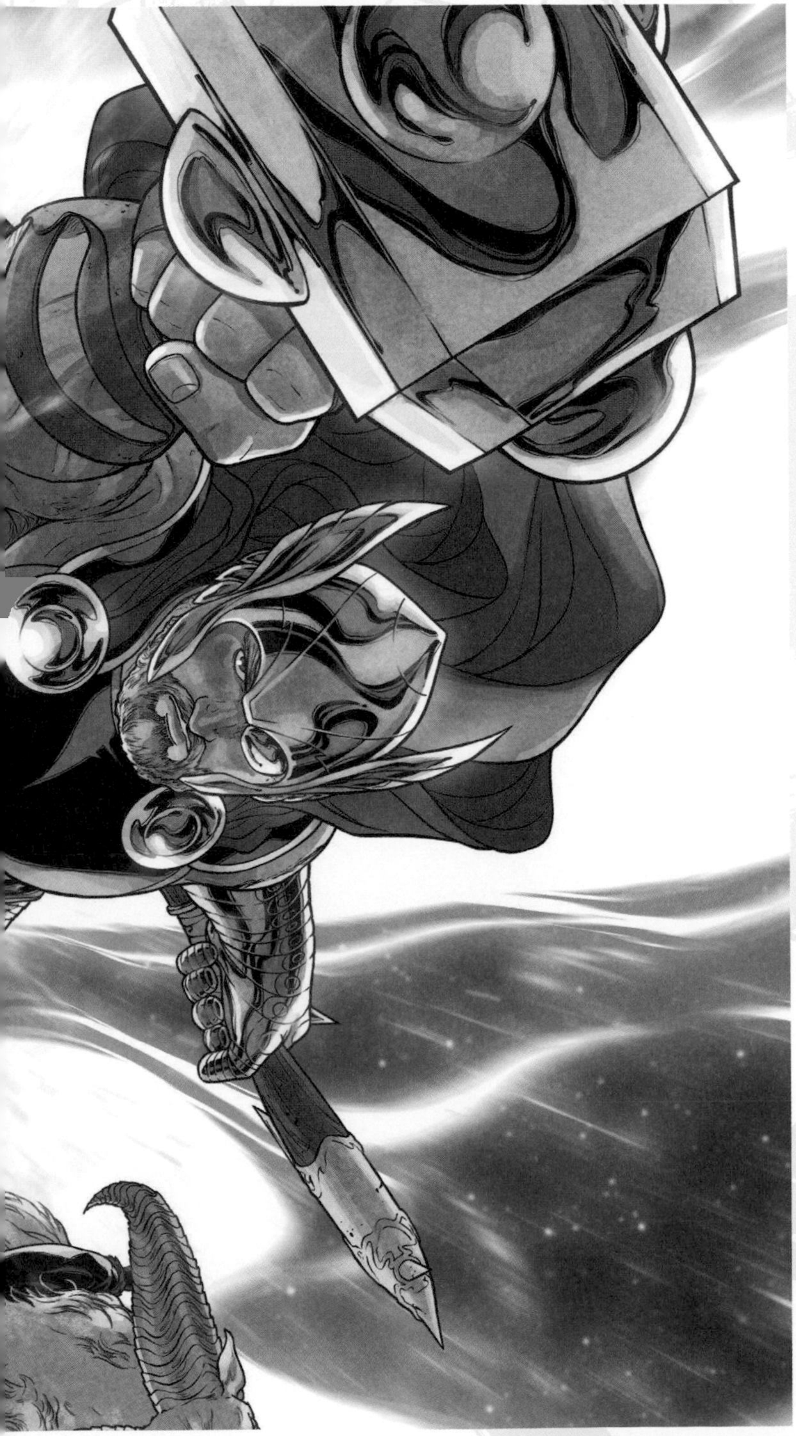

With her son sidelined, Freyja prepared to make a defiant last stand on the streets of New York City. Fighting alongside Earth's Super Heroes, the Asgardians engaged the enemy, hoping against hope they had the strength to hold the line against seemingly endless waves of Trolls, Frost Giants, and Dark Elves.

"We need to save the world." Captain America

While effectively mobilizing Midgard's defenses, Freyja was also determined to go on the offensive and she dispatched a squad of champions—Spider-Man, Wolverine, and Captain America among them—to retrieve Thor from the clutches of the Frost Giants. Their mission a success, the freed God of Thunder addressed a hastily convened war council at Avengers Mountain and took charge. "There is only one who will lead this fight," he declared. "And his name is Thor!" Ultimately, however, it wasn't a solitary Thor who turned back the tide of darkness, it was four unique Thors: a storm of Thunder Gods.

Thor Corps
Odinson teamed up with the Goddess of Thunder and his past and future selves to take on the nigh-infinite might of Malekith.
War of the Realms #6, Aug. 2019

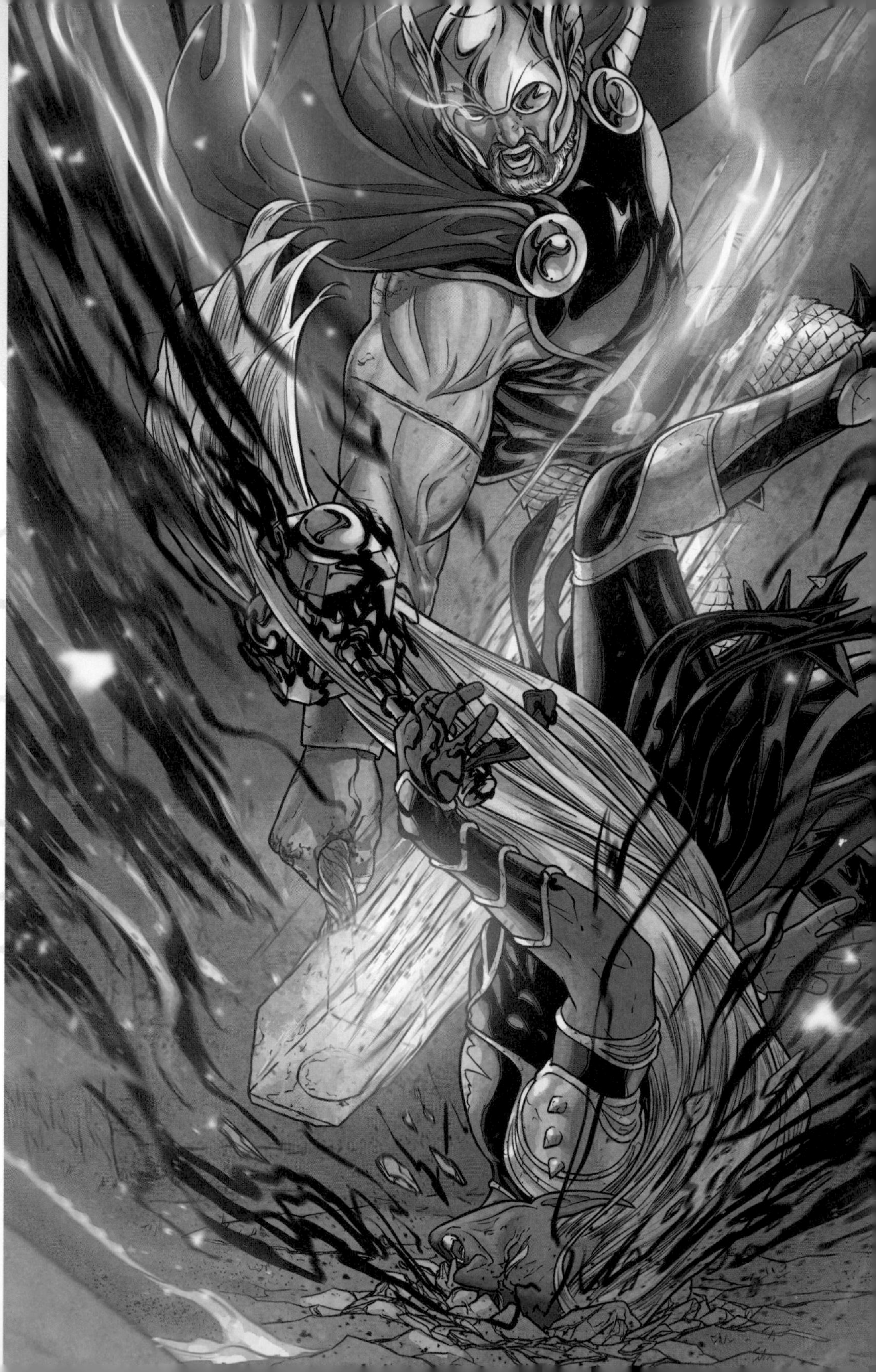

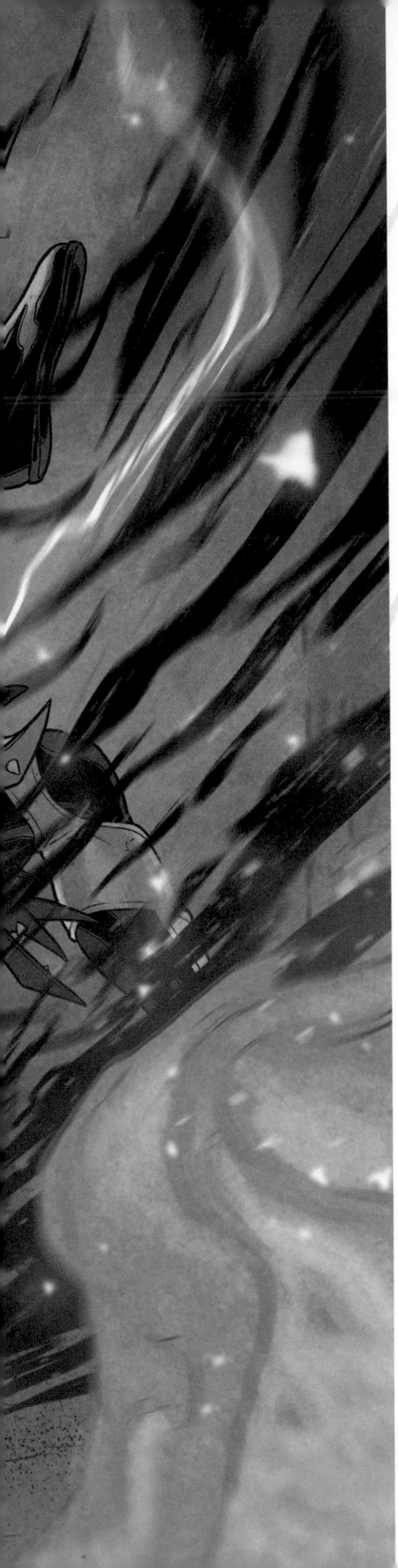

Having earlier recognized that he faced seemingly impossible odds, Odinson had again communed with the World Tree. It transpired that following Asgardia's destruction, a seed of Yggdrasil had taken root in the sun and Odinson braved the heat of the raging star to learn how best to defeat Malekith. As before, a sacrifice was required in exchange for this wisdom, and Thor willingly surrendered his right eye and the last piece of Mjölnir to the inferno.

"All hail... All-Father Thor." Odin

The offering proved its worth for Thor learned that Malekith would be unable to withstand the power of multiple Thunder Gods. Odinson used the Fantastic Four's time-travel technology to recruit a version of himself from the past and one from the far-flung future. Jane Foster had also taken up arms, wielding the Mjölnir of an alternate reality to become Thor for one last time. And so Malekith fell before the combined might of the four Thunder Gods. Odinson delivered the decisive blow, revealing he had not idly given up the last remnant of Mjölnir. Rather, he had used the sun's power to forge it into a complete hammer, a pristine weapon that he now used to devastating effect. In victory, Thor was declared the savior of the Ten Realms and pronounced Asgard's new ruler.

Knockout blow
Wielding a newly forged Mjölnir, Odinson ended Malekith's bid for universal conquest with one swift strike.
War of the Realms #6, Aug. 2019

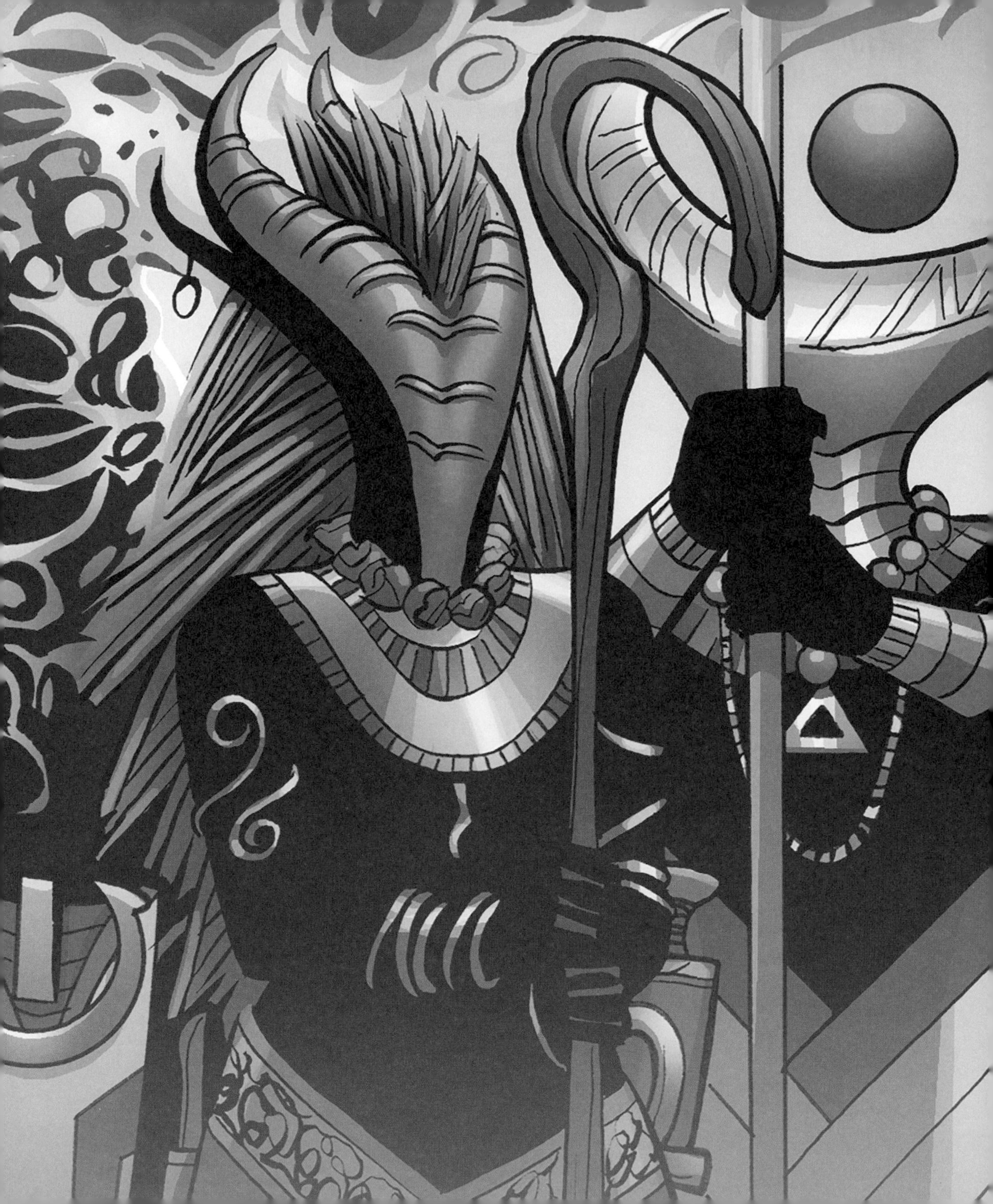

The Orisha: Bast's Pact

At the dawn of early man, Bast of the Orisha agreed to protect the warrior Bashenga in exchange for worship. Together they established the Black Panther Cult, a lineage of heroic rulers that endures to this day.

In an ancient time lost to human memory, wanderers made their way through East Africa. Their explorations brought them into contact with the Originators, mystical beast folk who were distantly related to the Elder Gods. Foremost among the Originator tribes were the Simbi—snake-men who resembled the serpentine god Set, the Anansi—ferocious-looking man-spiders, and the gorilla-like Vanyan.

The earliest encounters between the Originators and humans were largely friendly, but competition for natural resources increased tensions between the two groups. Eventually, some minor dispute sparked a brutal war. At first, it seemed the powerful and savage Originators would be easy victors, but heroic warriors soon rose up to defend their fellow humans from attack. Empowered by the faith of their followers, these women and men were miraculously transformed into a new pantheon of hero-gods, the Orisha.

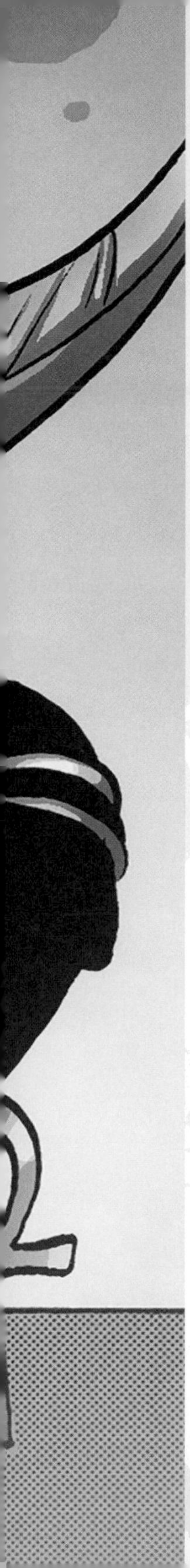

Out of Africa
The Orisha, such as Mujaji the Life-giver and Ptah the Shaper, were given form and substance by the faith of early East African explorers.
Black Panther #13, Jun. 2017

Empowered by their worshipers, the Orisha fought the Originators. War god Kokou led the way, followed by Mujaji, the giver and taker of life, who released a raging flood to sweep away whole armies of Originators. Most formidable of all was the panther goddess Bast, who struck with a savage fury and did much to turn the tide of battle in favor of the humans. The Orisha banished the defeated Originators to a netherworld beyond the mortal plane, and then spent the next few millennia guarding the gates to this mystical prison. In time, the war slipped into legend, and the humans who devoutly worshiped the Orisha forgot that their land had ever belonged to anyone else.

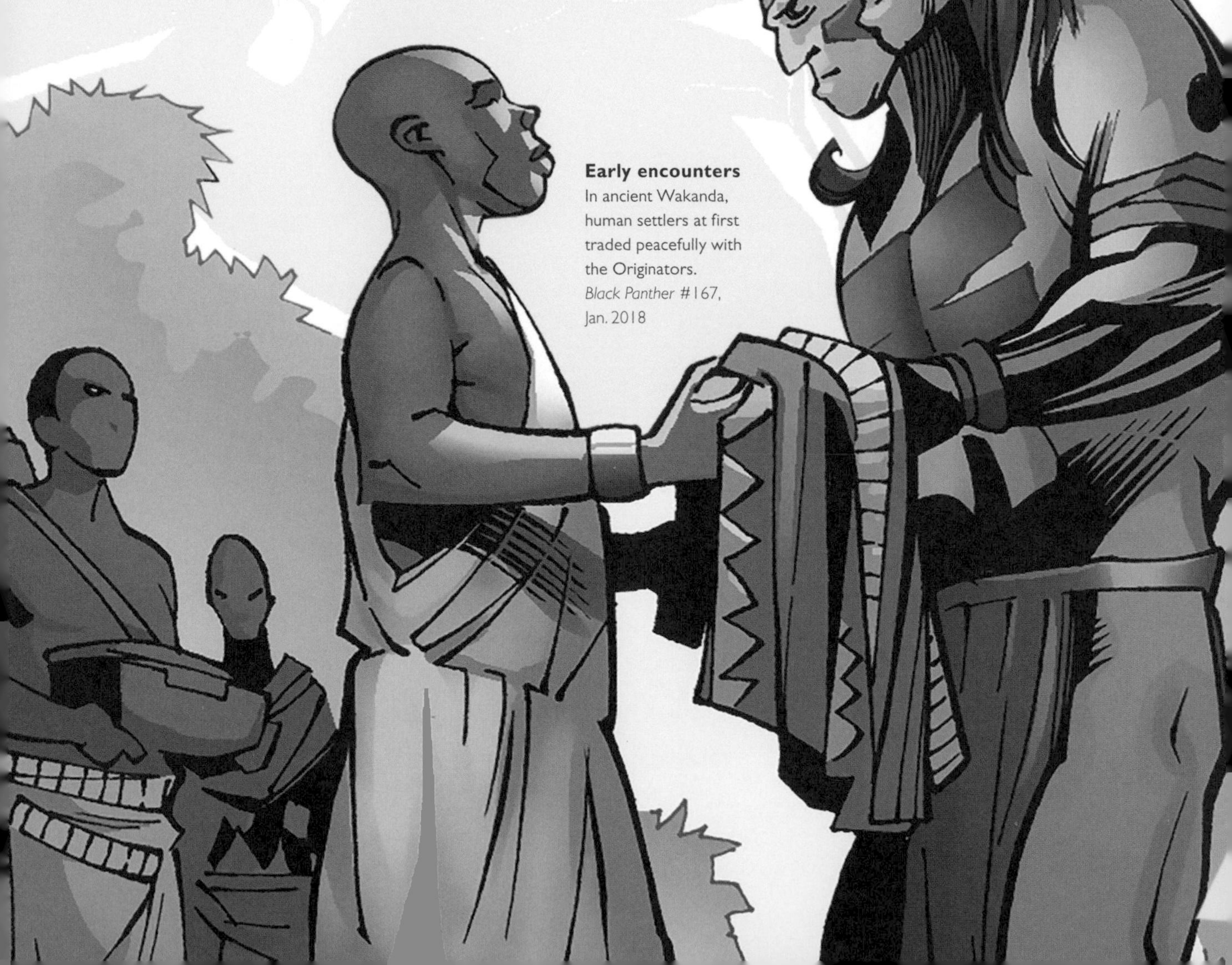

Early encounters
In ancient Wakanda, human settlers at first traded peacefully with the Originators.
Black Panther #167, Jan. 2018

Around the time of the Originator's defeat, a meteor crashed to Earth, tearing up the landscape and forming a great mound. Laced with the mineral element Vibranium, the fallen rock possessed several remarkable properties. It absorbed kinetic energy and emitted radiation that mutated those who dared to venture too close, transforming them into horrific "demon spirits." Rallying his tribe, the visionary leader Bashenga vanquished the monsters and established a warrior clan dedicated to the preservation of the great Vibranium Mound and the protection of the innocent people who lived in its shadow.

Bast was impressed with Bashenga's courage and, looking for devoted worshipers to be custodians of her legacy, she proposed a special pact. In exchange for supplication, Bashenga and his tribe would receive divine protection. Bashenga agreed and, donning the sacred panther robes in Bast's honor, he became the first in a long line of leaders who derived their authority from the panther goddess and her power. With the creation of the Black Panther Cult, the land finally became known as Wakanda, an isolated and fiercely independent nation that worshiped Bast but also honored the entire pantheon of the Orisha.

Taking offence
Some unknown disagreement sparked conflict between the Originators and the humans, leading to all-out war.
Black Panther #167, Jan. 2018

Harnessing the power of Vibranium, Wakanda developed advanced technology many years before other countries and this frequently attracted the predatory interest of would-be colonizers. Following in Bashenga's footsteps, successive rulers donned the ceremonial armor of the Black Panther to repel invaders or to root out spies. Over the years, Wakanda kept its secrets by being resolutely isolationist, holding closely to traditions and customs that kept it safe from outside interference for many centuries.

In fact, the past continued to be a tangible presence in Wakanda as each new leader, thanks to Bast's influence, was able to commune with their predecessors. A city of mausoleums was constructed near Lake Nyanza, and this Necropolis formed a nexus with the ancestral plane through which the current Black Panther could commune with the Black Panthers of ages past. This ghostly Royal Council of Elders—filled with the spirits of women and men of great wisdom and experience—was instrumental in steering Wakanda through many difficult times.

"Bashenga was... wise and fearless." Black Panther (T'Challa)

In recent years, T'Challa assumed the throne of Wakanda upon the death of his father, T'Chaka, at the hands of the villainous Ulysses Klaw. From the beginning, T'Challa's reign was tumultuous, with the young ruler torn between his scientific calling and his nation's devoted worship of the Orisha. What's more, T'Challa's duties as Black Panther, and as a member of the Avengers, frequently took him abroad.

Cult following
Protected by Bast's divinity, Bashenga created the Black Panther Cult, establishing a lineage of warrior-leaders that kept Wakanda safe for centuries.
Black Panther: Marvel Legacy Primer, 2017

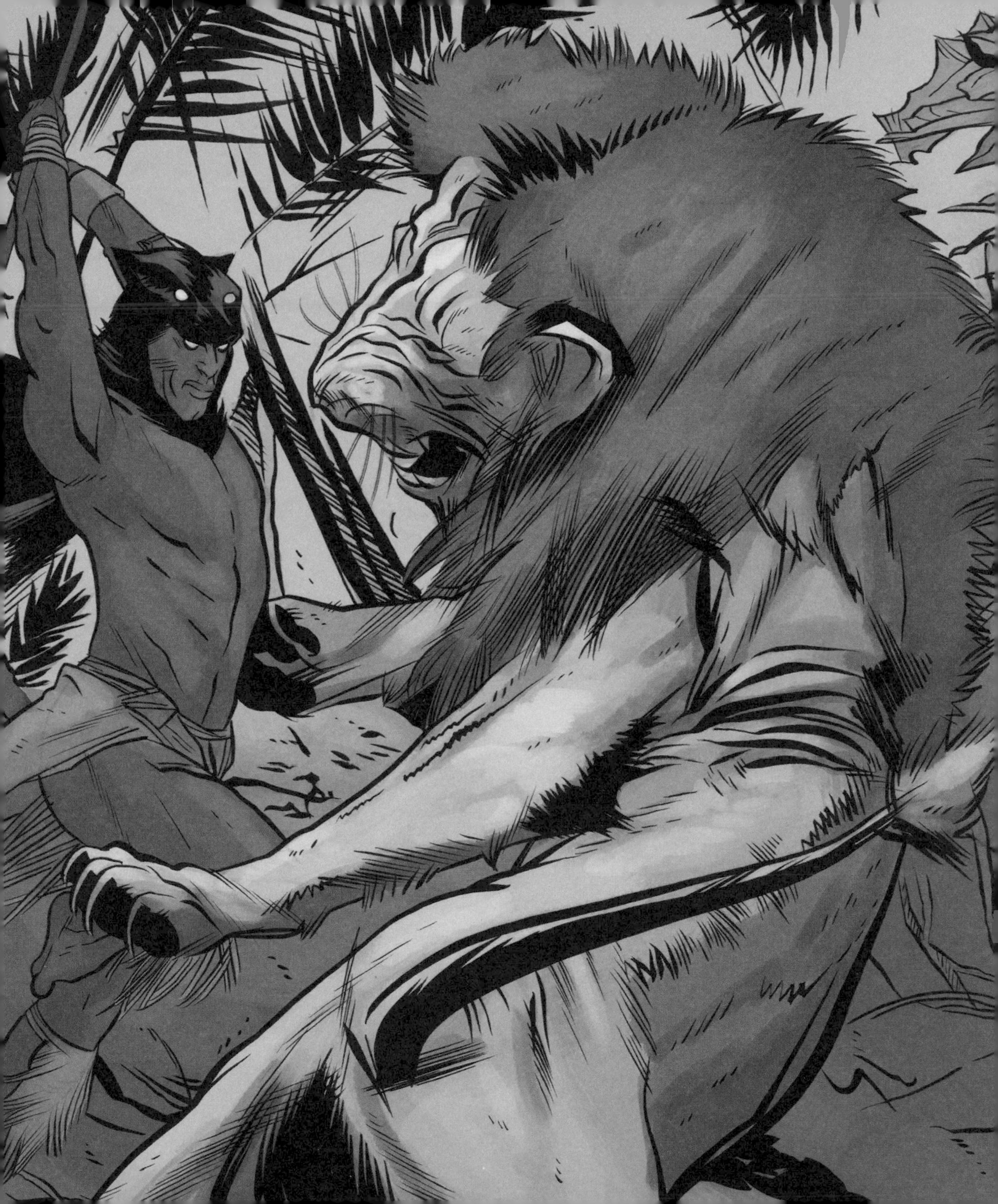

As a consequence, there were some in Wakanda who openly questioned their monarch's commitment to the nation. Did T'Challa care more about the outside world than he did his own people?

Eventually, after struggling through war with the kingdom of Atlantis and an alien invasion, the people of Wakanda cried out for change. T'Challa forestalled all-out revolution by championing democratic reforms: convening a constitutional council and promising to transform Wakanda into a constitutional monarchy. It seemed the country's troubled times were finally at an end, but even greater tumult would soon rock the nation to its foundations and bring into question everything Wakandans believed about themselves.

"From time immemorial, the Gods of Wakanda... have safeguarded us." Black Panther (T'Challa)

During Wakanda's woes, the Orisha had been conspicuously absent and rumors swirled among the devout that the gods had abandoned their people. The failure of crops, followed by a relentless torrent of rain, seemed to confirm that Wakanda no longer enjoyed the blessing of its divine guardians, even their own panther deity Bast. T'Challa himself found the absence of the Orisha troubling and he set out to investigate the matter. His quest took him deep into the jungle, where he found a mystical gateway spewing out dozens of enraged Simbi. Although initially bemused by the barbaric snake-men's sudden attack, T'Challa was thankful for a rare opportunity to unleash his full strength and he swiftly subdued his otherworldly foes.

As he lay stricken in the dirt, one of the defeated snake-men delivered an ominous warning: "The Orisha in flight. The gate unmanned. The Originators return."

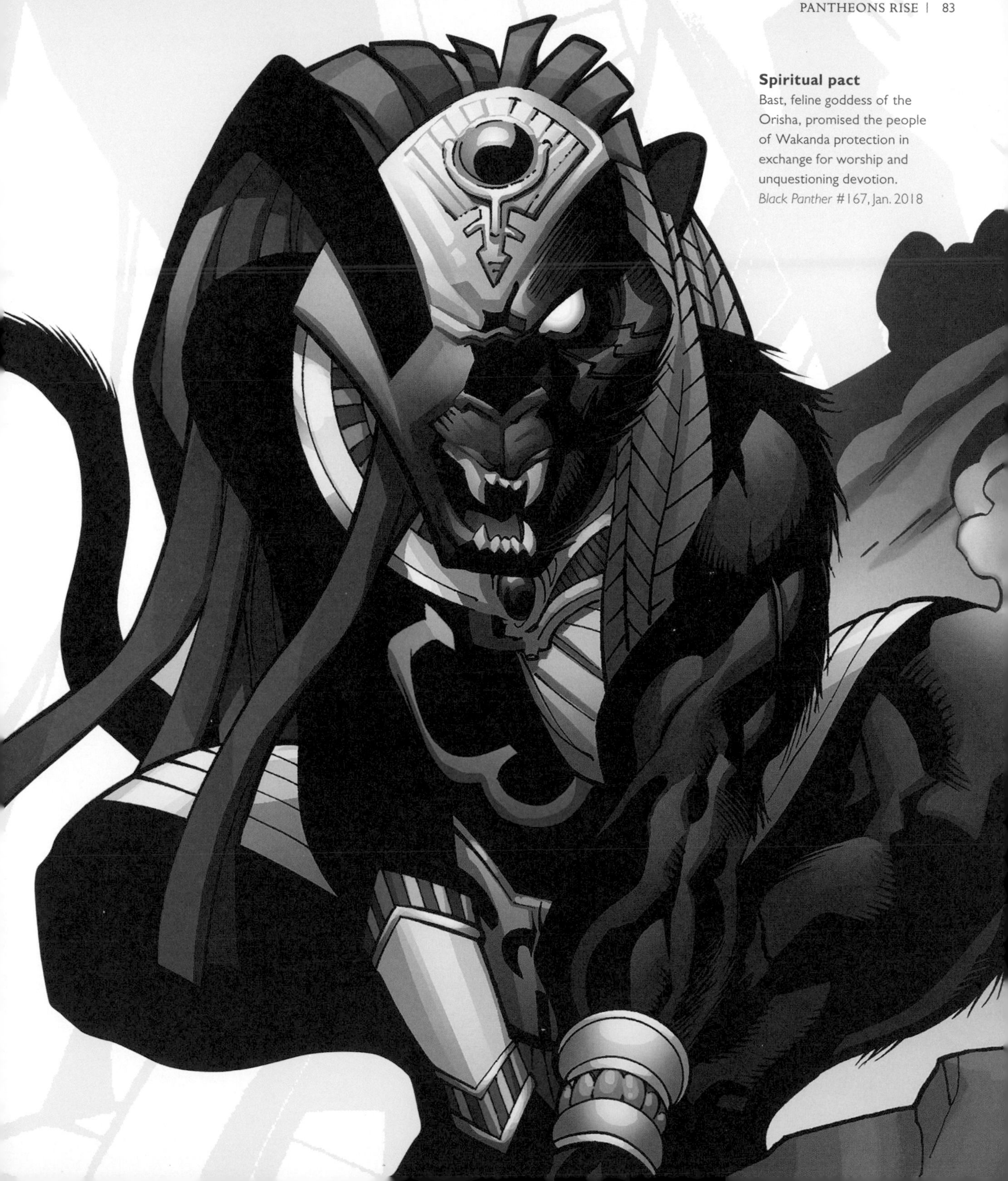

Spiritual pact
Bast, feline goddess of the Orisha, promised the people of Wakanda protection in exchange for worship and unquestioning devotion.
Black Panther #167, Jan. 2018

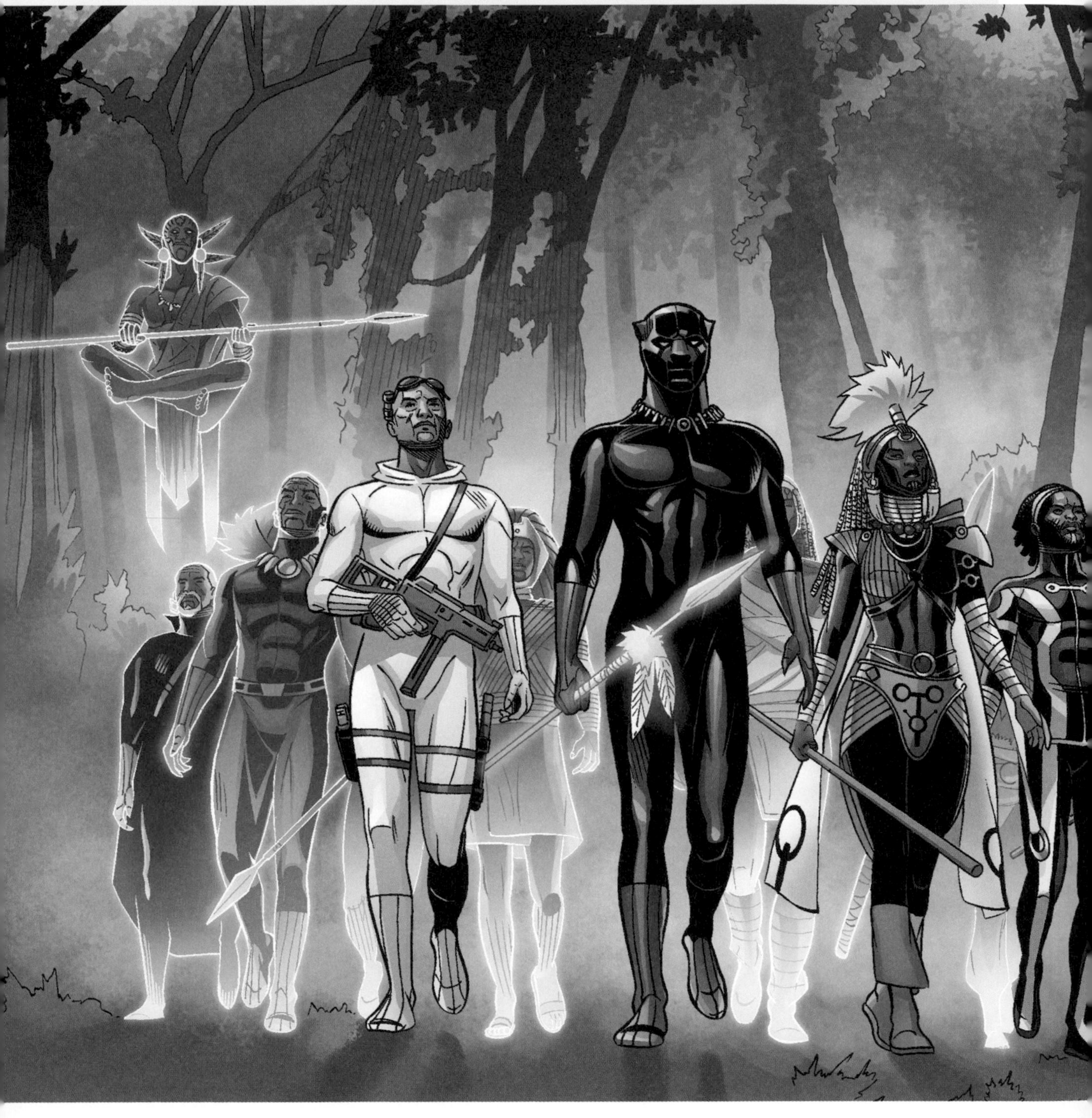

While puzzled by this pronouncement, T'Challa's immediate concern was the still-shimmering transdimensional gateway, and he called on a group of sorcerer-shamans to close the portal. As part of the spell to barricade the gate, and to smite the Originators who were still pouring through in great numbers, the shamans prayed to the Orisha. Their incantation worked: the gateway was closed. But in addition to killing the snake-men, the spell also killed the shamans. It seemed the Orisha had declined to answer the sorcerers' entreaty for divine protection.

Consulting with the spirits of the Royal Council, T'Challa confirmed that the Orisha had, indeed, vanished from the mortal plane, leaving Wakanda particularly vulnerable. Soon, more gateways opened up across the entirety of the country. No longer imprisoned by the Orisha, the aggrieved Originators were free to return to the Earthly plane and they did so with a vengeance, determined to wrest back control of their ancestral homeland.

To help push back the invaders, T'Challa recruited his ex-wife, Storm of the mutant Super Hero team the X-Men, and the wizard Zawavari to his cause. Storm had long been beloved by the people of Wakanda and her climate-controlling abilities proved invaluable in dealing with the crisis. She bent the winds to her will and quelled the raging torrents. With each success came greater adulation, and Storm used her popularity to urge the people to continue to support their sovereign-protector: T'Challa, the Black Panther. While the heroes held the line against the Originators, they were unable to achieve a decisive victory. Furthermore, their efforts to inspire the people were undermined when some Wakandans turned their backs on the Orisha, rejected the word of Bast, and embraced the violent teachings of a mysterious new god called Sefako.

Ancestral army
With Wakanda under attack, Black Panther drew strength from his ghostly predecessors and rallied his allies, including spy-chief Akili, his sister Shuri, and the mutant Manifold, in resolute defense of the nation.
Black Panther #11, Apr. 2017

Seeking to learn more about his mystical foes, T'Challa journeyed to the Djalia, the astral plane of Wakandan memory, with his sister Shuri. There the warrior-siblings were greeted by a spirit who took on the form of Queen Mother Ramonda. Recognizing T'Challa as a seeker of knowledge, the spirit revealed to him the truth about the Originators and their long-forgotten war with the Orisha.

"They offended the Originators. And so there was war." Mother of Wakandan memory

T'Challa was shocked by the revelation that his ancestors had been complicit in the removal of an entire race from their lands, but the memory-ghost told him now was not the time for recriminations. The past was the past and what mattered most was the future. While T'Challa may have sympathized with the plight of the Originators, the creatures still represented a dire threat to Wakanda's current inhabitants. Many would die if the Originators were allowed to run amok across the kingdom.

T'Challa returned to the mortal realm with a renewed sense of purpose. He gathered together his allies—Storm, Shuri, Zawavari, and the reformed villain Thunderball among them—and raced to meet the ever-growing army of Originators. The warring parties clashed on the dried-up bed of Lake Nyanza. This once-fertile oasis had become a desert, as it had been in ancient times, due to the mystical influence of the Originators.

At first, it seemed as if the invaders had the upper hand, but Storm unleashed all her extraordinary mutant powers to bring down a deluge of truly epic proportions.

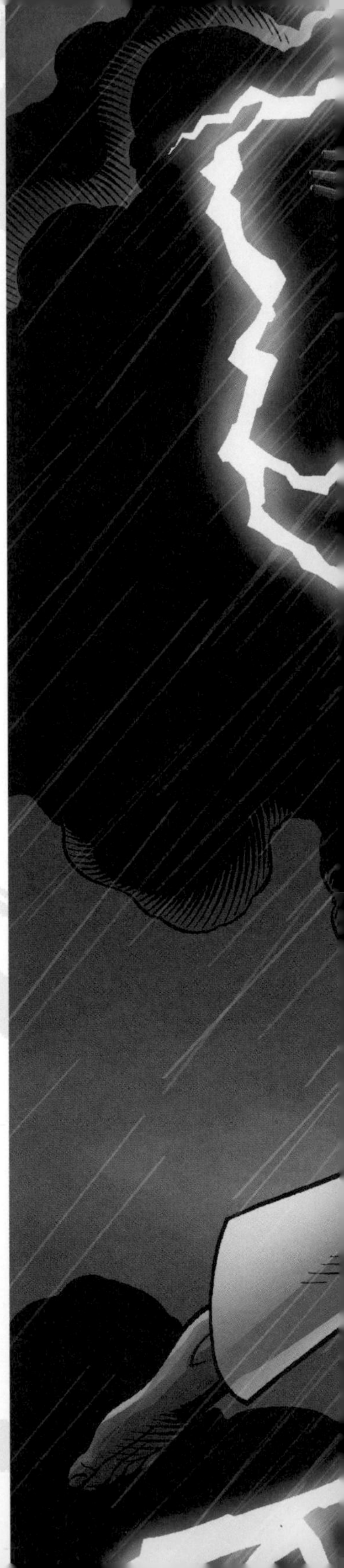

Storm rider
Storm used her climate-controlling powers to help tame the runaway weather brought on by the invading Originators.
Black Panther #16, Sep. 2017

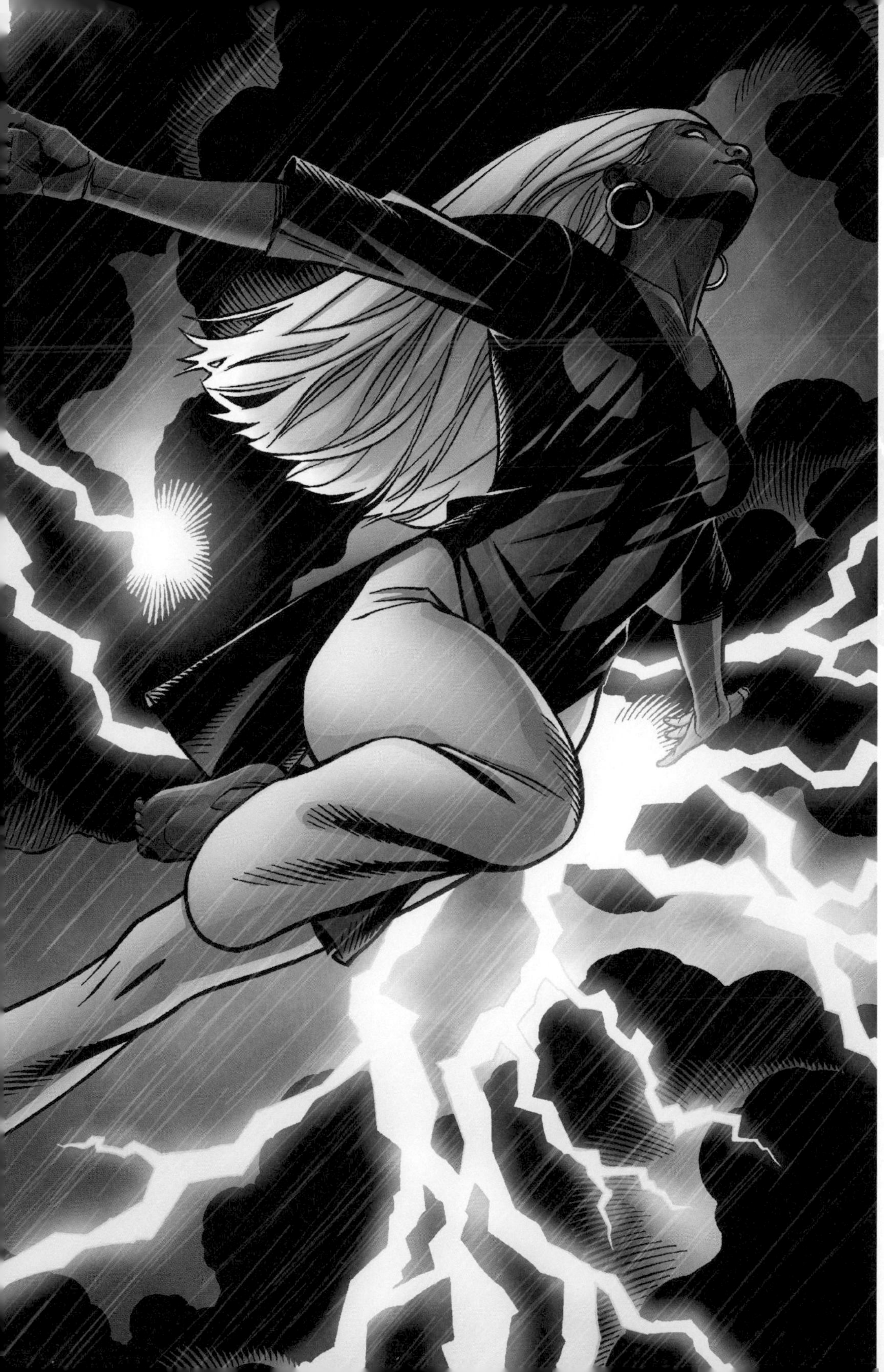

Rain and hail lashed the Originators, causing them to flee back through a gateway. Victory seemed assured, but when Storm and Shuri ventured close to the still-open portal, they were startled by an emerging figure. Storm recognized him instantly as the Adversary, a powerful, capricious, demon-like entity she had battled in her days with the X-Men.

> **"The time of my dominion is now!"**
>
> Adversary

Following an earlier defeat, the Adversary had been cut off from the material world. He found himself in the same realm as the banished Originators. Calling himself Sefako, he had helped them break through the unguarded gateways. In freeing the Originators, the Adversary had also freed himself, and he now planned to take advantage of the Orisha's absence and sow endless discord.

The Adversary struck at Wakanda's defenders, burying Storm beneath tons of rubble. Since childhood, she had suffered from claustrophobia and her sudden confinement caused Storm to panic, unable to use her powers to free herself. T'Challa called on his former love to have faith, to believe in herself as he and the people of Wakanda believed in her.

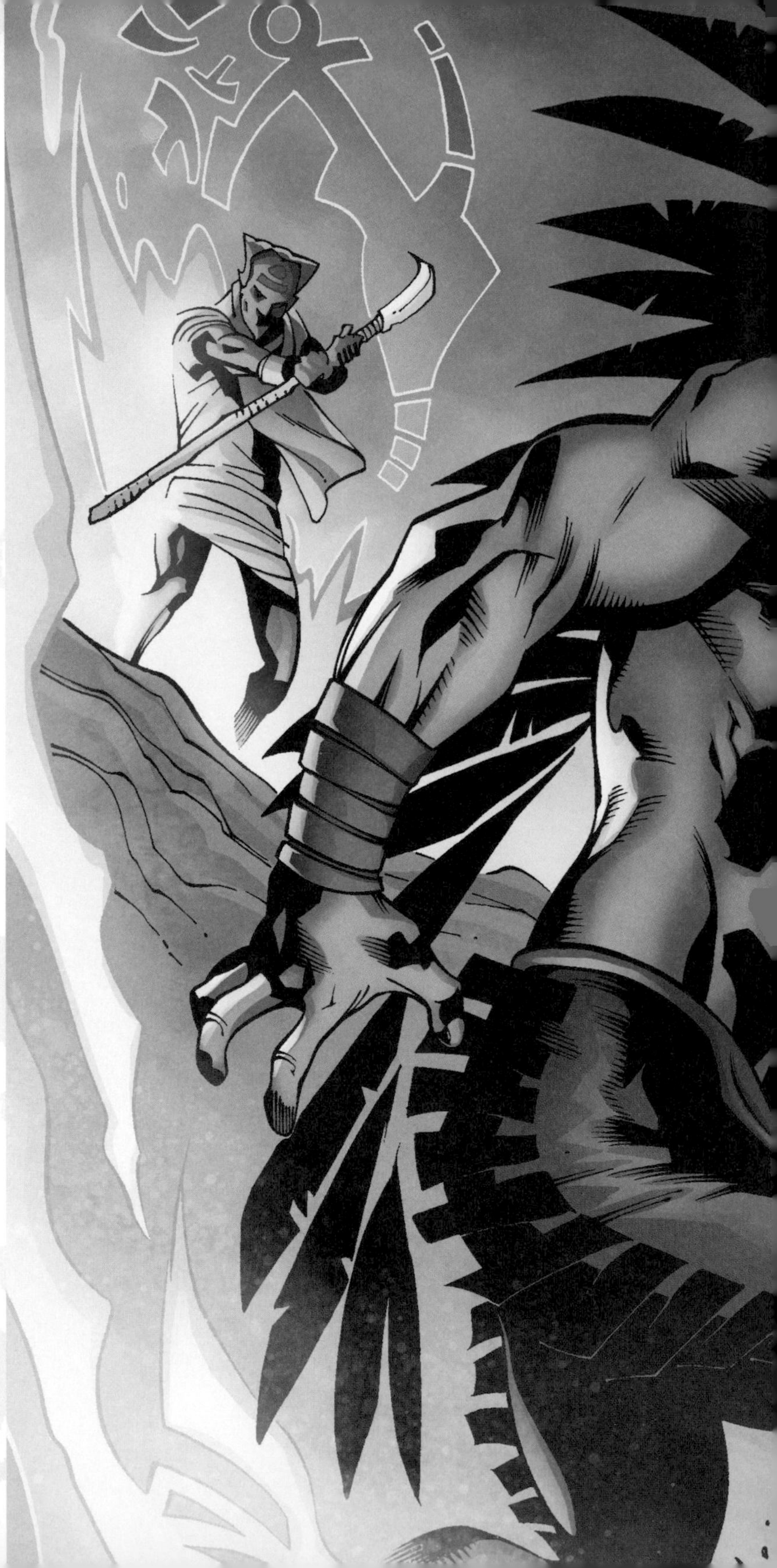

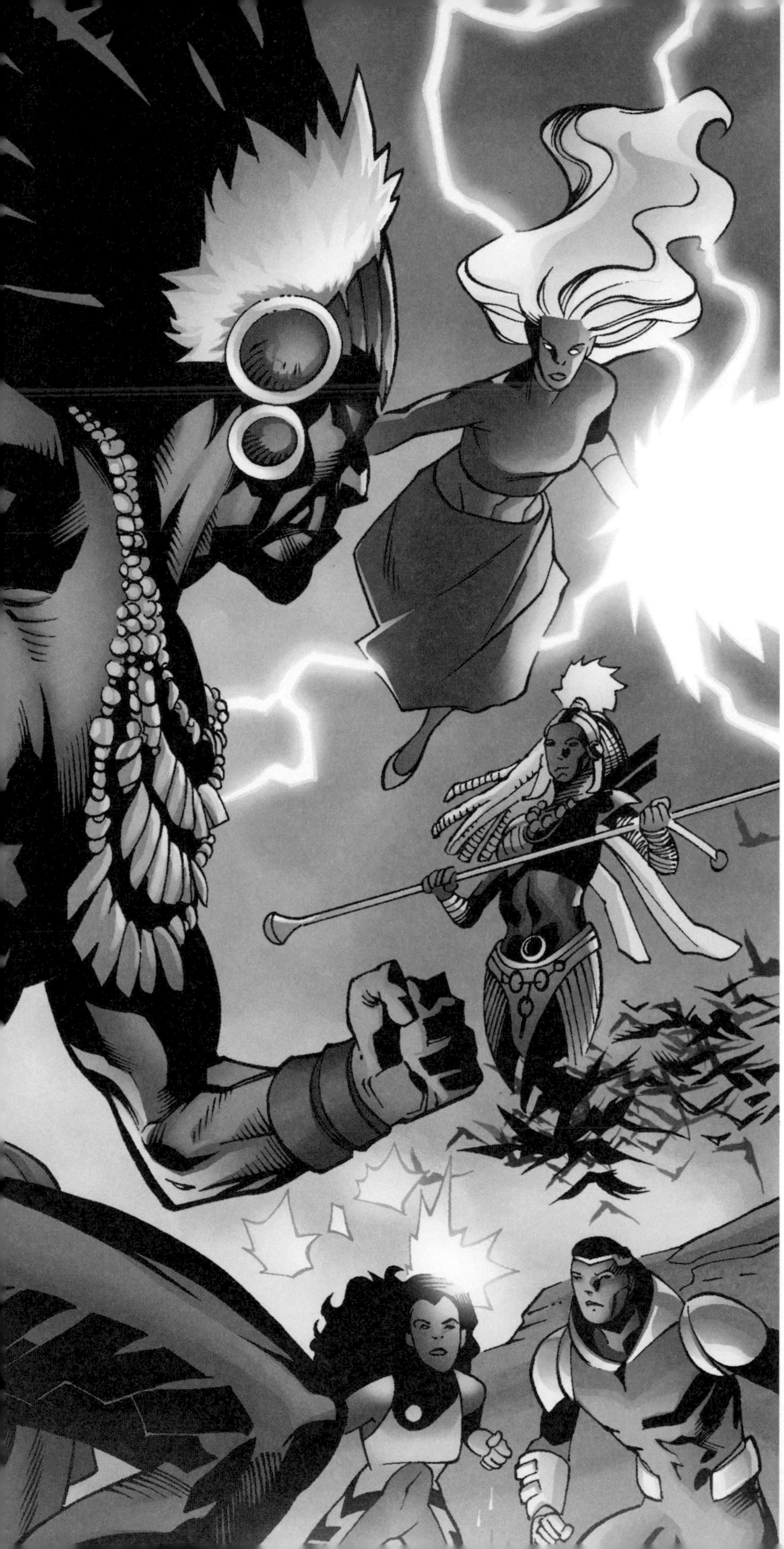

At their king's radio command, Wakandans from every walk of life prayed for their Goddess of the Storm. This communal act of worship empowered Storm, amplifying her mutant powers, and allowed her to burst free of her prison. Taking to the skies, Storm unleashed a fearsome barrage of lightning bolts at the Adversary, casting him back into the last remaining gateway and sealing it off forever.

The threat of the Adversary was over, but the Orisha were still missing, and it remained unclear why they had forsaken their people. Even as T'Challa celebrated a great victory, he knew that his kingdom had entered a dangerously unpredictable era. The certainties of old had proved illusory and the benevolence of the gods could no longer be relied upon.

Adverse reaction
Wakandan defenders Zawavari, Storm, and Shuri stood ready to send the demonic Adversary back to his otherworldly prison.
Black Panther #172, Jun. 2018

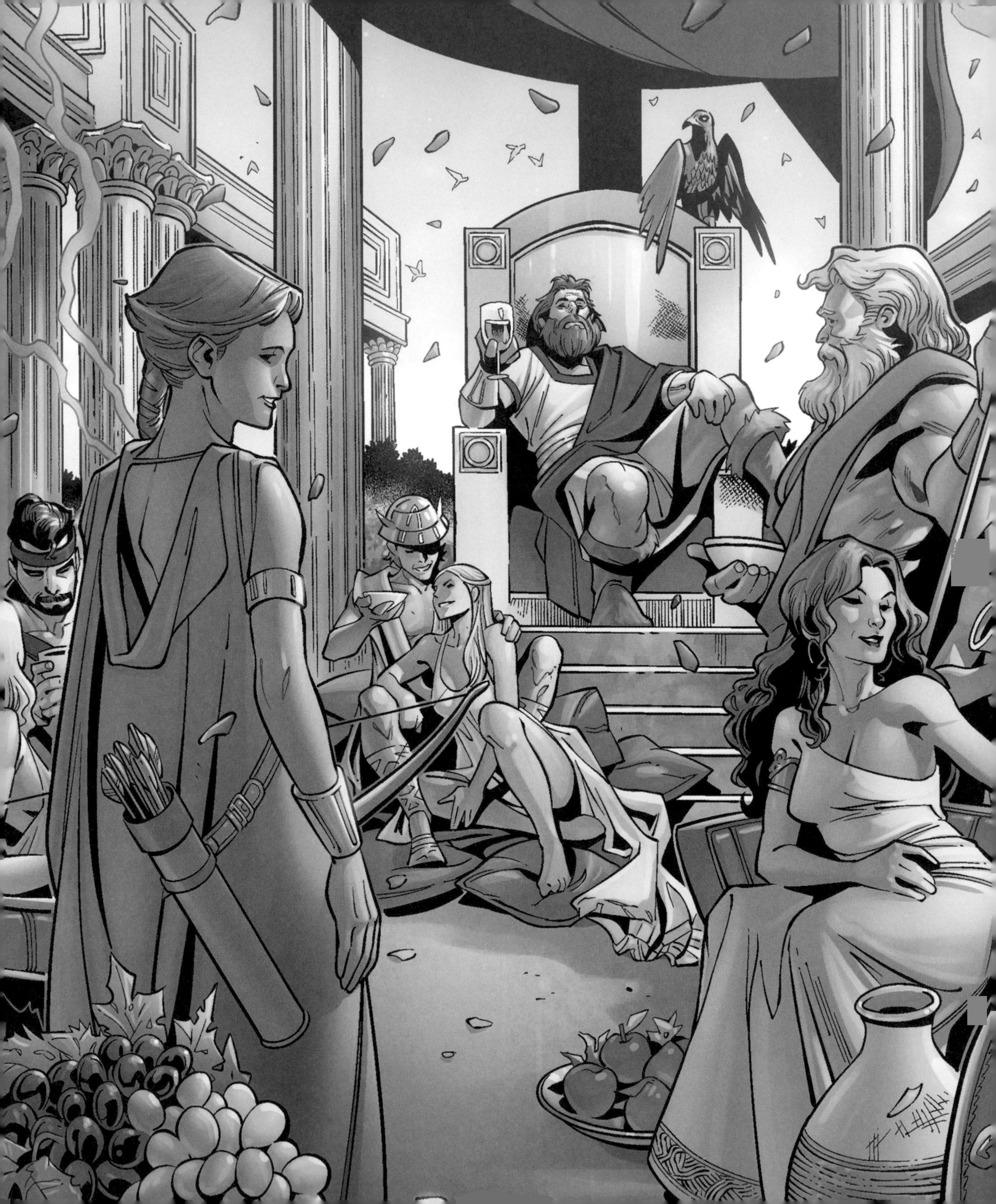

The Olympians: Clash of the Pantheons

Although his fellow Olympians had retreated from the mortal realm, the high-spirited demigod Hercules was increasingly drawn back to Earth, often finding himself in conflict with the Asgardian God of Thunder.

Worshiped by the inhabitants of Ancient Greece and the Roman Empire, the gods of Olympus influenced the affairs of humankind for many centuries. Residing in a "pocket" dimension adjacent to Earth, they traveled to the mortal realm via numerous nexus points, the most widely used being atop Mount Olympus in Greece. Once he had established himself as the unchallenged ruler of the Olympians, Zeus took Hera as his queen. Pluto was assigned to rule over the underworld, Neptune to command the seas, and Demeter to watch over the land. This arrangement provided stability and, luxuriating in the worship of countless multitudes, the Olympians flourished and grew ever stronger. However, in time, their hegemony was challenged and came to an end. With humankind developing apace and new faiths emerging, the Olympians increasingly clashed with rival pantheons, particularly the Asgardian gods of Northern Europe and the Heliopolitans of Egypt.

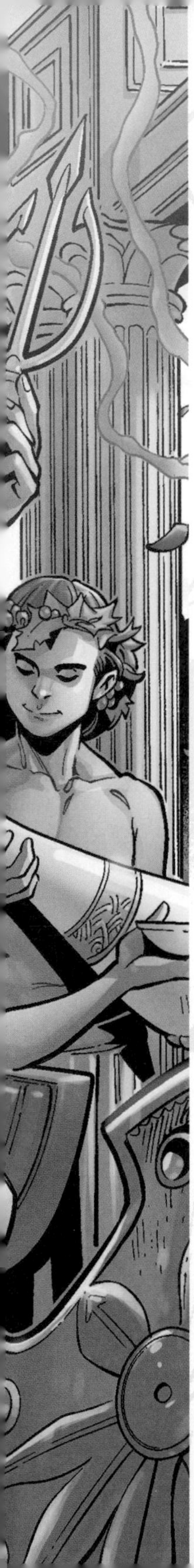

Holding court
At peace in their mystical realm, the gods of Mount Olympus enjoyed the lavish hospitality of Lord Zeus at seemingly endless courtyard parties.
Avengers: No Road Home #1, Apr. 2019

To avoid needless conflict, and with Zeus' blessing, the Olympians gradually withdrew from Earthly affairs. Safe and secure in Olympus, they watched humanity's progress from afar, occasionally nudging the mortals in the right direction. Generally, though, they were passive onlookers, idly watching the world turn endlessly on its axis.

Hercules, Zeus' son to the mortal Alcmena, viewed Earth differently to his fellow gods. For him, the world of his birth was an endlessly fascinating orb. Even after he had been accepted into the Olympian pantheon, Hercules frequently adventured on Earth, most notably when he joined Jason's crew of Argonauts and completed his legendary Twelve Labors.

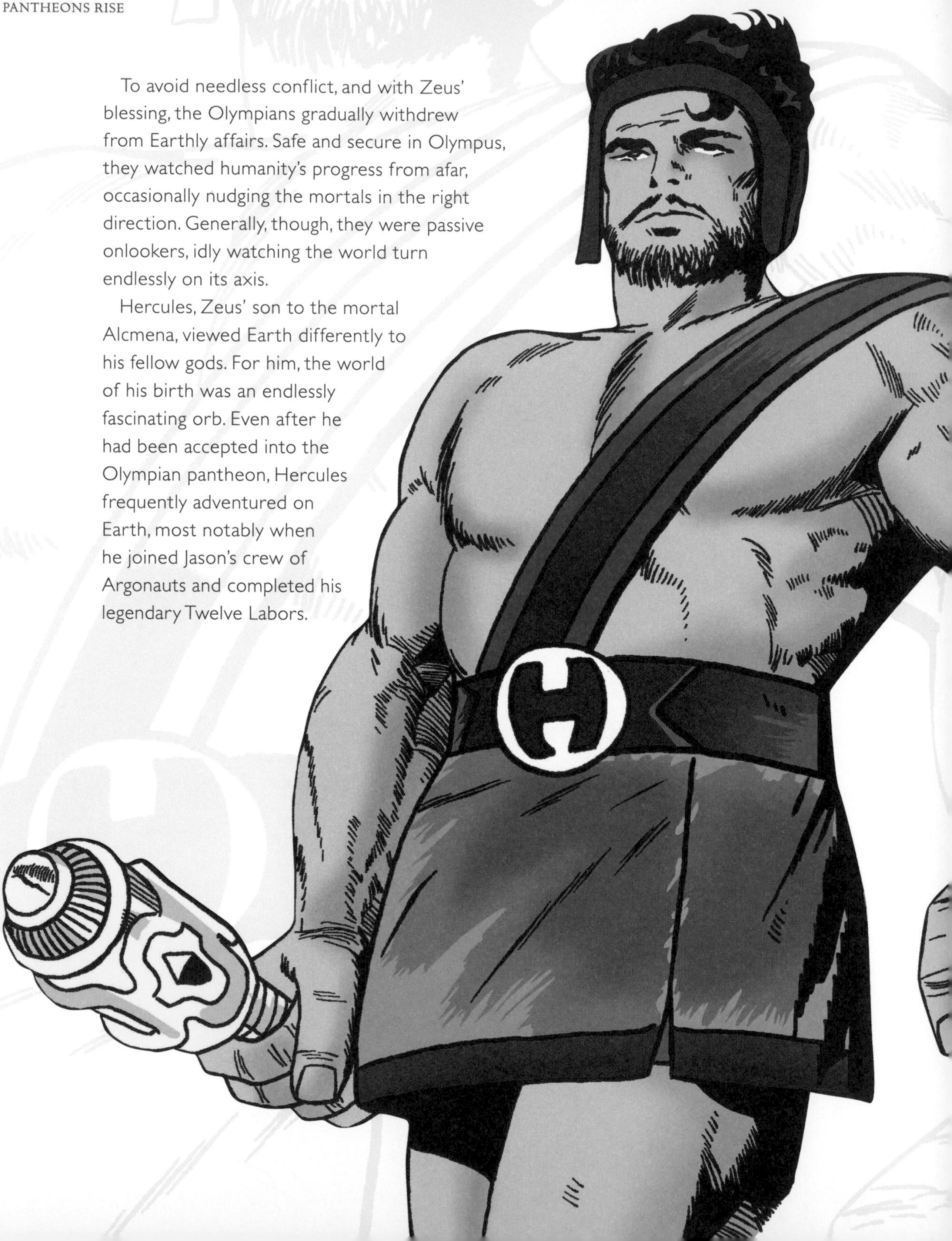

Blessed with tremendous strength, Hercules was confident to the point of hubris, and his brash, bombastic nature frequently led to misunderstandings and violent confrontations with similarly headstrong individuals. Over the years, he clashed with the Asgardian Thor several times. Their first eventful meeting occurred so far back in time that the encounter became the stuff of legends even to the gods of Olympus and Asgard.

While still relatively young—long before he learned humility on Earth—Thor thirsted for endless exploits. Hearing whispers that a portal once linked Asgard to Olympus, the God of Thunder traveled to Jotunheim in search of the legendary gateway. It didn't take him long to find it and, as fate would have it, he arrived just in time to deter a band of Storm Giants from entering the portal and invading Olympus.

Thor's battle with the Storm Giants caused a rockslide, however, and he was sent plunging through the gateway. He soon found himself in Olympus, surrounded by sights and sounds that were unfamiliar, yet still reminiscent of far-off Asgard. Searching for a way home, the God of Thunder met a figure standing at a bridge. The stranger introduced himself as Hercules and refused to let Thor cross the bridge until he had passed the other way. Thor was equally determined to cross over first, and an exchange of insults swiftly became a brawl. Boulders were hurled through the air and marble pillars crushed to dust, but neither champion managed to gain a decisive advantage.

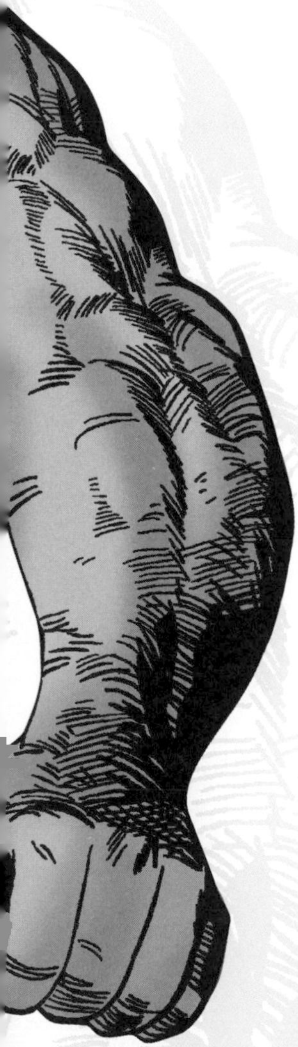

Thrill seeker
The demigod Hercules found the pastoral nature and sedate pace of Mount Olympus stultifyingly dull. Throughout his long life, he frequently sought adventure on Earth.
Thor #124, Jan. 1966

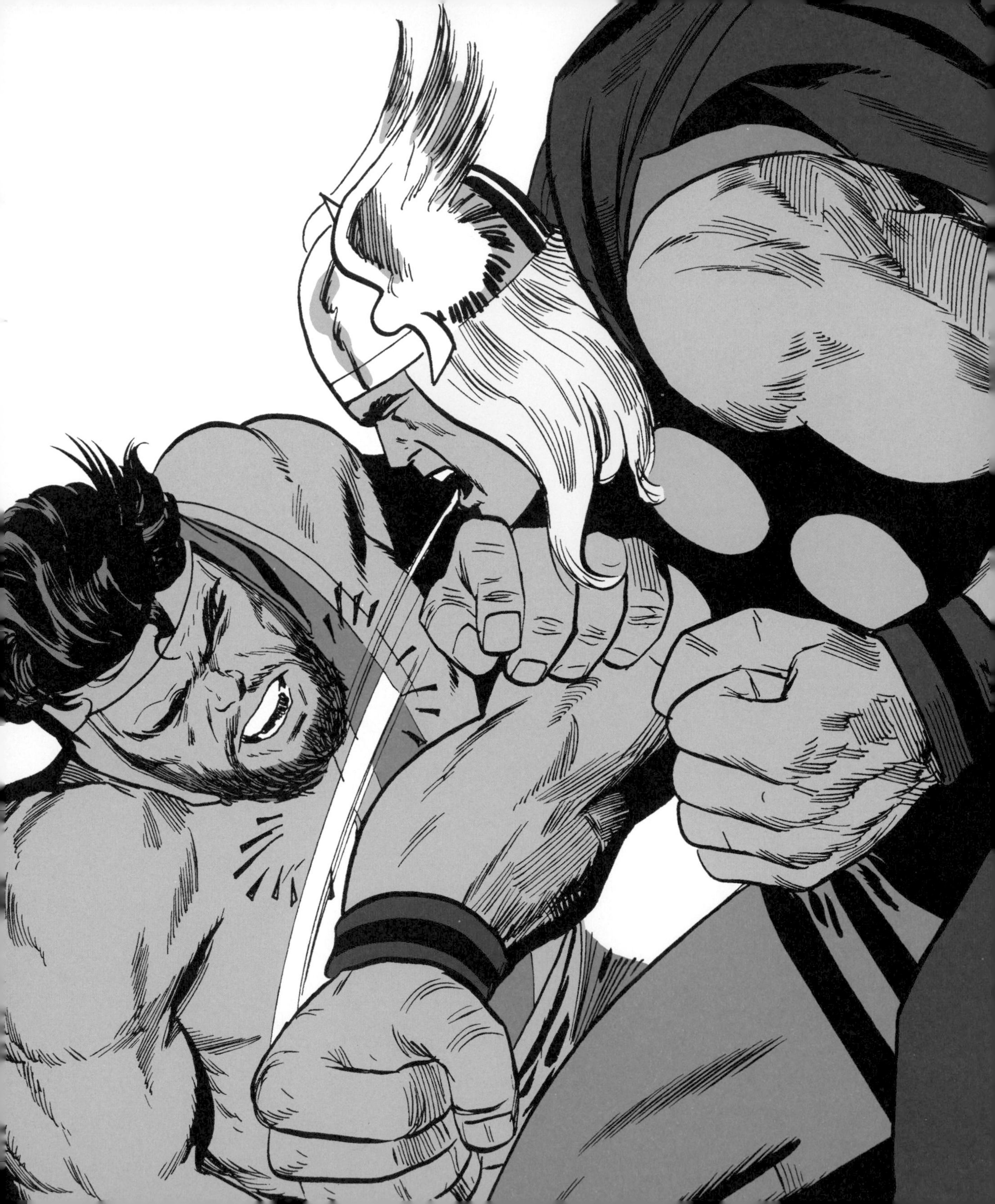

"Thor defeated by Hercules? Never!" Thor Odinson

The warriors' noisy squabble swiftly drew the attention of Zeus, who stepped between the combatants and ordered them to cease fighting. Once tempers had cooled, Zeus teleported Thor back to Jotunheim. Almost immediately, the transdimensional trip began to fade from the God of Thunder's memory, as if it had been no more than a dream. His mind clouded by Zeus, Thor forgot his first fractious meeting with Hercules, but the altercation set a pattern that would continue far into the future.

When devotion to the Norse gods was at its height, Thor answered the urgent prayers of Viking warriors and traveled to Midgard to aid them in a war with a mysterious new enemy. He found his followers fighting a band of Ancient Greeks who had voyaged to Scandinavia in search of fresh conquests. Thor's intervention turned the tide of battle in favor of the Vikings. In response, the Greeks called on their own gods for salvation, summoning mighty Hercules from Olympus.

Thor and Hercules clashed, but they were too evenly matched for either to win the battle. Still, both were determined to prove to their followers that they—and by implication, their whole pantheon—were the strongest. With this in mind, Thor offered Hercules a temporary truce. He proposed that they end hostilities for now and only resume the fight once they had time to gather together their respective pantheons for an all-out war between the gods of Asgard and Olympus. As confident as ever in his own superiority, Hercules agreed to Thor's terms.

Headstrong heroes
Seemingly cast from the same divine mold, Hercules and Thor were both impulsive and foolhardy. Early encounters between the pair invariably descended into brawls.
Thor #126, Mar. 1966

Back in Asgard, All-Father Odin was angered by his son's rash behavior and refused to marshal the forces of the Golden Realm for a war that he believed was misguided and fueled by sheer pride and arrogance. His words found an echo in Olympus, where Zeus also dismissed the very notion of conflict. However, true to his mischievous ways, Loki used a spell to temporarily assume the form of Thor. He attacked unsuspecting Olympus and then fled back into the night. Enraged by this brazen provocation, and not realizing he had been tricked into action, Zeus declared open war on Asgard.

"So, it's war thou desirest, my son?" Zeus

Some time later, the rival armies met on a rocky battlefield that floated in a region of space far beyond the realm of mortals. Thor led the charge for the Asgardians while Hercules rallied the Olympian forces. The battle raged for two Earth days, with neither side of immortals willing to rest or give ground.

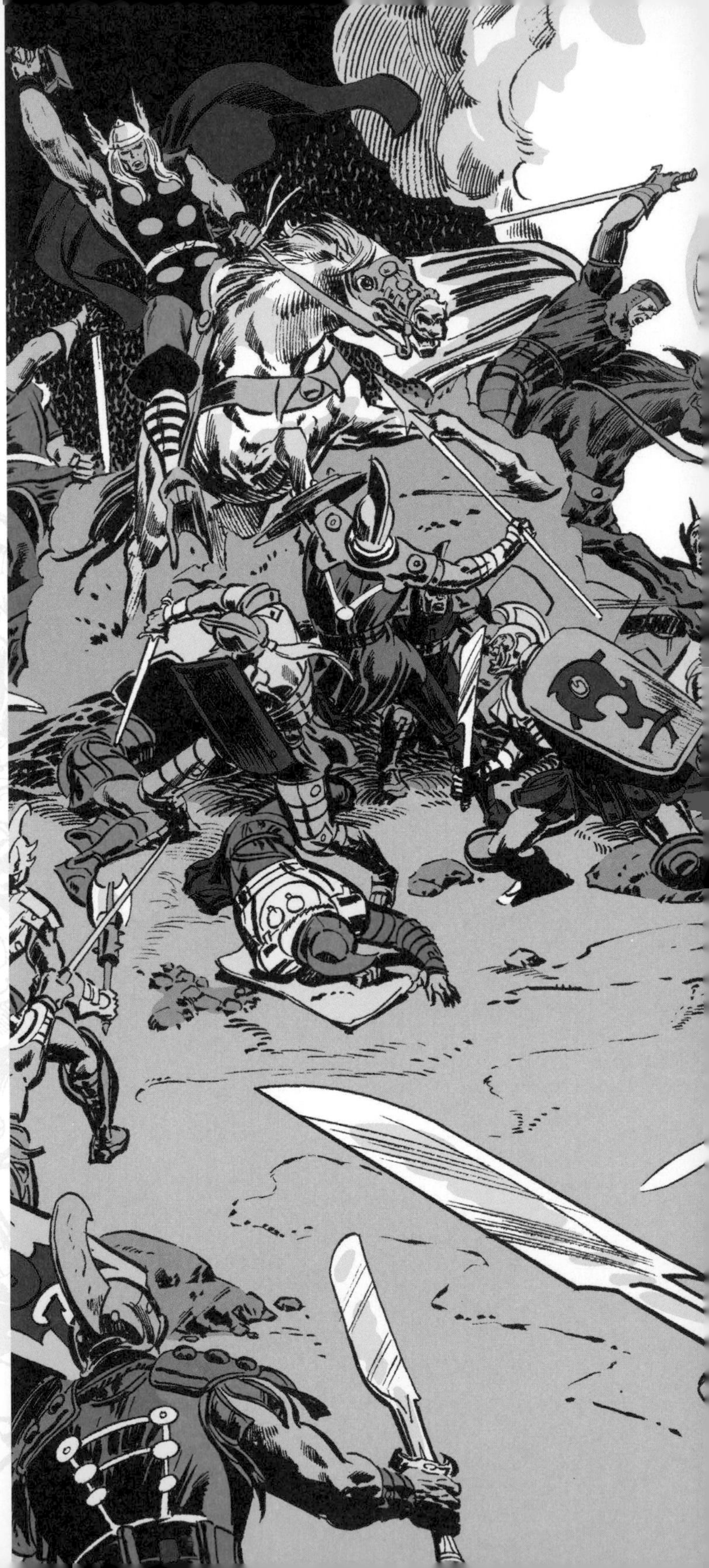

War gods
With ever-faithful Balder the Brave at his side, Thor led the charge against the Olympian gods, determined to prove that Asgard was mightier than Olympus.
Thor Annual #15, Sep. 1976

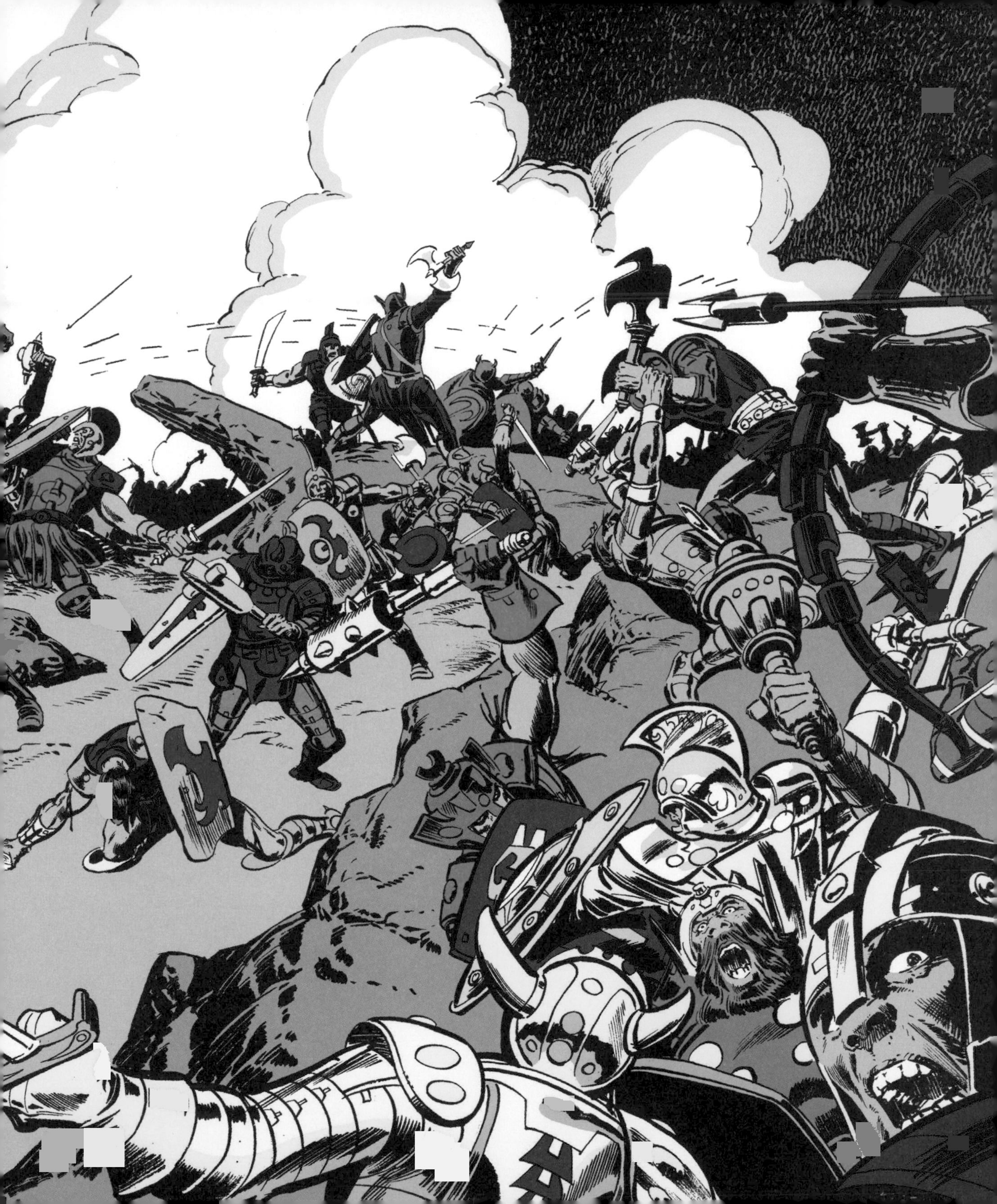

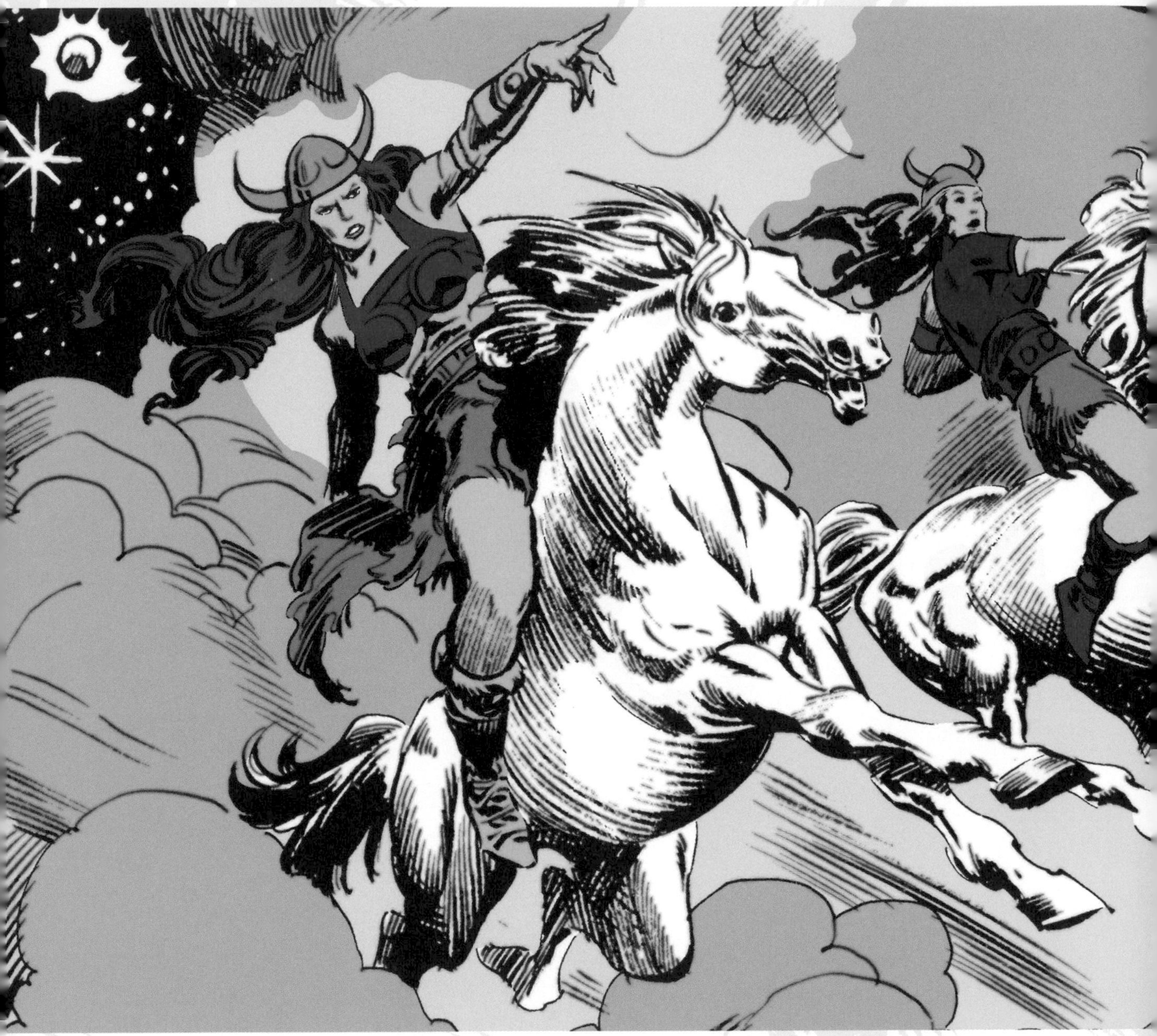

Choosers of the slain
The Valkyrie, riding their steeds at the battle between Asgard and Olympus, took the bravest of the fallen to Valhalla, the land of the honored dead.
Thor Annual #15, Sep. 1976

In the end, with the Valkyries whisking the souls of the dead to distant Valhalla, the somber pitch of a Norse battle horn signified victory for the Asgardians. Thor was triumphant, believing he had won the right for the Asgardians to replace the Olympians as the gods of Greece. Odin begged to differ, though, and he forbade his son from traveling to Ancient Greece to pronounce the islands a protectorate of Asgard. Thor ignored his father's wishes and journeyed to Greece. He expected to receive adulation from his new subjects, but was met with ill-disguised contempt. Furthermore, the longer he stayed in Greece, the weaker he became, as if the land itself was sapping him of his immortal strength.

Returning to Asgard, Thor sought answers from the All-Father. Odin explained that it was impossible for an Earthly pantheon to simply supplant another. The faith of the Greeks sustained the Olympians while the power of the Olympians protected the Greeks. The two were intrinsically linked, just as the Asgardians were tied to the Vikings. As it happened, the whole affair, including the apparent defeat of the Olympian gods, had been orchestrated by Odin and Zeus to teach their errant sons a much-needed lesson about the reality—and the limits—of divine power.

"Gods believe in men and men believe in gods." Odin

While both Hercules and Thor were chastened by the experience of war, it still took many centuries for them to fully appreciate the wisdom of their fathers. Even in the modern era, the godly princes continued their nonsensical rivalry. The turning point came during Thor's early days as an earthbound Super Hero. Zeus, like Odin before him, tired of his son's carousing, dispatched Hercules to Earth where he hoped the demigod would find an appropriate outlet for his strength and passionate nature.

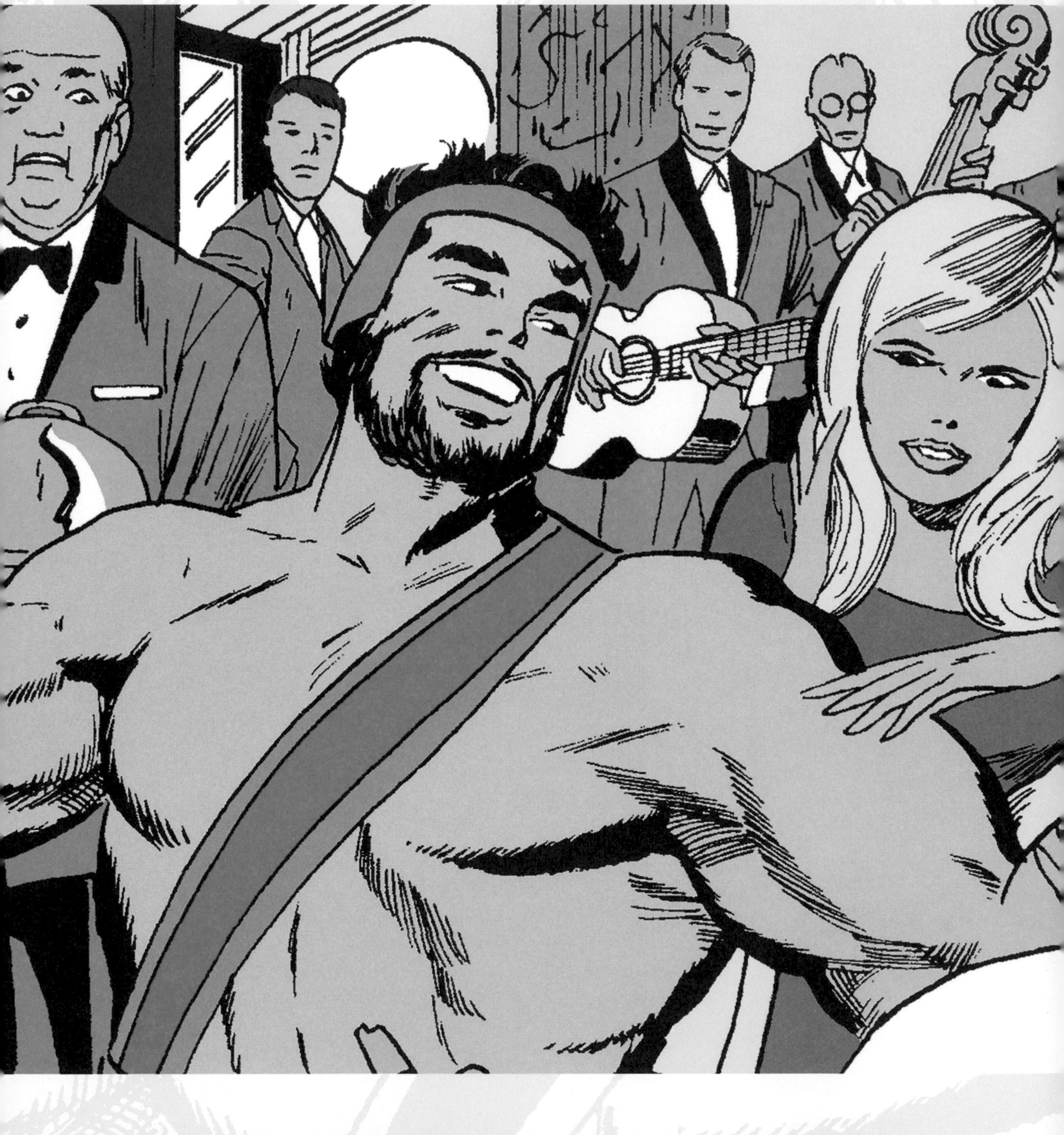

Unfortunately, Hercules' thirst for food and drink was greater than his desire for righting wrongs, and he spent much of his time dining in New York City's most expensive restaurants.

While enjoying the best the city had to offer, Hercules met Jane Foster and attempted to impress her with tales of his legendary past. Witnessing Hercules' seductive ways, Thor grew jealous and an exchange of angry words inevitably escalated into a fight. This time, though, the two gods were not evenly matched. Odin had stripped his son of half his strength as punishment for revealing his Don Blake identity to Jane. Reduced in this manner, the God of Thunder was easily felled by Hercules.

Watching the duel was a Hollywood talent scout. Impressed with Hercules' prowess, the agent offered him a movie contract, suggesting that fame and fortune awaited in Hollywood. Not wishing to deny the world an opportunity to appreciate his greatness, Hercules agreed to accompany the scout back to the film capital of the world. At Stardust Studios, the demigod walked out onto an elaborate set and was amazed to learn that the blockbuster movie was supposedly about his own mythic adventures.

Food of the gods
Hercules' first trip to New York saw him sampling fare from the city's finest eateries while regaling fellow customers with stories of his legendary past.
Thor #125, Feb. 1966

Beguiled by a charismatic producer, Hercules wasted little time in agreeing a deal. As soon as his signature was on the contract, though, a chill descended across the film lot. The producer removed his sunglasses to reveal his true identity as Pluto, Lord of the Underworld. Hercules had not agreed to appear in a movie—rather, he had signed a contract to replace his divine uncle as Lord of Hell.

For centuries, Pluto had been looking for some way to escape the burden of his infernal office and, thanks to Hercules' gullible nature, he was finally free. Hercules protested, denouncing Pluto's trickery. But it was no use, according to the dictates of Olympus, the contract was binding. The only way for Hercules to escape his fate was for some champion to come to his defense. An increasingly desperate Hercules sought help from his Olympian cousins, but he was rebuffed at every turn. Even the war god Ares was disinclined to cross swords with the devilish Pluto.

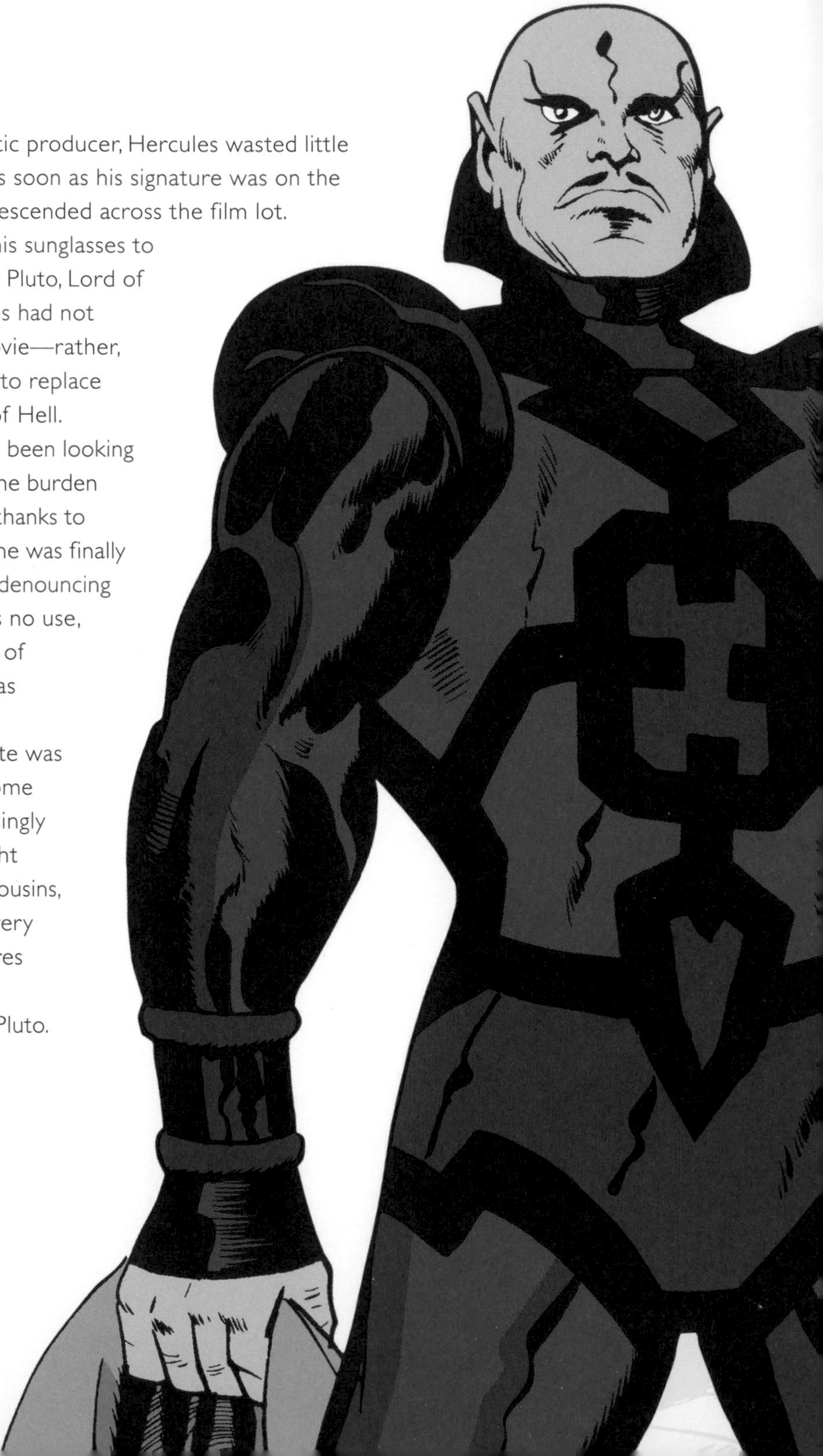

Hercules' salvation, when it finally did arrive, came from a most surprising source. Thor had recovered from his defeat at the hands of the Olympian. He and his father had enjoyed a rapprochement, and the God of Thunder was back to his full strength. Now Odin revealed an ancient Asgardian prophecy to his son. It said that Thor would languish in limbo until the Winds of the World called him to do battle on behalf of another.

"Pluto! Thor, Son of Odin, accepts thy challenge!"

Thor Odinson

So, as foretold, Thor traveled to the empty realm and waited patiently to be summoned. At the designated time, the winds carried words of defiance to his ears. Amazingly, it was the voice of Hercules, who was being dragged into the underworld, but was still railing against Pluto's deception. Impressed by Hercules' courage, Thor flew to his former rival's side. He took on Pluto's armies and caused so much damage that the imperious Lord of the Underworld feared his realm might fall into permanent ruin. Seeing no alternative course of action, Pluto reluctantly released Hercules from his hellish contract.

Back on Earth, the Olympian and the Asgardian set aside their differences, with Hercules going on to replace Thor as a member of the Avengers. While their relationship would continue to be competitive—and still combative on occasion—it was now built firmly upon a hard-won respect for one another.

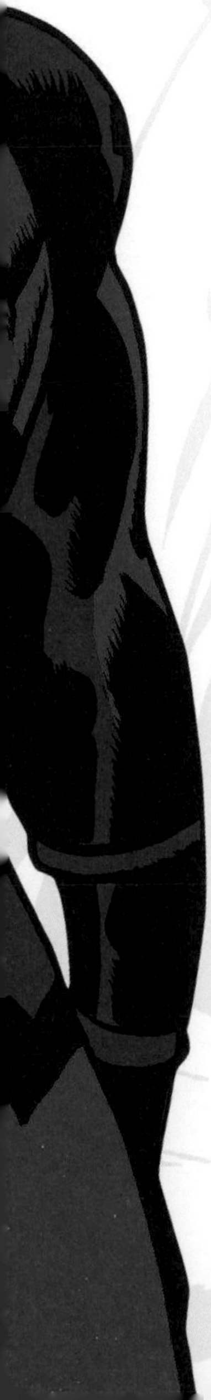

Retirement plan
Pluto, Oympian Lord of Hell, was tired of his infernal responsibilities and sought to trick Hercules into taking his place as custodian of the underworld.
Thor #164, May 1969

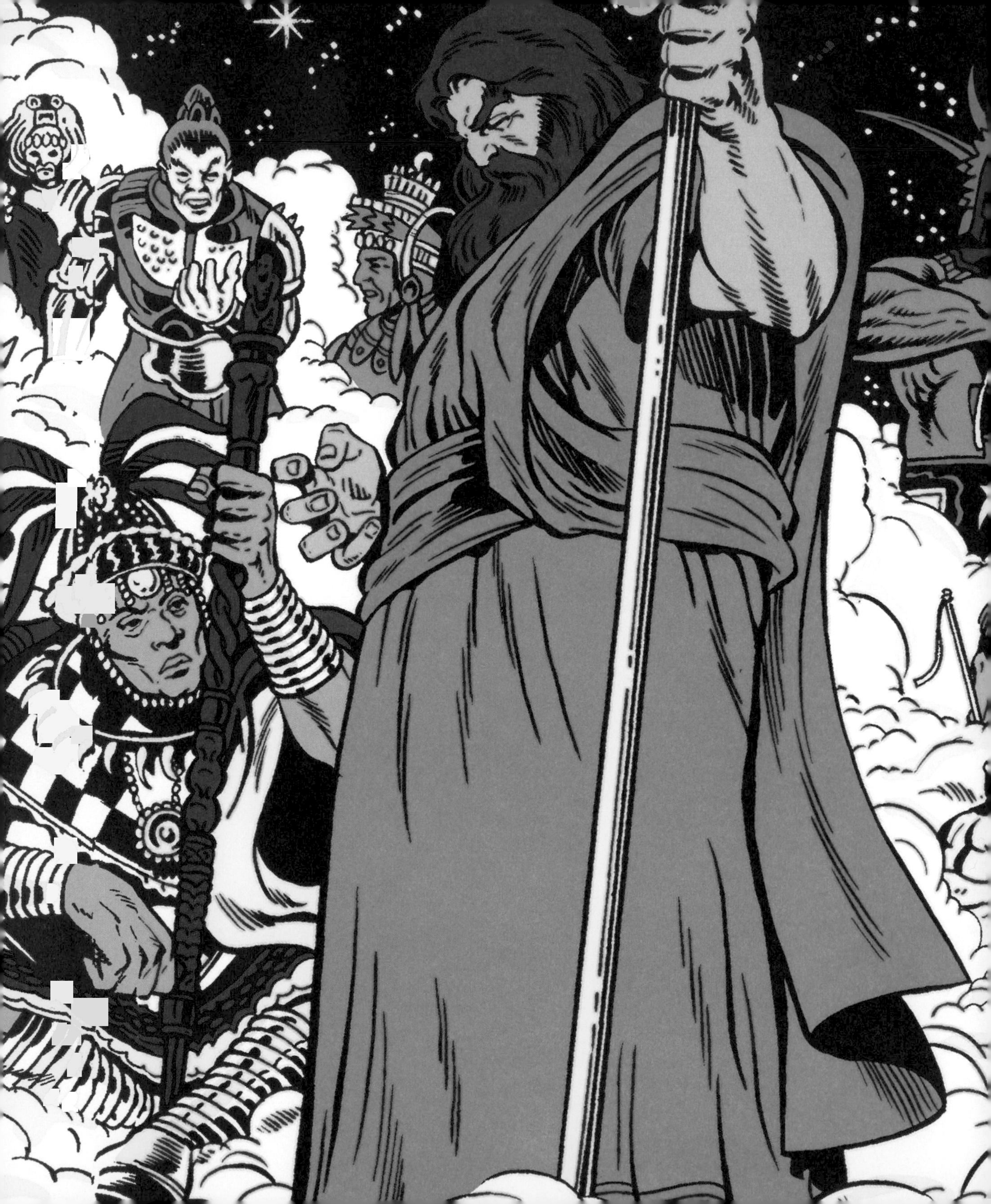

The Council of Godheads

Fearing the power of the Celestials, All-Father Odin called upon Earth's rival pantheons to set aside their differences. The Council of Godheads was convened to consider how best to deal with the threat of the enigmatic space gods.

In approximately 1000 CE, when the Celestial Third Host came to Earth to further study the results of its genetic tampering, All-Father Odin ruminated on how best to deal with the extraterrestrial interlopers. He knew from his experience at the time of the First Host that any direct assault on the Celestials would be easily rebuffed. What's more, he feared any precipitous action on his behalf might cause the Celestials to abandon their work altogether and wipe away humankind as if it were little more than a failed experiment. And, of course, without humanity to sustain them, Earth's gods would soon perish as well.

Seeking the wisdom of his peers, Odin assembled the heads of all the godly pantheons to discuss matters. It was the first time in history that such a divine council had been convened, and this very fact spoke of the seriousness of the threat that was posed by the Celestials. After much discussion, it was agreed that Odin, Zeus, and Vishnu would confront the space gods and demand they leave Earth.

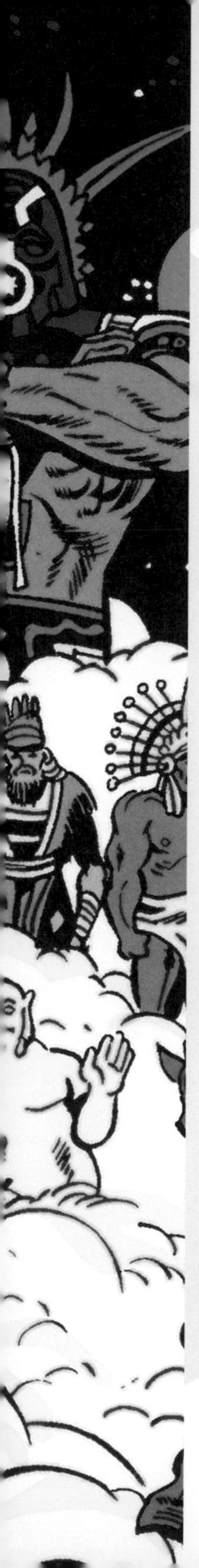

Wise council
The Olympian Zeus (center) discussed matters with Mayan god Itzamna at the first meeting of the Council of Godheads, as the masked native American deity Tomazooma looked on.
Thor #300, Oct. 1980

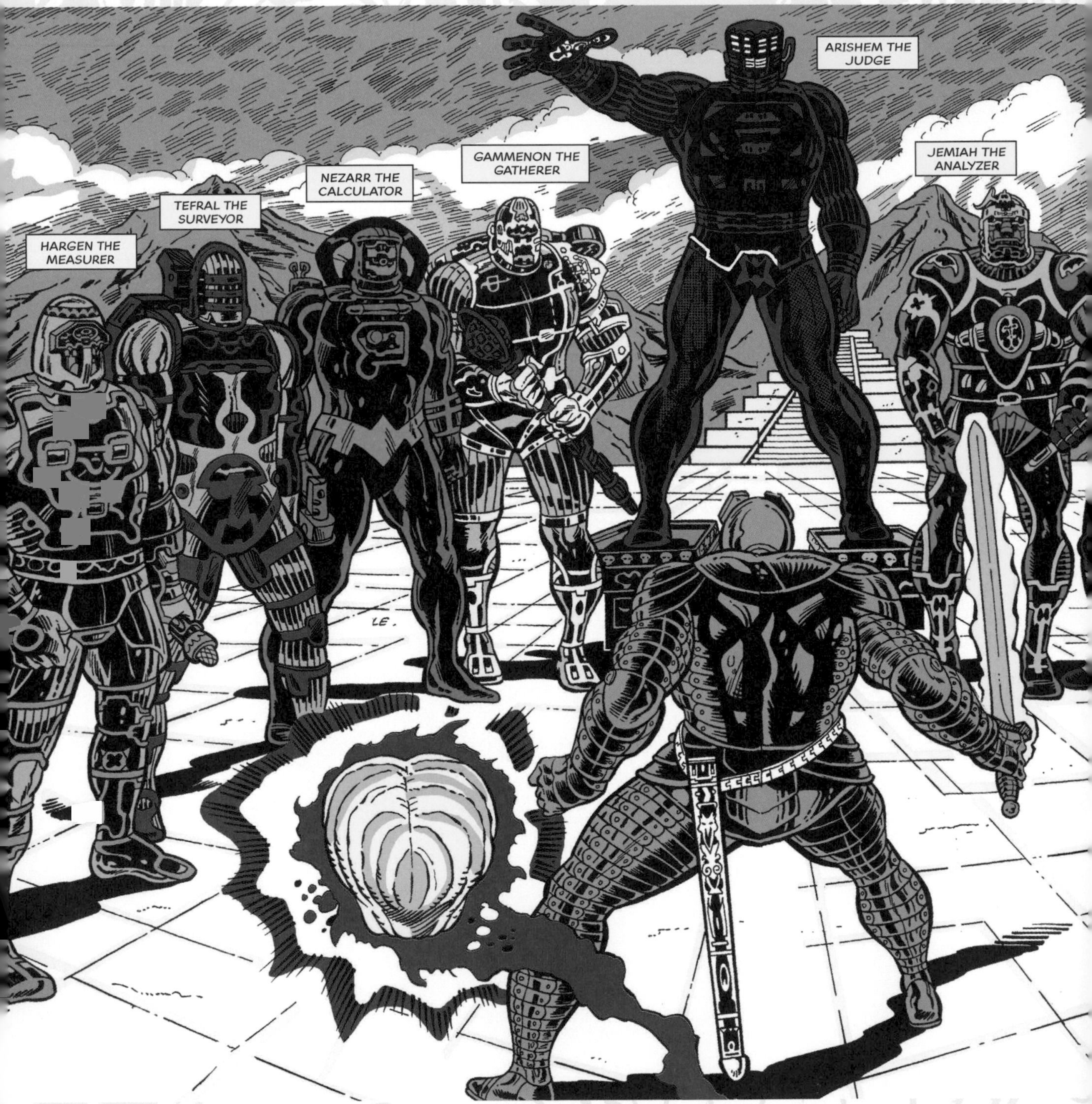
HARGEN THE MEASURER
TEFRAL THE SURVEYOR
NEZARR THE CALCULATOR
GAMMENON THE GATHERER
ARISHEM THE JUDGE
JEMIAH THE ANALYZER

ESON THE
SEARCHER

ONEG THE
PROBER

ZIRAN THE
TESTER

Riding a gleaming chariot and with a thunderous storm announcing their arrival, the godly envoys approached the Third Host base in the Andes mountains. Landing before the Celestial Arishem, they delivered their ultimatum. "Our kind stands united in its defiance of your designs on our world," Odin boldly announced.

Before another word could be uttered, the Eternal Ajak interceded and urged the gods to be cautious, that even their might was insignificant in comparison to that of the Celestials. As if to illustrate this point, Arishem projected an image into the minds of the three gods. The vision showed the pathways connecting Earth to the immortal realms in ruin, and the implication could not have been clearer. The Celestials had the power to cut off the gods from humanity and would do so if pressed.

Recognizing it was not the right time for open conflict, the three gods bowed before Arishem, promising not to interfere with the Celestials' plan for humanity. Even if Vishnu and Zeus intended to keep their word, Odin did not. He spent the next millennium plotting to bring down the presumptuous space gods. As weapons of last resort, he created the nigh-indestructible Destroyer armor and forged the gigantic Odinsword. At the time of the Fourth Host, when the Celestials returned to pass their final judgment on Earth, Odin swiftly put his plan into action. He imbued the Destroyer with his own life force and that of his fellow Asgardians, causing the iron-like automaton to grow to a colossal size.

Battle plan
Odin formulated a stratagem to defeat the Celestials; the plan led him to take control of the Destroyer armor and pick up the Odinsword.
Thor #300, Oct. 1980

Brandishing the Odinsword, the Destroyer prepared to do battle with the Celestials. He was joined by the Eternals, who had finally realized they could no longer be passive observers to such monumental events. In the form of the Uni-Mind, they had determined that the best course of action was to defend humanity from the Celestials and, in their gestalt form, they flew to fight alongside Odin's Destroyer.

Although the Eternals' act was courageous, it was ultimately in vain. A combined blast from Celestials Gammenon and Jemiah shattered the Uni-Mind, leaving the Eternals unconscious on the ground.

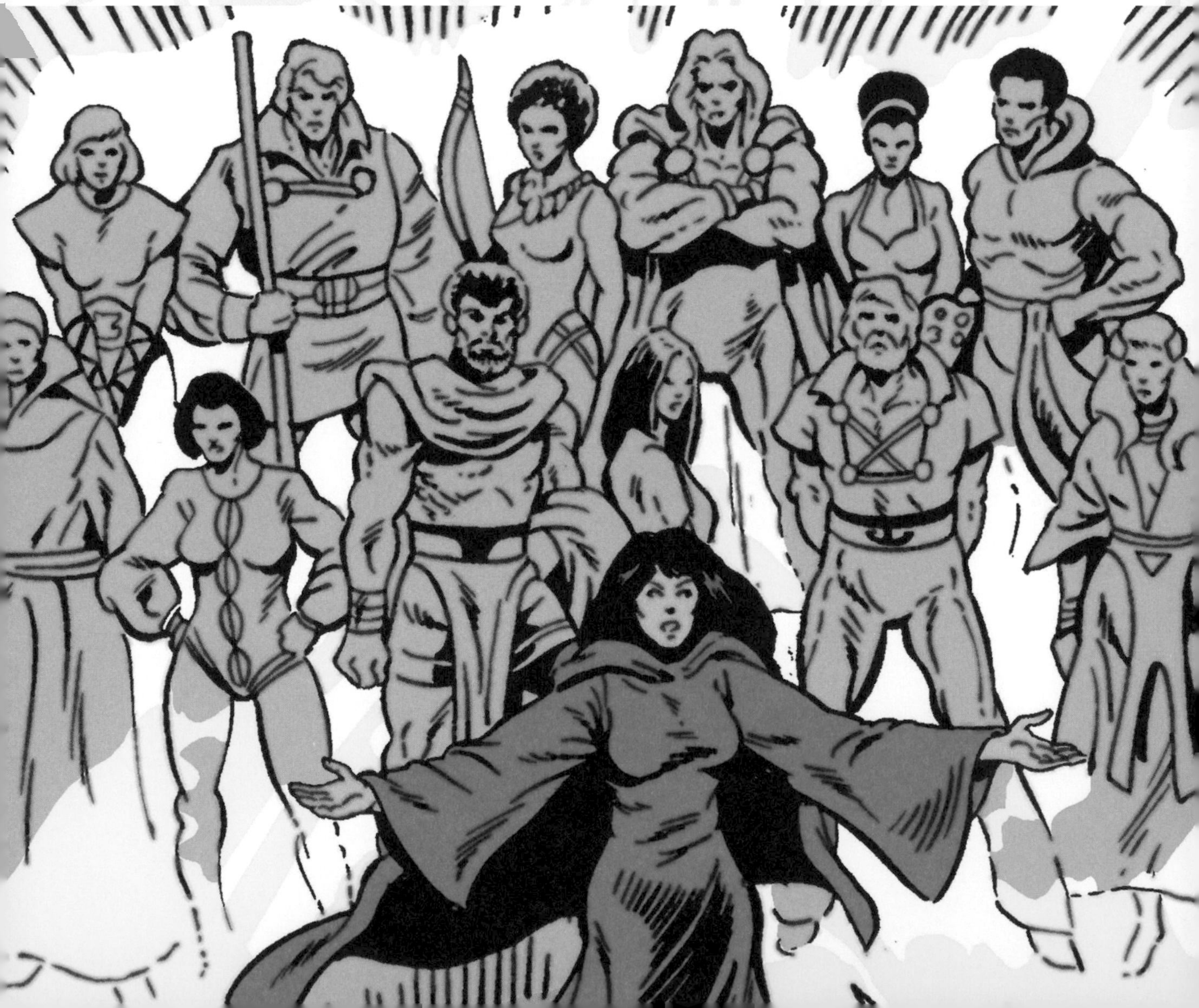

Empowered by Odin's warrior spirit, the Destroyer engaged the enemy directly, fighting its way into the very center of the massed space gods. But while it wielded the Odinsword to great effect, it was hopelessly outnumbered. When the Celestials successfully consolidated their fire, the Destroyer was melted into slag by the force of the unified blast.

Witness to the apparent death of Odin and the Asgardians was Thor, who had raced to the Andes upon learning of his father's plan. Enraged, Thor hurled Mjölnir at Arishem, sending the giant toppling to the ground. When the stunned Celestial struggled to regain his feet, Thor propelled the discarded Odinsword into his foe's chest. But even this wasn't enough to stop Arishem. The Celestial projected his own life force into the sword, reducing it to a pool of liquid metal.

"I am she who birthed you, Thor." Earth-Mother Gaea

As Thor prepared to meet his inevitable end, a new figure magically appeared on the battlefield. Earth-Mother Gaea introduced herself to Arishem and claimed Thor as her true-born son. She explained that, while Odin had planned to meet the Celestials with force, she and the goddesses of Earth had spent the last thousand years secretly seeking a more peaceful solution. They had nurtured the world's most accomplished individuals, whom she now presented to the Celestials as the pinnacle of human development. These so-called Young Gods were anxious to explore the cosmos, and so Gaea suggested that the Celestials take them under their tutelage. While the Young Gods learned more about the universe, the Celestials could study their reactions and expand their own knowledge.

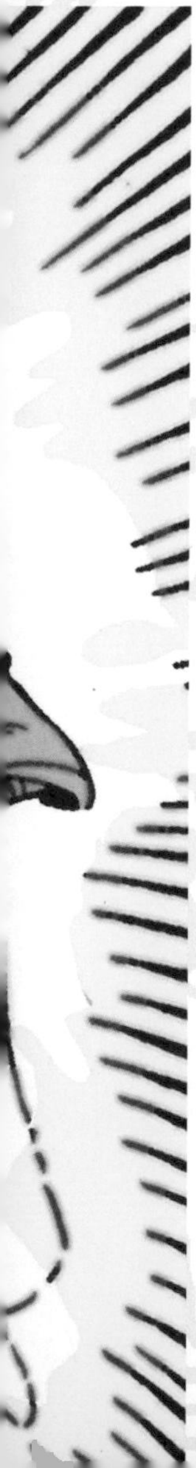

Young gods
Earth-Mother Gaea sought consensus rather than conflict, offering the space gods the finest examples of humanity if they agreed to depart.
Thor #300, Oct. 1980

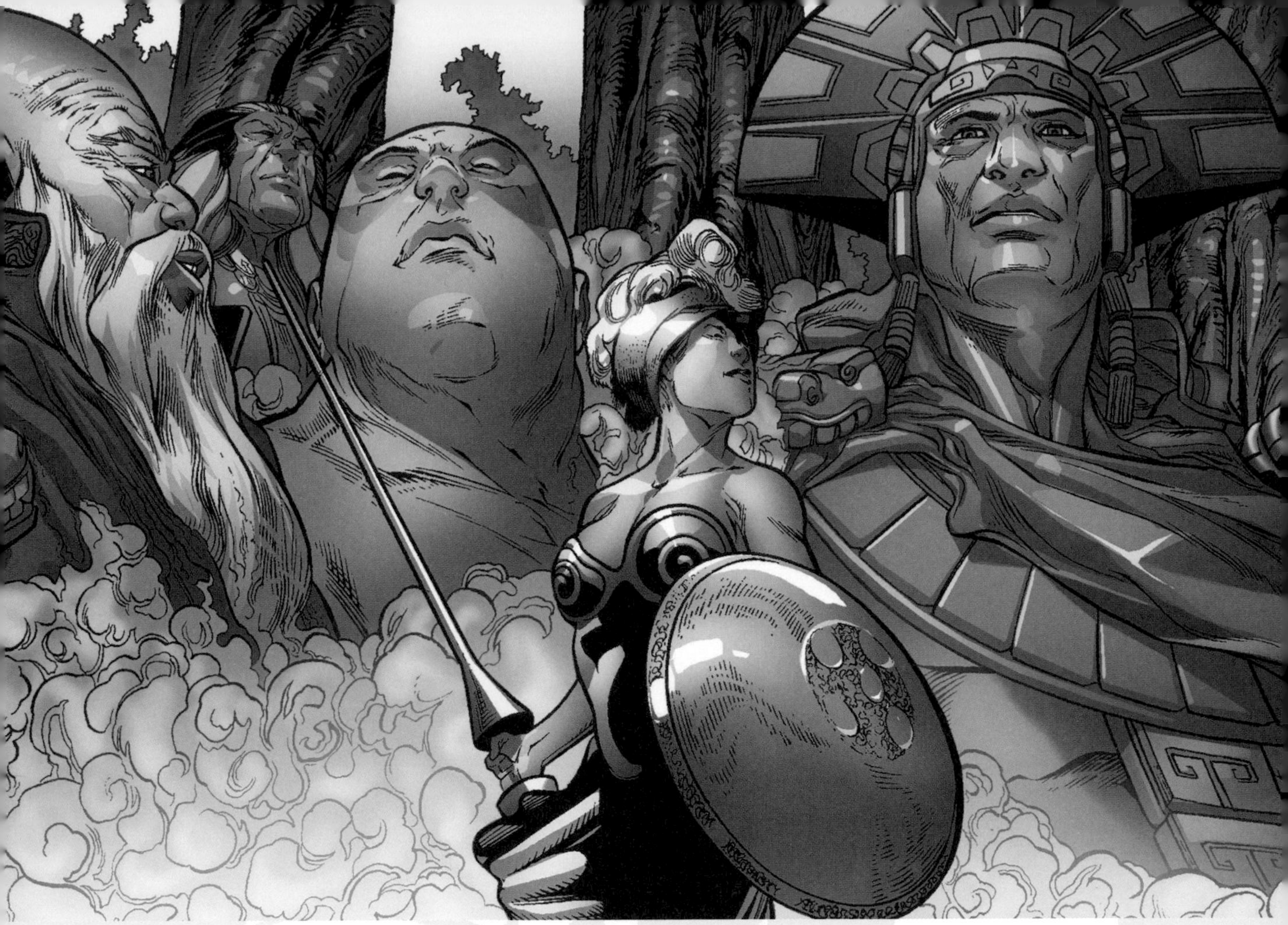

Arishem considered the offer and eventually agreed to Gaea's terms. He made his final judgment on the people of Earth, ruling in favor of their continued existence, and the Celestials and the Young Gods departed with little fanfare. The Celestials' last act on Earth was to use their power to cloud the collective memory of ordinary women and men, making them forget the space gods' most recent visitation. In the wake of the Celestials' departure, Thor visited each of Earth's pantheons, convincing them to donate a portion of their own godly essences to resurrect Odin and the Asgardians. Back in Asgard, Thor and his fully restored fellow gods celebrated their great victory. Meanwhile on Earth, the Eternals and the Deviants, as well as their human cousins, faced a future that was hopefully free of the Celestials and their meddling ways.

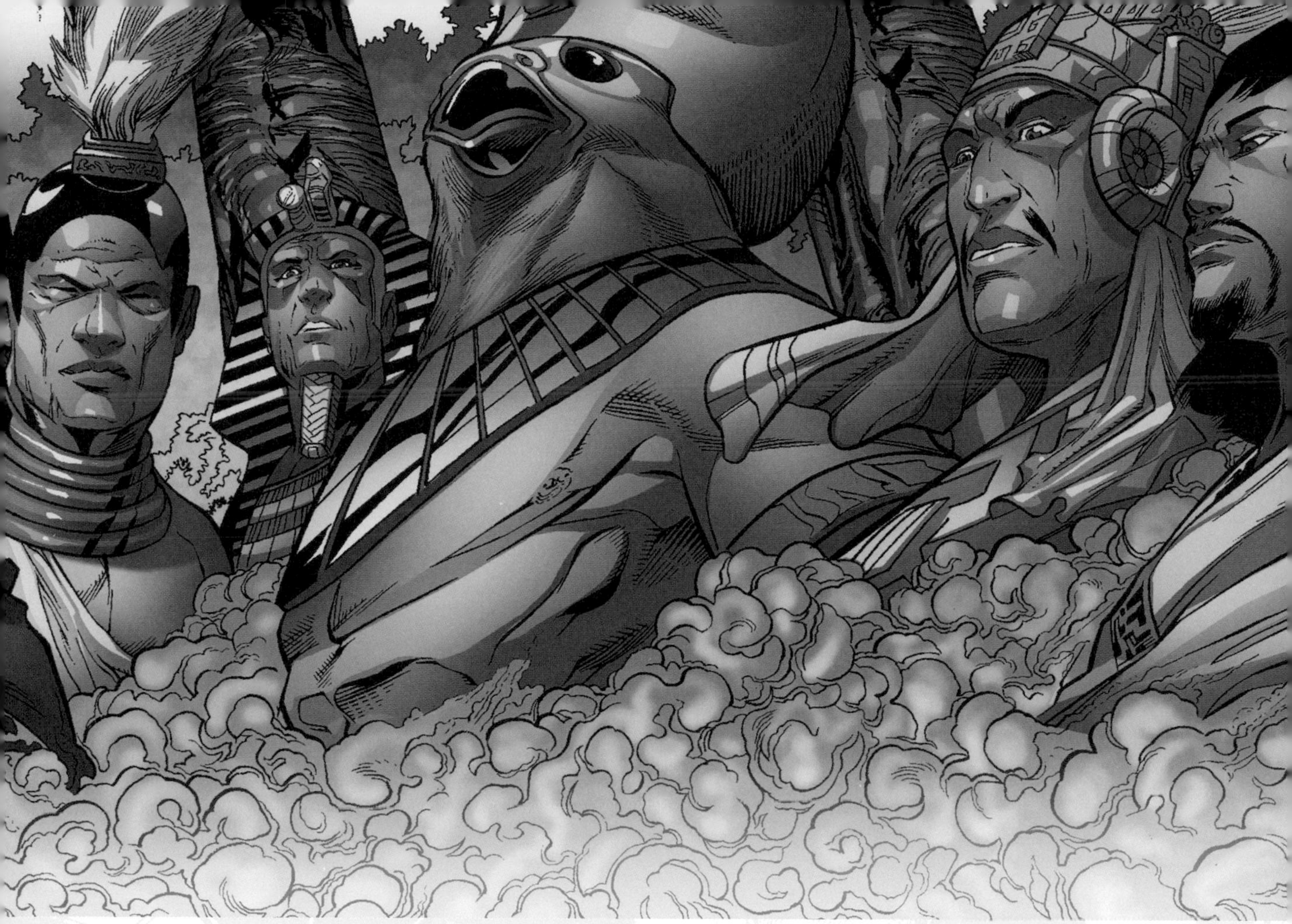

Call to arms
Delivering a message of dire peril, the Olympian Athena addressed the full Council of Godheads.
Incredible Hercules #116, Jun. 2008

The Council of Godheads continued to be the venue in which the godly hosts met to discuss existential threats and matters of cosmic importance. When the ancient Demogorge was revived by a coalition of death gods, the council feared he would consume the godly pantheons without thought. In response, they dispatched a team that included Thor, Horus, and Quetzalcoatl to apprehend the God-Eater. After successfully completing their mission, they returned the Demogorge to his place of slumber within the sun.

Sometime later, the Olympian Goddess of Wisdom, Athena, convened a meeting of the council to discuss an unparalleled threat posed by the extraterrestrial Skrulls. A Deviant race created by the Celestials in the distant past, the Skrulls had used their shape-changing abilities to become the dominant species on their homeworld of Skrullos and extend their realm into outer space.

Now, with their empire in chaos, the Skrulls had infiltrated Earth, capturing and replacing many of Earth's leading figures and heroes. The embedded Skrulls operated in secret for many years and when the main Skrull fleet arrived in orbit, they finally dropped their disguises in preparation for a full-scale invasion.

Athena feared that victory for the Skrulls would mean victory for the Skrull gods and that Earth's pantheons would find themselves replaced by extraterrestrial immortals. To avoid this dire fate, she proposed a preemptive strike, arguing that the Council of Godheads

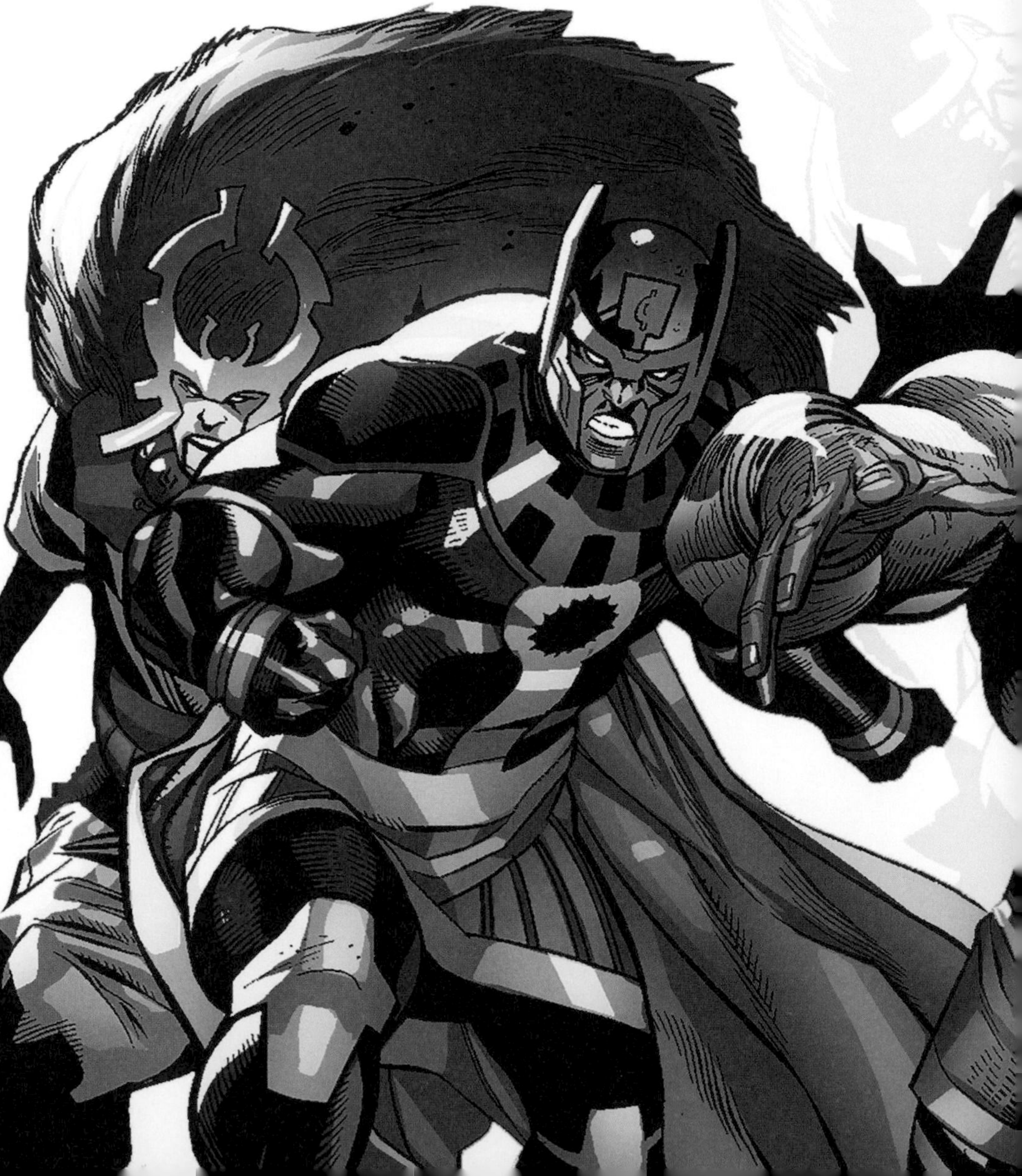

God Squad
Chaos lord Amatsu-Mikaboshi, Eternal Ajak, the Demogorge, and boy-genius Amadeus Cho were among Hercules' crew on a quarrelsome voyage across the Dreamtime.
Incredible Hercules #120, Oct. 2008

should send a band of gods and demigods to eliminate the Skrull deities Sl'gur't and Kly'bn. The plan was accepted and, with Thor and the Asgardians thought to be vulnerable to Skrull infiltration after their recent resurrection, Hercules was chosen to lead the so-called "God Squad" on its urgent, clandestine mission.

The council selected the Eternal Ajak, the reawakened Demogorge, Northern goddess Snowbird, and chaos lord Amatsu-Mikaboshi to accompany the Olympian. Also on the hastily assembled team was Hercules' friend and faithful ally, the human boy-genius Amadeus Cho.

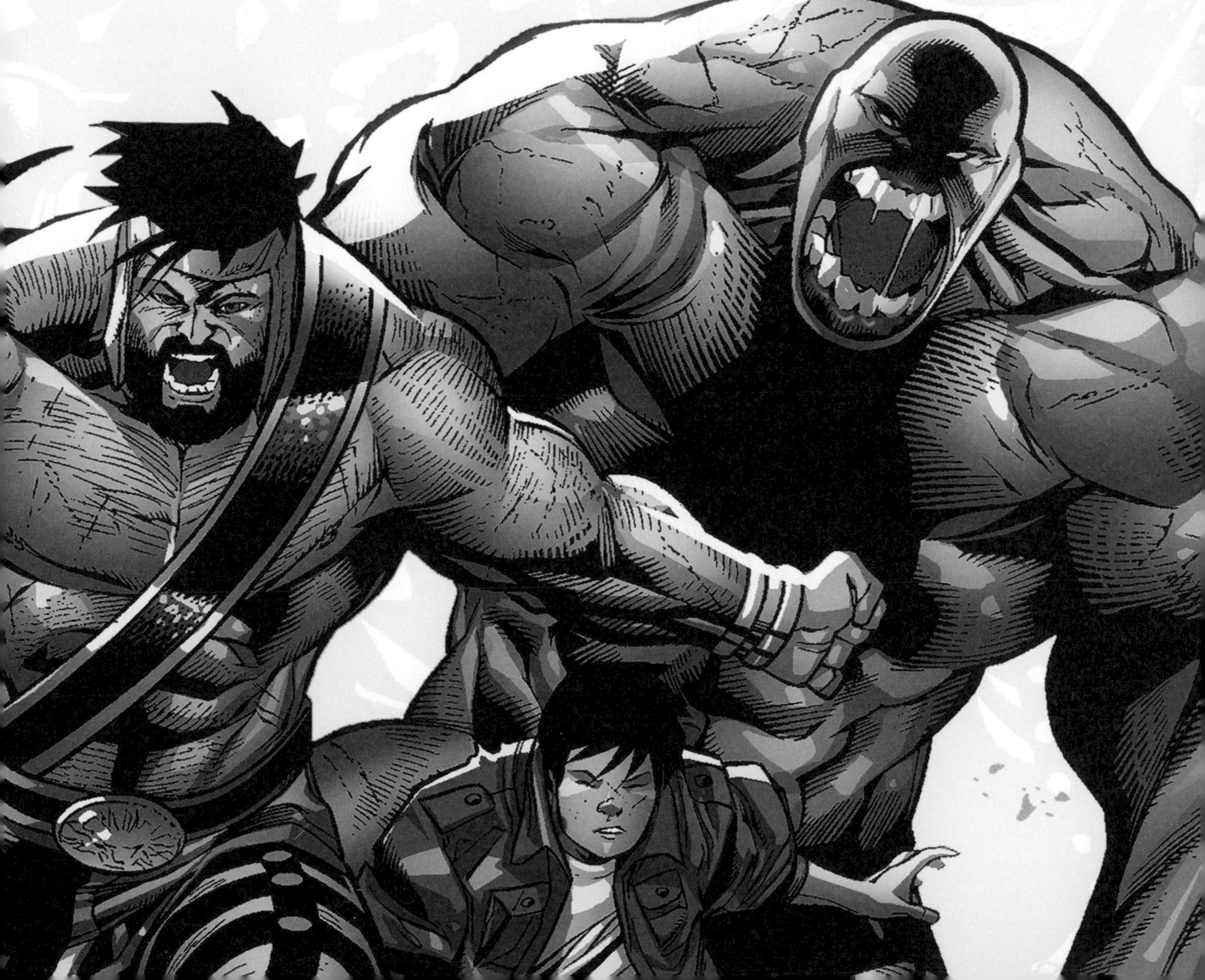

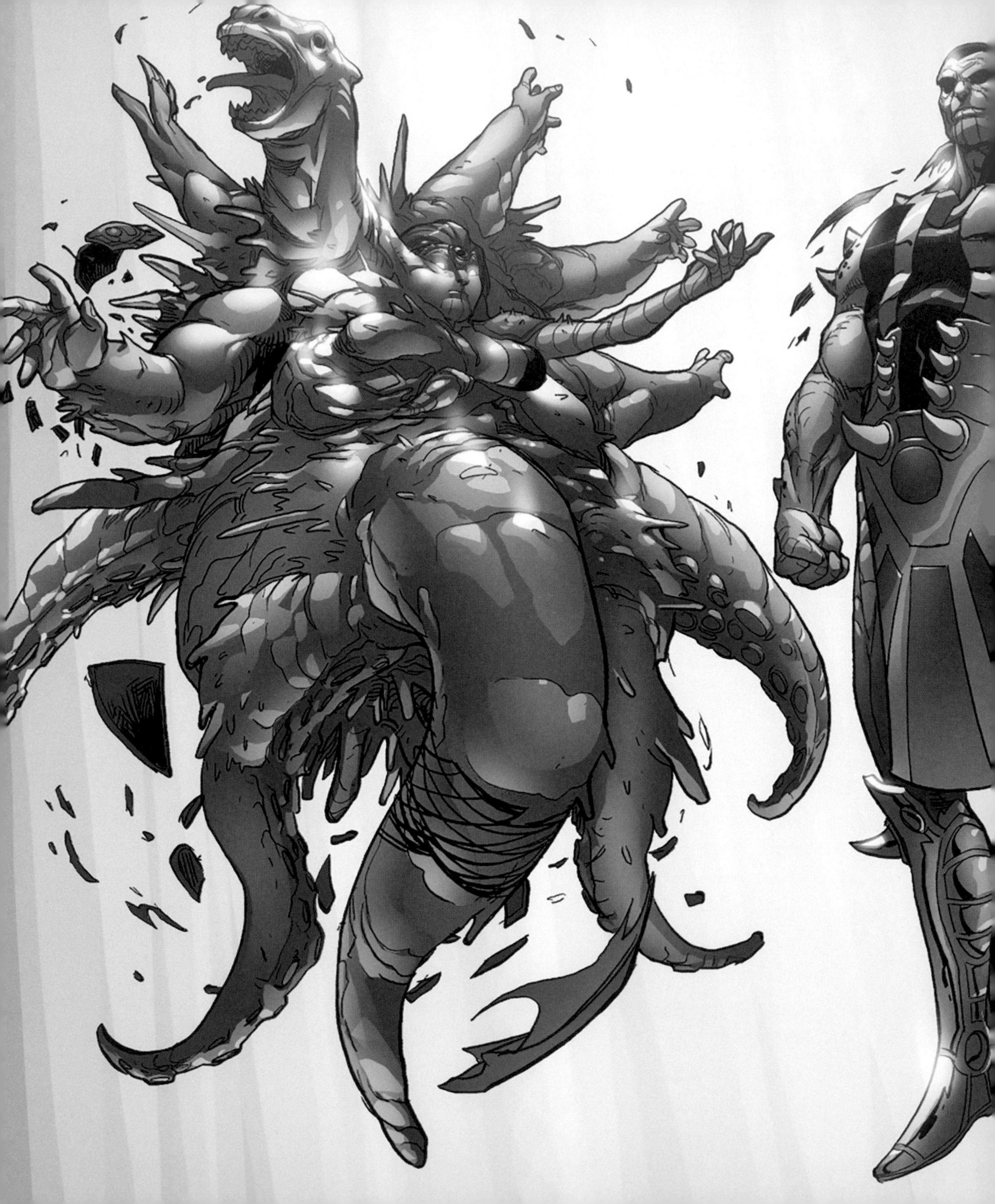

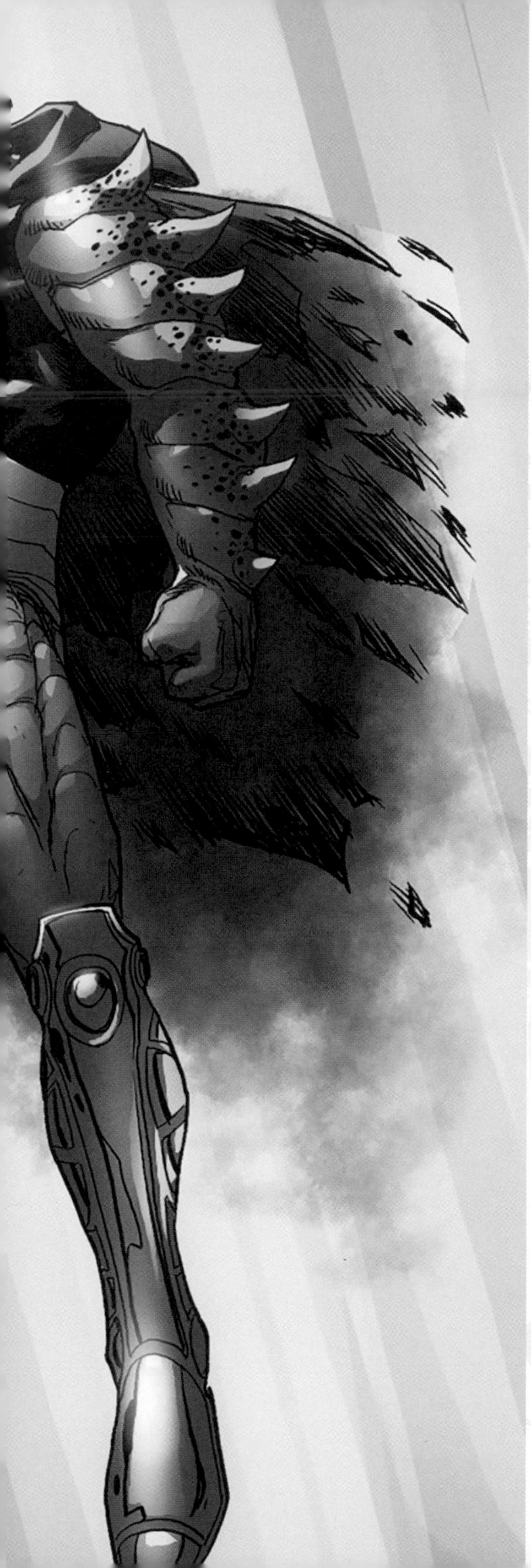

The domain of the Skrull gods was located somewhere in the Dreamtime, so the God Squad used a mystical galleon to sail across the ethereal realm, guided by a map stolen from Nightmare, Lord of Dreams.

"I'm ready to play god!" Hercules

The voyage was ill-tempered, old rivalries sparking conflict among the gods. Furthermore, there was a spy on their ship—a Skrull in the shape of Amadeus Cho's coyote pup, Kirby. When Hercules and the God Squad finally arrived at their destination, the Skrull gods were waiting. Feigning benign intent, Kly'bn introduced himself. He revealed that in ancient times, he had been the last Eternal on Skrullos, all the others slain by Sl'gur't and her Deviant followers. When Sl'gur't had arrived to kill him, Kly'bn had rejected her hatred and professed his love for her and all living things. Sl'gur't was so enchanted by Kly'bn's declaration that they were married, the power of their devotion to each other causing them to ascend to the heavens to become the Skrulls' first gods.

All he and Sl'gur't wanted to do now, Kly'bn explained, was spread their love to other worlds. Hercules rejected the extraterrestrials' misleading claim, pointing out that the Skrull gods' supposed benevolence would inevitably lead to the enslavement of humankind and the extinction of Earth's own pantheons.

Heavenly couple
The malformed Sl'gur't and handsome Kly'bn ascended to Skrull heaven after declaring their love for one other.
Incredible Hercules #120, Oct. 2008

A fierce fight ensued and, despite his Olympian strength, Hercules ultimately found himself overwhelmed by Kly'bn's vast array of Eternal powers. It was only when Hercules took inspiration from Amadeus Cho, an ordinary human facing extraordinary circumstances, that he finally gained the upper hand. With a helpful distraction from Snowbird, he was able to deliver a fatal blow to Kly'bn. Meanwhile, elsewhere in the Skrull Dreamtime, Amatsu-Mikaboshi gave vent to his chaotic instincts and savagely slaughtered Sl'gur't.

With the death of their gods, the Skrull invasion force found itself in a perilous situation. In their panicked and weakened state, the extraterrestrials were no match for Earth's Super Heroes, and they were soon forced back into outer space. Hercules and the God Squad returned home, but not to a hero's welcome. Their mission had remained a secret. Only the gods were aware of the life-and-death struggle that had occurred in the Dreamtime. As ever, the Council of Godheads sat above such mundane matters, operating on a level far removed from the daily concerns of ordinary mortals.

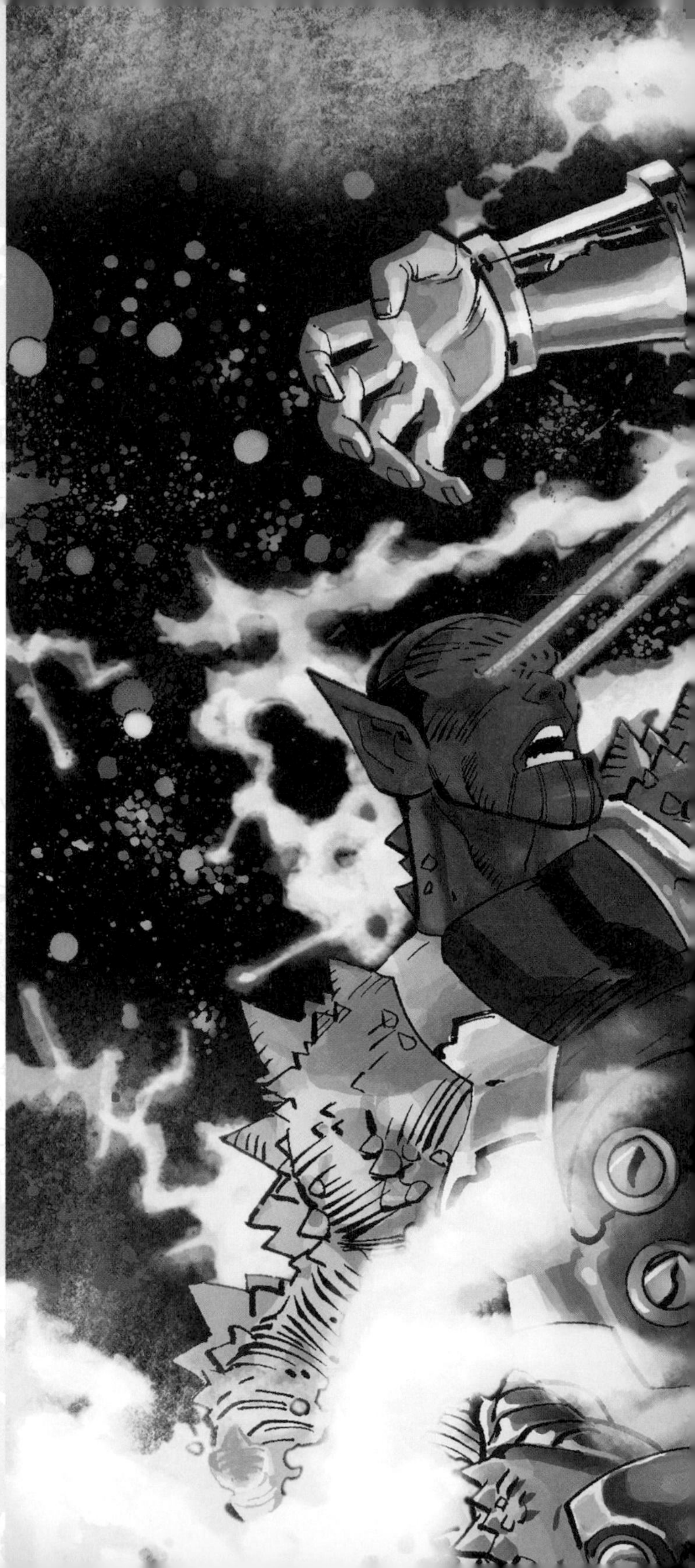

Divine intervention
Hercules engaged the Skrull god Kly'bn in hand-to-hand combat in a bid to end his rival's threat to Earth's pantheons.
Incredible Hercules #120, Oct. 2008

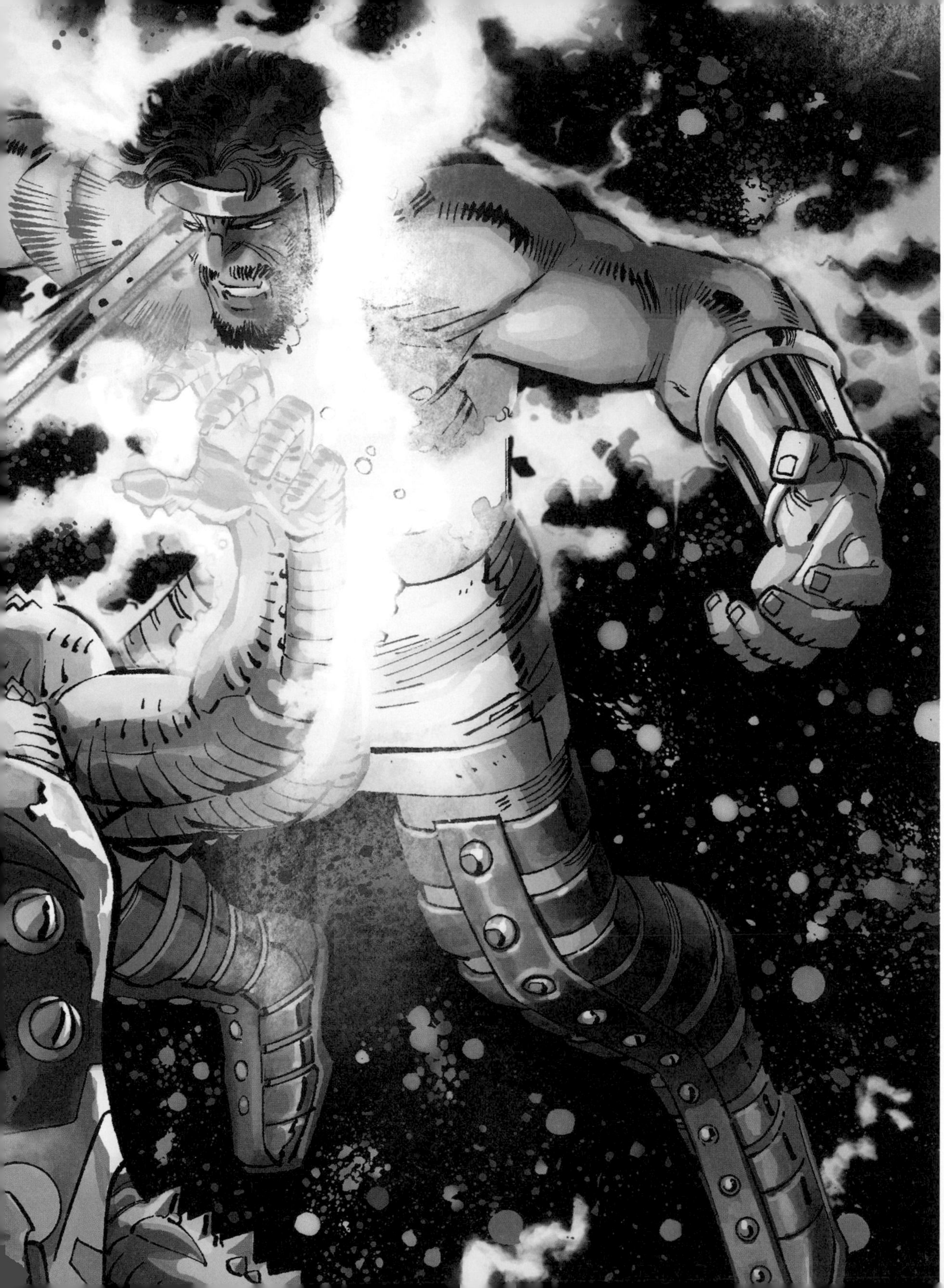

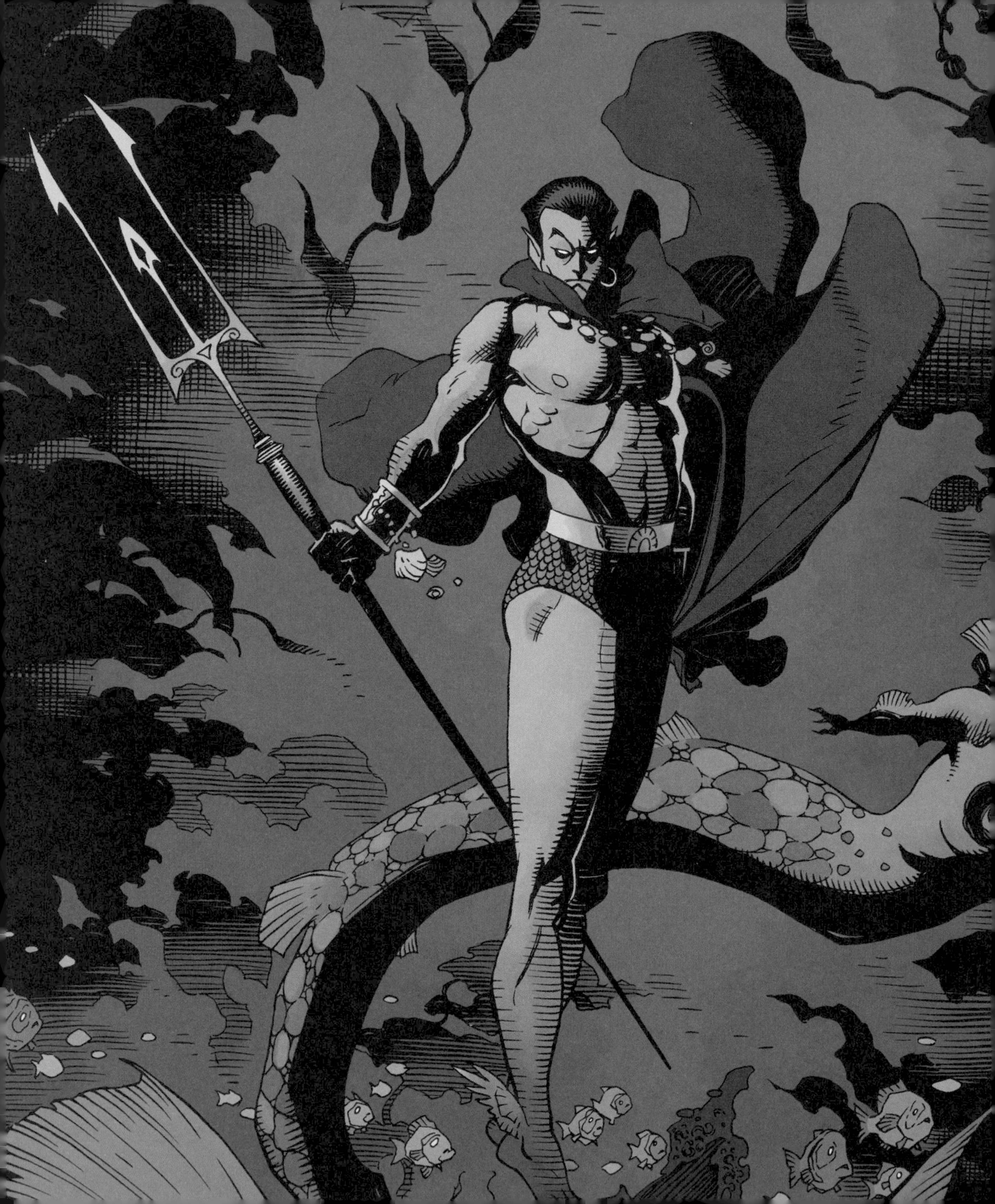

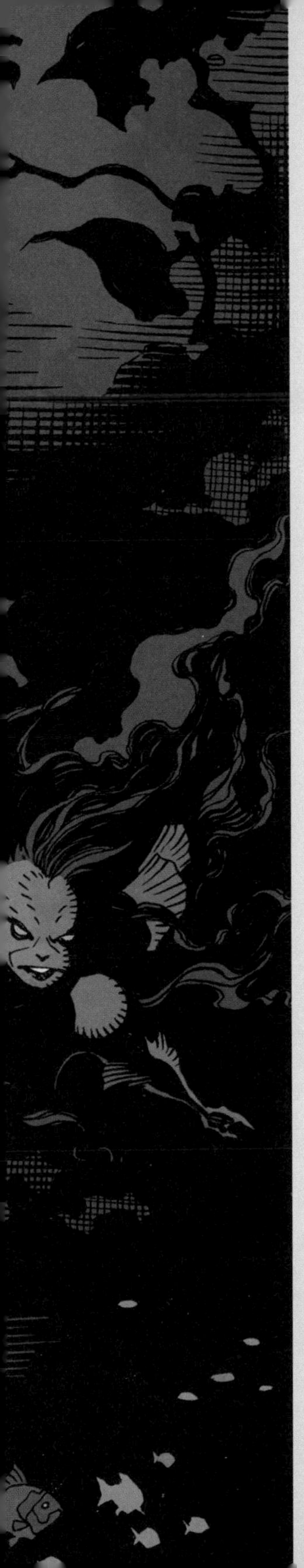

LEGENDARY HEROES

As the gods themselves intervened less directly in Earthly affairs, many mortal heroes filled the vacuum. Some, like the members of the Brotherhood of the Shield, employed advanced science in a never-ending battle against the forces of darkness. Others, such as the Black Knight and Captain Britain, were empowered by the otherworldly mage Merlin to uphold the values embodied by fabled Camelot. Even remote Atlantis gave birth to a unique individual in the regal form of Namor, the Sub-Mariner—one of the world's earliest mutant heroes.

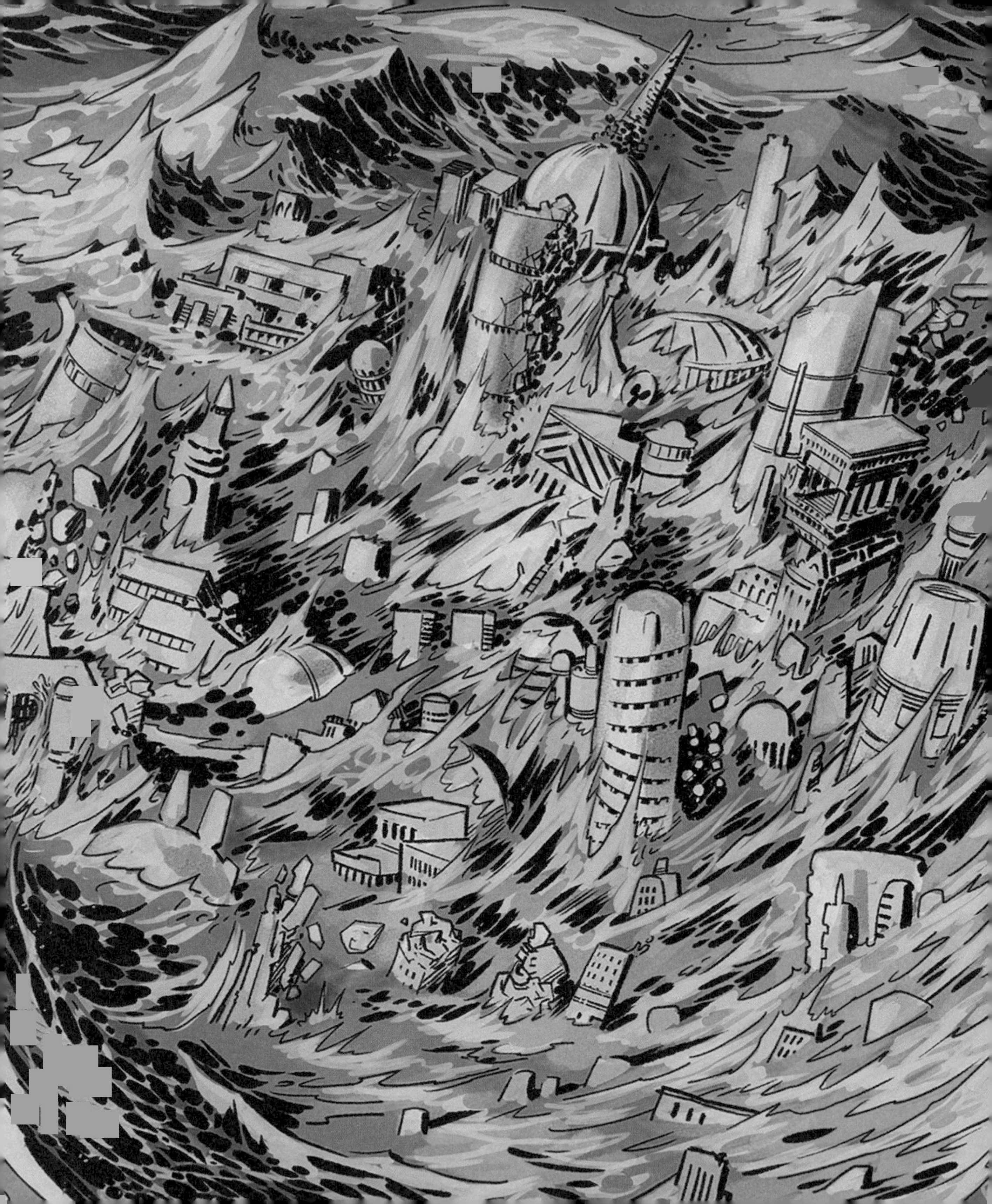

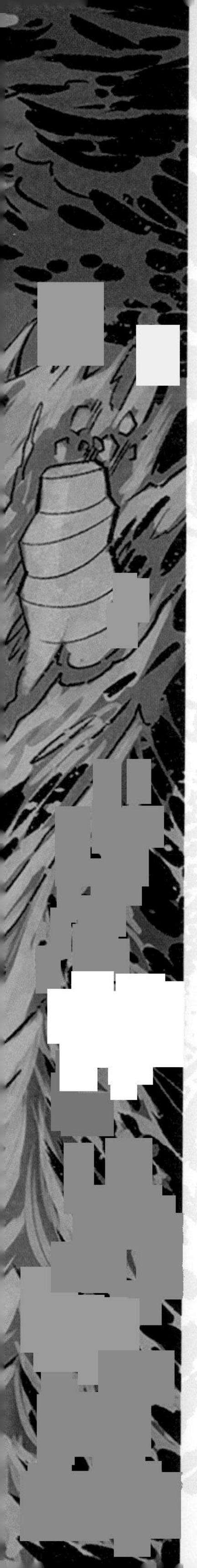

Cataclysm and Conflict

For centuries, Atlantis was bedeviled by strife and, even when unified under the rule of the Sub-Mariner, the sunken kingdom continued to be haunted by figures from the ancient past.

In addition to sweeping away the Deviant Empire, the Great Cataclysm of 18,000 BCE also sent the continent of Atlantis plunging to the ocean floor. One of the few human civilizations to remain free of the Deviant scourge, the continent and its capital had served as a vast repository of scientific and cultural knowledge. Centuries of expertise and insight were lost when Atlantis drowned beneath the waves. However, while the city itself was brought low in less than a week, a handful of Atlanteans miraculously survived the upheaval.

The survivors became water breathers, the first of a new offshoot of humanity that would eventually be classified as *Homo mermanus*. Whether the Atlanteans developed gills and an enhanced physiognomy as a result of some natural mutation, through the application of arcane science, or by sorcery, is unknown, but their sudden adaptation allowed them to flourish beneath the waves. With Atlantis in ruins following the catastrophe, the survivors abandoned the city to become a nomadic people, spreading across the great oceans of the world. Over the centuries, rare sightings of *Homo mermanus* inspired many legends about aquatic merpeople.

Washed away
Unleashed by the Celestial Second Host, the Great Cataclysm of 18,000 BCE sent Atlantis, the pinnacle of human civilization, crashing to the ocean floor.
History of the Marvel Universe #1, Sep. 2019

Thousands of years after it sank, Atlantis was repopulated by the descendants of the original inhabitants. In time, the revived city became the hub of an elaborate network of underwater cantons and principalities. Just as it had on the surface, war shaped the history of sunken Atlantis, with rival warlords frequently vying for dominance. The continual infighting reached its apex at the start of the 20th century, when aquatic barbarians forced Emperor Thakorr to abandon the original Atlantis and establish a gleaming new city in the icy waters beneath Antarctica.

When the expedition ship *Oracle*, under the command of Captain Leonard McKenzie, became trapped by Antarctic ice, depth charges were deployed to free the stricken craft. Unfortunately, the new city of Atlantis was located directly below the vessel and the ensuing explosions caused significant damage. Enraged, Thakorr ordered his daughter to dispatch a cadre of warriors to investigate the source of the deadly blasts. Not wishing to endanger those under her command, Princess Fen swam to the surface herself, imbibing a potion that allowed her to breathe above the waves for five hours at a time. While staying on the *Oracle*, and seeking to better understand the surface dwellers, Fen fell in love with Captain McKenzie. The pair were married, but their happiness was fleeting. Fearing for his daughter's safety, Thakorr ordered a team of Atlantean warriors to forcibly retrieve Fen from the surface. Unfortunately, the crew of the *Oracle* were killed in a confrontation that swiftly turned violent.

Some months later, while still grieving the senseless loss of her husband, Fen gave birth to a fair-skinned boy she named Namor, the Avenging Son. Namor was the world's first human-Atlantean hybrid, capable of breathing both on land and in the sea. He was also a mutant, with an ability to fly through the air with the force of a missile.

Between two worlds
Following a romance with a surface-dweller, Atlantean Princess Fen gave birth to a mutant boy, Namor.
History of the Marvel Universe #2, Oct. 2019

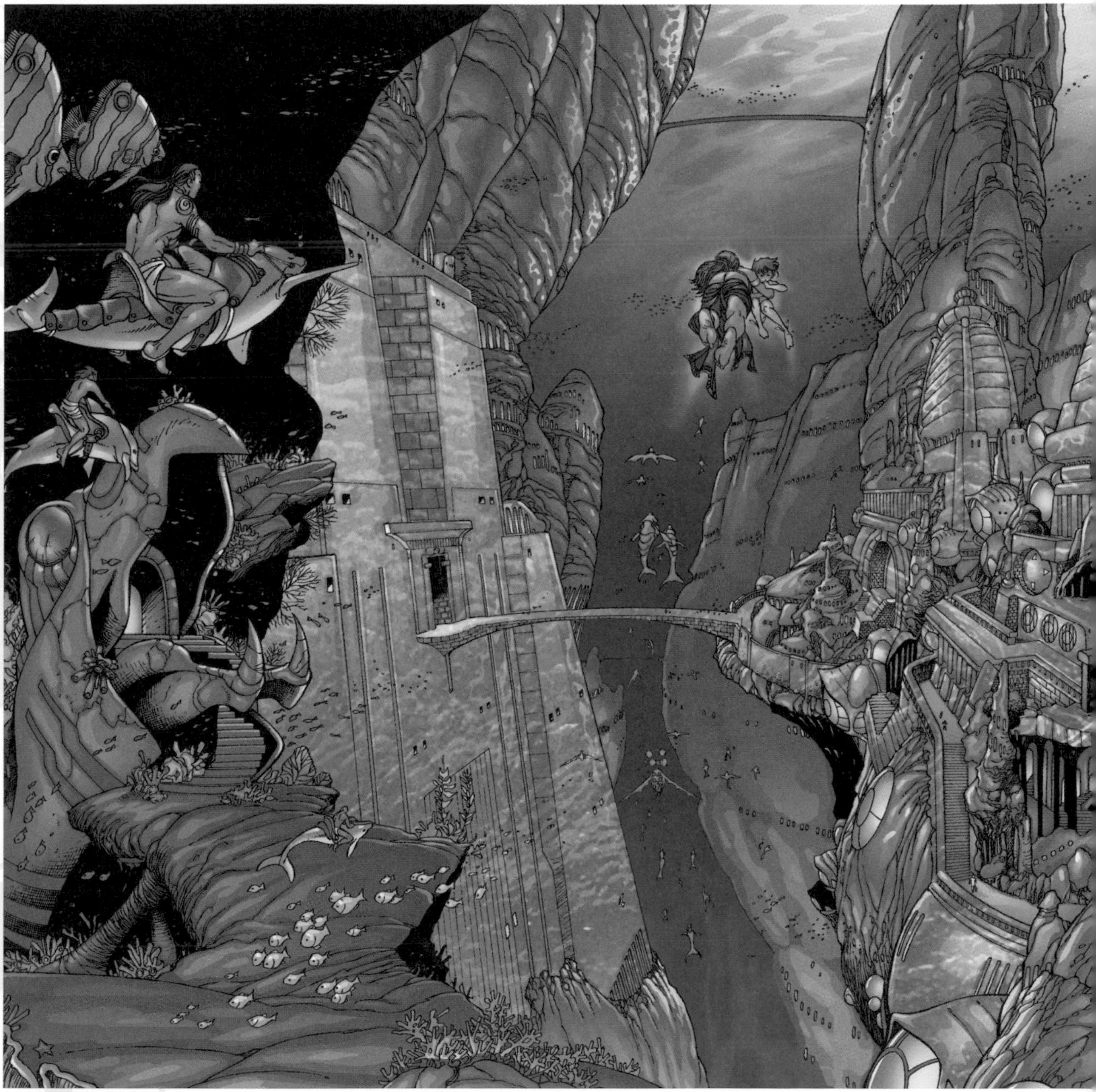

Royal outcast

Namor grew up shielded from the jealousy of pure-blood Atlanteans by his royal status and over-protective mother.

Namor #1, Jun. 2003

Raised under the influence of Emperor Thakorr, Namor developed an intense loathing of the surface world. As a young adult, he attacked New York City and disrupted shipping lanes in retaliation for what he saw as humanity's careless disregard of the world's oceans. Dubbed "the Sub-Mariner" by a hysterical press, Namor was considered a menace to the United States. All that changed, however, during World War II, when Namor joined the allies to fight alongside the likes of Captain America and the original Human Torch. His time as a member of the Invaders, battling to turn back the tide of tyranny, finally earned him a degree of acceptance from the surface world.

"Many are the tales written and whispered about me..." Namor, the Sub-Mariner

Perhaps inevitably, Namor's triumph was followed by his nadir. In the immediate post-war era, he wandered aimlessly for decades, his memories cruelly suppressed by a psionic villain called Destiny. Thanks to an intervention from the second Human Torch, Johnny Storm, Namor regained his wits and raced back to Atlantis. He found the city in ruins—destroyed by humanity's reckless nuclear tests—and its people scattered across the ocean floor.

His distrust of the surface world rekindled, Namor resumed his campaign against humanity's interests. However, after finally reuniting his lost subjects, he concentrated his efforts on rebuilding Atlantis and establishing himself as its sovereign leader. Because of his human heritage, Namor was never universally accepted. Some Atlanteans viewed him as an outsider, and the new king's relationship with his own people was often as tense as his dealings with the surface world. Events came to a head when it appeared that Namor had abandoned his subjects to an uncertain fate, fleeing Atlantis when the realm was overwhelmed by creatures from the mythic past.

From the depths
As a young adult, Prince Namor was obstinate and reckless, frequently turning his back on Atlantis to strike at the surface world.
Namor #1, Jun. 2003

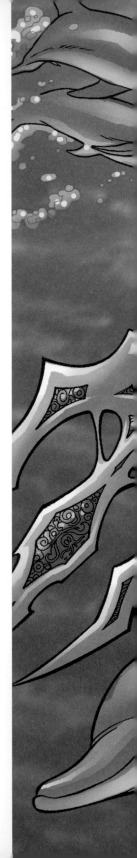

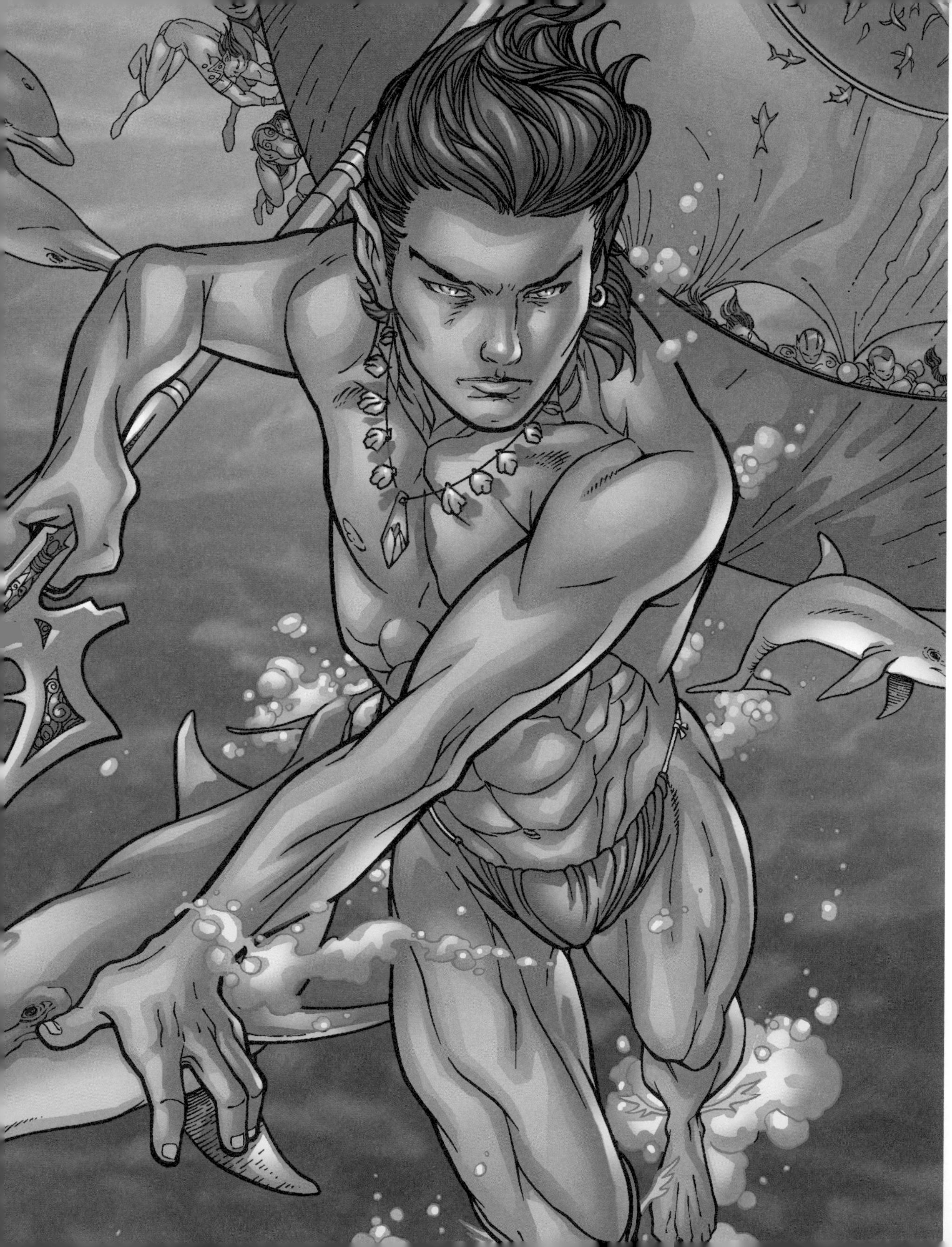

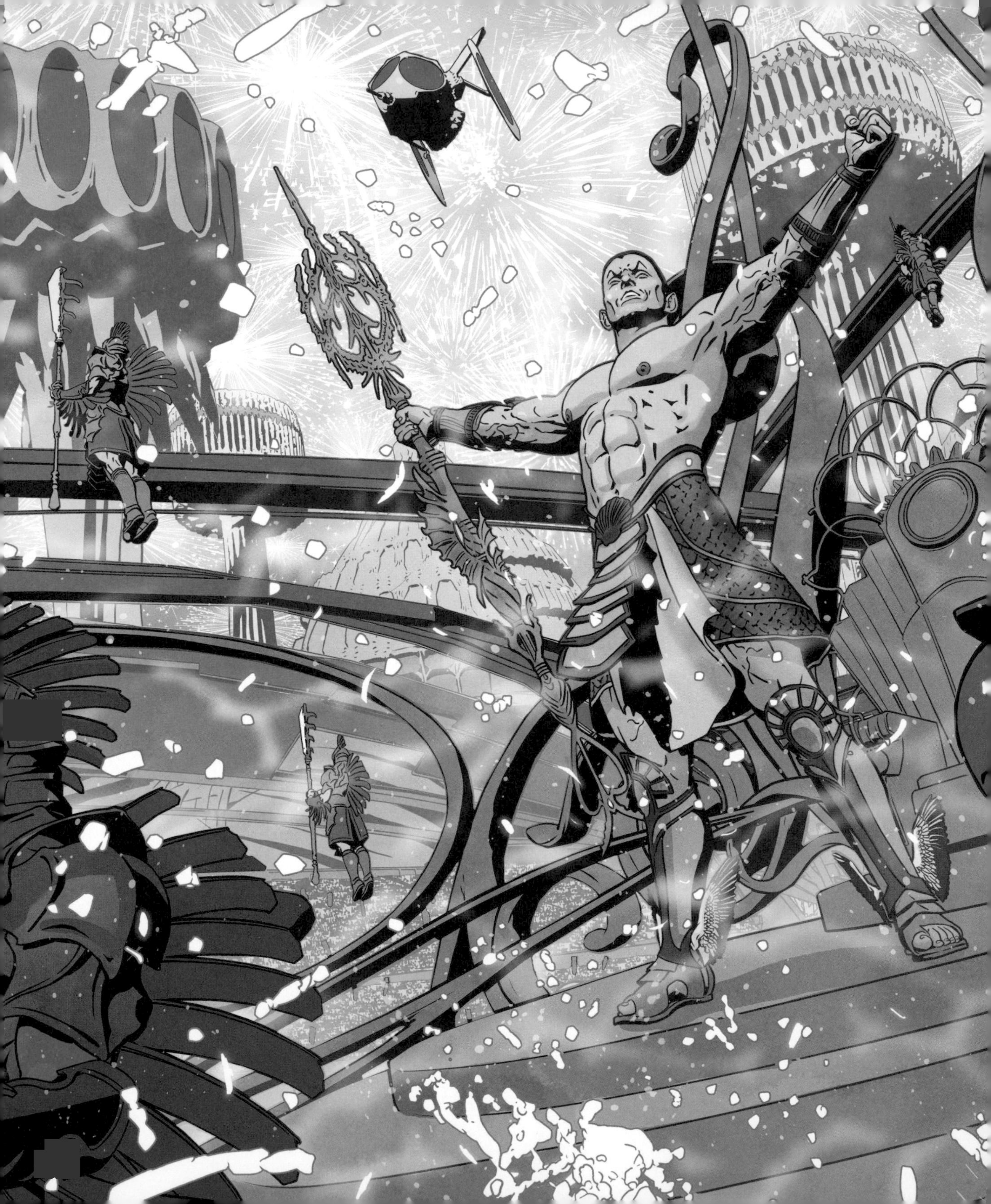

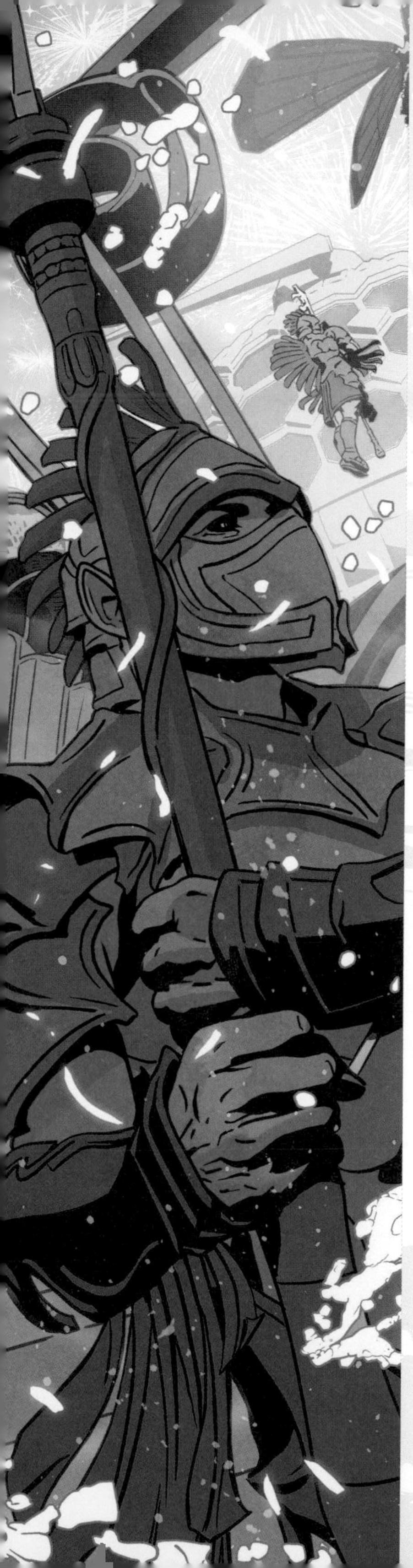

Using arcane sorcery, Sin—the nefarious Red Skull's villainous daughter—freed the Asgardian Serpent God of Fear from its long slumber beneath the Atlantic Ocean. As a result, a tremendous wave of terror flowed over the world, causing consternation and mass panic. Moreover, the Serpent God bestowed hammers of immense power on seven individuals, each chosen specifically for his or her ability to sow fear and discord. One of the recipients was Namor's long-term nemesis, the barbarian Attuma, who used the power of the hammer to take on the aspect of a legendary Atlantean figure, Nerkkod, the Breaker of Oceans. Entering into an alliance with the Undying Ones, ancient demons distantly related to the original Elder Gods, Attuma conquered Atlantis and subjugated its citizens.

"Your fear... poisons the water." Attuma (as Nerkkod)

Facing overwhelming odds, and gripped by the irrational dread unleashed by the Serpent God, Namor fled the city. As he escaped, Attuma's words echoed in his ears. "Never forget that you still drew breath while your city crumbled and your people suffered." Namor's actions were not solely driven by fear, however. He also recognized the scale of the challenge that lay ahead. He would need powerful allies if he were to ever win the day, and so he formed a new team of Defenders with Doctor Strange, the mutant Loa, the spacefaring Silver Surfer, and Lyra, the Savage She-Hulk.

Mighty monarch
In modern times, Namor embraced his responsibilities as underwater sovereign, vowing to rule his aquatic people with equanimity and protect them from harm.
Nick Fury #4, Sep. 2017

Almost immediately, the heroes came under assault from the Undying Ones. The demonic spirits took possession of countless sea animals, warping their bodies into grotesque shapes. Although Namor and his fellow Defenders could unleash their full might upon the misshapen leviathans, they had to be more restrained when it came to a fresh enemy. Some of the Undying Ones used captive Atlanteans as their corporeal vessels, taunting Namor as they marched relentlessly forwards, weapons drawn, crying "Our king… How could you let us be taken?"

Rather than causing despair, though, these words strengthened Namor's resolve and banished his fear. Finally accepting his responsibilities as a leader, the King of Atlantis held the line against the advancing troops. He used minimal force to subdue them, knocking many unconscious. This gave Doctor Strange enough time to concoct a spell that was successful in transporting the Undying Ones back to their otherworldly realm. With his allies in retreat, Attuma was forced to abandon Atlantis with his few remaining forces. The Defenders gave chase and, as his fellow heroes rounded up Attuma's confederates, Namor delivered a decisive, crushing blow to the villain. Separated from his hammer and severely wounded, Attuma fled the battlefield.

In the aftermath of his victory, Namor looked to the safety and security of his people. While others would deal directly with the Serpent God—the Asgardian Thor ultimately wielding the Odinsword to defeat the creature—the King of Atlantis would take time to rebuild his realm and regain his people's trust.

Making waves
Transformed into Nerkkod, the Breaker of Oceans, the barbaric Attuma drove the Sub-Mariner from his undersea kingdom.
Fear Itself: The Deep #3, Oct. 2011

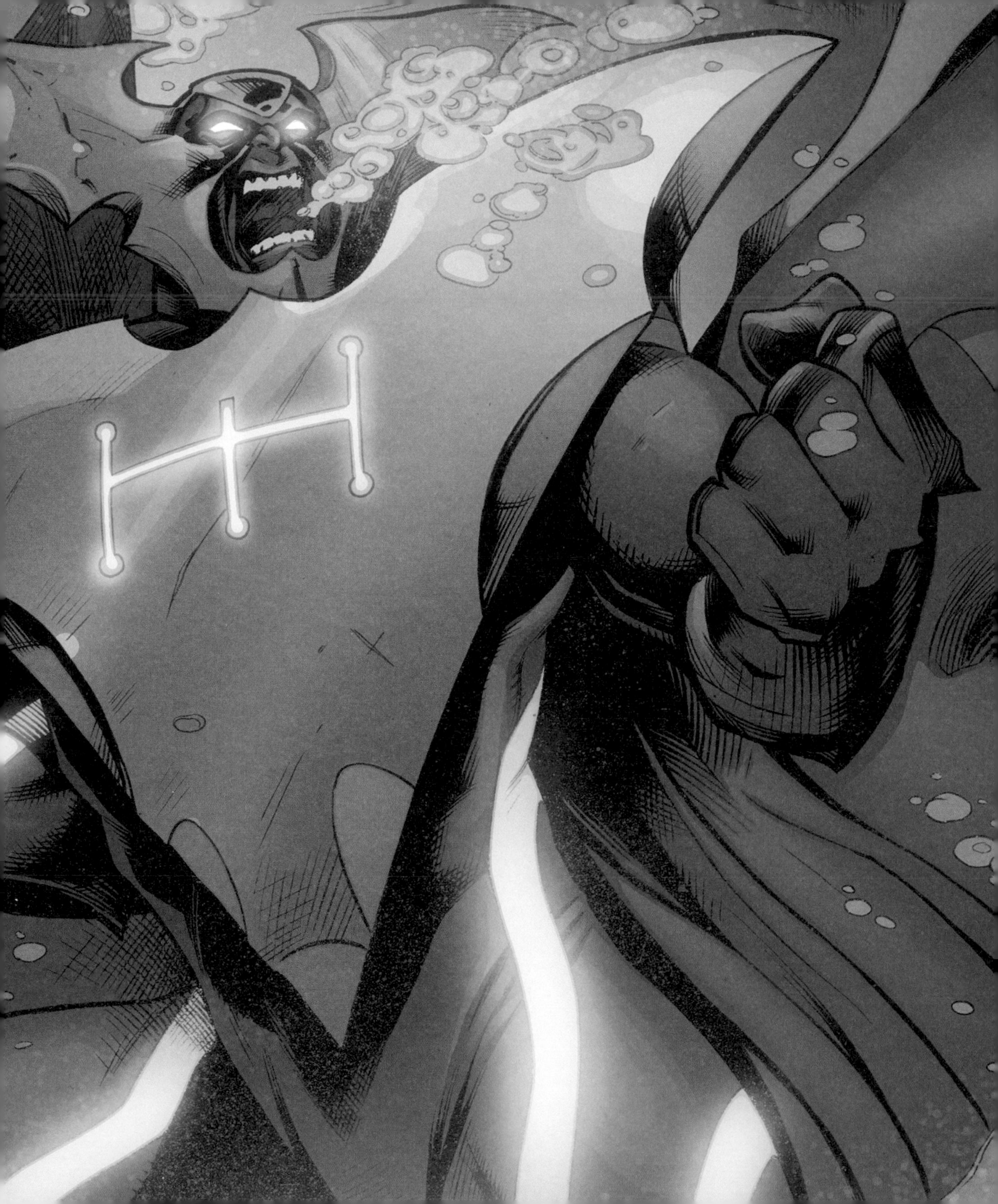

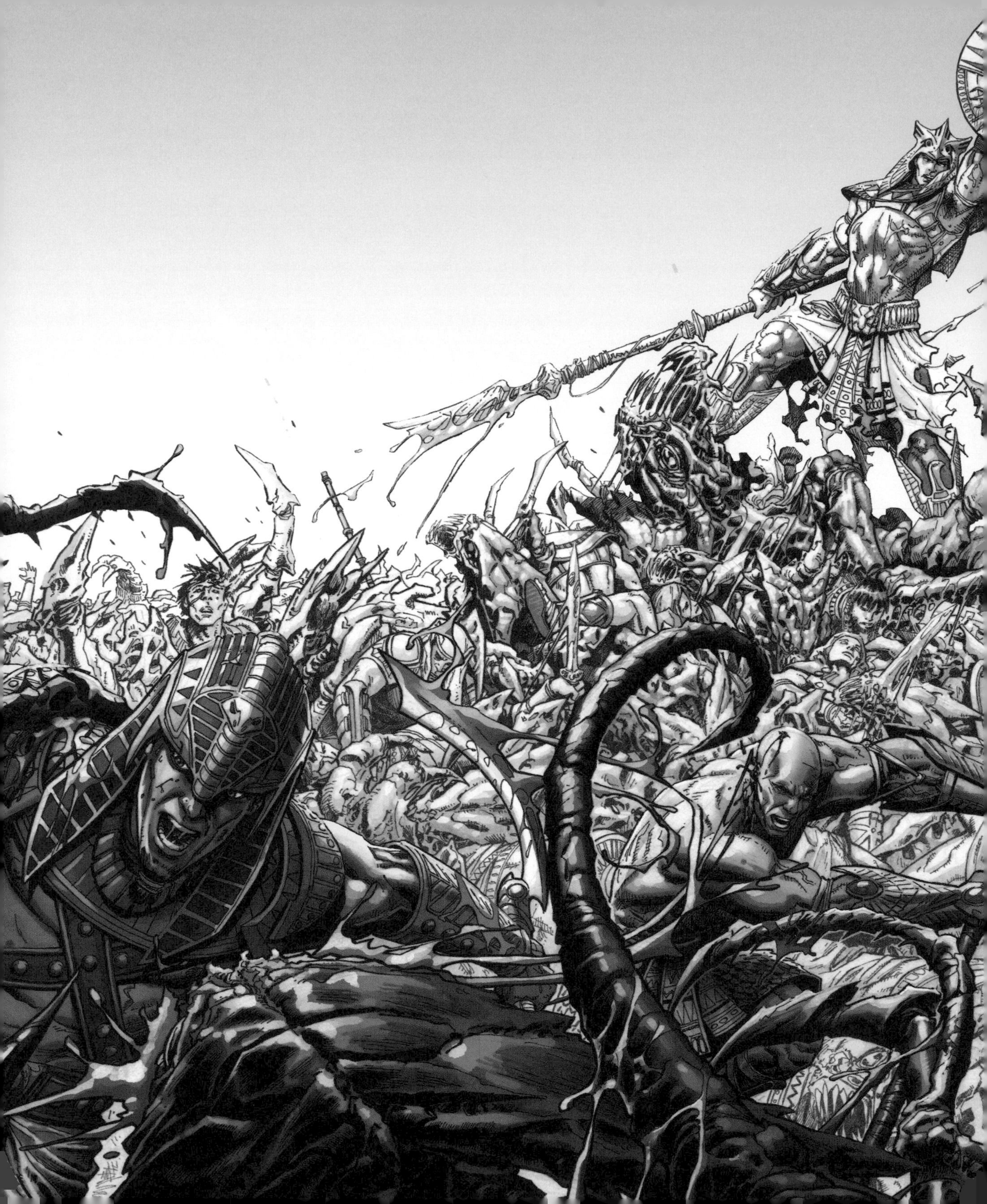

Sword and Shield

Throughout its history, the world has had countless secret guardians. Cloaked in shadow, these selfless individuals have gently guided human civilization and left behind legendary tales that inspire to this day.

When alien parasites known as the Brood threatened to first overrun ancient Egypt and then the entire world, a warrior called Imhotep refused to yield to the marauding creatures. He formed a mighty army that successfully repelled the invaders. After personally killing the Brood Queen in 2620 BCE, Imhotep formed the Brotherhood of the Shield, an organization tasked with protecting humanity from extinction-level threats.

More than a simple warrior clan, the Brotherhood of the Shield counted philosophers and learned women and men among its ranks. Operating in secret, the group sought to steer humanity toward an enlightened future, one free from ignorance and fear. Over the centuries, some of history's greatest thinkers served as members of the Brotherhood. Circa 200 BCE, the Greek inventor Archimedes utilized his vast intellect to transform the Colossus of Rhodes into a giant exoskeleton that he then wore to battle a marauding Kree Sentry, successfully destroying the extraterrestrial interloper. Some three centuries later, the Chinese statesman and polymath Zhang Heng embraced his responsibilities as a leading member of the clandestine organization to engage in a deep philosophical discussion with a visiting Celestial.

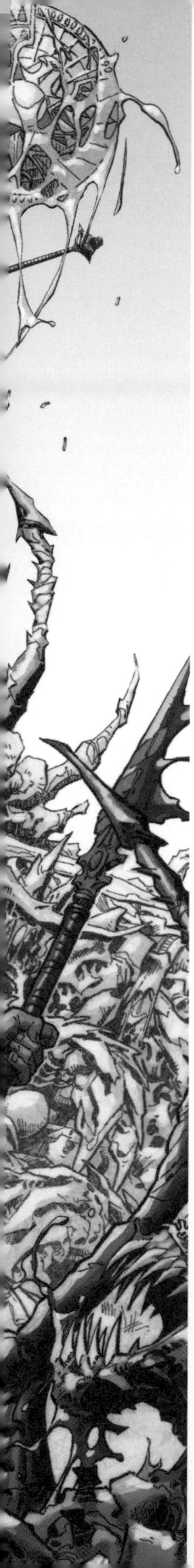

Shield bearer

In ancient times, Egyptian warrior Imhotep raised an army to fight off the alien Brood and then founded the Brotherhood of the Shield.

S.H.I.E.L.D. #1, Jun. 2010

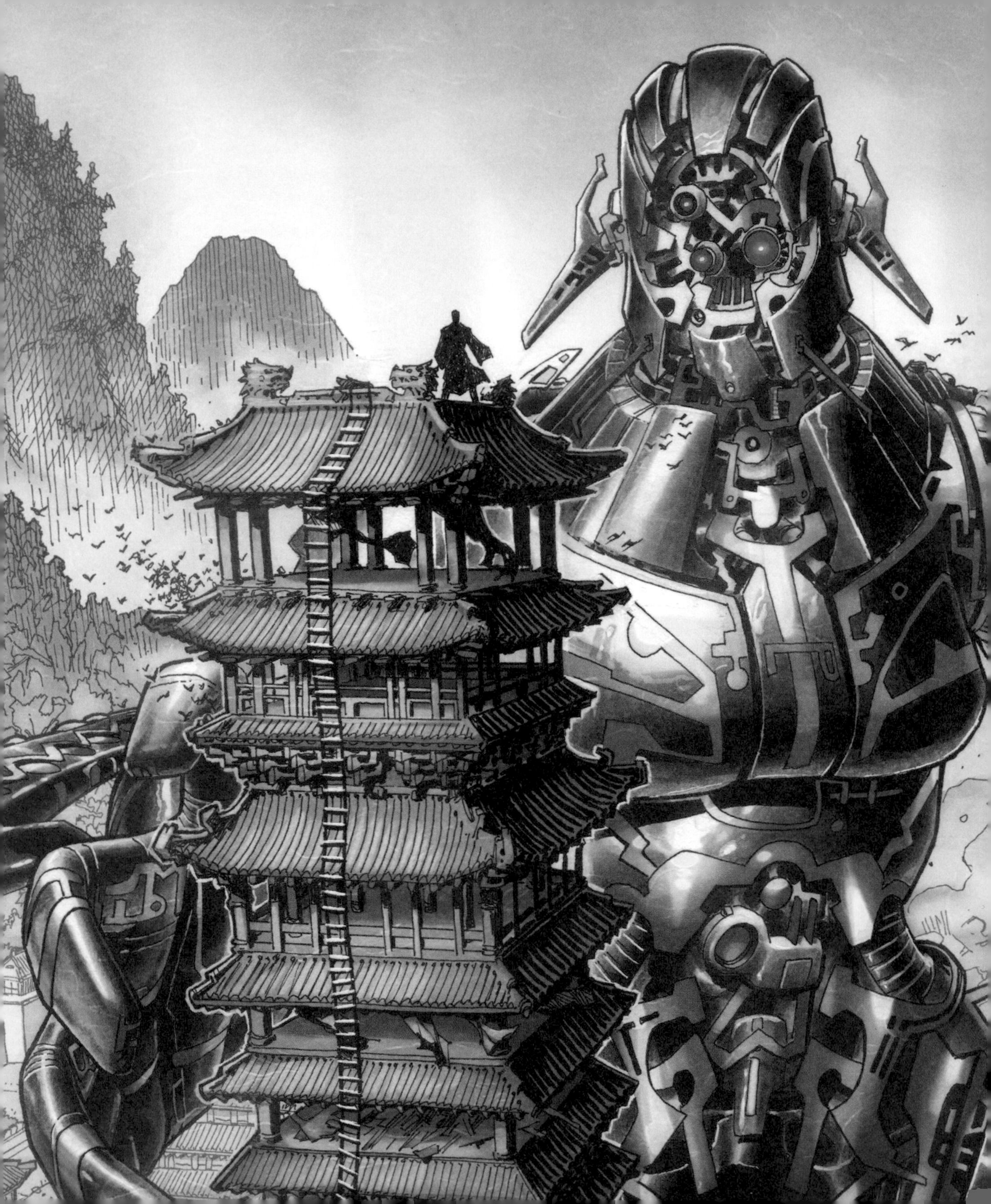

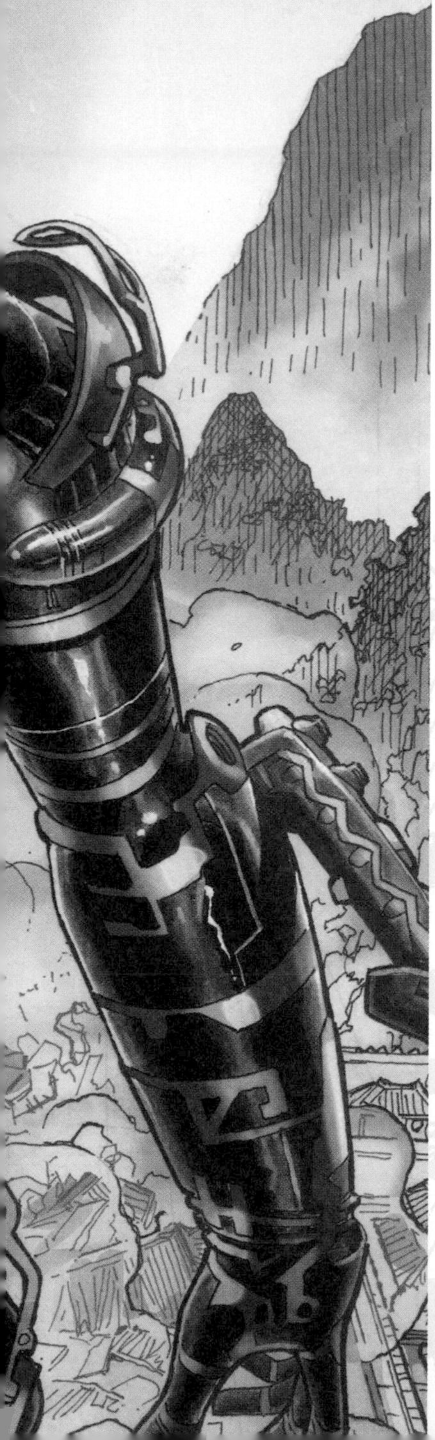

The towering space goddess was in the final stages of pregnancy, and the cosmic forces unleashed by the impending birth would likely tear the world apart. Zhang Heng argued for humanity's right to exist and he ultimately convinced the Celestial to give birth safely inside the Earth's sun.

Around 750 CE, the renowned Persian scientist Jabir ibn Hayyan assumed leadership of the Brotherhood of the Shield. He sought to build a machine that would contain all of humankind's hopes, dreams, and aspirations. His experiment ran awry, however, and his invention drained the life force from thousands of erudite individuals. With the Brotherhood's ranks so sorely depleted—and with so much knowledge seemingly lost forever—the world entered a dark age of ignorance.

The Renaissance, some 750 years later, brought with it fresh hope, however, and the likes of the futurist Leonardo da Vinci and the astronomer Galileo committed their lives in service to the Brotherhood of the Shield. During his tenure as leader of the Brotherhood, Leonardo da Vinci was particularly concerned about the Celestial fetus that had been growing in the sun since Zhang Heng's time. He invented a mechanical flight suit that would take him into outer space to investigate matters further, but promptly vanished during his inaugural voyage.

A century after Leonardo's disappearance, Sir Isaac Newton was recruited into the Brotherhood and swiftly rose through the ranks to become leader of the High Council. In his quest for arcane knowledge, he stumbled upon the secret formula for the legendary Elixir of Life, which he used to extend his allotted life span indefinitely. Immortality gave Newton a clarity of thought, and plenty of opportunities to mull over seemingly intractable problems. He eventually devised the Quiet Math, a unique formula that predicted future events. Using this, and the prophecies of Nostradamus, Newton divined that the world would end in the year 2060. He called this revelation the Silent Truth.

Up close
In the year 114 CE, Zhang Heng constructed a huge tower so that he could converse face-to-face with a visiting Celestial.
S.H.I.E.L.D. #1, Jun. 2010

Armed with this foreknowledge, Newton set about restructuring the Brotherhood of the Shield. Abandoning its outward-looking ways, the cabal became insular, ever more secretive and hidebound by tradition. While it still sought to defend humanity from external threats, it did so only in preparation for an inevitable end. According to Newton, the Brotherhood's primary task was to now usher the world toward its preordained future. Of course, this philosophy ran contrary to the Brotherhood's founding principles— that all men and women were masters of their own destiny—and there were murmurings in opposition to Newton's bleak ideology.

"I am a builder of great things." Leonardo da Vinci

The rebels found an unlikely leader in the form of Leonardo da Vinci, who miraculously reappeared in the year 1956. In addition to his flight suit, the inventor had created a temporal bridge, which he had used to traverse the centuries and arrive at this critical juncture for the future of the Brotherhood. For a while there was an uneasy peace between Leonardo and Newton, both leaders seeking to persuade their brothers to the righteousness of their particular cause. During this time of détente, Leonardo freed the Celestial Star Child from inside the sun and sought to use the universal language of mathematics to communicate with the seemingly unfathomable space god.

Sun seeker
Renaissance man Leonardo da Vinci used a flying machine of his own invention to investigate matters within the sun.
S.H.I.E.L.D. #1, Jun. 2010

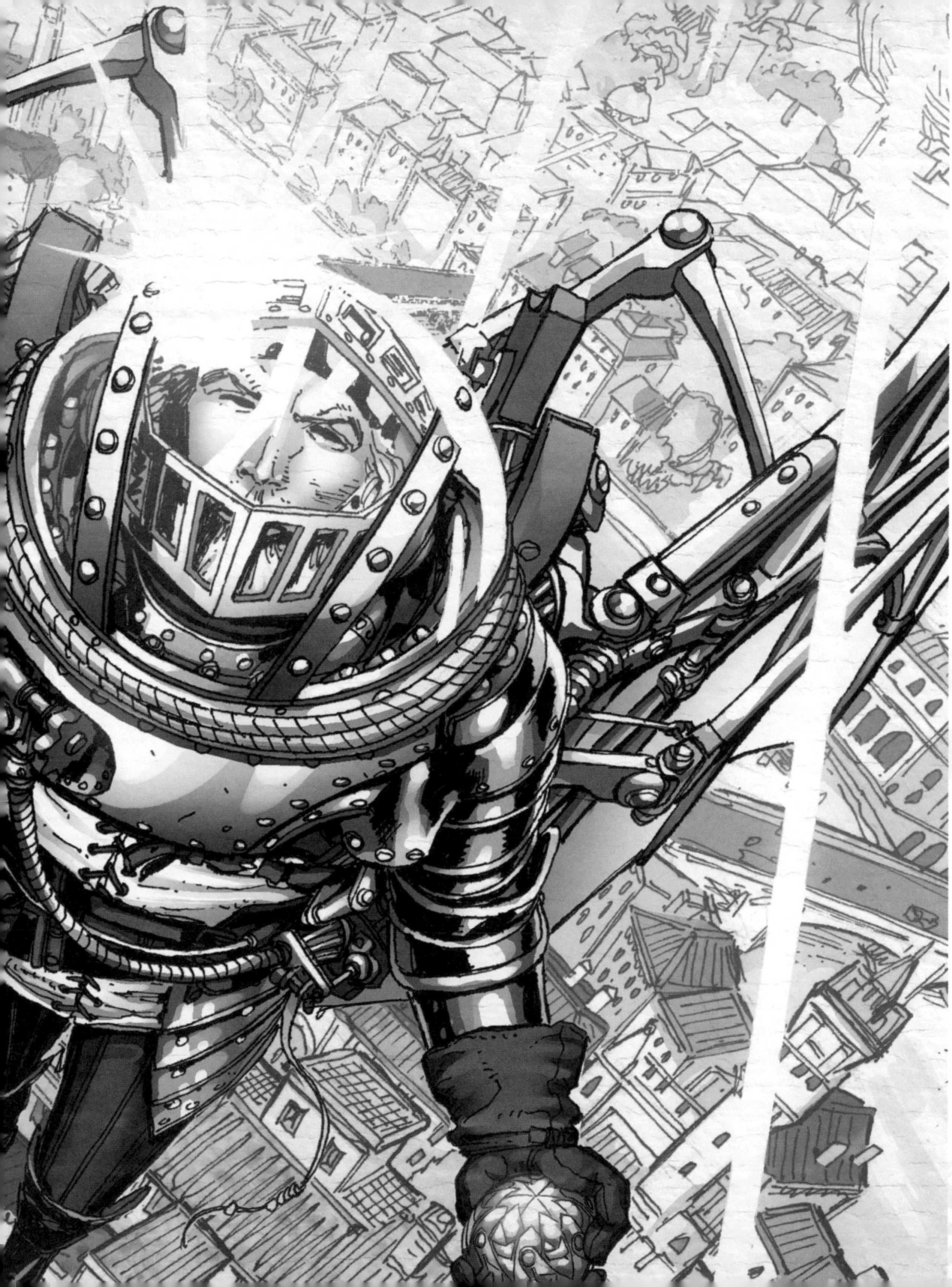

Eventually, and perhaps inevitably, all-out war broke out between the Brotherhood's two competing sects—with armed factions clashing on the streets of Rome. During the ensuing chaos, the Celestial Star Child caught sight of Newton's Quiet Math equations and was driven insane as a result. The now-colossal creature wrought mindless destruction on the city until two recent Brotherhood inductees—Howard Stark and Nathaniel Richards—used an advanced cannon they had devised to stop him in his tracks.

Meanwhile, with his forces in disarray, Newton sought sanctuary at the supposed end of time. Traveling to 2060, he discovered that the future was far from set, and that there were many probable outcomes.

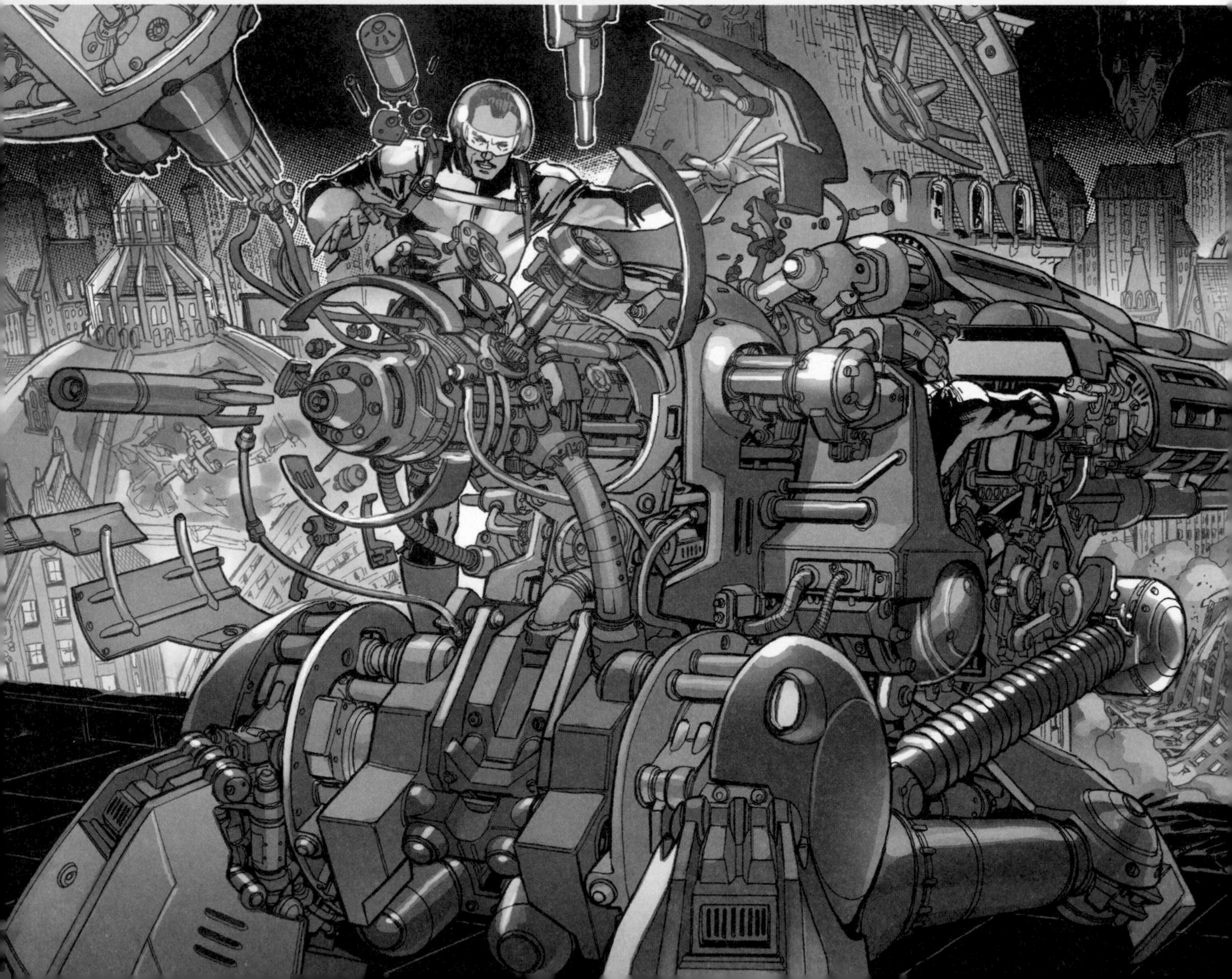

In a quantum universe there was a myriad alternative timelines, each as valid as the next. With Stark, Richards, and other allies at his side, Leonardo followed Newton into the future and successfully trapped him in a post-apocalyptic realm that most resembled the austere world predicted by the Silent Truth.

Once he returned to the 20th century, Howard Stark made a document of events as a permanent record for his young son, Tony—who would one day become the armored adventurer Iron Man. Stark Snr. encouraged his son to believe in a future of endless possibilities, pointing out that the first step toward achieving a better tomorrow was imagining a better tomorrow.

Child care
Howard Stark and Nathaniel Richards engineered a cannon powerful enough to take care of a rampaging Celestial Star Child.
S.H.I.E.L.D. #3, Dec. 2010

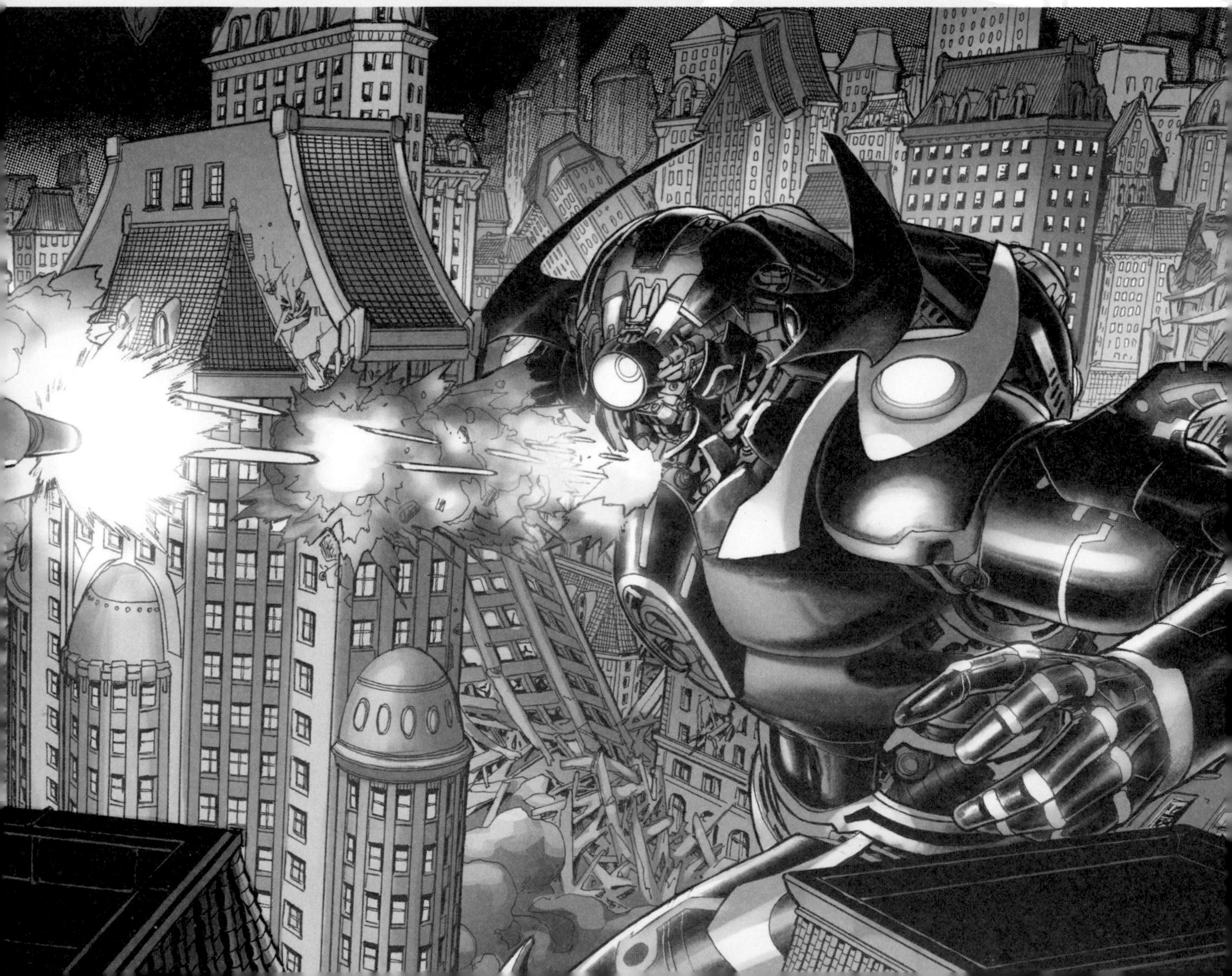

"Everything begins with an idea." Howard Stark

And, true to this doctrine, Howard Stark refashioned the covert Brotherhood of the Shield for the modern era. He helped form an extra-governmental agency with a remit to defend civilization from all existential threats. Several millennia after Imhotep first raised a shield, the warrior's steadfast dream lived on in the form of a new super-spy organization that was originally dubbed Supreme Headquarters, International Espionage, Law-Enforcement Division, or, more succinctly, S.H.I.E.L.D.

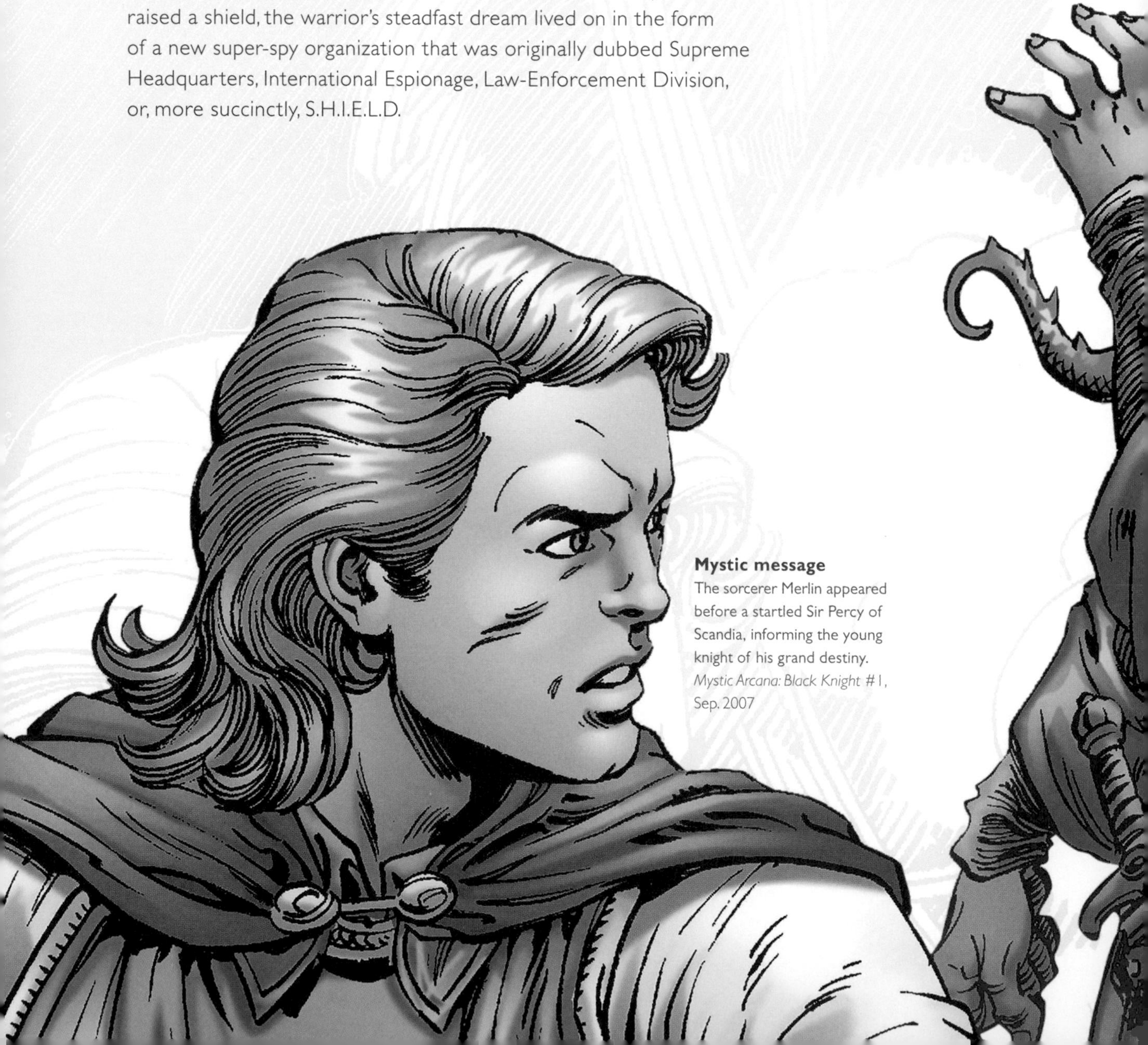

Mystic message
The sorcerer Merlin appeared before a startled Sir Percy of Scandia, informing the young knight of his grand destiny.
Mystic Arcana: Black Knight #1, Sep. 2007

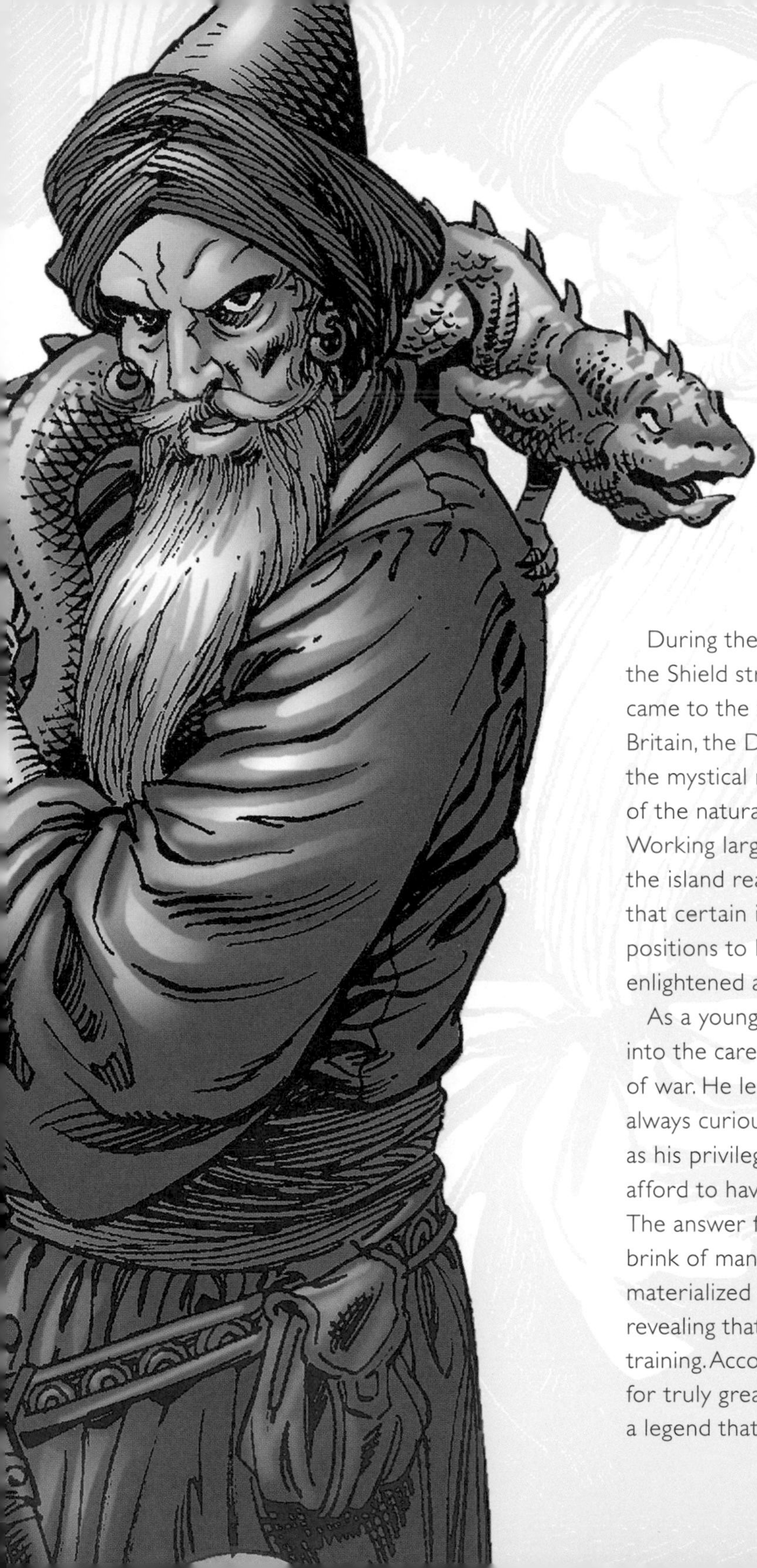

During the Dark Ages, when the Brotherhood of the Shield struggled to reassert itself, other forces came to the fore to keep humanity safe. In ancient Britain, the Druids were a force for good. Linked to the mystical realm of Avalon, they were caretakers of the natural world and custodians of the future. Working largely in secret, the Druids steered the island realm in a positive direction, ensuring that certain individuals found themselves in key positions to lead the country into a more enlightened and prosperous era.

As a young boy, Sir Percy of Scandia was given into the care of the Druids and trained in the arts of war. He learned his lessons well, but Percy was always curious as to why he was studying warfare, as his privileged position meant that he could afford to have others do his fighting for him. The answer finally came when Percy was on the brink of manhood. The otherworldly mage Merlin materialized suddenly before the novice knight, revealing that it was he who had arranged the boy's training. According to Merlin, Sir Percy was destined for truly great things, and he would give rise to a legend that would echo down through the ages.

The next step in fulfilling his heroic future took Percy to fabled Camelot where, under firm instructions from Merlin, he played the fop whenever he attended King Arthur's court. Initially confused by his mentor's orders, Percy understood the plan better when Merlin gifted him a suit of ebony armor with a face-concealing helmet.

As Percy, the Prince of Scandia would act the fool, listening all the while for potential palace intrigue and plots, but as the mysterious Black Knight, he would raise his sword and shield in defense of King Arthur's court. And, thanks to his cunning misdirection, no one ever guessed that the two men were actually one and the same.

When Merlin's divinations revealed that Camelot was fated to fall into ruin at some indeterminate point in the future, he armed the Black Knight with the Ebony Blade, an enchanted sword forged from the metal of a fallen meteor. The mage hoped the sword, which had the capacity to disrupt magical energies, would help the Black Knight delay the inevitable end of King Arthur's reign. Wielding his new blade with gusto, the Black Knight turned back countless threats, frequently foiling the machinations of Arthur's sorceress half-sister, Morgan le Fay.

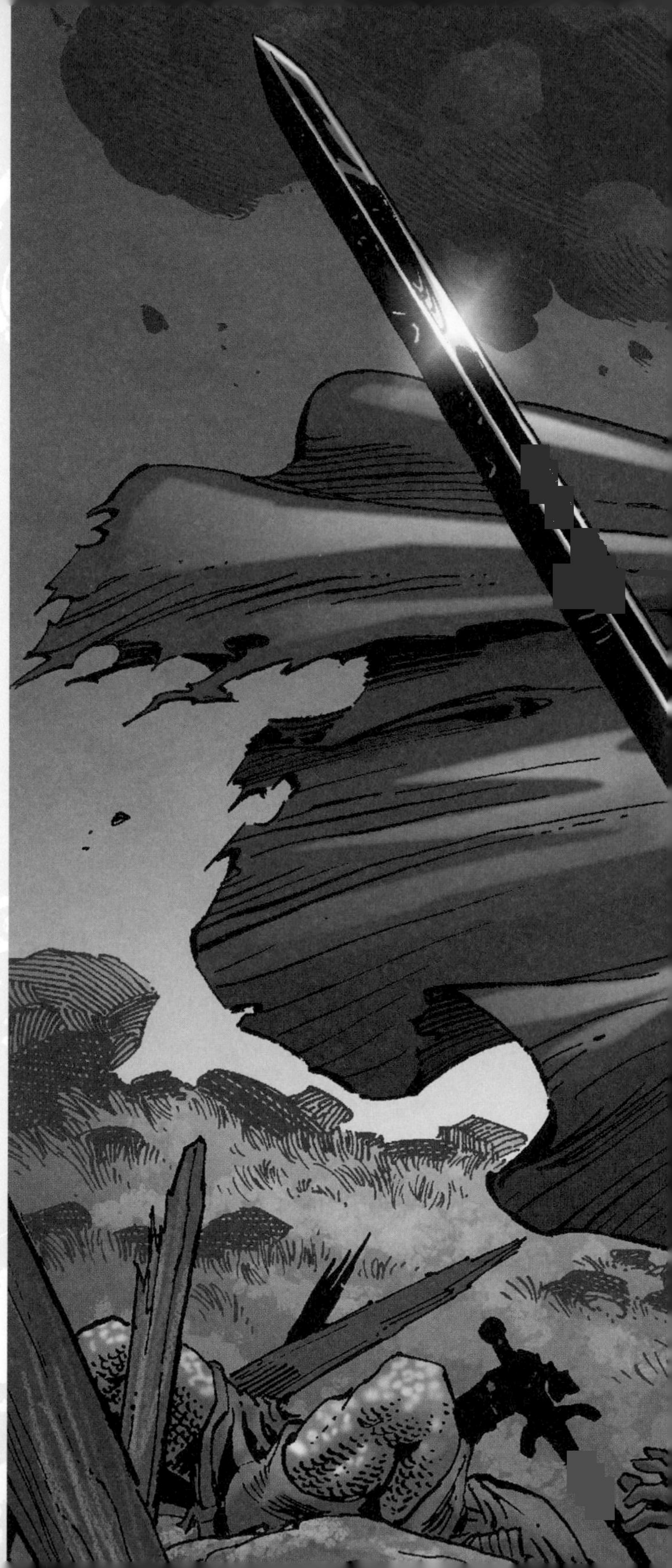

Sword and sorcery
Wielding the enchanted Ebony Blade, the Black Knight fought a tireless battle to defend Camelot from the forces of evil.
Mystic Arcana: Black Knight #1, Sep. 2007

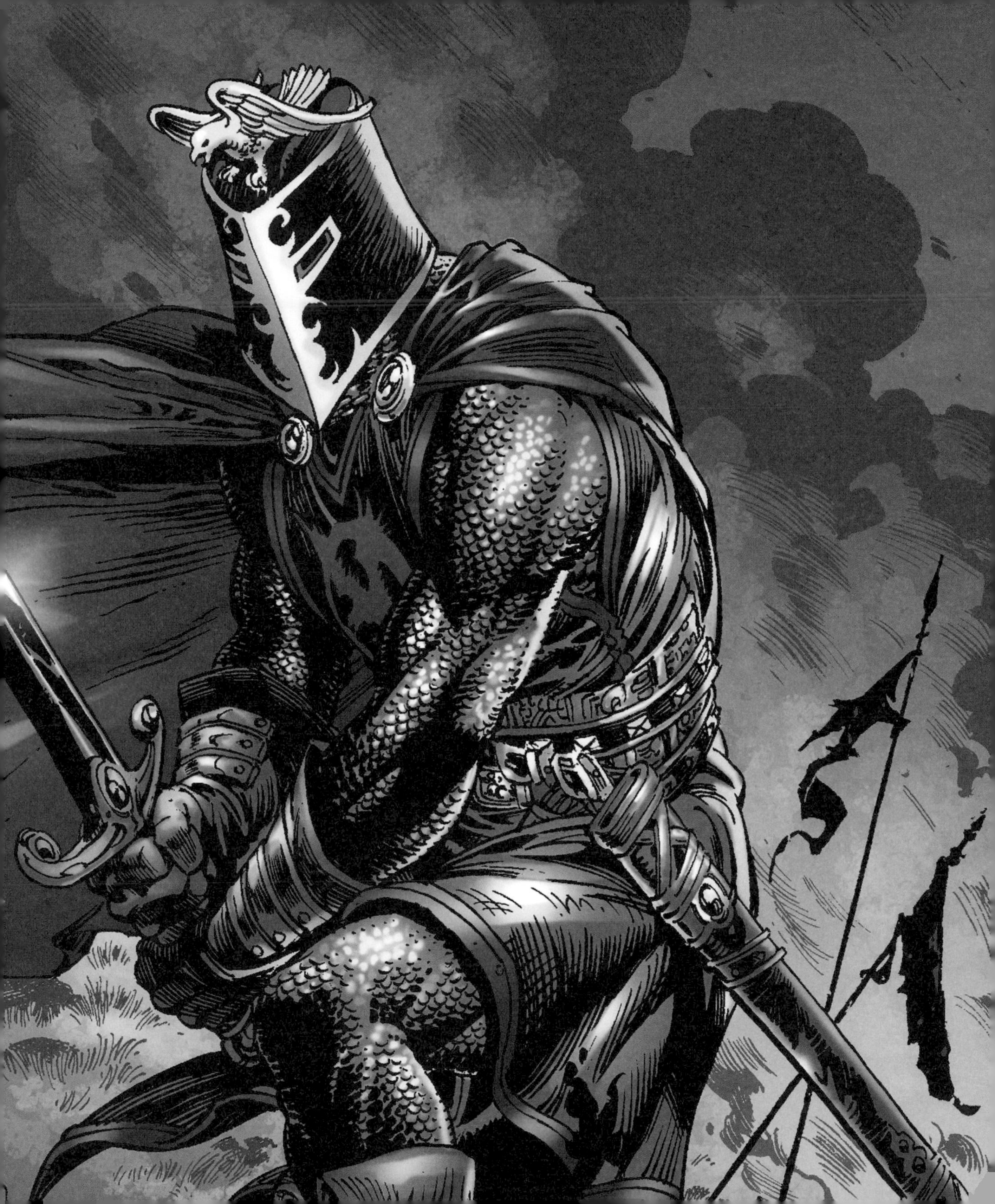

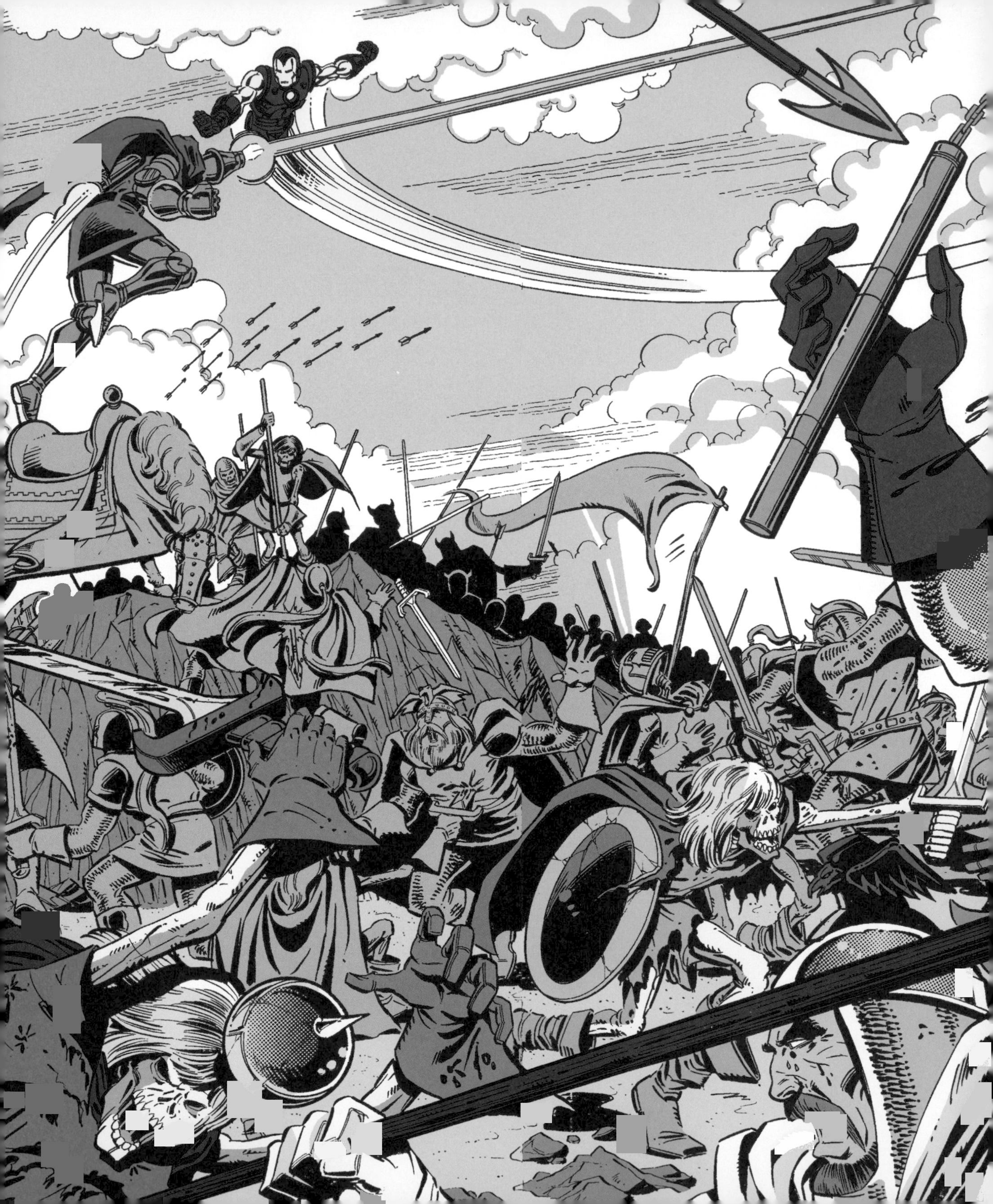

The Black Knight couldn't be everywhere at once, however, and when his heroic responsibilities briefly took him away from the kingdom, Morgan le Fay seized the moment to strike. Although trapped inside her stone keep by Merlin's spells, she still possessed formidable magical resources. Summoning her mystical strength, the sorceress caused Merlin to fall into a deep slumber and raised a terrifying army of the dead to march upon Camelot.

King Arthur rallied his knights, but the situation was bleak. Fortunately, in the Black Knight's absence, another armored hero came to the defense of the realm. A time-displaced Iron Man miraculously appeared to help save the day. The red-and-gold Avenger had been battling Doctor Doom in the 20th century and, during the confrontation, the pair had inadvertently activated the villain's time-travel platform. Arriving in Camelot, Iron Man instinctively sided with King Arthur while Doctor Doom joined forces with Morgan le Fay, hoping she would share her supernatural knowledge as part of their grand alliance.

Ultimately, Morgan le Fay's sorcery proved no match for Iron Man's science. The hero used his advanced repulsor tech to cut through her unliving army— and to tame her savage dragon—and restore order to King Arthur's realm. With the battle won, Iron Man and Doctor Doom agreed to a temporary truce, pooling their scientific knowledge, and the circuits of their respective armors, to build a time machine and return to the modern world.

Medieval warfare
Stranded in medieval times, the villainous Doctor Doom led Morgan le Fay's army of the dead into battle, while heroic Iron Man rallied King Arthur's knights.
Iron Man #150, Sep. 1981

Some time later, the end finally arrived for Camelot. King Arthur was murdered by his treacherous nephew, Mordred, and the fabled citadel itself was set ablaze by the villain's henchmen. The Black Knight watched as Camelot burned, horrified by the day's tragic events. In the end, he was also killed, stabbed in the back by Mordred.

As Sir Percy breathed his last, Merlin arrived to ease his passing. He informed the hero that his service to a higher ideal had not been in vain. He revealed that centuries hence, Sir Percy's descendant, scientist Dane Whitman, would pick up the heroic gauntlet and continue the fight for justice as the new Black Knight.

"It burns... Camelot burns!" Black Knight (Sir Percy)

Thousands of years after the fall of Camelot, Merlin once again empowered a remarkable individual to stand as Britain's primary defender against the forces of darkness and ignorance. Taking the form of a ghostly apparition, with his ethereal daughter, Roma, at his side, Merlin appeared before the startled eyes of a research student named Brian Braddock. The young scientist had been mortally wounded during a terrorist assault on a remote nuclear facility. In a mad scramble, he had escaped into the wild Darkmoor countryside, but he was now lost and on the verge of death. Merlin offered Braddock a final chance at life—all he had to do was choose between the Amulet of Right and the Sword of Might. The correct choice would bring salvation, the wrong choice would bring death. In his delirium, and rejecting all thoughts of senseless warfare, Braddock grasped the amulet and was instantly transformed into Captain Britain.

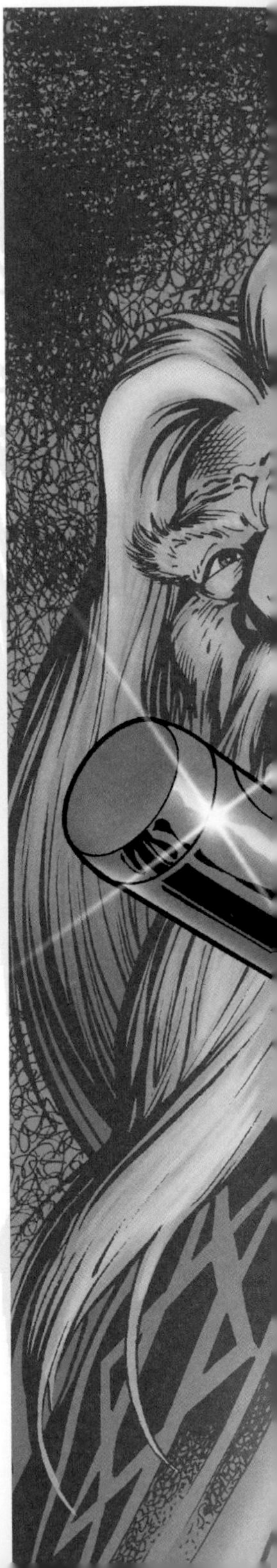

Living legend
Brian Braddock was transformed into Captain Britain: a modern-day hero who embodied King Arthur's chivalrous values.
Captain Britain: Legacy of a Legend, Oct. 2016

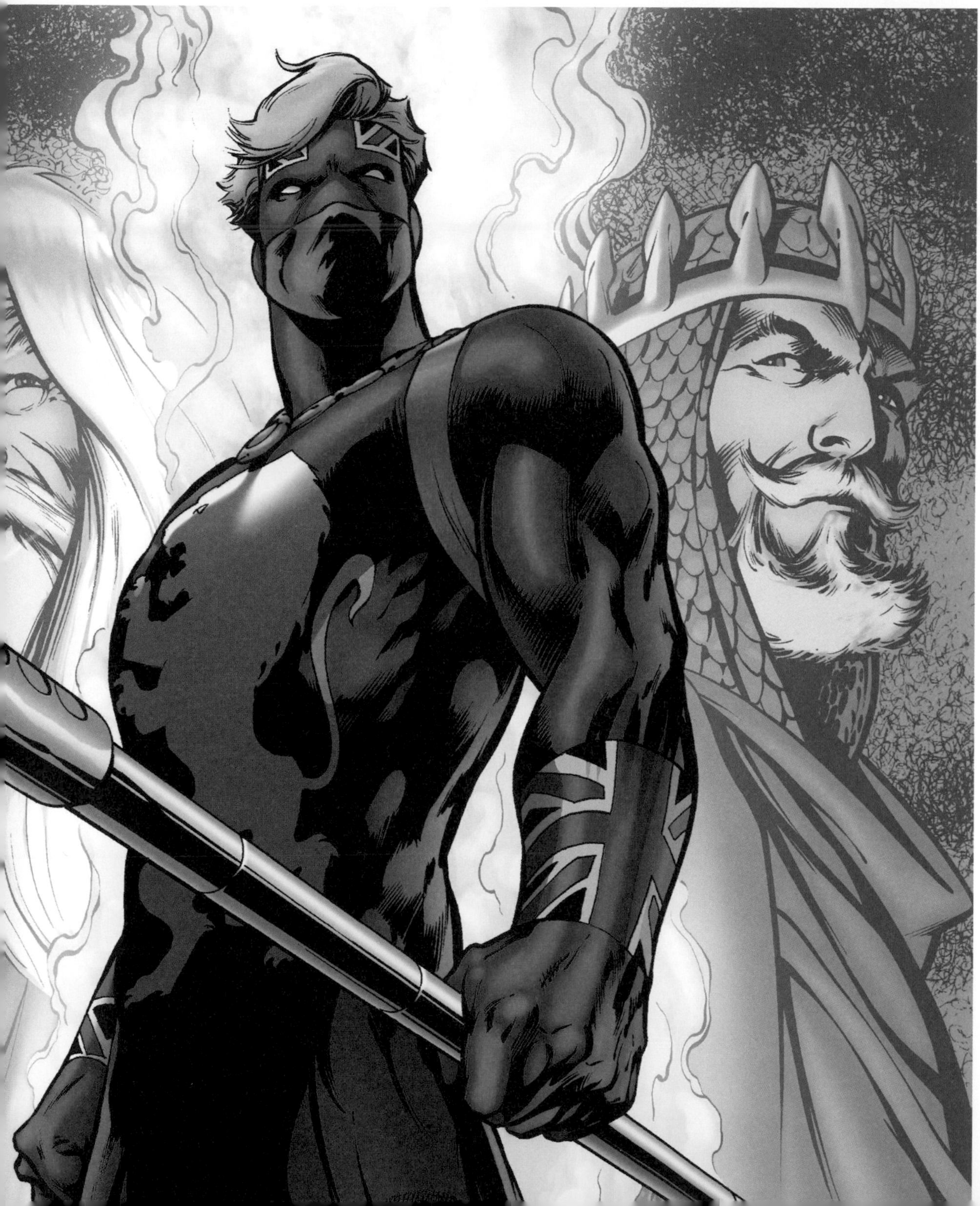

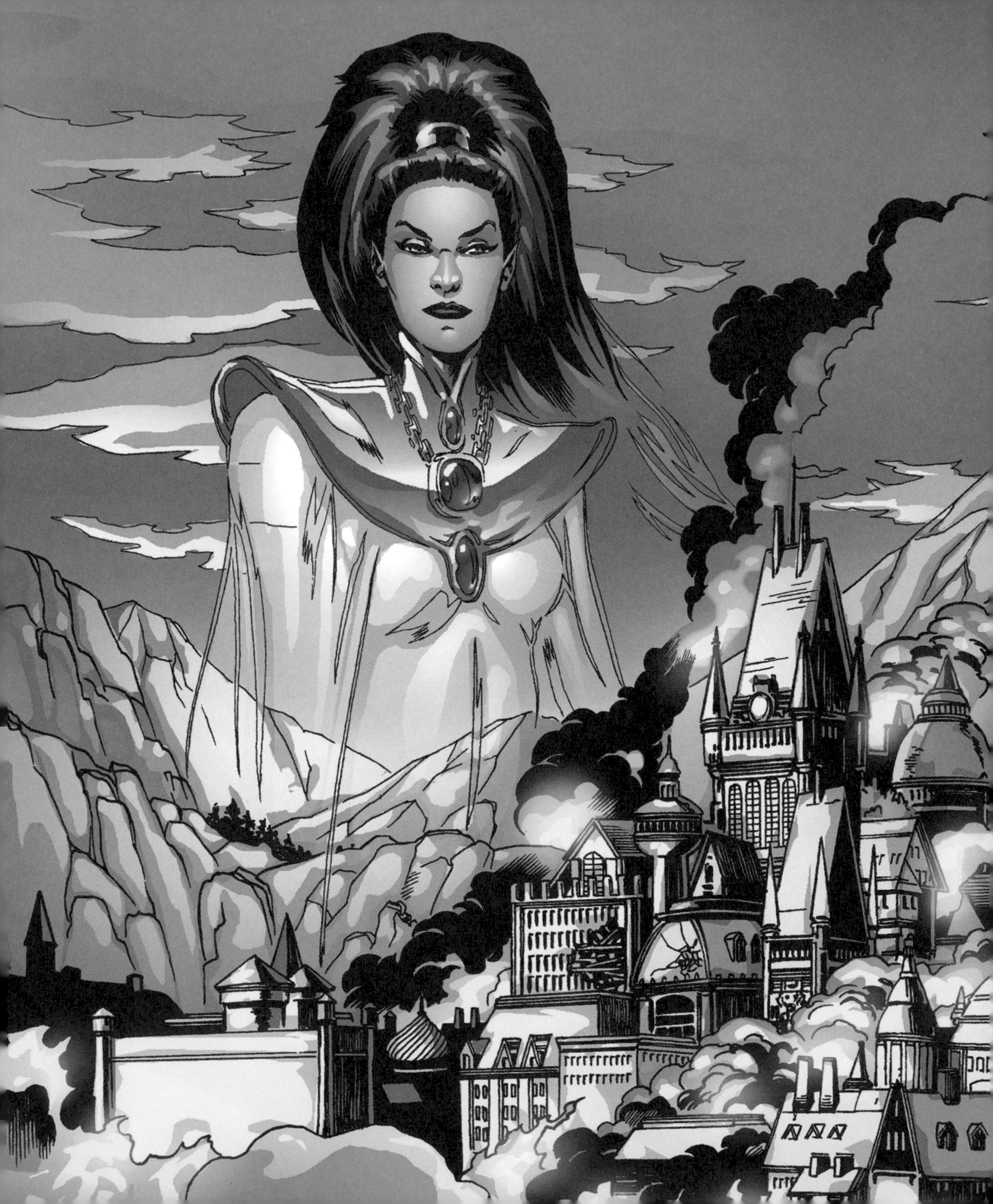

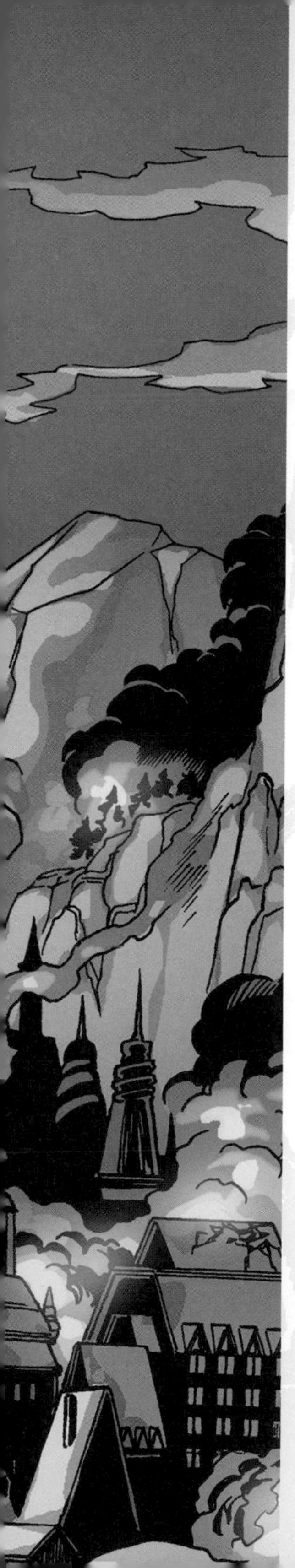

"Choose, Brian Braddock—the amulet or the sword." Merlin

Surging with mystical power, and with a defensive quarterstaff as his primary weapon, the neophyte hero easily repelled the terrorists from the nuclear power plant, going on to have an illustrious career as Britain's premier Super Hero. Over time, Captain Britain learned more about his magical benefactors and their origins. Merlin and Roma were cosmic guardians, immortal custodians of Otherworld, an extra-dimensional realm that included the Isle of Avalon and was sustained by the hopes and dreams of the British people. What's more, Otherworld existed at a vital nexus point where science and sorcery were indistinguishable from one other. Consequently, the realm sometimes resembled a fairy-tale kingdom—replete with elves, sprites, and other mythical creatures—while on other occasions, it took on the aspect of a sterile, high-tech world.

Merlin, or Merlyn as he sometimes preferred, proved to be just as mercurial as his realm. In his role as Omniversal Guardian, he had established the Captain Britain Corps, ensuring that there was a different Captain Britain stationed on the variety of different Earths throughout the Multiverse. Ostensibly, the Corps was created as a force for good, the embodiment of universal values, but Merlin frequently deployed it in service to his own agenda. Merlin believed he knew what was best for the cosmos and would brook no dissent. This attitude frequently led to disagreements with Brian Braddock about the nature of free will and the desirability of personal agency. Roma, in contrast to her father, was far more benign and, whenever Merlin was away plotting his intricate schemes, she would rule over Otherworld with an even hand.

It was sheer madness to think that Roma would ever turn against the interests of Otherworld, but it indeed became a bleak reality during one of her father's frequent absences. Seemingly gripped by a violent derangement, she murdered several members of the Captain Britain Corps and unleashed a wave of relentless cyborg warriors upon Otherworld.

Devilish daughter
Usually a benign and just ruler, Merlin's daughter, Roma, suddenly turned on the people of Otherworld, fomenting war and burning cities.
Excalibur #1, Feb. 2001

As Roma's army lay waste to the land, it spread a techno-organic virus that turned others into cyborgs and transformed Otherworld's gleaming minarets and majestic castles into mechanized factories, belching out pollution. After surviving an assassination attempt by Roma's henchmen, Brian Braddock led the fightback against the emergent tyrant. Along with his twin sister Betsy, who possessed mutant psi-powers, and a small band of surviving Corps members, he journeyed from Earth to Otherworld. There, he was reunited with the Sword of Might, which was finally revealed to be King Arthur's legendary weapon, Excalibur.

Once again rejecting thoughts of needless conflict, Braddock wielded Excalibur to heal, not harm. Utilizing the sword's magical properties and his own strength of will he purged the techno-organic virus, restoring Otherworld's inhabitants to their natural forms. He was also able to see through a hologram that enveloped Roma, revealing the true villain to be an old foe, the computerized entity known as Mastermind. After freeing Roma from the malevolent Mastermind's possession, Captain Britain directly faced the rogue AI. Unfortunately, Mastermind overpowered his rival with ease and was exultant at the prospect of victory. However, when he grasped Excalibur's hilt, the sword's magical energy disrupted his circuitry and closed down his systems for good. Sorcery had, on this occasion, proved more potent than science.

Once order was fully restored to Otherworld, Brian Braddock returned to Earth and resumed his career as a costumed adventurer. Peace was not to last, however, and civil war once again consumed Otherworld. Morgan le Fay conscripted Brian Braddock into the internecine conflict, forcibly making him her armored champion. In response, he bequeathed the Amulet of Right to his sister, and Betsy Braddock became the new Captain Britain, a hero with a truly legendary pedigree.

Family business
Mutant hero Betsy Braddock inherited the Amulet of Right to become the latest Captain Britain.
Excalibur #1, Dec. 2019

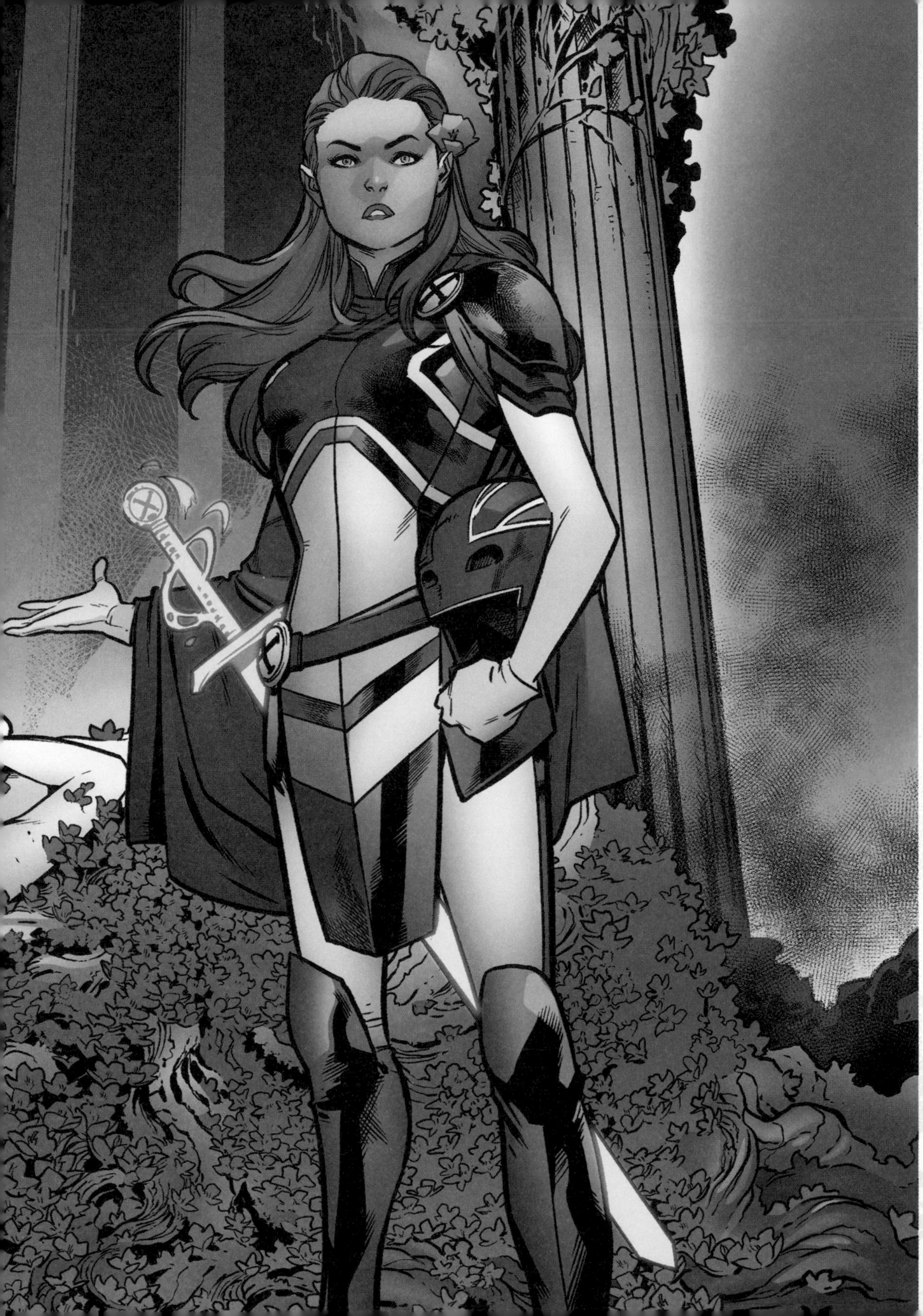

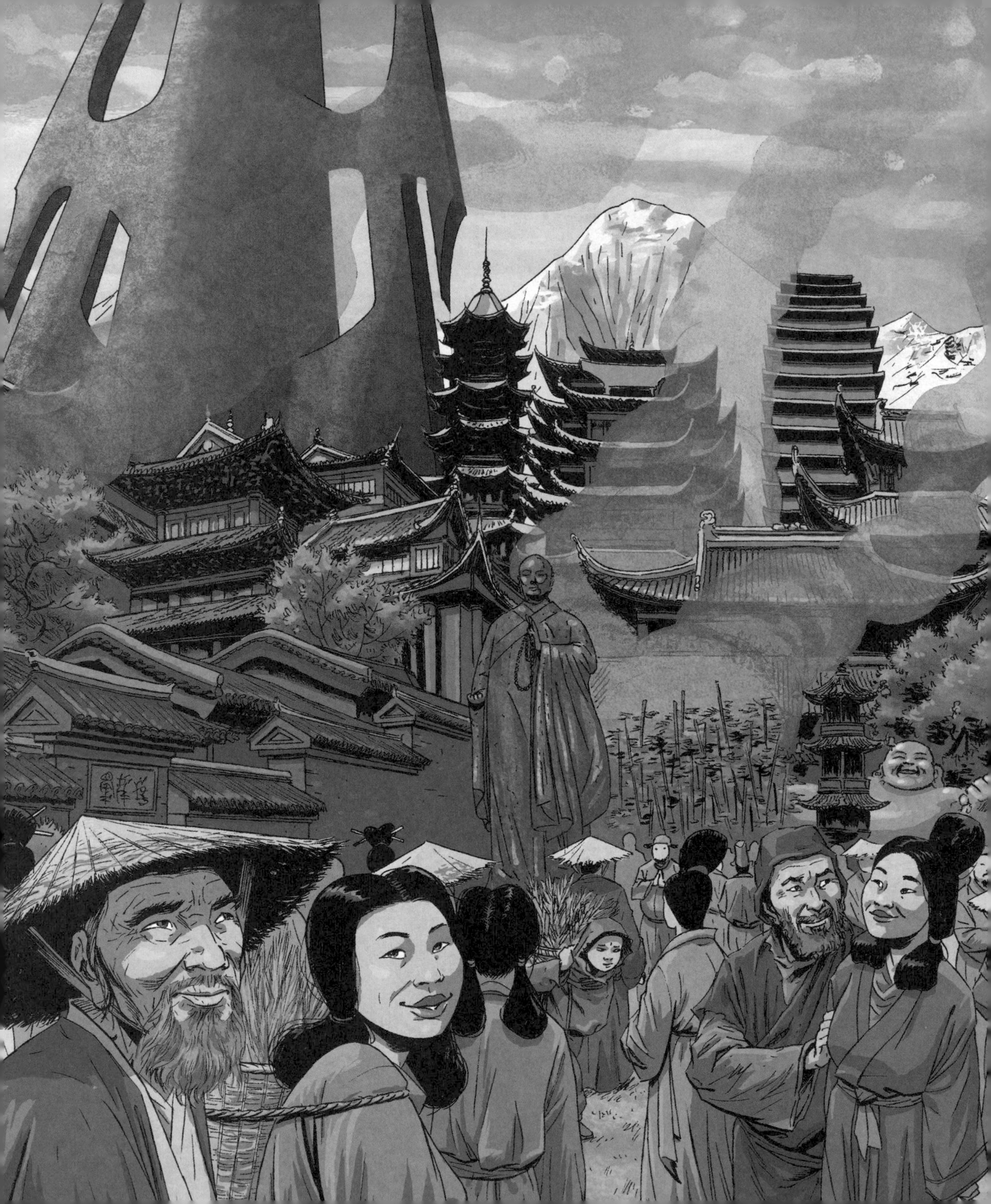

The Immortal Iron Fists

Mythical K'un-Lun was seemingly cut off from the Earthly plane. However, despite the city's supposed splendid isolation, many of its sons and daughters had a direct influence on the wider world.

Located in a pocket dimension adjacent to the mortal realm, K'un-Lun was one of the Seven Capital Cities of Heaven. Home to a race of hardy immortals, K'un-Lun only appeared on Earth once every decade, with access to the city being gained through a mystical portal that materialized in the Himalayan mountains. Since prehistoric times, K'un-Lun had selected the most skillful martial artist of the day to serve as the city's protector and champion—the Immortal Iron Fist.

To achieve this venerated rank, potential candidates had to defeat the magical dragon Shou-Lao the Undying in combat. By absorbing the creature's life force—its chi—each successful fighter would gain an ability to channel the dragon's strength and deliver blows of unimaginable force. Often, an Iron Fist's hands were said to become "like unto a thing of iron." Each Iron Fist served for decades, defending K'un-Lun from outside interference and attacks. They were also expected to fight in the Tournament of the Heavenly Cities, a ceremonial contest that occurred once every 88 years when the stars aligned and the seven divine realms merged into one.

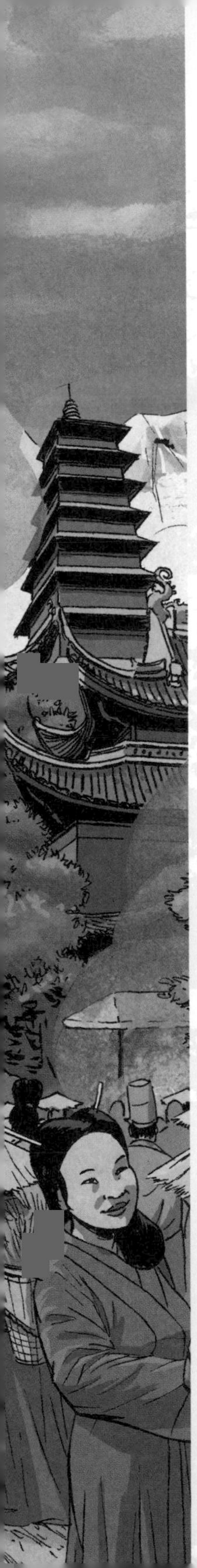

Mountain retreat
Appearing in the Himalayas once every ten years, the mystical city of K'un-Lun was home to a race of divine immortals.
The Immortal Iron Fist #24, May 2009

While some women served as the Iron Fist, it was a rare occurrence, and it was even more unusual for a commoner to be granted the honor. K'un-Lun's ruling elites were reluctant to give up their privilege, ensuring that only those they saw fit had access to the power of the Iron Fist. All that changed around 1545 CE, when Wu Ao-Shi, a young woman who had been raised in an orphanage, bested Shou-Lao and won the title. Her time as Iron Fist was short, however, as she found herself torn between her duties to K'un-Lun and her loyalty to her lover, a young fisherman who had provided for her before she absorbed the power of Shou-Lao. A humble individual, the fisherman was disturbed by Wu Ao-Shi's new life of violence and conflict. Packing up his meager belongings, he fled K'un-Lun to find a new life of his own on Earth, one that was free from potential strife. While the portal was still open, Wu Ao-Shi followed, wanting to prove to her lover that he meant more to her than the title of Iron Fist.

"I come to take that which only I may own!" Iron Fist Wu Ao-Shi

Unfortunately, when she emerged into the world, she was unable to locate any trace of the fisherman. Finding herself in unfamiliar surroundings, and with no other viable means of support, she became a mercenary, selling her formidable fighting skills to the highest bidder. Her new career took her to Pinghai Bay on a mission to liberate a fishing village from tyrannical pirates. Her first attempt at overthrowing the Pirate King ended in failure and capture, however, and she was paraded in disgrace through the streets of the village. As fate would have it, the fisherman was witness to his beloved's humiliation. He poisoned Wu Ao-Shi's guards and set her free to exact her terrible revenge. Using her chi to infuse her arrows with mystical fire, Wu Ao-Shi burned the pirate fleet to ash. Finally reunited, the Immortal Iron Fist and her lowly fisherman spent the rest of their days together in wedded bliss, with Wu Ao-Shi becoming famous the world over as the Pirate Queen of Pinghai Bay.

Centuries after Wu Ao-Shi escaped K'un-Lun to forge a new destiny for herself, another Iron Fist followed in her stead. Orson Randall was born shortly after his parents' experimental airship crashed in K'un-Lun during the city's manifestation in the latter years of the 19th century. The boy was adopted as a member of the city and he trained in the martial arts, going on to serve as Iron Fist.

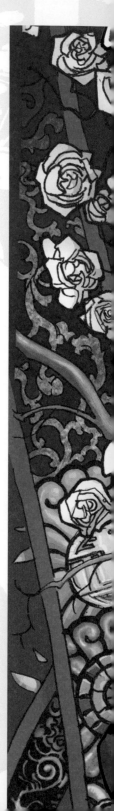

Female empowerment
Wu Ao-Shi rose from humble beginnings to claim the power of the Iron Fist as her own.
The Immortal Iron Fist #7, Aug. 2007

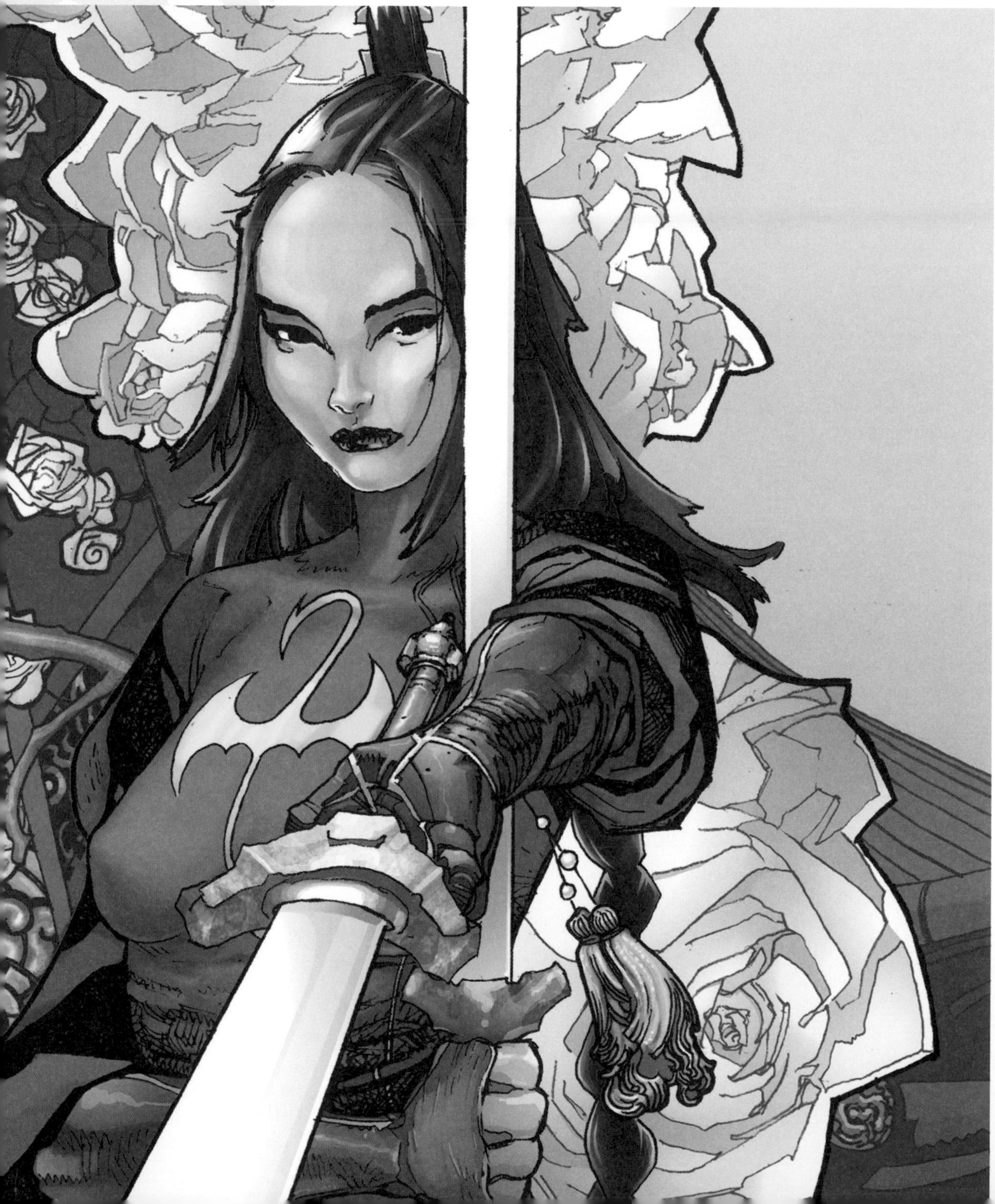

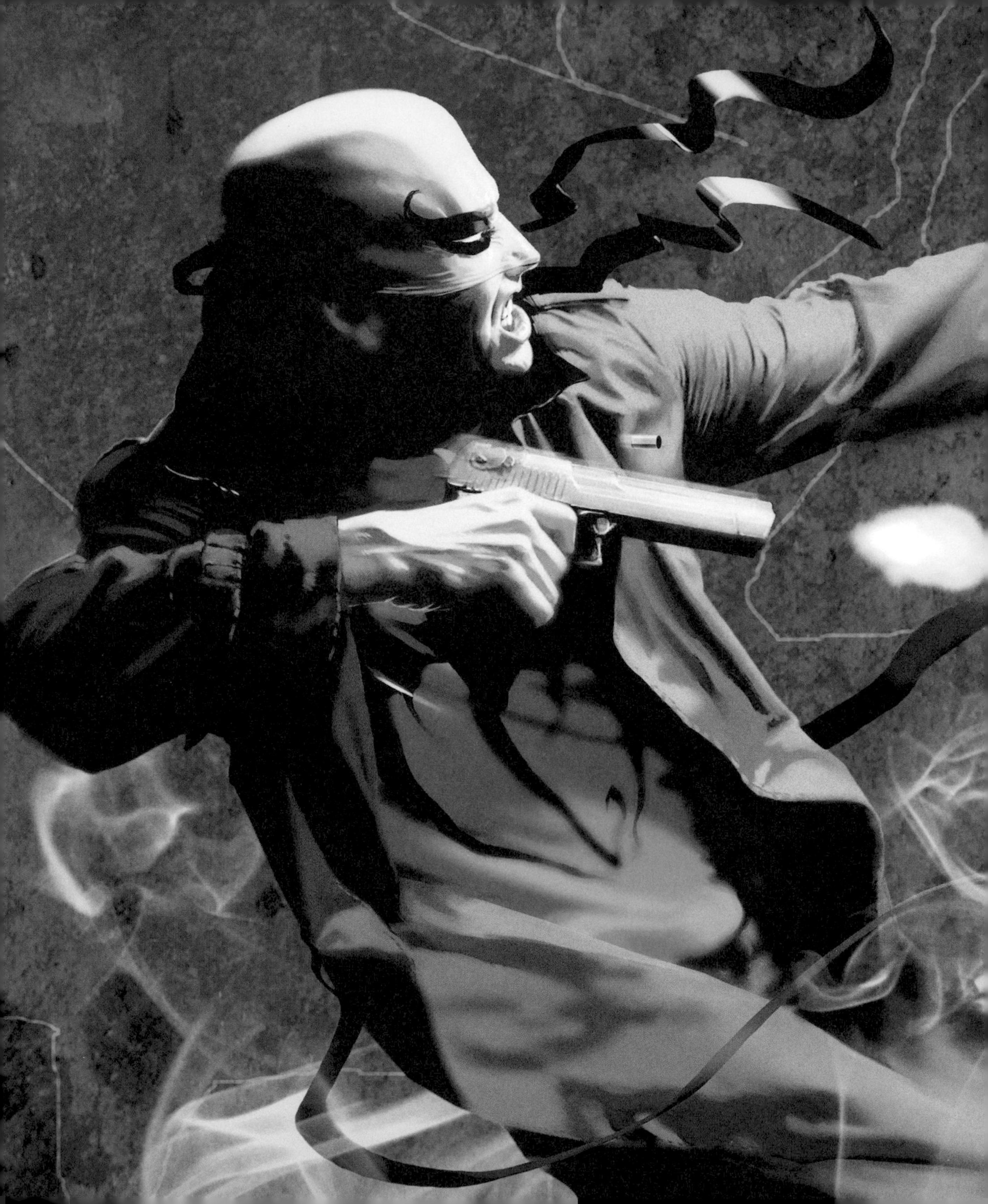

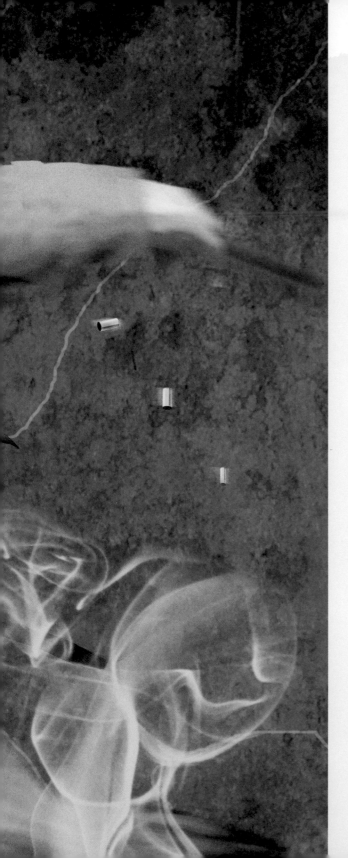

When World War I broke out, Orson left his mystical home to fight for the allies alongside other adventurers like Union Jack and the Phantom Eagle. At war's end, Orson was recalled to K'un-Lun. The wholesale slaughter he had witnessed in Europe had changed him, however, and he was sickened by the very thought of violence. He refused to participate in the Tournament of the Heavenly Cities and an attempt to escape his duty inadvertently led to the death of a rival participant in the contest. Hunted by the forces of the heavenly realms, Orson returned to Earth—an Iron Fist forever haunted by his strife-torn past.

"Some very powerful people want me very dead." Iron Fist Orson Randall

During a period of aimless wandering, Orson adopted an orphan whom he named Wendell Rand. Finding fresh purpose, Orson taught young Wendell everything he knew about the martial arts, the duo going on to have many adventures together as members of a crime-busting team known as the Confederates of the Curious. Wendell was fascinated by his guardian's tales of exotic K'un-Lun and he longed to visit the city. Orson cautioned against such a trip, however, reminding his young charge that he was still stalked by the rulers of the mystic realm.

Crime buster
In the early days of the 20th century, Iron Fist Orson Randall escaped K'un-Lun to fight crime and combat mystical threats in the wider world.
The Immortal Iron Fist: Orson Randall and the Green Mist of Death #1, Apr. 2008

Following one particularly bitter argument, Wendell ran away. After deducing the next time K'un-Lun would appear on Earth, Wendell journeyed to the Himalayas and entered the city. Keeping his close association with Orson a secret, Wendell announced his intention to become the next Iron Fist. He trained alongside other adepts and impressed his tutors with his fighting prowess. However, when the time came for him to confront Shou-Lao the Undying, he panicked and fled the city in disgrace.

Years later, Wendell attempted to return to K'un-Lun with his wife, Heather, and their nine-year-old son Danny. The trip proved disastrous, and both Wendell and Heather died as they searched fruitlessly for the city in the snowbound mountains. Young Danny survived, though, and was taken in by the people of K'un-Lun. He followed in Wendell's footsteps and trained ferociously to meet the challenge of Shou-Lao. Unlike his father, he was triumphant, taking the dragon's chi to become the latest outworlder to serve as K'un-Lun's Immortal Iron Fist.

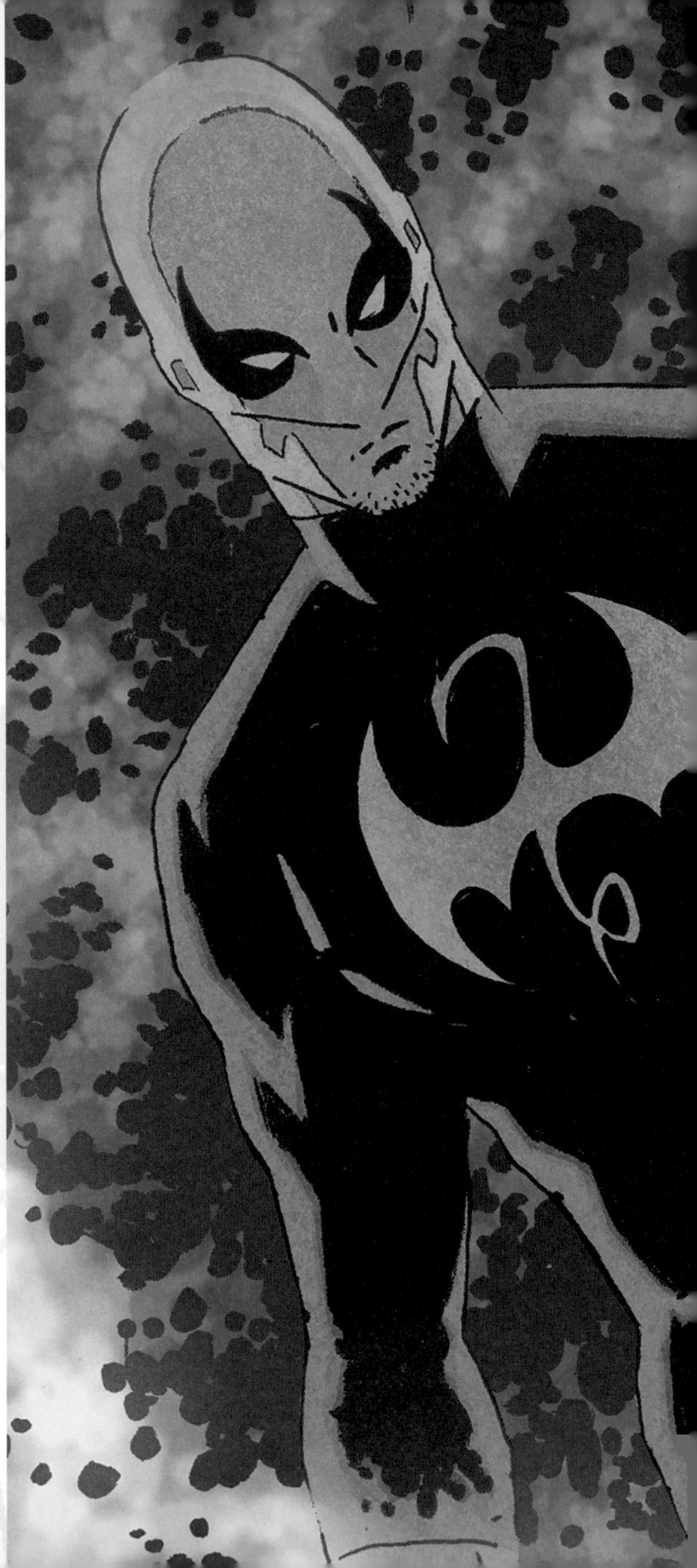

Living weapon
In modern times, Danny Rand inherited the mantle of Iron Fist, channeling the power of an immortal dragon to become one of the world's greatest martial artists.
The Immortal Iron Fist #6, Jul. 2007

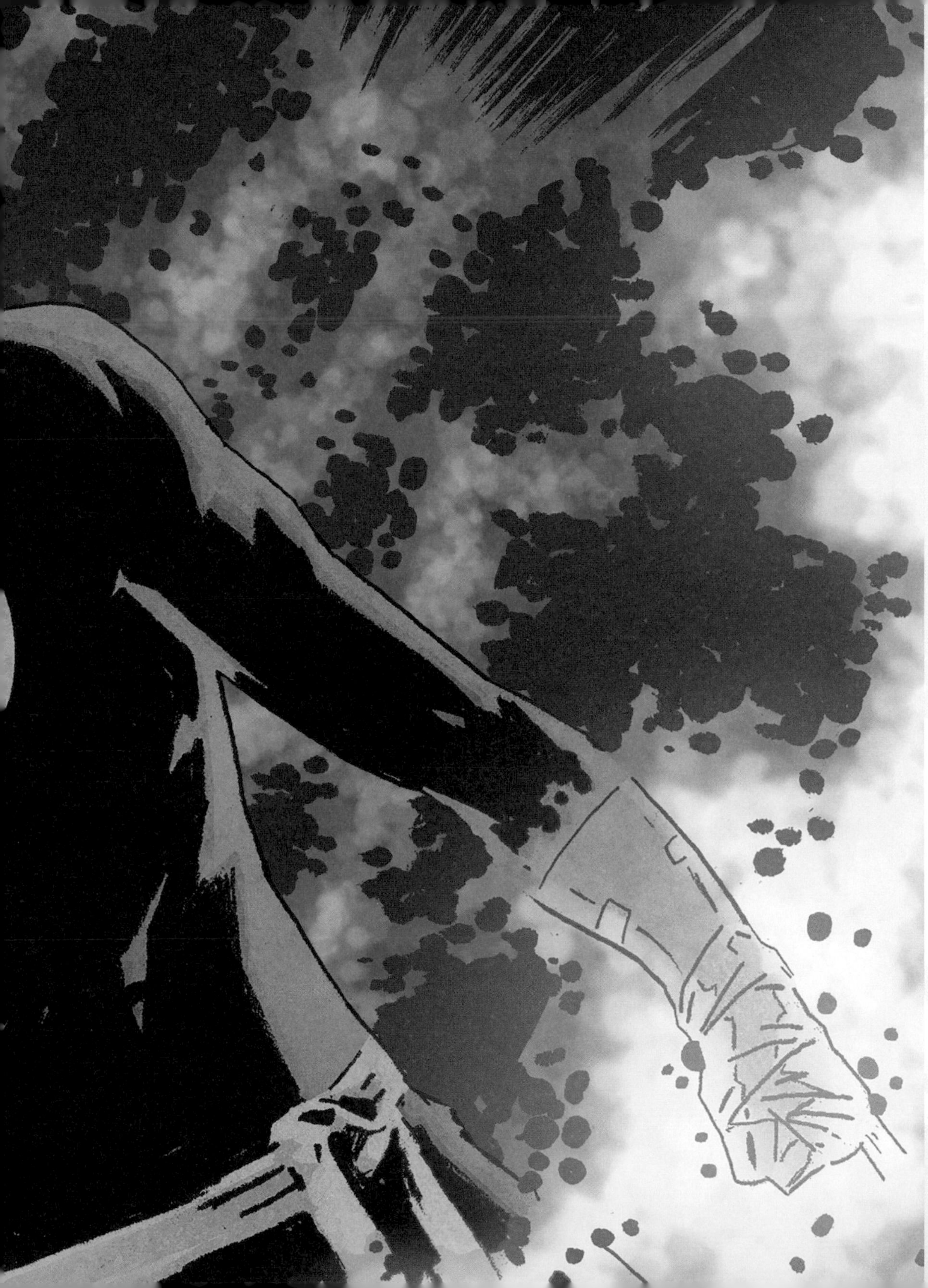

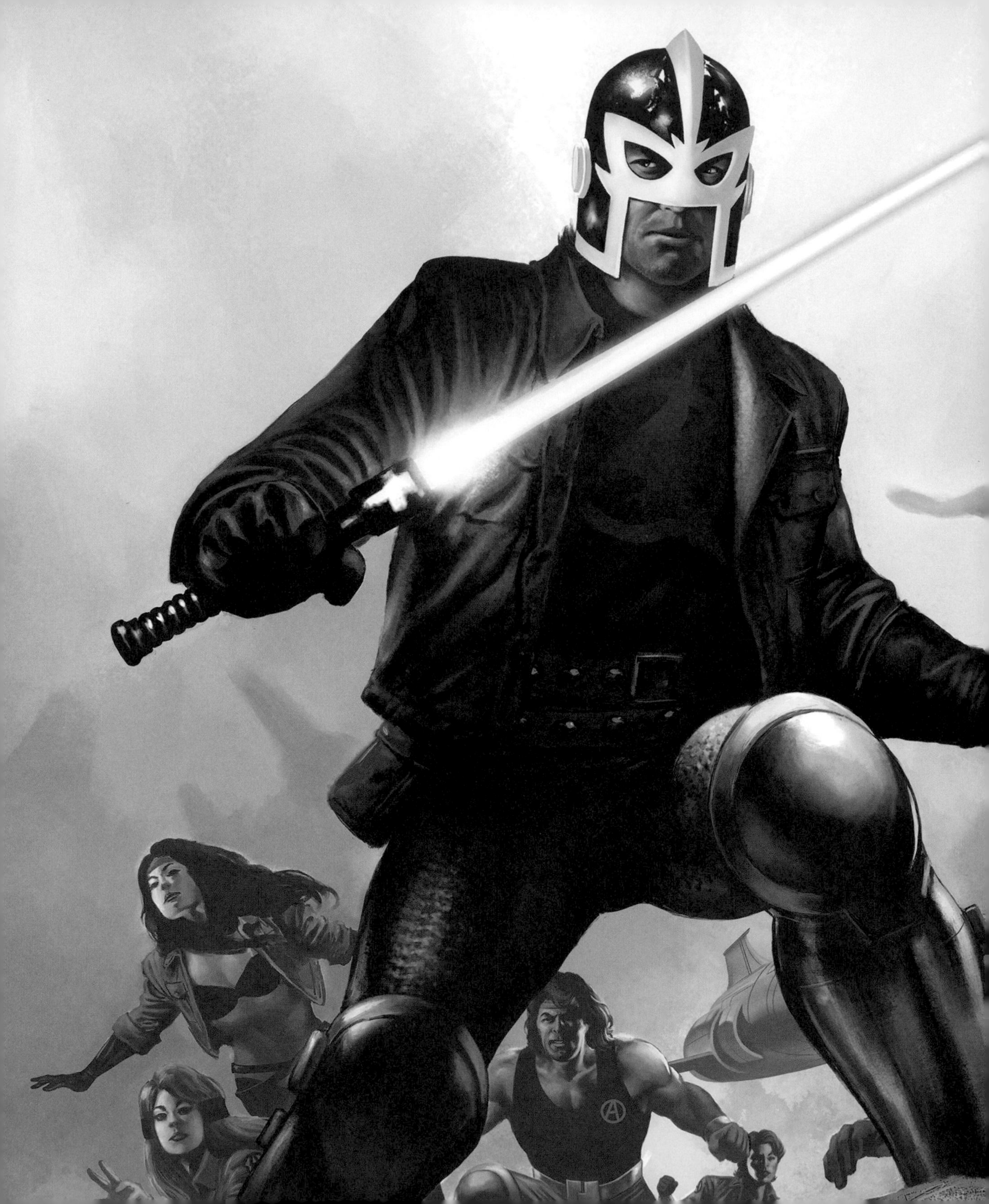

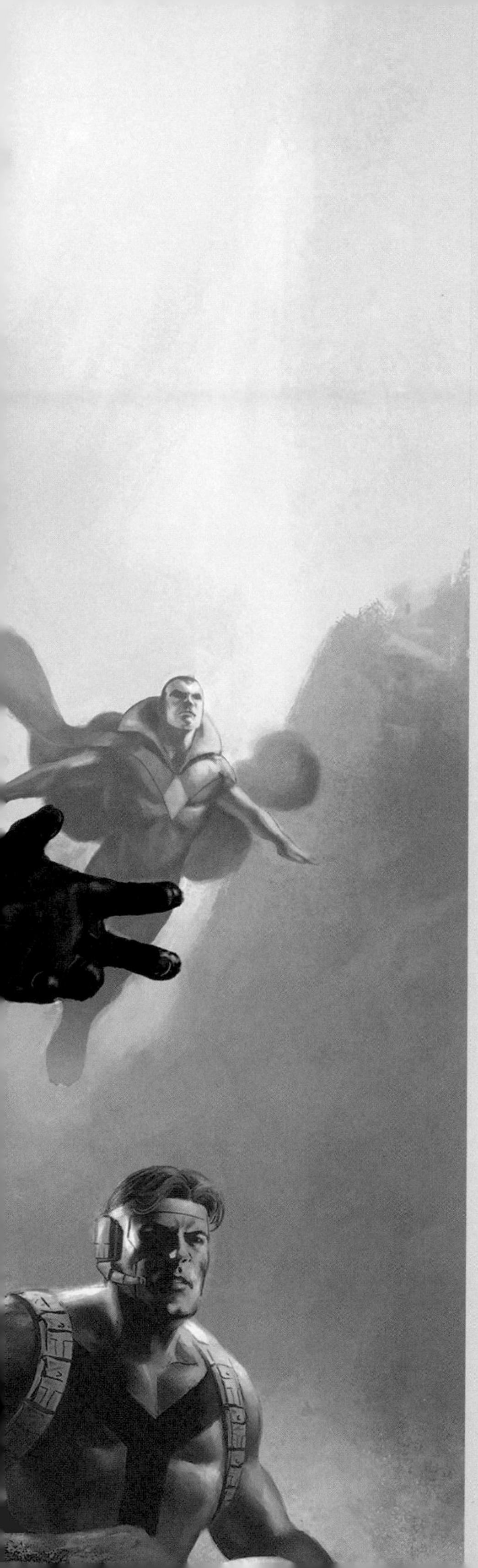

ETERNAL HEROES

Tendrils of the mythic past reached down through the ages to influence the modern era of Super Heroes. Immortals like the Eternal Sersi were recruited into the Avengers to fight alongside true demigods like Thor and Hercules. Dane Whitman, the latest incarnation of the legendary Black Knight, inherited his ancestor's magical sword and fought to uphold the values of the heraldic tradition. Meanwhile, Doctor Stephen Strange followed in the wake of Agamotto to become the latest—perhaps the greatest—Sorcerer Supreme.

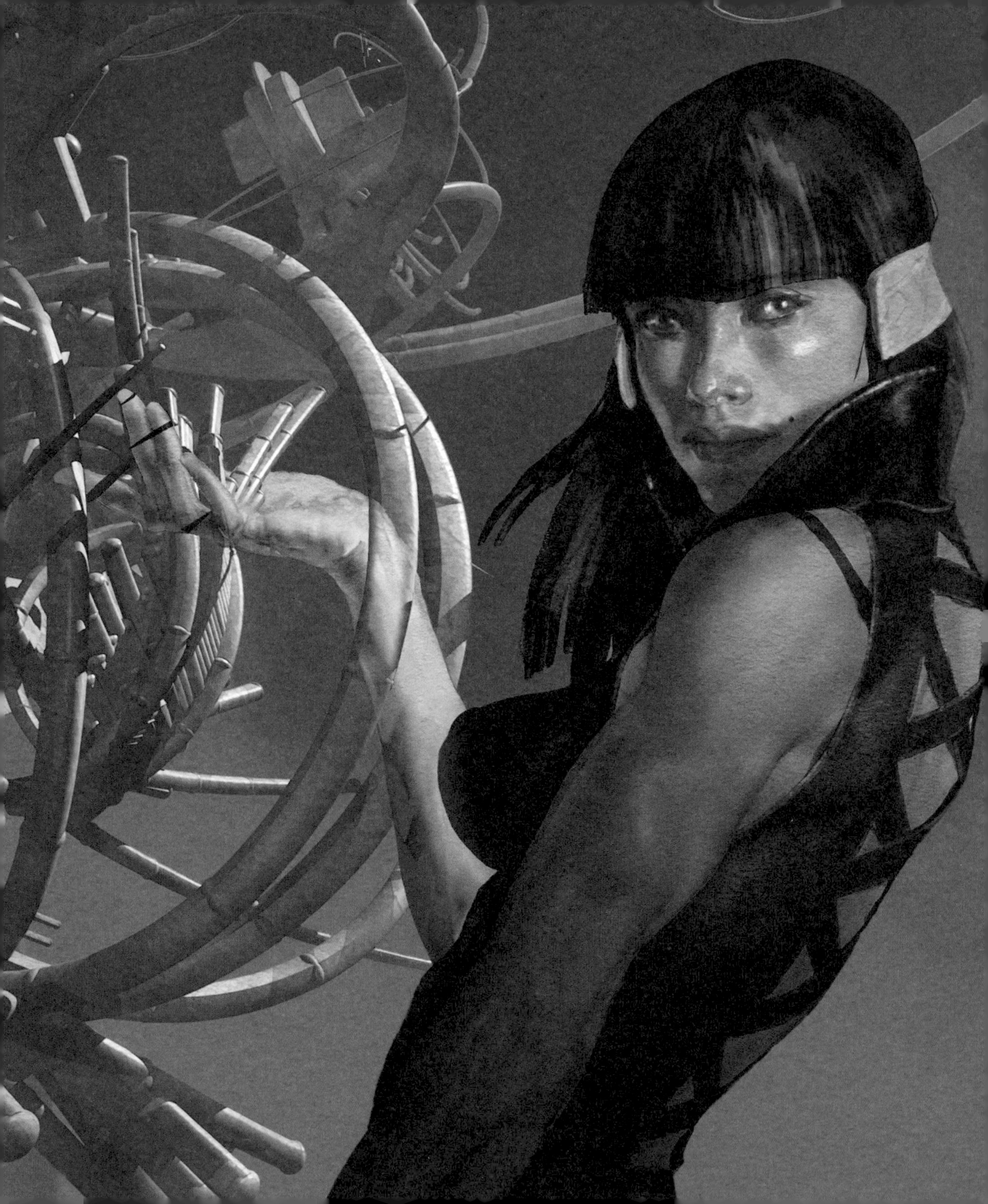

Love and Loss

During their shared time as Avengers, Sersi and the Black Knight became embroiled in a complex web of intrigue that threatened to shatter their sanity and tear the team apart.

Following the Deviant attack on New York City and the eventual departure of the Celestial Fourth Host, the Eternal Sersi resumed her customary life of leisure. Her role as an events organizer and party planner brought her into contact with some off-duty Avengers, including Captain America, with whom she flirted outrageously. The no-nonsense hero was resistant to Sersi's charms, however, and somewhat disdainful of her hedonistic ways. Stung by the hero's gentle rebuke, and wanting to prove herself the equal of any human hero, Sersi uncharacteristically accepted an offer to join the Avengers. Her ability to manipulate matter proved invaluable to the team and she helped defeat numerous villains, swiftly earning the respect and admiration of her new colleagues.

While acknowledging the serious nature of her new role, Sersi continued to greet the world in an open and engaging manner. She brought a relaxed informality to the Avengers and was instrumental in eliminating some the group's unnecessary rules and excessive bureaucracy. In time, the Eternal found herself romantically attracted to her teammate, the scientist-adventurer Dane Whitman. The latest incarnation of the Black Knight, Whitman was a longtime associate of the Avengers who had recently returned to the team in order to give meaning and structure to his often-chaotic life.

Psi siren
Following a life of leisure, the Eternal Sersi found a fresh outlet for her potent psionic abilities as a member of the heroic Avengers.
Eternals #2, Sep. 2006

An American by birth, Whitman was a descendant of Sir Percy of Scandia, but it was only later in life that he learned of his familial connection to the legendary hero of Camelot. Ironically, Whitman's formative years were characterized by a rejection of all superstition and an abiding belief in the power of science to solve humanity's problems. As a student, he earned advanced degrees in physics and other disciplines before going on to become a world-class engineer and geneticist. Only when he inherited the family's ancestral castle in England did his absolute faith in the rational world begin to falter.

While exploring the ancient fort's labyrinth of dungeons, the American became lost and hopelessly disoriented. Before his startled eyes, a wraith-like figure materialized, the apparition seeming to be a knight from medieval times. Struggling to comprehend what was happening, Whitman stuttered, "Who… are you? What do you want of me?" In answer, the spirit replied that it was the ghost of Sir Percy of Scandia and that it had been instructed by the wizard Merlin to anoint Whitman as the new Black Knight. Whitman was skeptical at first, holding on to the possibility that he was in the grip of a particularly vivid hallucination, but his doubts faded when he finally held the Ebony Blade. Having been ordered by his spectral ancestor to retrieve the sword from a crypt, Whitman could feel the weapon pulsing with arcane power and, in that critical moment, his life changed forever. The certainties of the past, built as they were upon a bedrock of scientific belief, crumbled away. Whitman's world view had been blown wide open and he now embraced a fresh destiny, one filled with supernatural wonders and the promise of endless adventure.

Back in the United States, Whitman created an arsenal of technologically advanced weapons to aid him in his forthcoming crusade against the forces of darkness. He even employed the very latest in genetic engineering techniques to create a wondrous winged horse he named Aragorn.

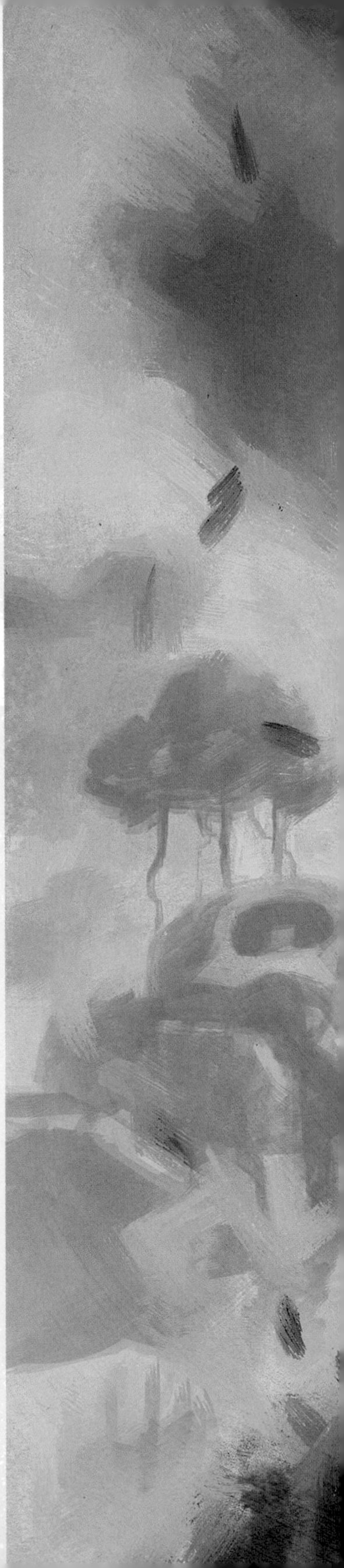

Heroic legacy
Scientist Dane Whitman embraced the supernatural power of the Ebony Blade to become a modern-day heraldic hero.
Black Knight #1, Jan. 2016

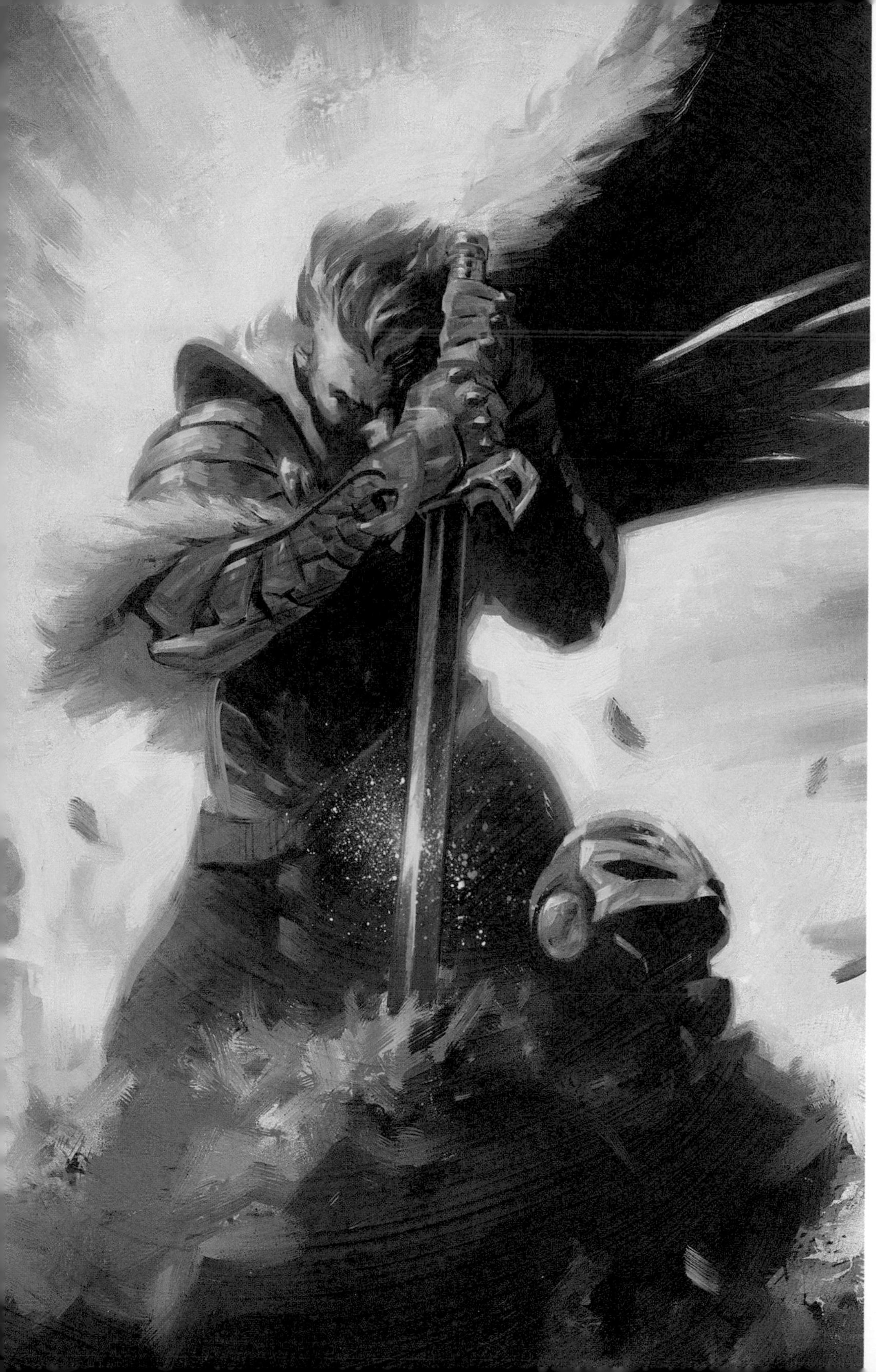

After helping the Avengers defeat the Masters of Evil and the time-traveling Kang the Conqueror, the modern-day Black Knight became a reserve member of the team. Whenever the Avengers faced overwhelming odds, he was called upon to add his mighty sword arm—and equally prodigious brain power—to the group effort.

During a confrontation with the Asgardian sorceress known as the Enchantress, Whitman's soul became trapped in limbo where it languished for what seemed, to the hapless hero, like an eternity. He was eventually freed from the timeless realm by the power of the Evil Eye, an ancient relic that had recently been rediscovered thanks to a combined endeavor from the Avengers and the Defenders.

"The Black Knight shall live again." Black Knight (Dane Whitman)

The Black Knight resumed his heroic career, but he came to suspect that the Ebony Blade was having a malign influence on his actions. Whitman turned to Doctor Strange for aid, and the sorcerer swiftly determined that the sword had acquired a curse in medieval times, becoming corrupted by the blood of slain evildoers. Now the Ebony Blade threatened to drive Whitman mad—to stain his immortal soul—every time it tasted blood in battle. Acting on this information, Whitman reluctantly returned the blade to the vault in his castle and, when he finally joined the Avengers as a full-time member, he wielded a high-tech laser sword as a replacement weapon.

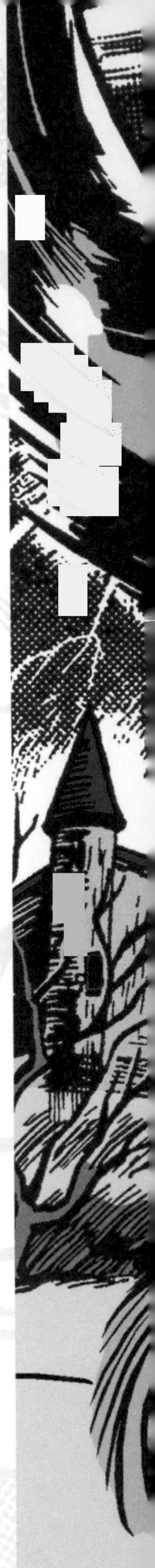

Winged wonder
The new Black Knight flew into action astride winged Aragorn, a genetically engineered stallion that resembled a mythological creature from medieval times.
Marvel Super-Heroes #17, Nov. 1968

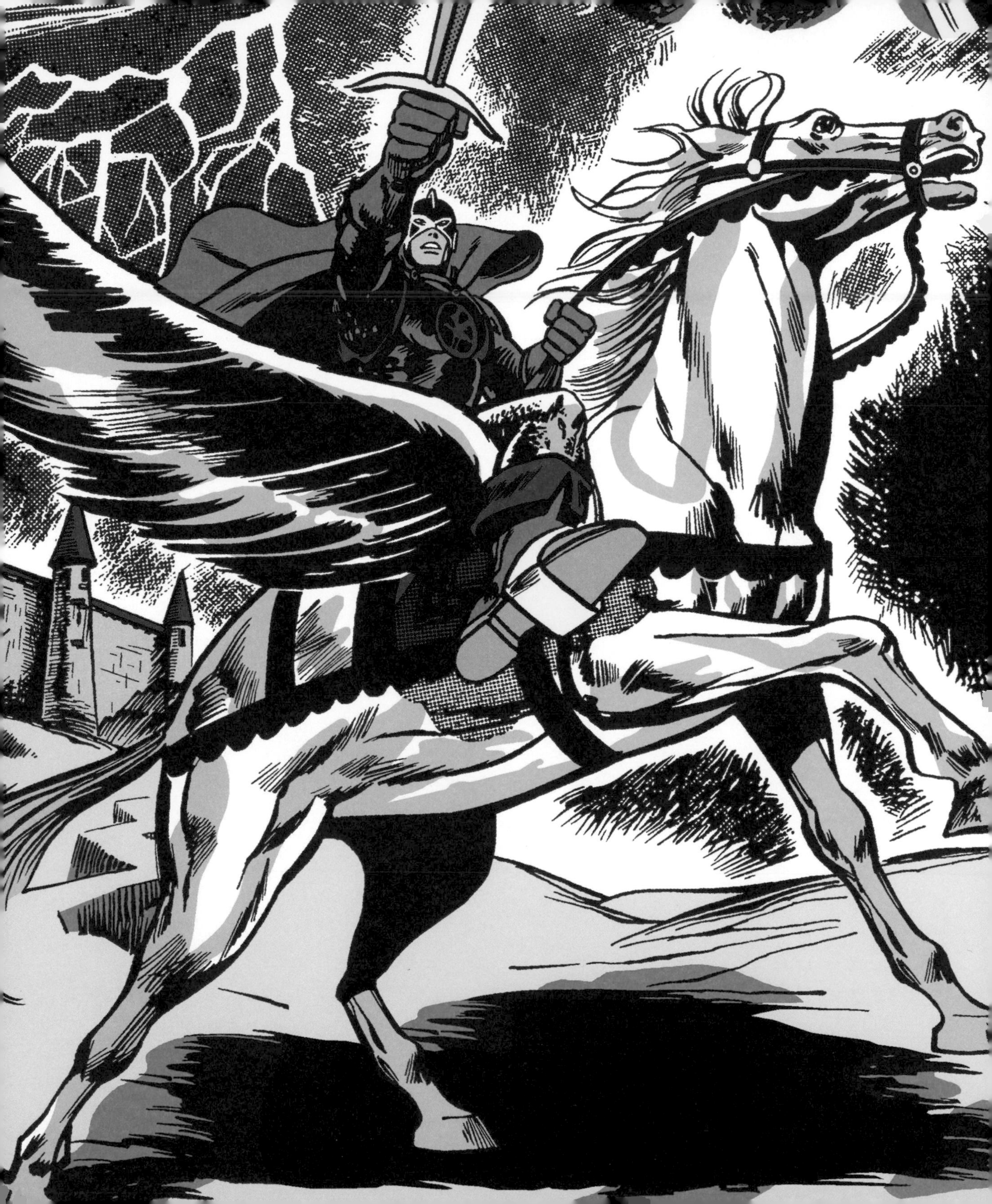

Humble beginnings
Although evolved from common bacteria, the Brethren was a proud and noble race led by Thane Ector, who embodied his people's warrior ethos.
Avengers #334, Jul. 1991

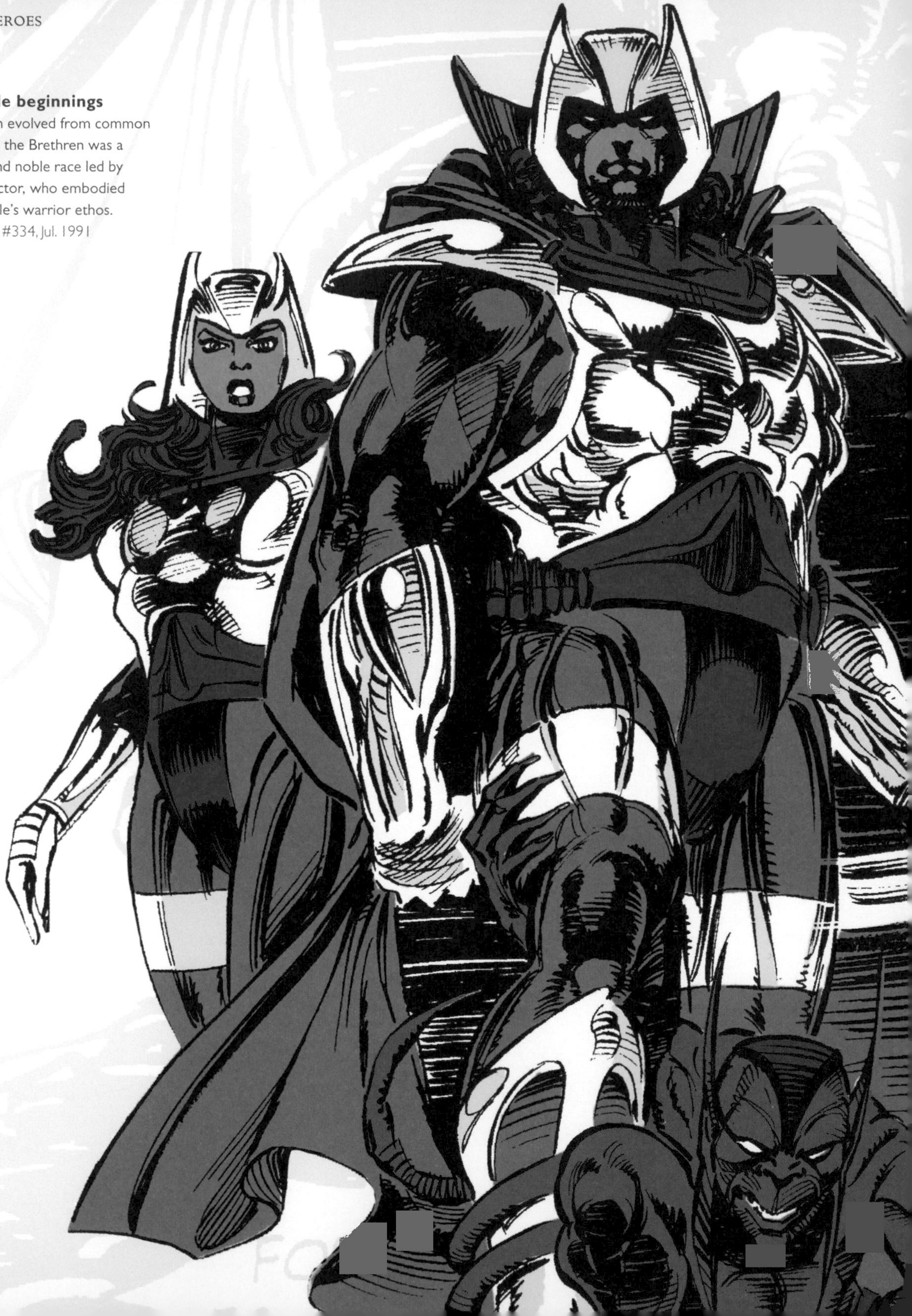

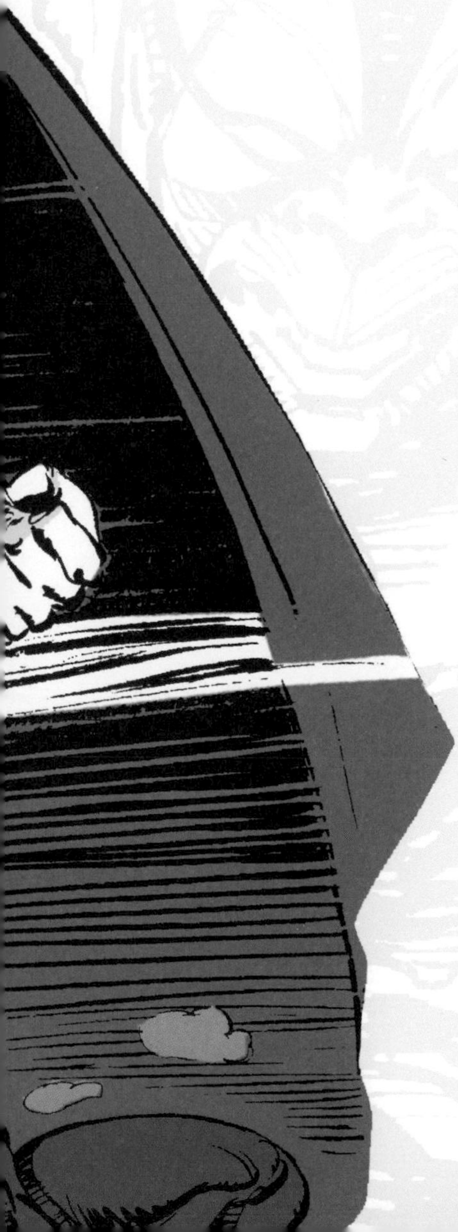

When Whitman moved into Avengers Mansion in New York City, he met Sersi for the first time. A close bond soon developed between the pair, but Whitman was torn between his attraction to Sersi and his deeper feelings for another new Avenger, Crystal.

Early in her time on the team, Sersi was astonished to learn that the Celestials had not only experimented on anthropoids in the distant past, but had also used common bacteria as the genetic basis to create a race of enhanced humanoids dubbed the Brethren. The Celestial Arishem would unleash the warlike Brethren upon planets he judged unworthy. With brutal efficiency, these humanoids would swoop down from the sky and eradicate every living thing, leaving behind worlds that were no more than dry, empty husks.

The Celestials apparently lost interest in their deadly genetics experiment at some point, and the Brethren were set free to roam the universe. The extraterrestrial villain known as the Collector eventually added them to his vast repository of unique artifacts and extraordinary individuals. Sometime later, in a bid to wipe out most of humanity so that the surviving specimens would make suitably rare additions to his cosmic museum, the Collector sent the Brethren to Earth. The Avengers struggled to hold back the invaders, but the tide of battle turned when Sersi sensed a connection with the Brethren leader, Thane Ector. As both had been created by the Celestials, they could form a Uni-Mind and, when they shared a single consciousness, Sersi was able to convince Thane Ector to turn on the Collector. Still in the shared form of the Uni-Mind, the Eternal and the Brethren leader jointly assaulted the fiend, causing the Collector to abandon his plans and flee.

"Help me... I think I'm going insane." Sersi

Sersi may have saved planet Earth by her actions, but victory seemingly came at the cost of her own mental stability. She grew increasingly violent, apparently killing three people during episodes of deep psychosis. She tried to hide her deteriorating condition from her teammates, but the Avengers realized something was amiss and they turned to Sersi's fellow Eternals for advice.

Arriving from Olympia, Ikaris announced that Sersi had fallen victim to the Mahd W'yry, a debilitating mental illness that gripped some Eternals as they grew older. By forming a Uni-Mind with an extraterrestrial, Sersi had prematurely brought on the disease. There was no known cure for the Mahd W'yry, and all the Eternals could hope to do now was stabilize Sersi's condition.

Without further discussion, Ikaris forged a strong mental bridge between Sersi and the Black Knight, making him her soul mate, or "Gann Josin" as the Eternals called it. Unfortunately, Dane Whitman was an unwilling participant in the process and he was resentful of the sudden imposition placed upon his free will. However, as Gann Josin, his mind was not his own, and he found himself uncontrollably, almost instinctively, protective of Sersi. Also, as time progressed, their psychic bond meant that he took on some of the burden of the illness, sharing and diffusing Sersi's emotional distress.

While the couple were struggling to better understand the bizarre turn of events, the Avengers came under a sustained assault from a mysterious villain known as Proctor. Although he struck indiscriminately at the Avengers, he seemed to have a particular interest in Sersi. The reason why became apparent when he was revealed to be the Dane Whitman of a parallel Earth. On his world, Proctor had willingly become Gann Josin to an alternative version of Sersi. When she eventually spurned him, putting intense strain on their psychic link, he was driven insane.

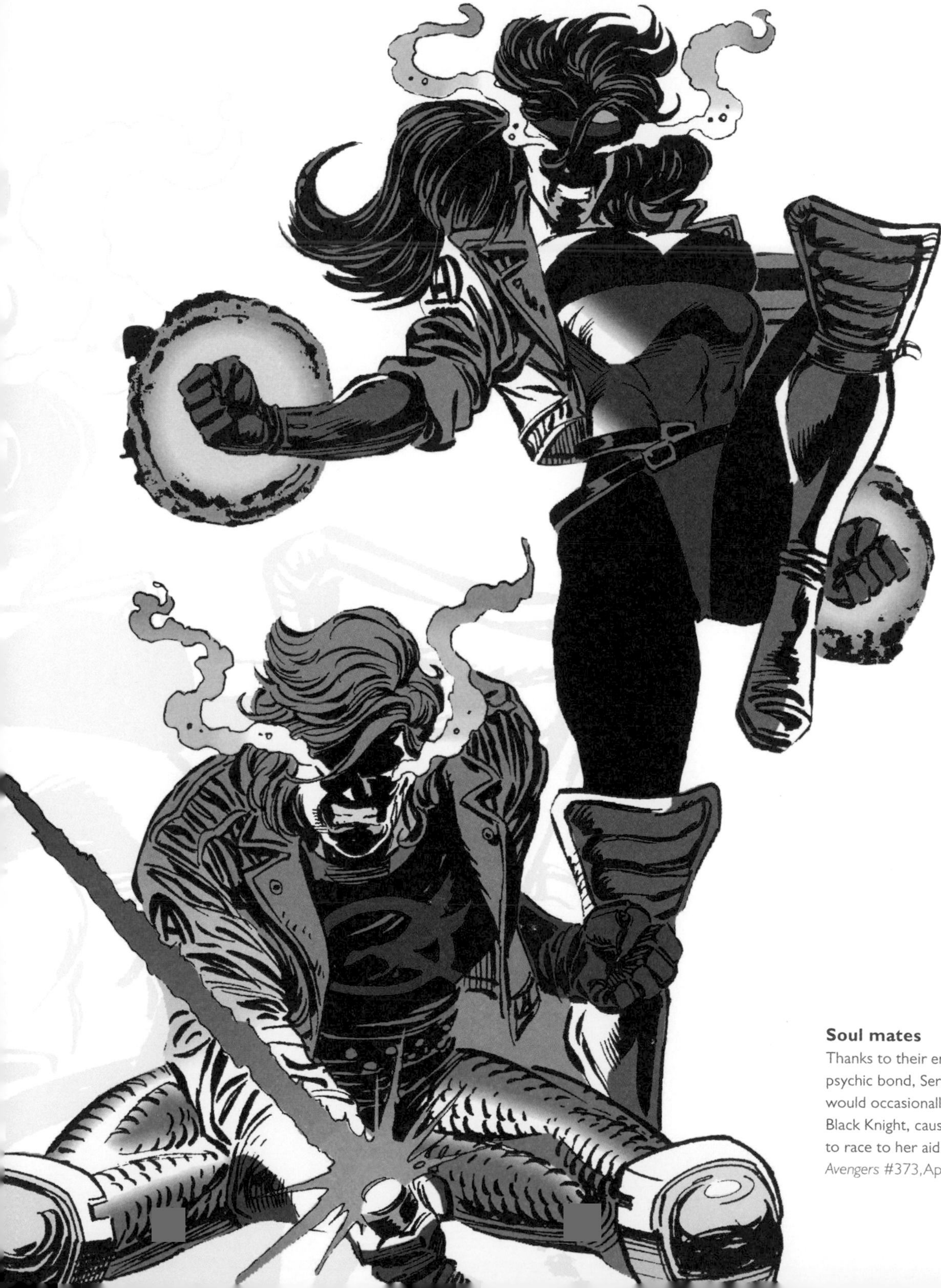

Soul mates
Thanks to their enforced psychic bond, Sersi's madness would occasionally infect the Black Knight, causing him to race to her aid.
Avengers #373, Apr. 1994

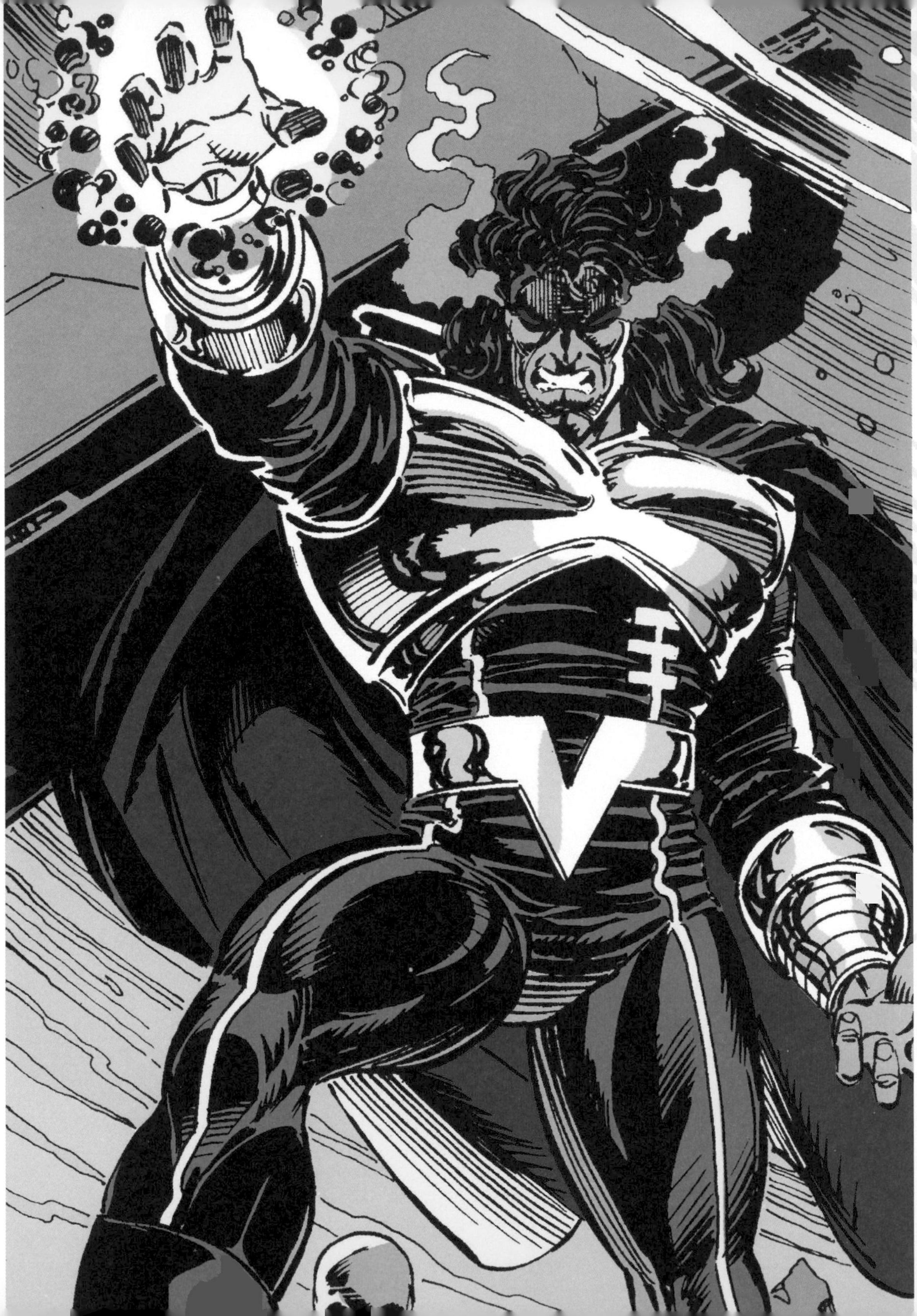

Rather than resisting the blood curse of his world's Ebony Blade, Proctor chose to embrace it, brutally slaughtering countless individuals and gaining formidable psychic abilities.

"I knew my revenge was justified!" Proctor

As Proctor became increasingly unhinged, so did his Earth's version of Sersi. Her mental powers became uncontrollable and she ultimately wrought destruction on their homeworld. Only Proctor survived the devastation, somehow escaping into the Multiverse. Confronted with an infinite number of alternative realities, he embarked on a frantic quest to eradicate every version of Sersi in existence. Amazingly, he succeeded in his deranged ambition except for the Sersi living on the primary Earth of the Multiverse.

Rather than dispatching the final Sersi in haste, however, Proctor wanted her to suffer. In fact, the villain had been responsible for all of Sersi's recent woes for the past several months. From the shadows, he had used his telepathic powers to subtly influence her actions. Slowly, he had broken down her mental barriers until it seemed like she was suffering from the Mahd W'yry. He was even responsible for killing her supposed victims, altering her memories so that she believed herself a murderer. After enjoying the Eternal's distress for a time, Proctor moved to the culmination of his elaborate plan.

Sinister stalker
Spurned by an alternative-reality version of Sersi, Proctor traveled the Multiverse on a lunatic quest to kill every iteration of his former lover.
Avengers #363, Jun. 1993

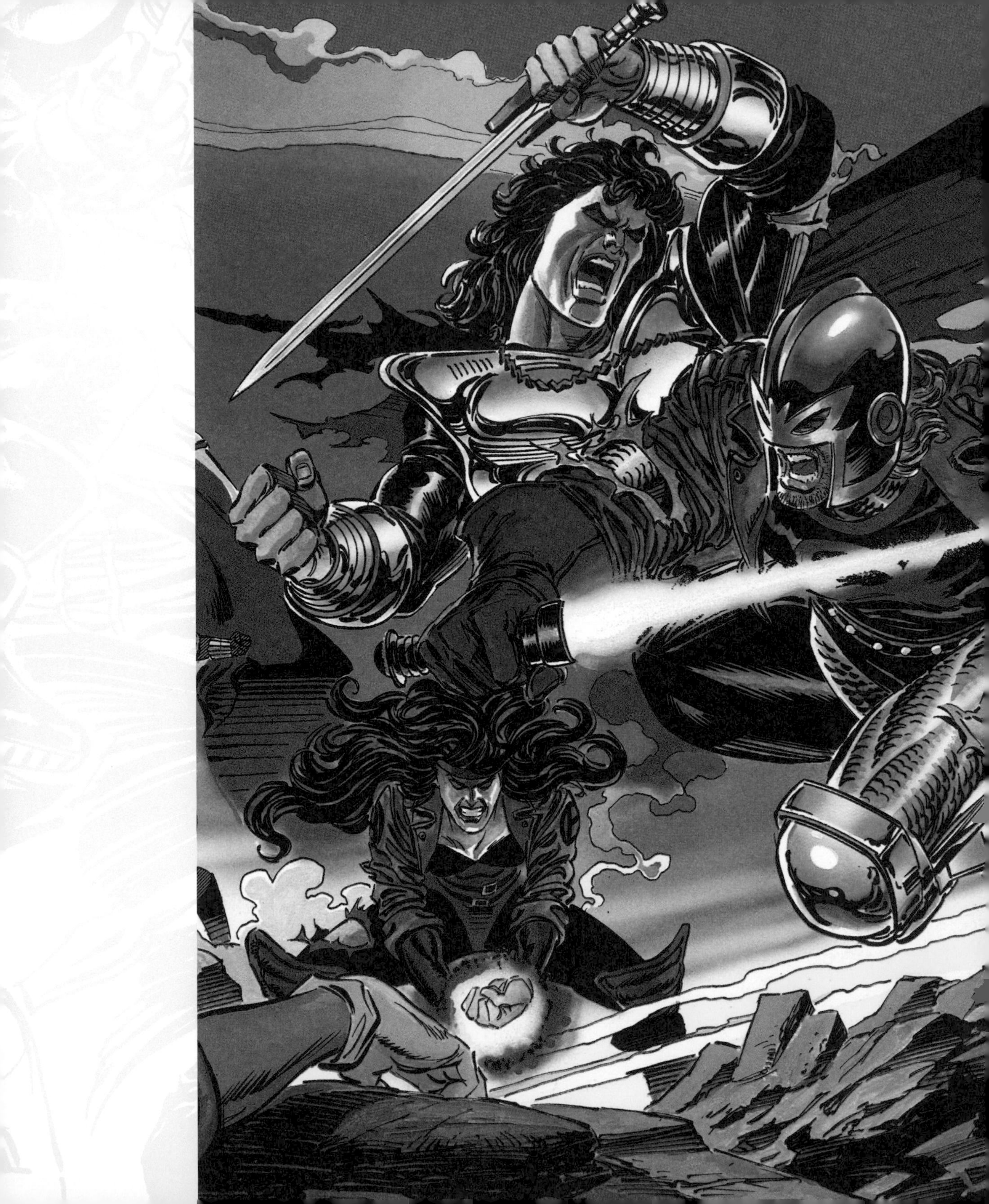

He kidnapped Sersi and drew on her power in an effort to violently collapse all of reality. The Avengers immediately raced to Sersi's aid, the Black Knight engaging his alternative-reality doppelgänger in direct combat. As Whitman activated his laser sword, Proctor unsheathed his Ebony Blade, which crackled with an ominous black energy. Proctor soon got the better of his foe, forcing Whitman to the ground. As she witnessed the Black Knight's life-and-death struggle, Sersi became enraged and she was able to break free of Proctor's mental cage. Snatching up the Ebony Blade, which Proctor had dropped during his fight with the Black Knight, she confronted the villain. Before Proctor had the opportunity to defend himself, Sersi killed him with his own cursed sword. "For all your victims," she announced, "I end your madness."

"We've all been Proctor's victims." Black Knight (Dane Whitman)

Following the defeat of Proctor, Sersi and Dane Whitman needed time away to ponder on what had happened to them. They journeyed across the Multiverse together, simultaneously exploring whether their feelings for each other were genuine or the by-product of Proctor's telepathic manipulations. Upon returning home, they parted company as close friends, but nothing more.

Dueling doppelgängers
Coming to Sersi's defense, the Black Knight crossed swords with Proctor, who still carried the cursed Ebony Blade.
Avengers #375, Jun. 1994

Dane traveled to Great Britain to resume his heroic career and soon found himself recruited into Britain's superhuman spy agency, MI13 (Military Intelligence, Section 13.) There, he fought alongside national heroes like Captain Britain, Spitfire, and Union Jack.

During the Skrull's worldwide assault, MI13 was instrumental in repelling the alien invaders from Great Britain. The Black Knight was at the vanguard of the counterattack. He fought off numerous extraterrestrials and found himself battling alongside a young medical doctor called Faiza Hussain. Struck by a blast from a Skrull energy weapon, Faiza had developed an uncanny ability to manipulate matter and immobilize individuals. She used her new gifts to great effect, helping to triage those wounded by the Skrulls. Later, after receiving King Arthur's legendary sword as a gift from Captain Britain, Faiza adopted the code name Excalibur. Joining MI13, she became Dane Whitman's heraldic steward, training to one day take over his duties as the Black Knight.

"The steward becomes the knight." Black Knight (Dane Whitman)

Sensing Great Britain was particularly vulnerable following the aborted Skrull invasion, the vampire Dracula seized the moment to strike. His undead legions had long been without a land to call their own, and the Prince of Darkness now saw the perfect opportunity to transform Great Britain—home to some of his most intractable foes—into a vampire nation.

Rule, Britannia!
Following a brief interdimensional sojourn, Black Knight Dane Whitman joined Great Britain's MI13 alongside Blade, Pete Wisdom, Captain Britain, Spitfire, and Excalibur.
Captain Britain and MI13 #15, Sep. 2009

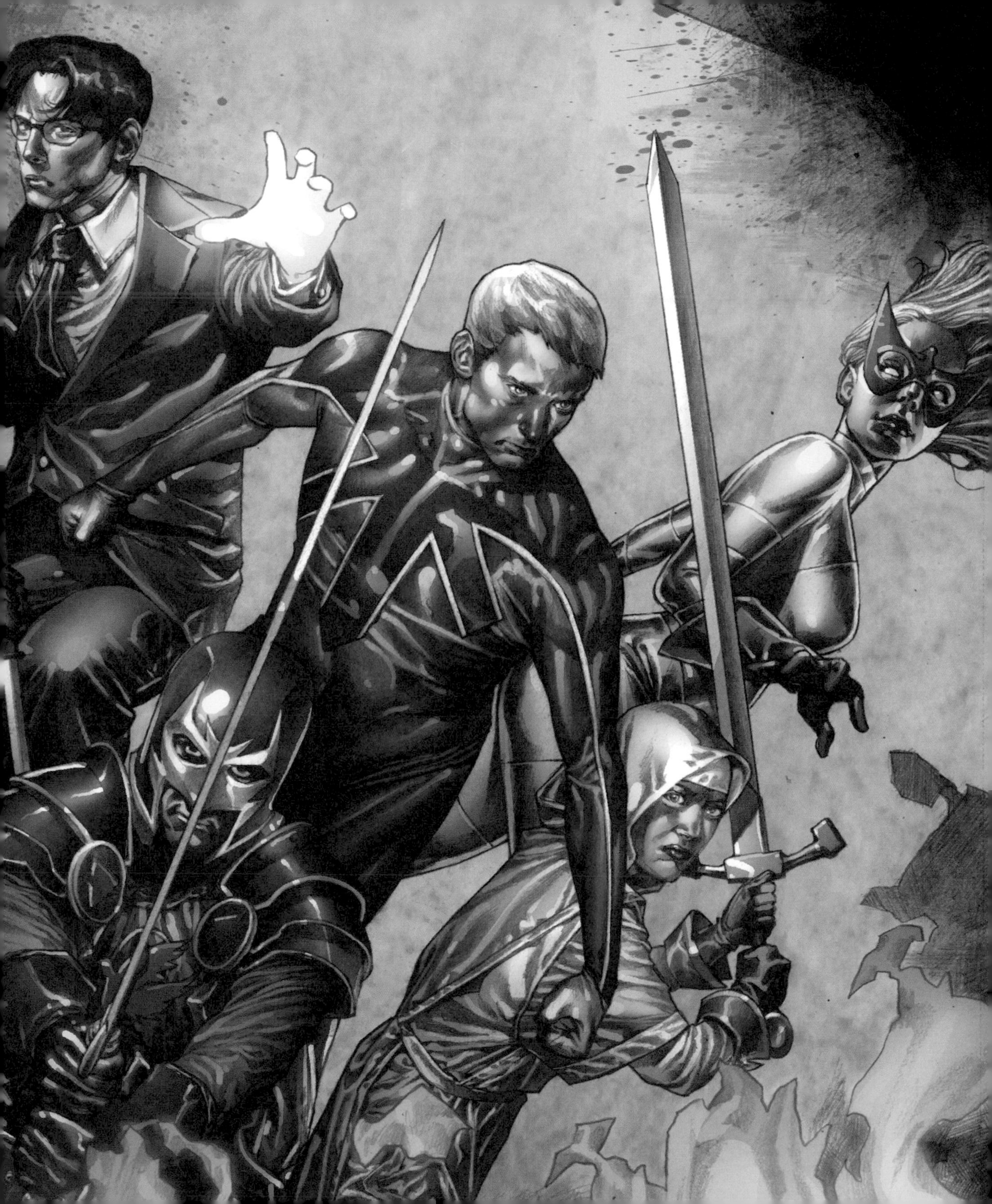

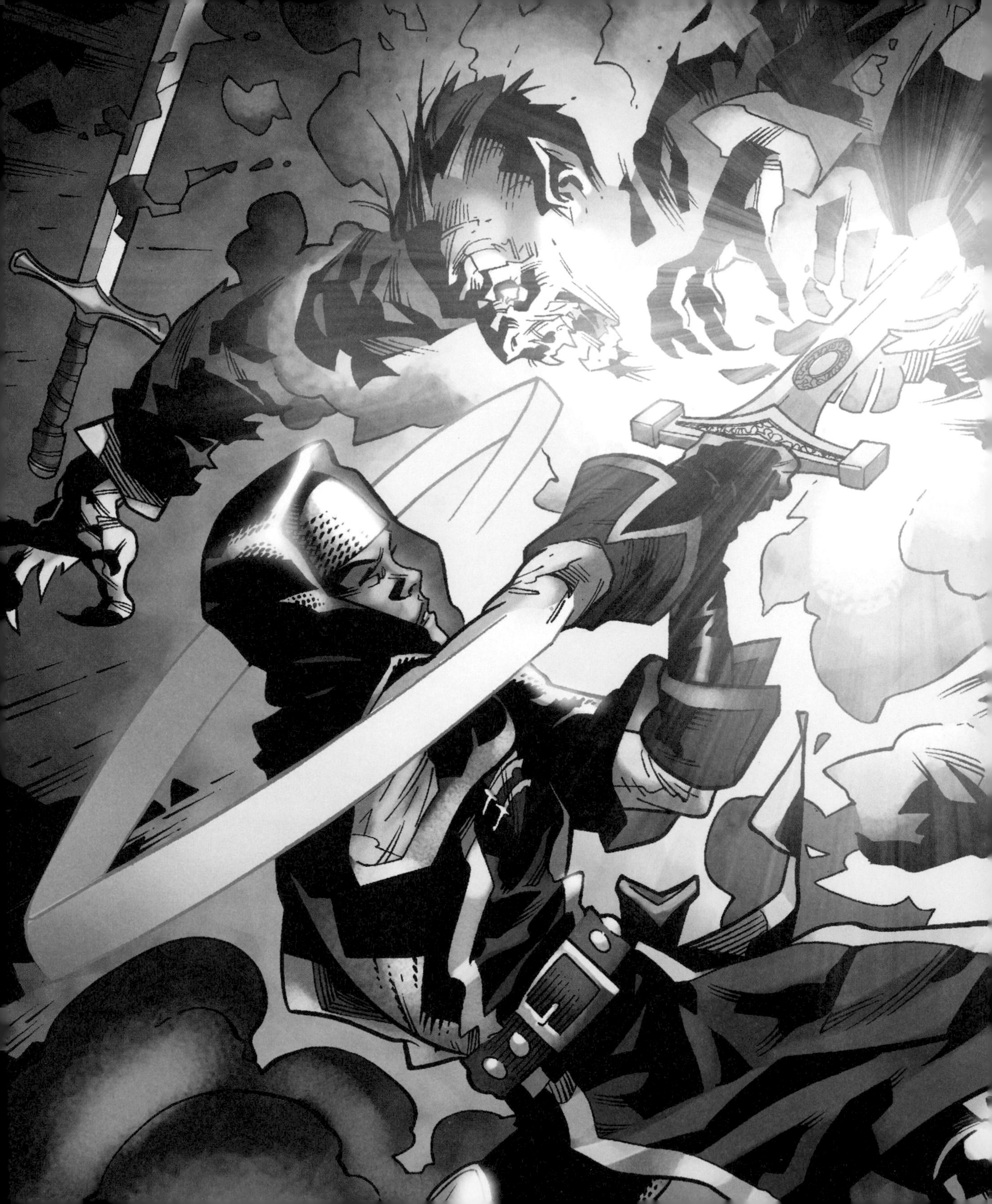

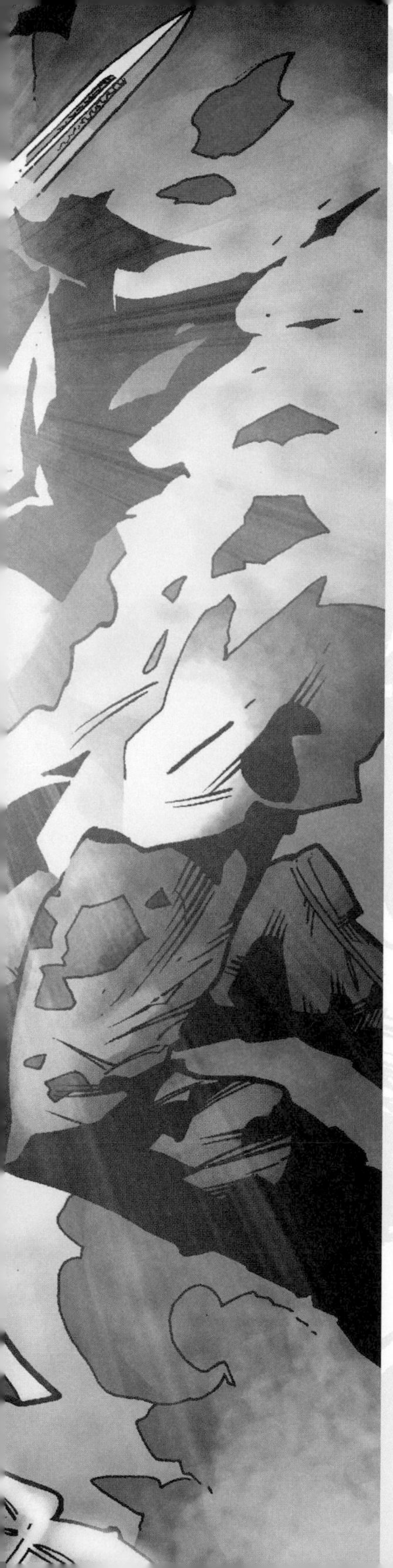

Recently, Dracula and his followers had found themselves barred from entry into the country thanks to a spell empowered by the skull of Quincy Harker, a man who had dedicated his long life—and now his death—to thwarting the machinations of the vampiric count. Under the power of the hex, Great Britain had been transformed into a single mystical residence that no vampire could enter without being personally invited. Obviously, Dracula's invasion plans could not go ahead while Harker's spell was still extant and so, employing magical means of his own, the vampire lord tracked down the skull's hidden location. Alerted to Dracula's plans, the Black Knight and MI13 raced to secure the skull, but they were too late. Shielded by a magical cloak, Dracula arrived and shattered Harker's skull into fragments. In that moment, the country became exposed to attack, and the vampiric invasion of Great Britain began in earnest.

"This is Excalibur... and I'm worthy of it." Faiza Hussain

From their orbit in outer space, Dracula's legions arrived in a vast armada of warships. The situation seemed hopeless—but Dracula's victory was fleeting. MI13's magicians had fooled him with a convincing hallucination. Harker's skull was still intact... and the anti-vampire spell still active. As the vampire fleet entered British airspace, the undead warriors burst into flames and were turned to ash in seconds. Dracula attempted to flee, but was cornered by Excalibur, who used her legendary sword to pierce the vampire's heart and end his nightmarish threat to her beloved homeland.

High stakes
The latest custodian of Excalibur, Faiza Hussain used the legendary blade to stab Count Dracula through the heart, saving Great Britain from the scourge of vampirism.
Captain Britain and MI13 #15, Sep. 2009

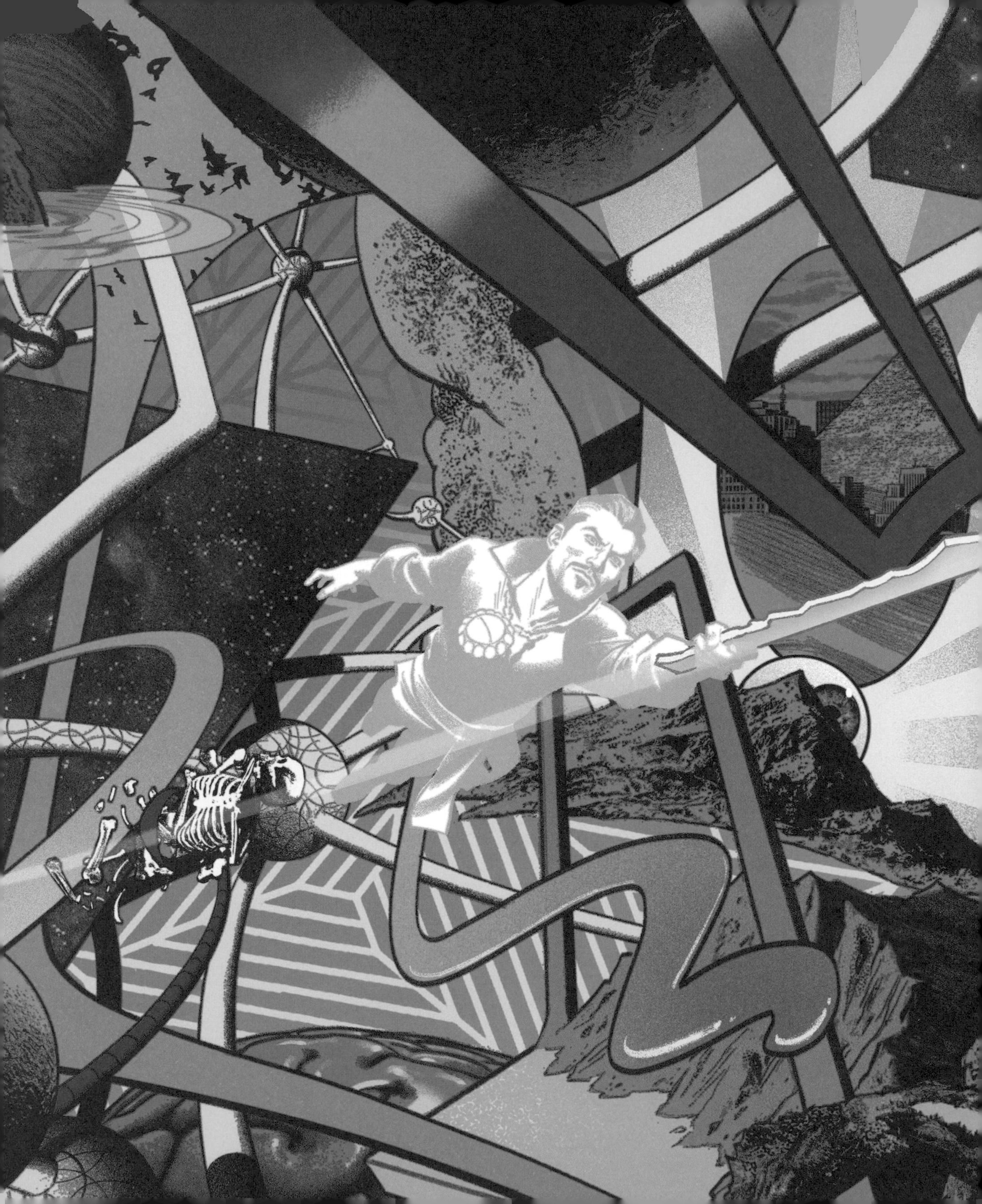

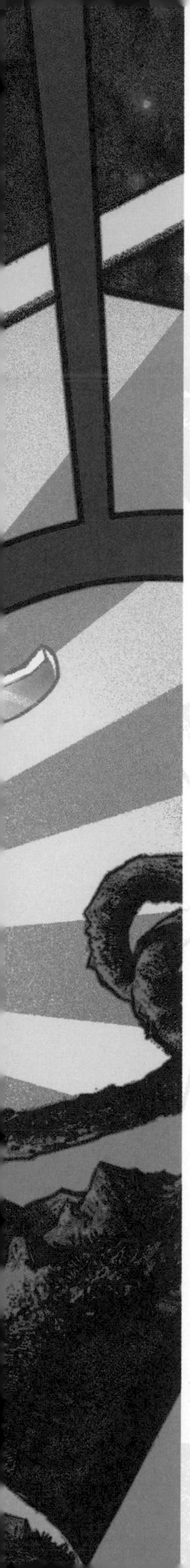

Doctor Strange: Magic No More

Drawing on the seemingly infinite power of arcane sorcery, Doctor Strange spent years battling the forces of darkness. But how would he cope when the well of magic unexpectedly ran dry?

Agamotto, Earth's first Sorcerer Supreme, created spells and magical artifacts that would well serve humanity's mystics for countless generations. One million years ago—around the time that the mighty mage was a member of Odin's Prehistoric Avengers—he fashioned a particularly potent talisman.

Empowered by the indomitable life essence of its creator, the Eye of Agamotto radiated a shimmering mystical light that could pierce through the veil of any disguise or illusion. The Eye could also track corporeal or ethereal beings by their psychic or magical aura, and it proved to be anathema to countless weak-willed demons, devils, and undying entities, all of who shrank before its "all-seeing" gaze.

When Agamotto abandoned Earth to join his mother, Oshtur, and the eldritch being Hoggoth, in the higher planes of reality, he left behind the Eye and other magical relics. These passed through the hands of numerous mystics until, in modern times, they became the primary weapons of Doctor Strange, who wielded them with a surgeon's skill in a seemingly endless fight against supernatural forces. Stephen Strange was just the latest in a long line of individuals to shoulder these responsibilities.

Supernatural sentinel
The latest mage to serve as Sorcerer Supreme, Doctor Strange would dispatch his astral self into the ethereal borderlands between realities, alert to mystical threats.
Doctor Strange: The Best Defense #1, Feb. 2019

After training to become a Master of the Mystic Arts, Strange inherited the role of Sorcerer Supreme when his mentor, the Ancient One, departed the mortal plane. Now serving as the Earth's preeminent mage, it was Doctor Strange's thankless task to maintain a constant vigil against otherworldly attacks and incursions.

One particularly persistent foe was Dormammu, the ruler of the Dark Dimension. He frequently tested the Sorcerer Supreme's mettle—and the world's supernatural defenses— in a bid to extend his dominion over the Earth. Following an early defeat, Dormammu had rashly promised Doctor Strange he would stop further attacks on Earth and, while he generally kept to that vow, he never stopped looking for ways to circumvent it.

On one occasion, rather than launching a direct assault, he infiltrated the Earthly plane by a particularly surreptitious route. Doctor Strange had recently sustained an eye injury in combat and Dormammu used the resulting scar tissue, which was as much mystical in nature as it was physical, as a means to cross over from his home dimension. Dormammu transplanted the smallest portion of his dark essence into the wound, where it festered and grew over time. When he was at full strength, Dormammu took control of Doctor Strange's body, locking out the Sorcerer Supreme's astral form.

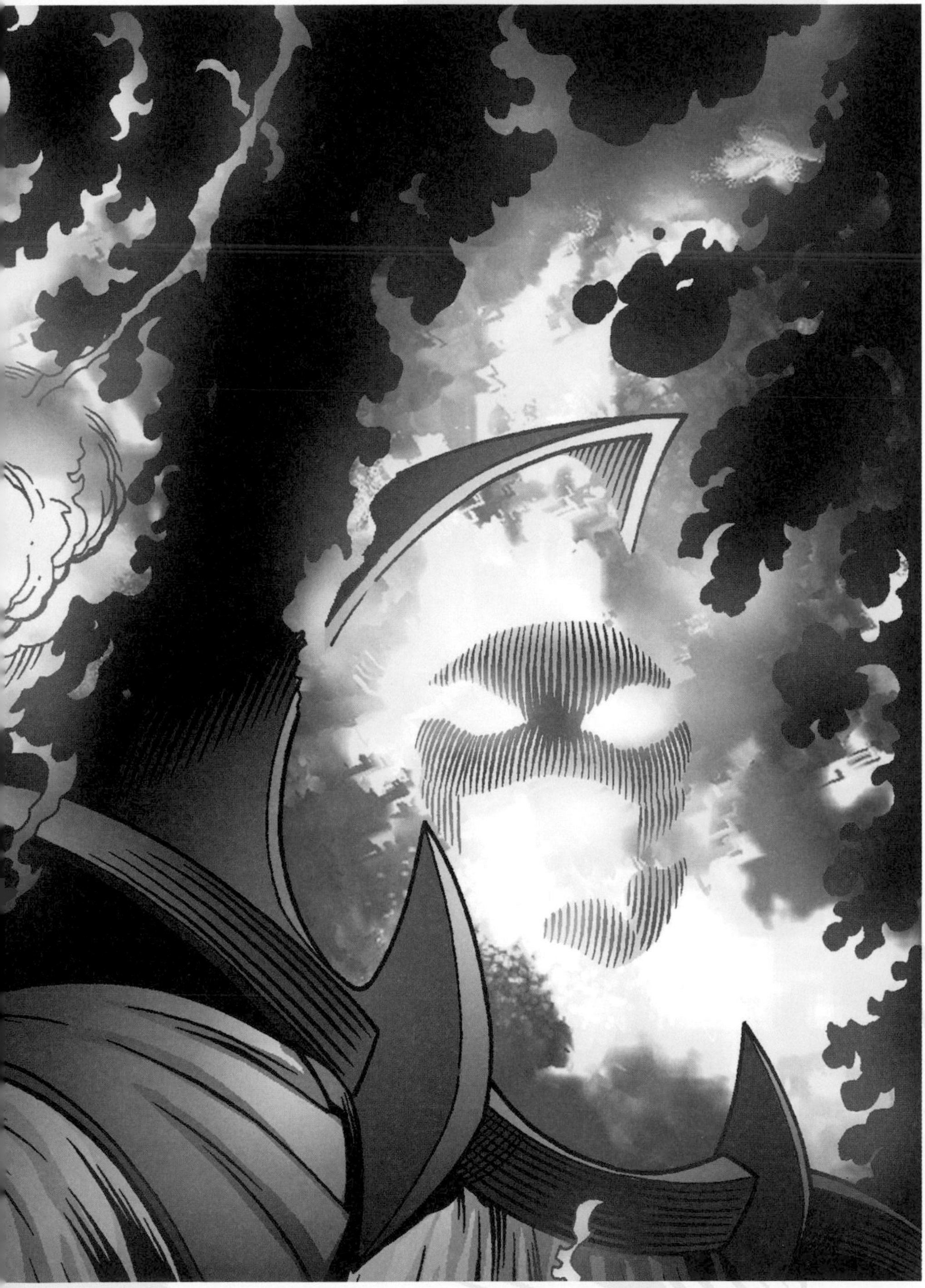

Burning ambition
Ill-fated individuals who sometimes stumbled into Dormammu's realm, such as the Sub-Mariner and Tiger Shark, found themselves held fast in his infernal grip.
Hulk #11, Jun. 2009

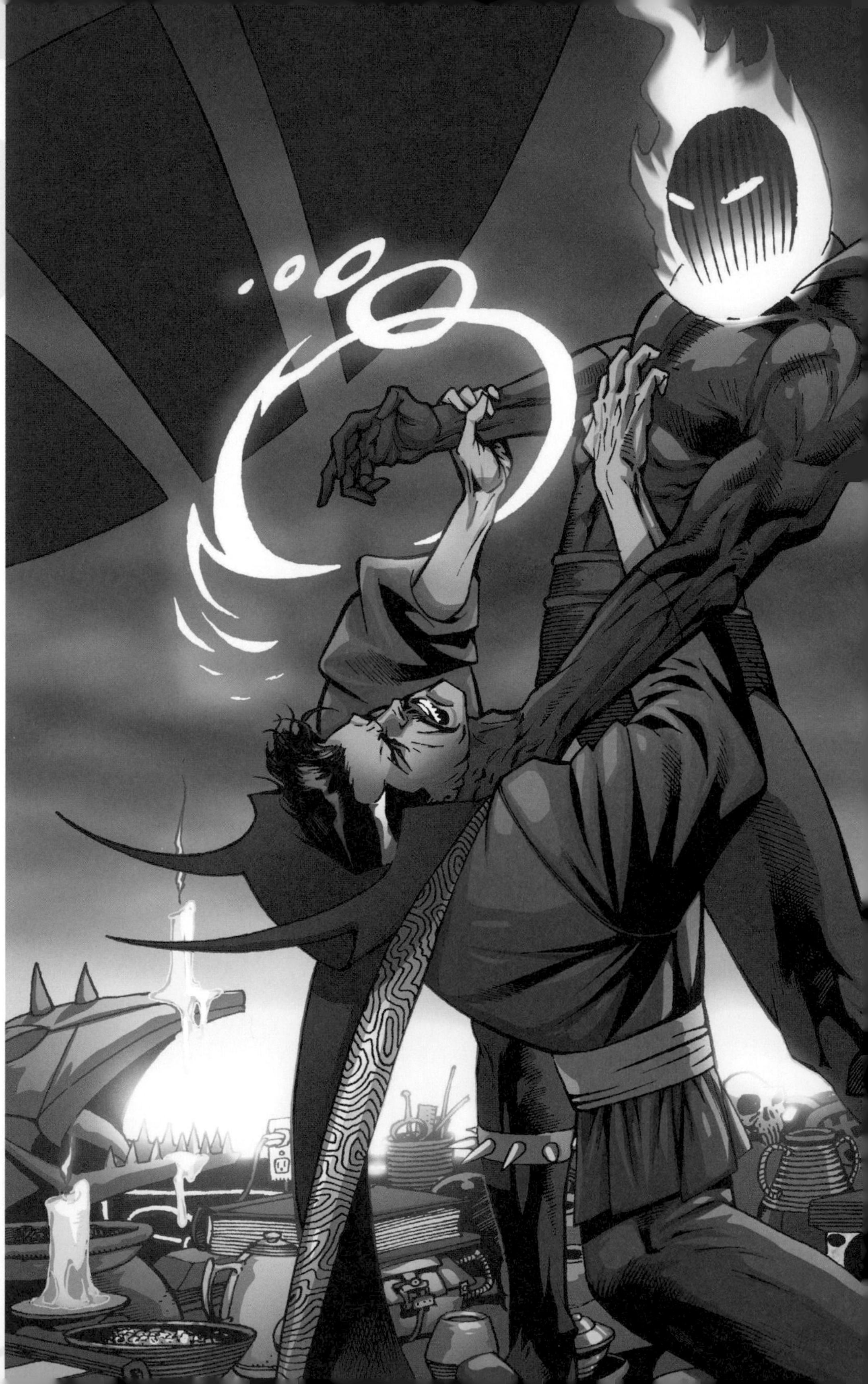

Dark days
Using Doctor Strange's body as a mystical conduit, the Dread Dormammu finally escaped his Dark Dimension.
Doctor Strange, Sorcerer Supreme #1, Nov. 1988

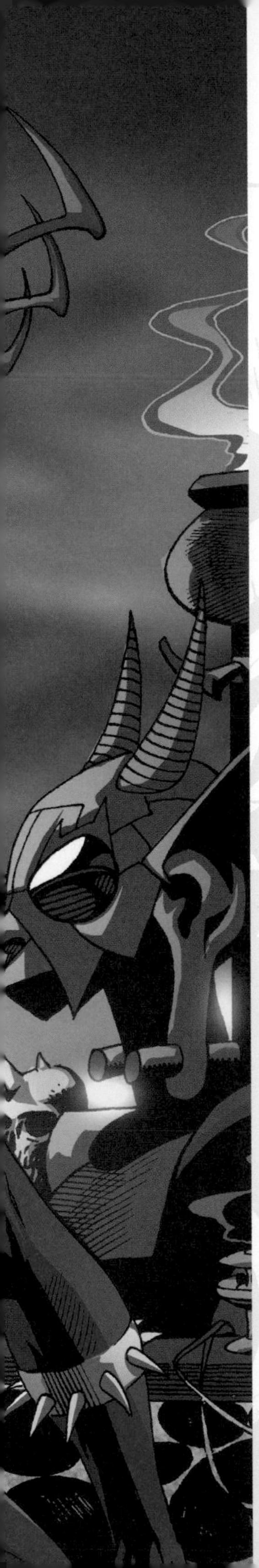

With cruel relish, the otherworldly despot announced to Strange: "Your body—your power—everything you are have now become the birthright of the Dread Dormammu!"

While Dormammu busied himself with his new plaything, unleashing a wave of tentacled horrors upon the Earth, Doctor Strange's consciousness found sanctuary in the most unlikely place. Hunted by Dormammu's demonic servitors, the magician's astral self hid in the body of a lowly sewer rat. In such a diminished form, Doctor Strange was virtually undetectable by magical means, but time was still of the essence. If Stephen Strange's ghostly form was not reunited with his body soon, he would simply cease to exist, his consciousness dissipating in the ether within 24 hours.

"Now—this world is mine!" Dormammu

Doctor Strange's first instinct was to contact fellow heroes in the Avengers and the Defenders, but in his rodent form he was unable to properly marshal his magical powers. What's more, as Dormammu tightened his grip on reality, he trapped more and more of Earth's guardians behind impenetrable barriers. Seeing no other possible recourse, Doctor Strange—Rodent Supreme—made ready to confront Dormammu directly.

In the end, though, the magician was far from alone. Alerted to Doctor Strange's predicament by Earth-Mother Gaea, the wiccan Topaz added her power to that of the weakened sorcerer. Their joint spells depleted Dormammu's power and, when Doctor's Strange's former lover, Clea, added her strength to the cause, the dread lord was finally expunged from Stephen Strange's body. The fiery demon retreated to his home dimension and Earth's Sorcerer Supreme was restored to full vigor. In the wake of his narrow victory, Doctor Strange rededicated himself to his mission. He vowed that no matter how many mystical horrors imperiled the Earth, he would always be there to meet them—and defeat them.

And so it remained for many years, with the Sorcerer Supreme drawing on a deep reservoir of spells and enchantments to keep humanity safe from otherworldly predators. There came a grievous time, though, when he could no longer rely on his traditional wellspring of mystical power. His talismans, including the All-Seeing Eye of Agamotto, began to falter, and his spells all ran dry. Shorn of his magical resources, Doctor Strange became an ordinary man facing truly extraordinary foes.

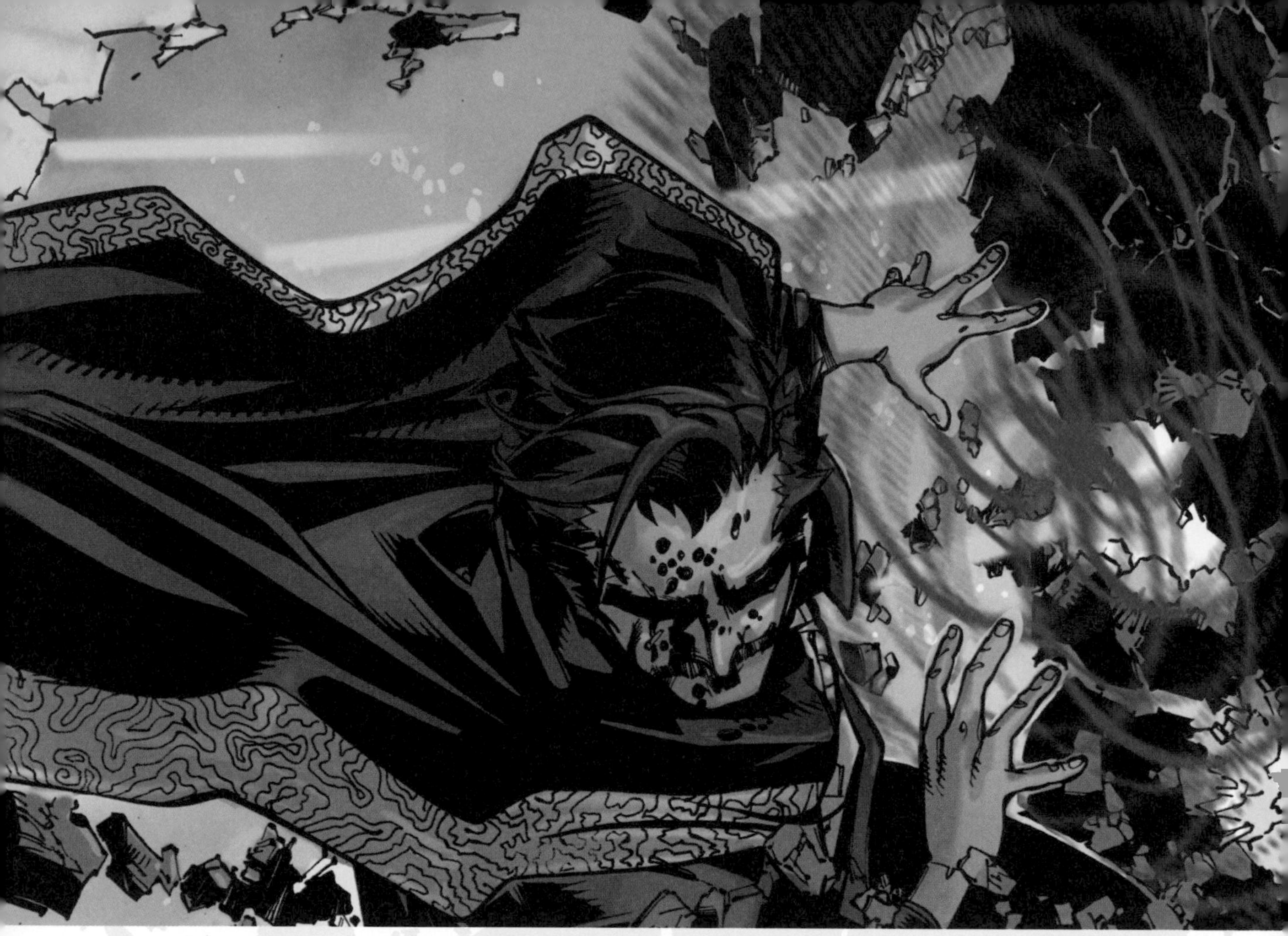

It began with a warning from the mages of other realities, something was moving through the mystical realms, eradicating magic and the sorcerers that used it. After traveling to another dimension to witness the devastation firsthand, Doctor Strange alerted his fellow mystics to the impending danger. Unfortunately, he sounded the alarm too late and Earth's magic users soon found themselves under a blistering assault from the forces of the Empirikul, a vast army of technologically advanced robots and AI constructs. Mystic heroes like the Scarlet Witch and Doctor Voodoo were among the first to be targeted, hunted relentlessly by cyborg Witchfinder Wolves. Doctor Strange also came under sustained attack, his Sanctum Sanctorum at 177A Bleecker Street in New York City invaded by the Imperator, the ruler of the Empirikul and commander of its automated armies.

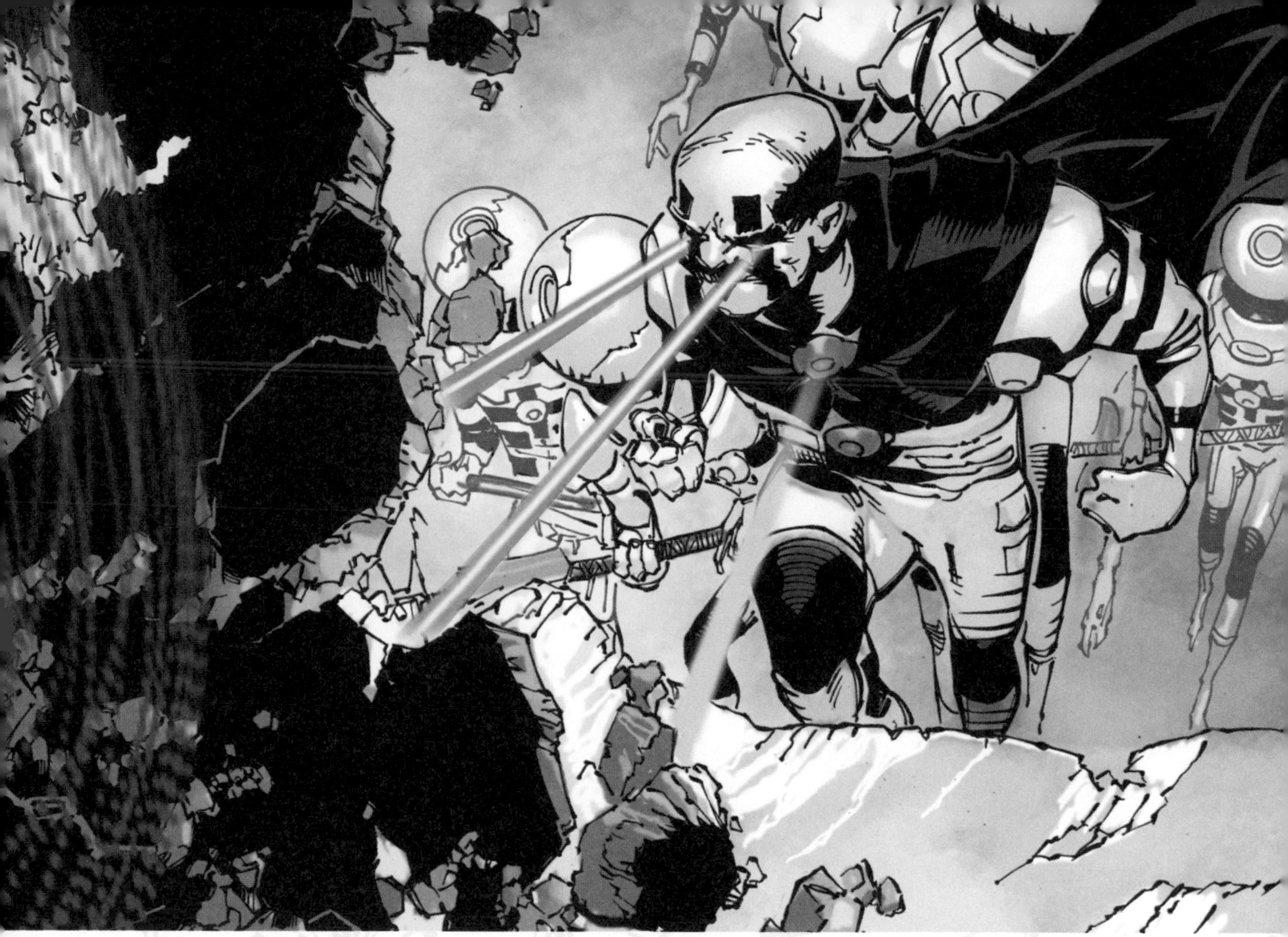

Flanked by a squad of powerful Eyebots, the Imperator cut through the Sorcerer Supreme's mystical defenses with ease. In a severely weakened state and on the verge of total defeat, Doctor Strange was forced to resort to extreme measures. Accessing Earth's network of ley lines, he tapped into the planet's magical core, taking on a near-infinite amount of mystical energy and becoming bloated with power. It was still not enough. The Imperator deflected Doctor Strange's desperate attack and took the now-debilitated Sorcerer Supreme prisoner.

The Empirikul had won, Earth's primary magical defender had been neutralized and Doctor Strange's own actions had all but depleted Earth's magical reserves. The well of mystic power was finally exhausted. To demonstrate the point, the Imperator tore Doctor Strange's Cloak of Levitation to pieces before the hero's astonished eyes.

Scientific advance
Led by the Imperator, the Empirikul's scientific forces targeted Doctor Strange in a bid to eradicate all magic in existence.
Doctor Strange #6, May 2016

While held captive, Doctor Strange learned that the Imperator was an other-dimensional orphan whose scientist parents had been sacrificed decades earlier to the dark god Shuma-Gorath. The couple had managed to save their baby son, however, and the Imperator had been given into the care of intuitive Eyebots. He spent his formative years in an artificial environment and, upon reaching maturity, he vowed to avenge his parents' deaths by removing every trace of magic from the universe. With the Eyebots' assistance, he created a huge fleet of starships and declared war on all things mystical, wielding science as his primary weapon.

"We burn you last, Doctor Strange." The Imperator

To celebrate his victory on Earth, the Imperator planned to burn Doctor Strange's Sanctum Sanctorum to the ground. However, the building proved remarkably resistant to damage, as if possessed by its own mystical aura. The source of this power was revealed when Eyebots ventured into the basement. There, they discovered a creature with many faces and a jet-black form that flowed like quicksilver. This was the embodiment of Doctor Strange's mystical suffering. Unbeknownst to the mage, the pain he had experienced in his many years of service had coalesced into a living entity, growing over time as the hero selflessly endured many physical and mental deprivations. While the Imperator was distracted by the presence of this bizarre monstrosity, an aged wizard called Monako arrived and successfully freed Doctor Strange from his bonds, teleporting him to safety.

All-seeing evil
Shuma-Gorath demanded absolute worship, killing the Imperator's parents for their heretical belief in science.
Doctor Strange #7, Jun. 2016

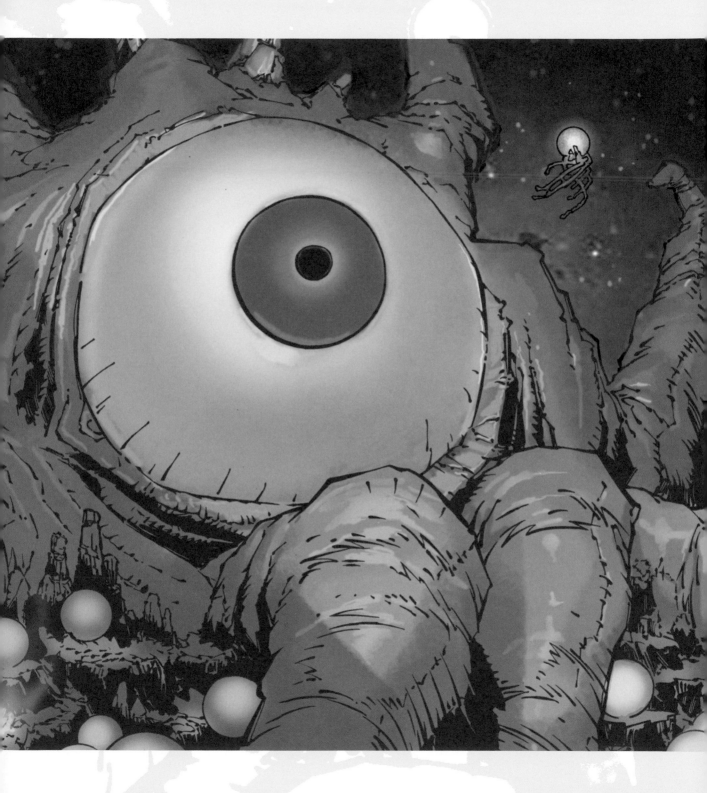

Unfortunately, the effort depleted Monako's reserves of mystical energy and he was himself captured and killed. Monako's spell transported the former Sorcerer Supreme halfway around the world and Doctor Strange soon found safe haven in a network of subterranean caves, alongside a handful of fellow mystics who had also survived the Empirikul attack. Stephen Strange rallied his newfound allies and organized a worldwide quest to locate and retrieve the world's few remaining magical icons. The mystics did not find much, and what they did recover was not particularly powerful, but given their dire predicament it had to suffice.

Armed with the Axe of Angarruumus and a few other basic weapons, Doctor Strange returned to his home to once again confront the Imperator. As before, the scornful super-scientist quickly gained the upper hand. However, when Doctor Strange embraced his own pain, willingly merging with the frightful creature in the basement, he finally amassed enough strength to overcome his foe. With the Imperator's defeat, the Empirikul robots ceased functioning. Victory had been won, but it had come at a truly terrible cost.

"If we won, why is the world still cold?" Doctor Strange

The Earth's supply of magic was now limited, and Doctor Strange faced an uncertain future. It was the last days of magic and the first days of a new era.

Hidden pain
Doctor Strange's mental anguish
and physical pain coalesced into
a hideous entity that lay hidden
in his basement, until it was
discovered by the Imperator.
Doctor Strange #9, Aug. 2016

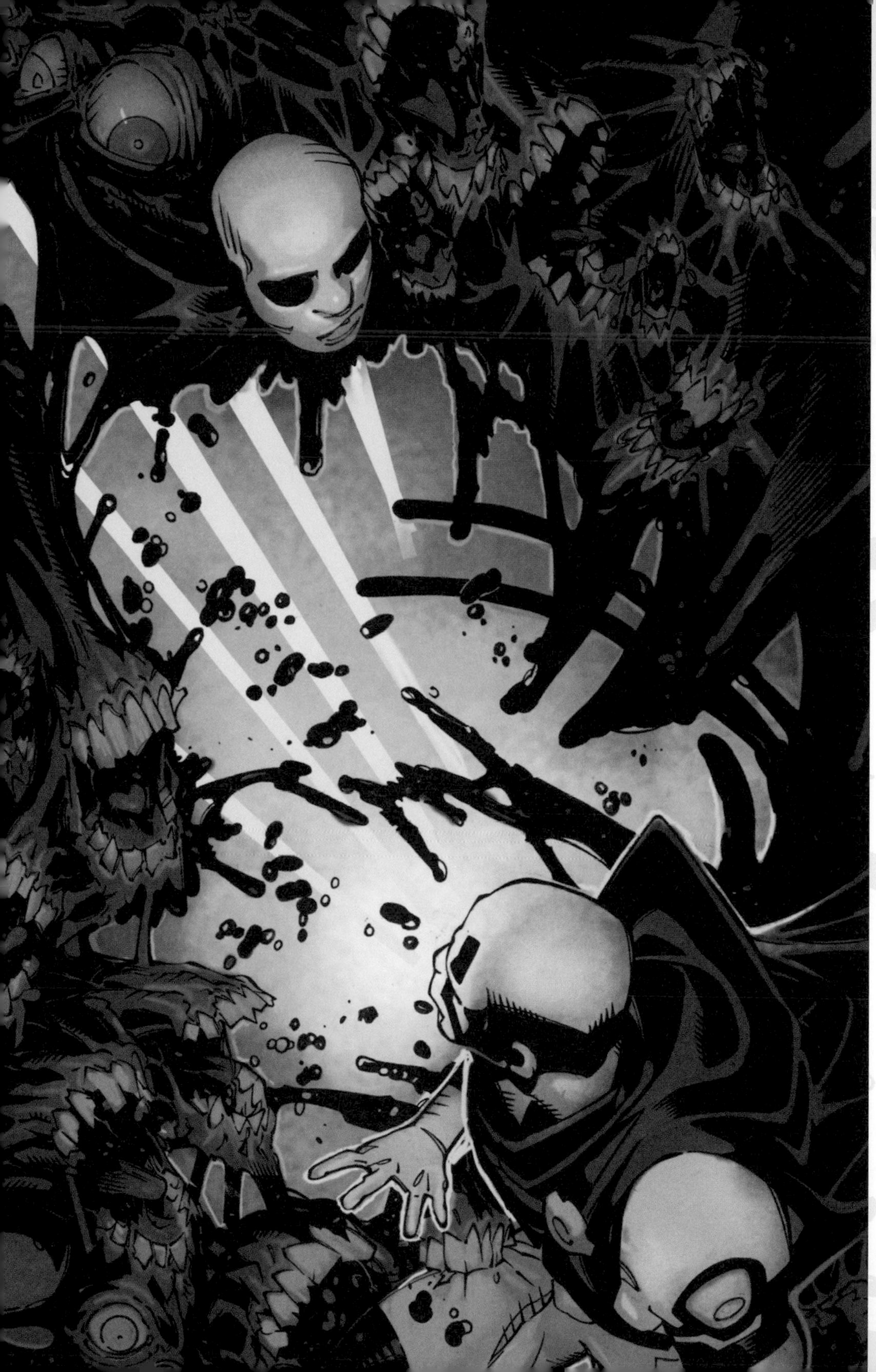

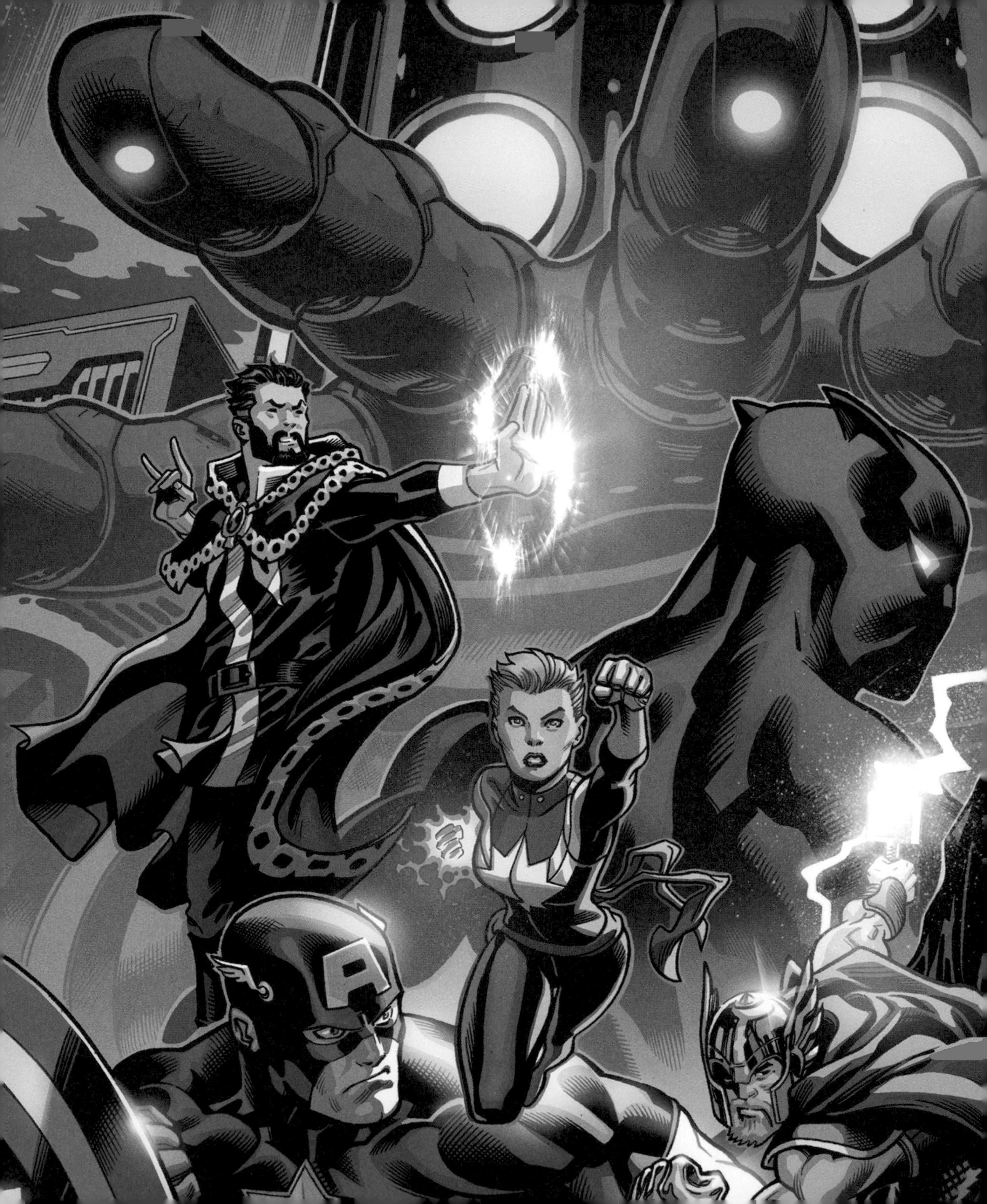

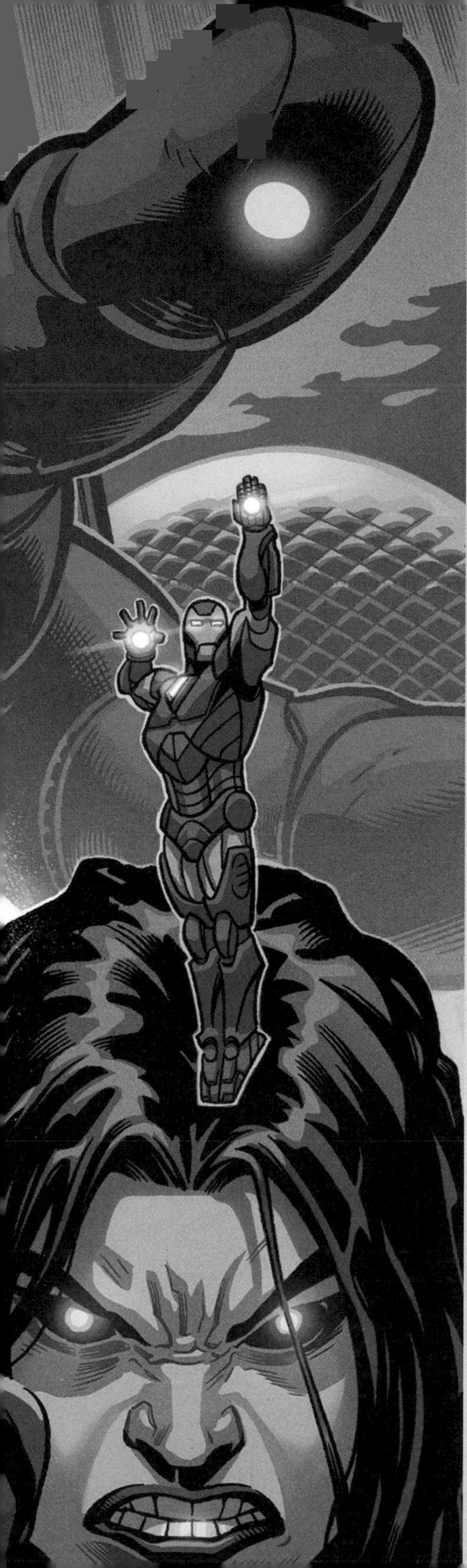

MODERN MYTHS

Dark gods and other living relics from the primordial past continue to shape the world of today. In recent times, the symbiote deity Knull awoke from eons of slumber to challenge the champion Spider-Man and the alien-bonded antihero Venom. Likewise, the monumental Celestials returned to Earth, their menacing, unexpected arrival prompting Captain America to rally his Super Hero allies and form a new squad of Avengers.

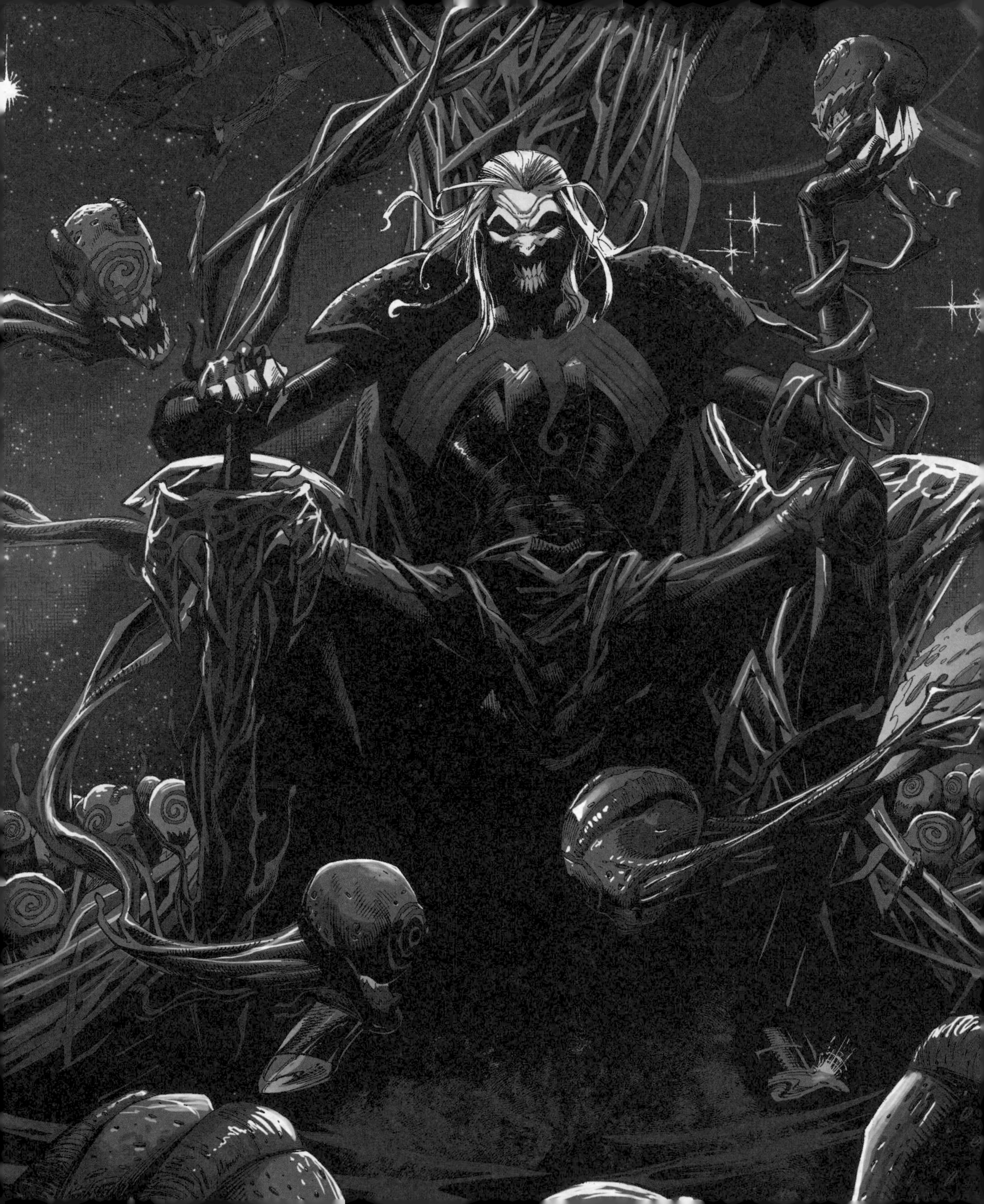

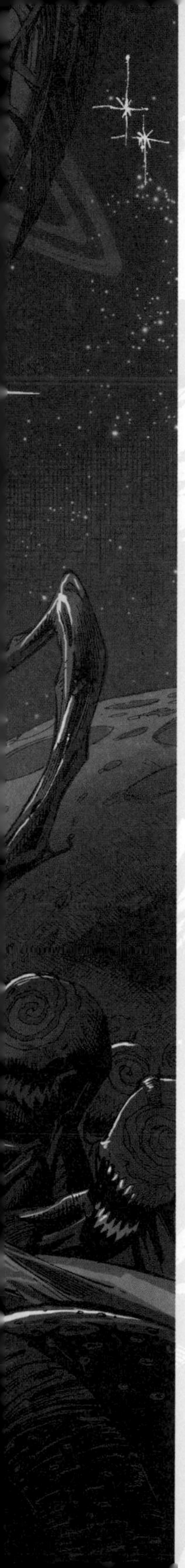

Knull and the Void

His solitary existence disturbed by the explosive chaos of the Big Bang, the malevolent Knull declared war on all living things, unleashing an army of symbiotic warriors upon the universe.

Knull was a god of the primordial darkness, the only being to exist before time itself began. He drifted through the void for an incalculable age, and was content in the monotony of his existence. However, the light of the Big Bang disturbed the evil deity's rest, and Knull grew increasingly angered as he witnessed his bleak kingdom overrun by life in a multitude of forms. Determined to fight back against the intrusion of light and life into his realm, Knull forged a sword of living darkness from his own shadow. He dubbed his weapon All-Black, the Necrosword, and used it for the first time to strike at a band of Celestials he had come across in the depths of space.

Knull successfully decapitated one of the space gods, but was swiftly cast aside by the cosmic giant's brothers. He was propelled back into his void, far away from the still-expanding universe of life. Knull was overjoyed to find himself in familiar territory, and pleased to discover the severed head of the Celestial adrift beside him. The dark god took the skull and transformed it into a gigantic foundry.

Bleak kingdom
Knull was a malign deity who presided over the void. His reign was absolute until the Big Bang disturbed the primordial darkness and released light and life into the universe.
Venom #3, Aug. 2018

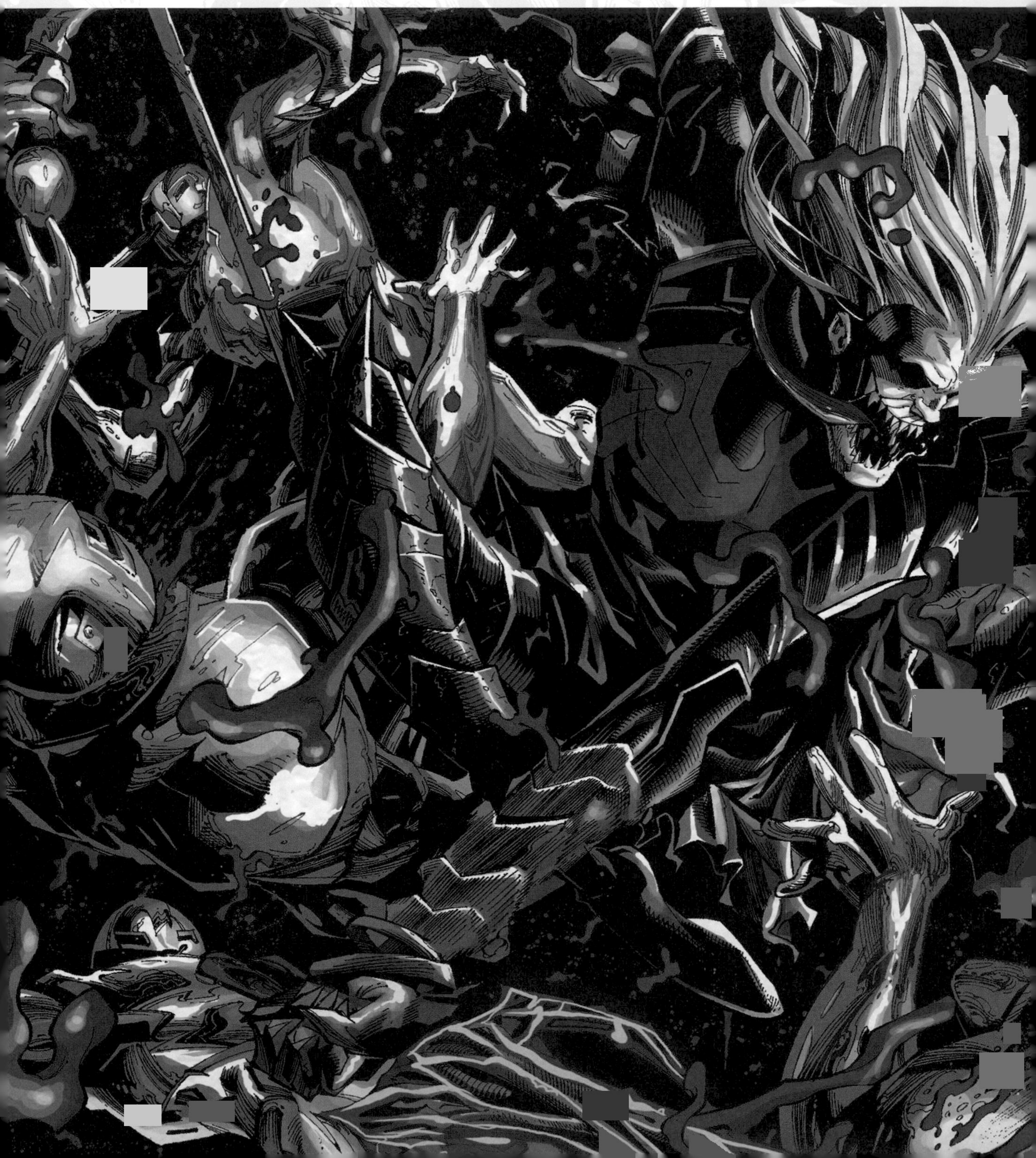

Drawing on the Celestial energies that still crackled within the hollowed-out cranium, Knull refined All-Black, tempering the metal and sharpening the blade to a razor's edge. He then forged a symbiotic suit of living armor from the eldritch darkness that was all around him. Suitably prepared, Knull went hunting. His prey were the godlike beings that now proliferated throughout the universe and who encouraged their followers to explore further the empty regions of space. Knull used All-Black to smite countless numbers of these new deities, building a fearsome legend throughout the cosmos. "Together we slit the throats of creation and choked a billion stars with the blood of the all-mighty," he boasted.

One particularly intense confrontation with a band of armored deities ran awry, however, and the dark god's bloody rampage came to a premature end. Severely wounded after being stabbed through the chest by one of the warrior gods, Knull crashed to a largely uninhabited planet. While Knull lay incapacitated, the semi-sentient All-Black bonded with a visiting alien called Gorr and was taken off-world. The armor's history, as it passed from one owner to the next, was subsequently recorded in a divine tome called the Saga of the God Butcher.

His power depleted by the fall, Knull remained semi-comatose for a century. Eventually, he regained enough strength to crawl out of the impact crater and explore his surroundings. He found he could bond with the planet's small, indigenous creatures, cloaking them in his own dark essence and turning them into obedient thralls. This act of symbiosis resulted in the creation of a communal hive mind with Knull at its center, controlling his slaves as if they were nothing but an extension of himself. The dark god birthed a vast horde of these symbiotes, sending them out into the cosmos. As a result of their shared psychic bond, Knull experienced everything his symbiotes did. At some point he discovered he could create symbiote dragons and thus spread his terror even further into the universe.

God slayer
Wielding All-Black, the Necrosword, Knull struck at the rapidly proliferating gods and godlings, cutting a bloody swathe across the early cosmos.
Venom #4, Sep. 2018

He sent one to Earth where, in the 6th century BCE, it bedeviled a band of Vikings and was dubbed the Grendel. Through the dragon's eyes, Knull could see that Earth had a particularly strong connection to the light of creation and he planned to burn the world to ash. The Vikings had a stout defender, however, in the form of a young God of Thunder. Thor stopped the monster's fiery onslaught with a lightning storm of unprecedented magnitude. The electrical maelstrom was so strong it severed Knull's connection with Grendel and all his other mind-controlled servants.

"Hold! Hold the Grendel back..." Viking warrior

Divorced from the hive mind the symbiotes sought out fresh hosts, bonding with creatures from many different worlds, and going on to develop their own independent culture. Some symbiotes even turned on Knull, imprisoning him at the center of an artificial planet they shaped from their own amorphous mass of bodies. This world became known as Klyntar, a term that meant "cage" in the symbiotes' own language.

Over the centuries, members of the symbiote race attempted to redeem themselves by acting to protect the universe they had once terrorized on behalf of their dark god. In time, they too became known as the Klyntar—and Knull was all but forgotten. The truth could not be buried forever, however, and events conspired to awaken Knull from his enforced slumber and unleash a revived Grendel upon the modern world.

Monster unleashed
When the dragon Grendel was revived, it swept through the concrete canyons of New York City—a creature of myth returned to life in the modern era.
Venom #2, Aug. 2018

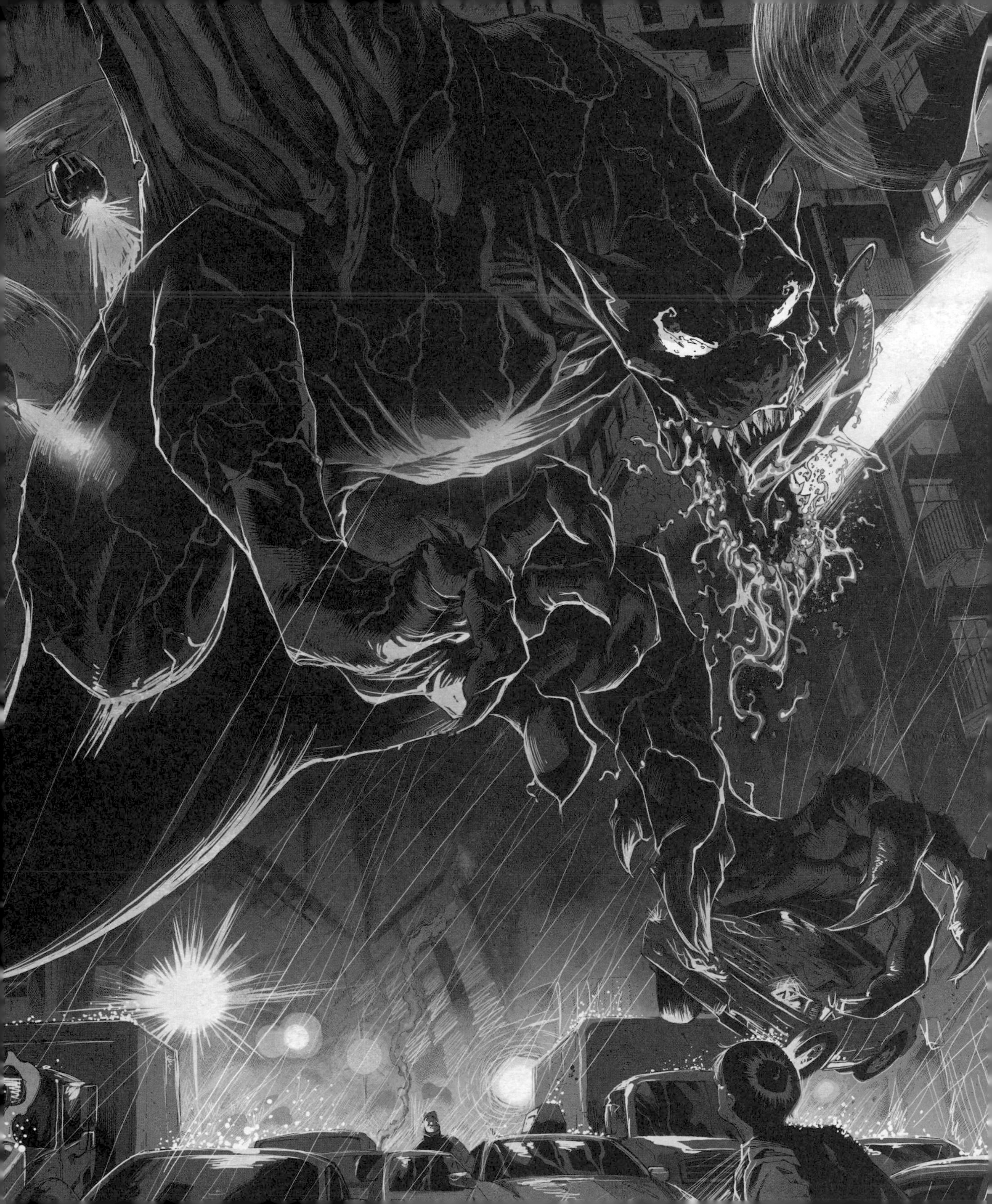

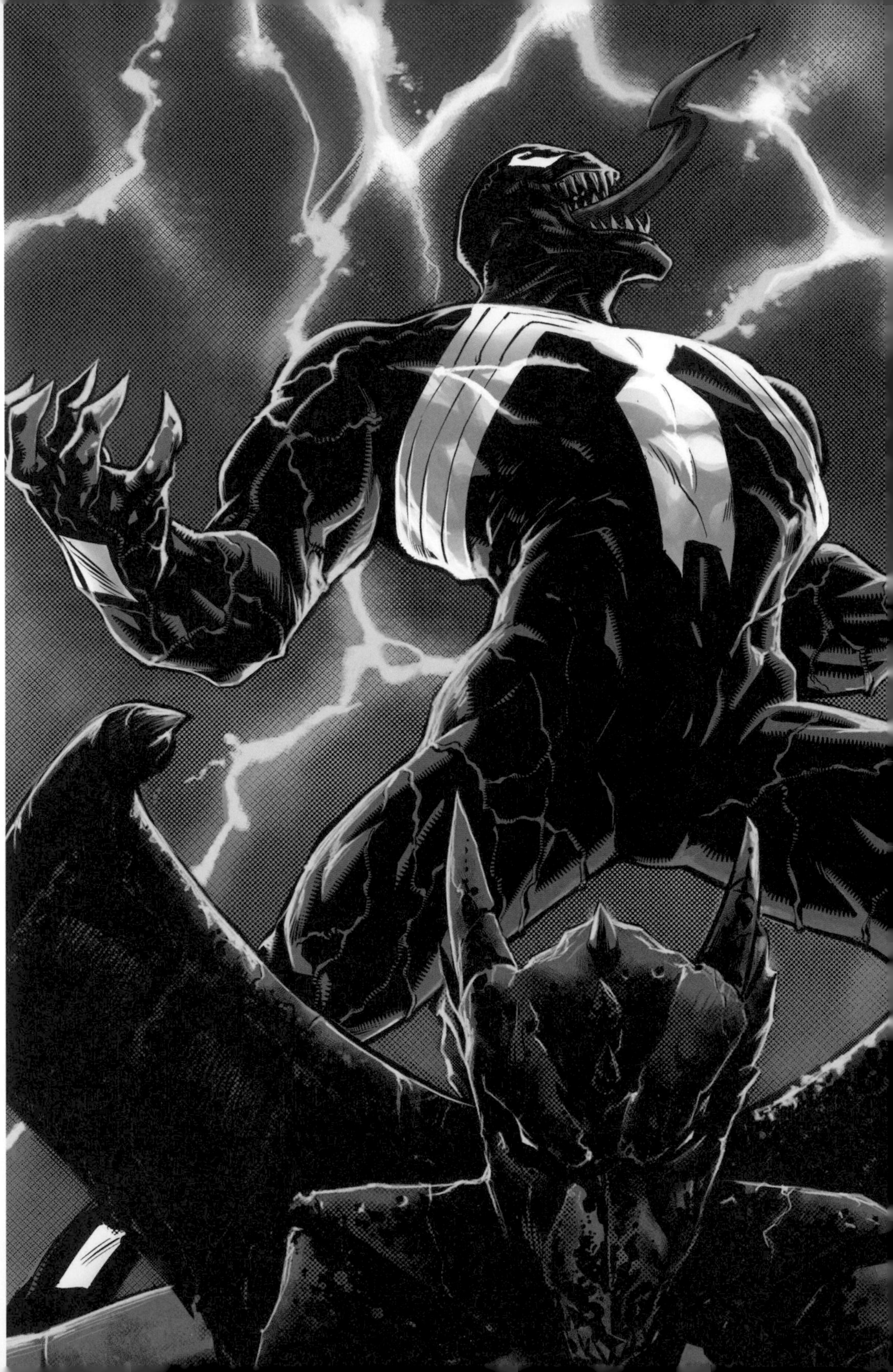

At the time of Earth's Vietnam War, agents from S.H.I.E.L.D. unearthed the body of Grendel and used its symbiotic properties to create a small team of deadly efficient Sym-Soldiers. While the enhanced fighters were put into cryogenic suspension at the end of the jungle conflict, they were briefly roused in the present day. This resurrection was detected by Knull, who was slowly reawakening inside his living prison. Establishing a psychic bond across the vastness of space, the dark god took control of the Sym-Soldiers and then projected his own essence into the inert form of Grendel. Wearing the dragon as an avatar, Knull took to the skies above Manhattan. He luxuriated in his newfound freedom and promised to rain fire upon the city.

"I became the hive mind. The god-host." Knull

Former journalist Eddie Brock found himself drawn to Grendel like a moth to a flame. For years, Brock had shared his life with a Klyntar symbiote. Linked together both emotionally and physically, the pair delivered a harsh form of street justice as the unconventional hero Venom. In ordinary circumstances, the symbiote covered its host like a jet-black costume and bestowed on him enhanced abilities similar to those of the hero Spider-Man. Now, though, the symbiote was acting unpredictably. Driven by an ancient race memory, it was compelled to merge with Grendel, to become part of the restored hive mind.

Venom rising
Eddie Brock merged with an alien symbiote to become the monstrous antihero Venom, bringing a harsh vigilante justice to New York City.
Venom #1, Jul. 2018

Although the symbiote resisted the call for a time, Brock feared he would soon lose his alien partner to the hive mind's malignant influence. Furthermore, he was horrified by the destruction he witnessed as Grendel rampaged across New York City. Teaming up with Miles Morales, a teenage hero who shared the Spider-Man identity with Peter Parker, Brock went on the offensive.

Symbiotes were particularly vulnerable to cacophonous sound and Brock hoped Morales' unique "venom blast" would be loud enough to subdue Grendel. Unfortunately, the beast recovered almost immediately from Spider-Man's sonic assault. Knull was growing stronger all the time, and he was now able to manifest on Earth. Although his body was still caged in the Klyntar, his consciousness appeared before a startled Brock and Morales. He taunted them and revealed that his ultimate plan was to fly Grendel across the depths of space and liberate his corporeal form from its confinement.

Recognizing Knull's power was growing exponentially, and that the dark god posed a threat to all of creation—not simply Earth—Brock chose to flee rather than engage in a direct confrontation he knew he could not yet win. He took Morales with him; the teenager was in a weakened state following the release of his venom blast. Leaving Morales to recover, Brock armed himself with a huge arsenal of explosives and returned to the fight. He detonated all his ordnance and the resulting explosion was powerful enough to stun Grendel. While the creature was compromised, Brock locked it in a blast furnace and burned it alive. This broke Knull's connection to Earth, leaving the dark god still trapped in his cosmic cage. Brock had won the day—had saved the world—but Knull was now fully awake. A primordial god had been reborn in the modern age.

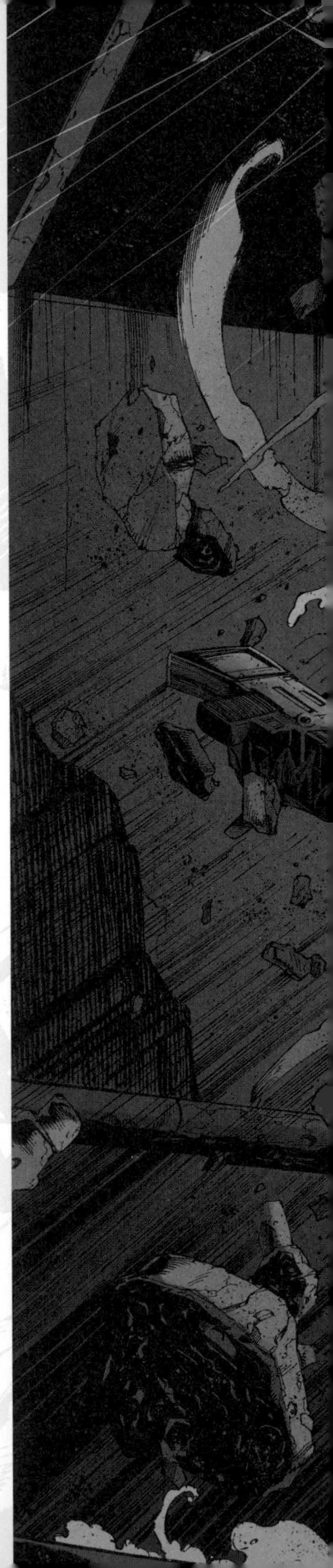

Jaws of death
Braving Grendel's gnashing teeth and fiery maw, Venom planned to detonate a huge arsenal of military-style ordnance and subdue the slavering monster.
Venom #6, Nov. 2018

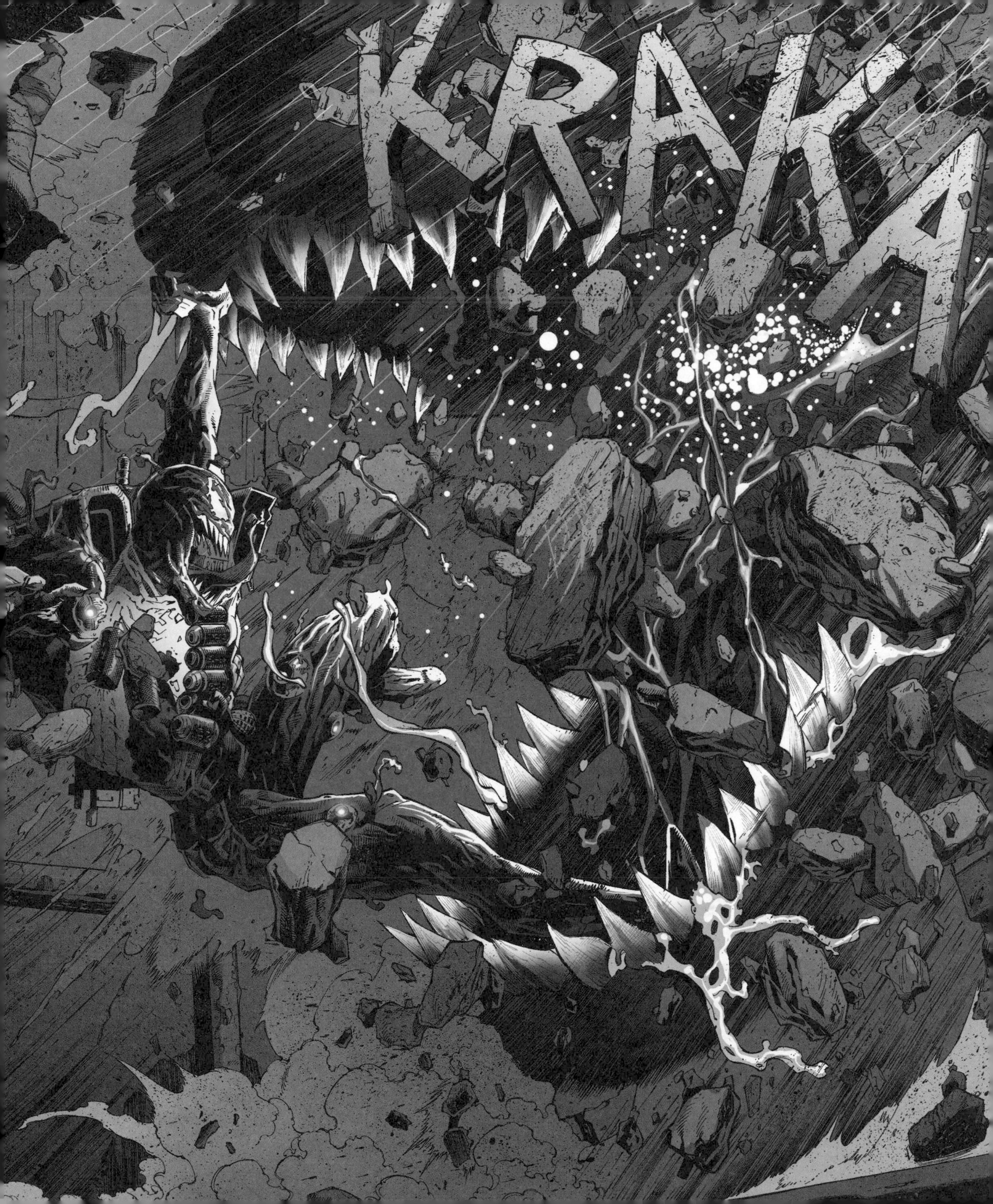
KRAKA

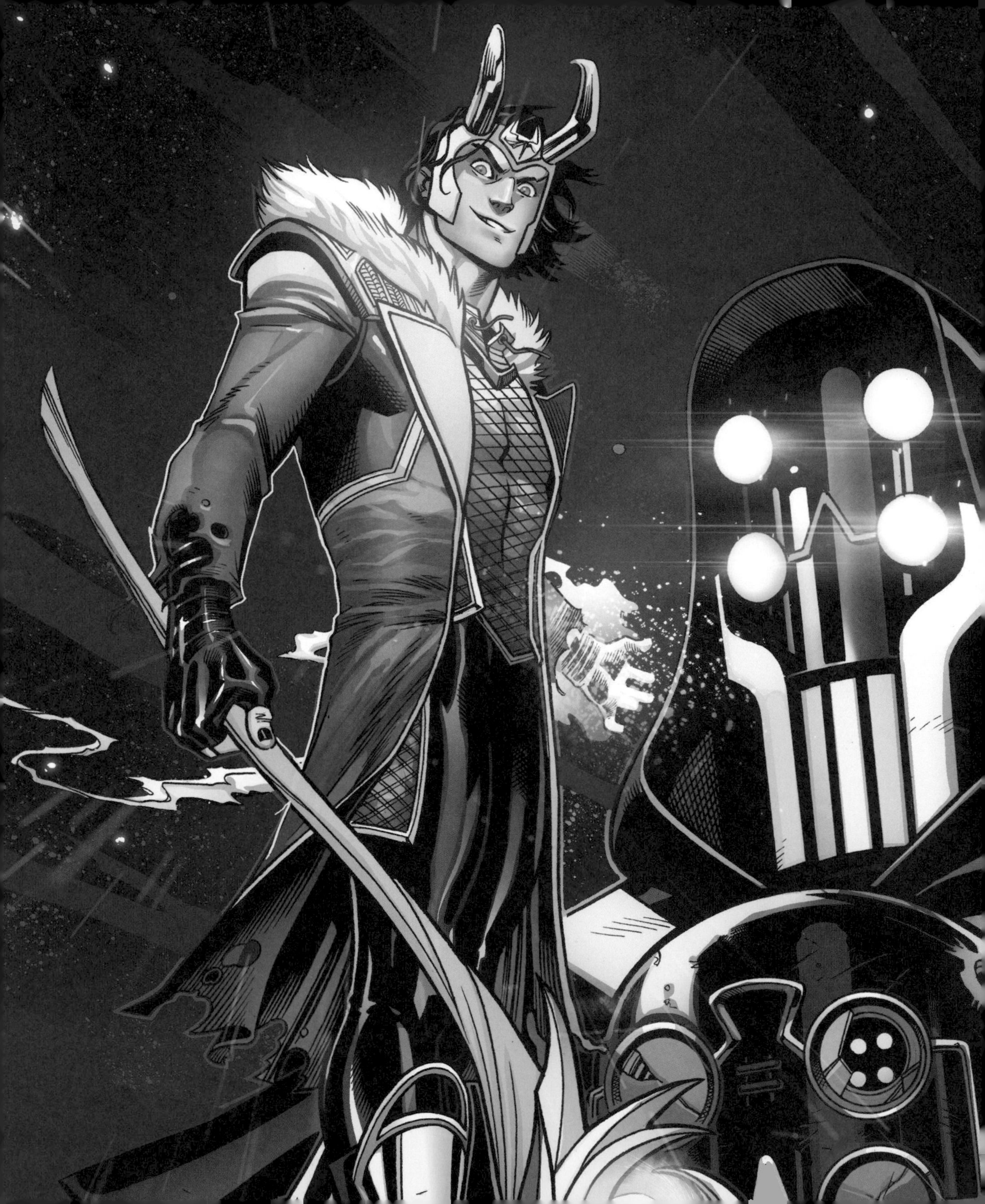

The Final Host

As a new race of Dark Celestials descended from the stars, humanity's ultimate destiny was revealed and a fresh team of Avengers was forged from the fires of a conflict sparked in the prehistoric past.

Throughout his long reign, All-Father Odin enjoyed regaling the court of Asgard with tales of his legendary exploits. He would tell of monsters slain and quests fulfilled—of heroic compatriots and devilish foes. In time, these stories became little more than background noise, as familiar to Asgardians as the everyday events of their own lives. Thus, many of the gods stopped listening to their king's epic sagas. Loki, though, spurned as he was by the nobility of the Golden Realm, sat quietly and attentively, absorbing each and every word. In this way, he learned of his adoptive father's adventures on primeval Earth and how the Prehistoric Avengers had killed the mad Celestial Zgreb and buried his body underground.

In modern times, the God of Mischief finally acted upon this knowledge. He planned to steal the fallen Celestial's energies, but was amazed to discover that Zgreb was not dead, but dormant. The alien Horde infestation was still rife within him, artificially maintaining his life. What's more, the insect-like Horde had proliferated, crawling beyond the Celestial's inert body to establish a network of underground nests. Loki revived Zgreb and took him into outer space. Together, they sought out other Celestials, who quickly succumbed to the Horde and were transformed into malevolent caricatures of their former selves—Dark Celestials.

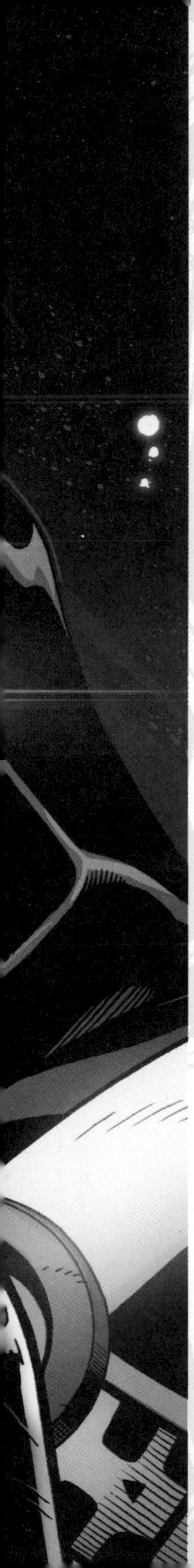

Delivering darkness
God of Mischief Loki helped create a new race of Dark Celestials, bringing his so-called Final Host to Earth to eradicate humanity.
Avengers #2, Jul. 2018

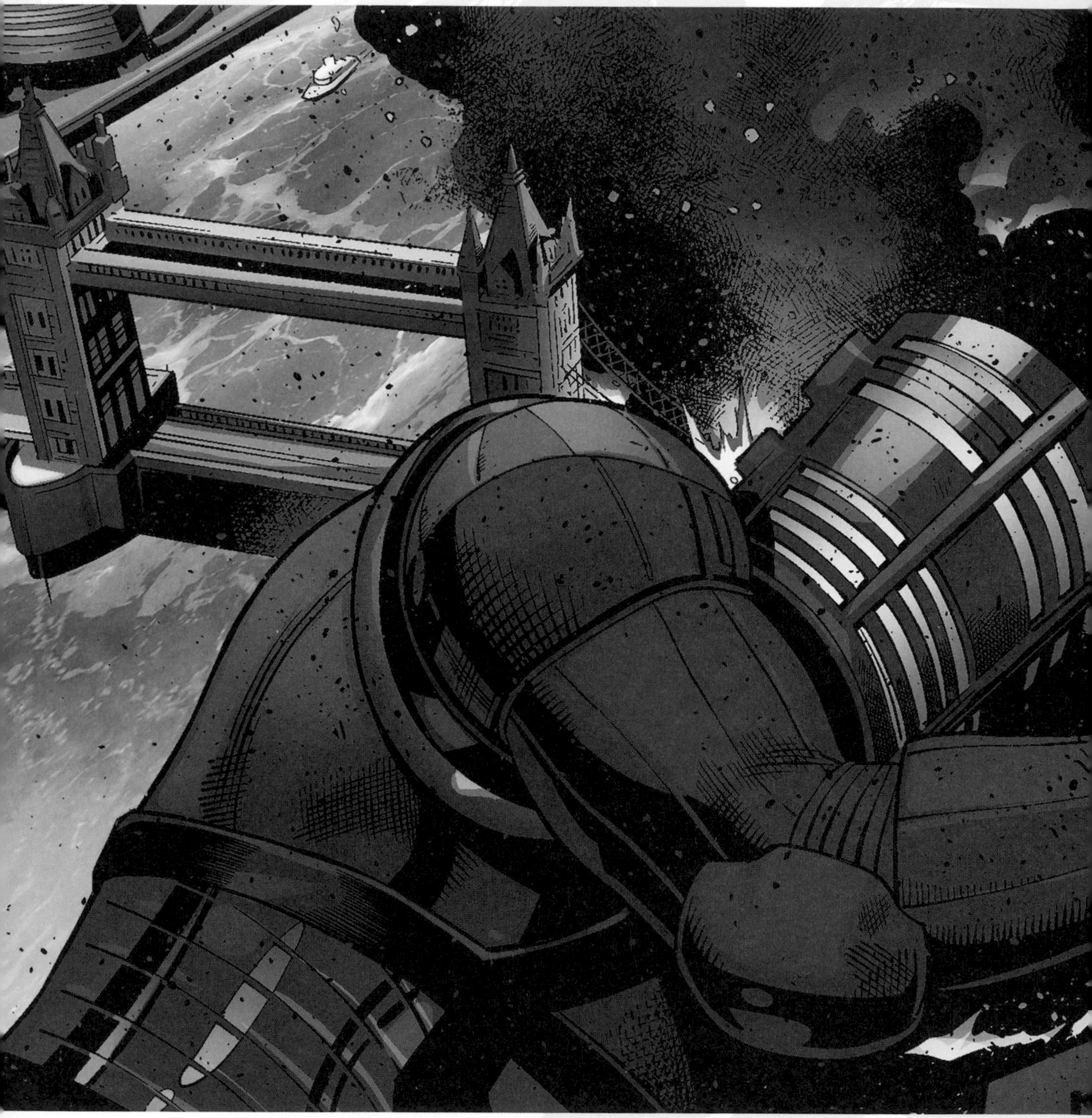

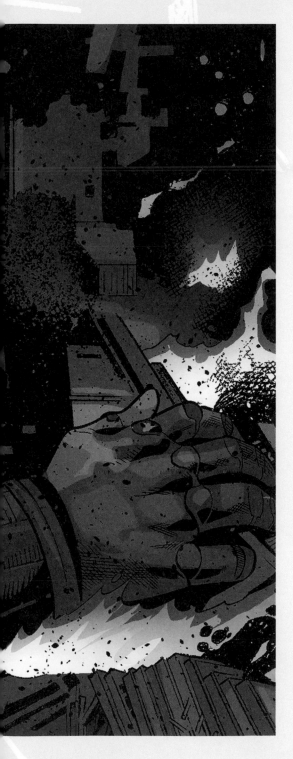

Those who could not be turned were killed and dropped on an unsuspecting world. And so, gargantuan space gods rained down upon the Earth, destroying landmarks and causing panic.

Responding to the emergency, Captain America urged Iron Man and Thor to join him in a reformed Avengers squad. The team had fallen apart in recent times, the strains of so many existential crises finally taking their toll and breaking the bonds of fellowship. Now Captain America asked his old friends to set aside any lingering differences and lead by example. Taking inspiration from the veteran hero's words, they agreed, and the Avengers were reborn. Joined by the photon-powered Captain Marvel, the new team did all it could to minimize the damage caused by the falling space gods.

The Avengers soon discovered that one of the stricken Celestials, Eson, was still alive, although badly wounded and lying prostrate across the breadth of the Hudson River. Before the heroes could decide what to do next, Loki and his Dark Celestial allies appeared in the skies above New York City. The God of Mischief announced it was the time of the Final Host, and that he had brought the Dark Celestials to Earth to wipe away the bothersome scourge of humanity. A brief battle ensued, but Loki and the Dark Celestials easily repelled the Avengers' attack and then retreated to faraway Siberia to instigate their genocidal plans.

Fallen gods
The monumental Arishem was just one of numerous space gods who were sent crashing to Earth as a prelude to the Dark Celestials' invasion.
Avengers #5, Sep. 2018

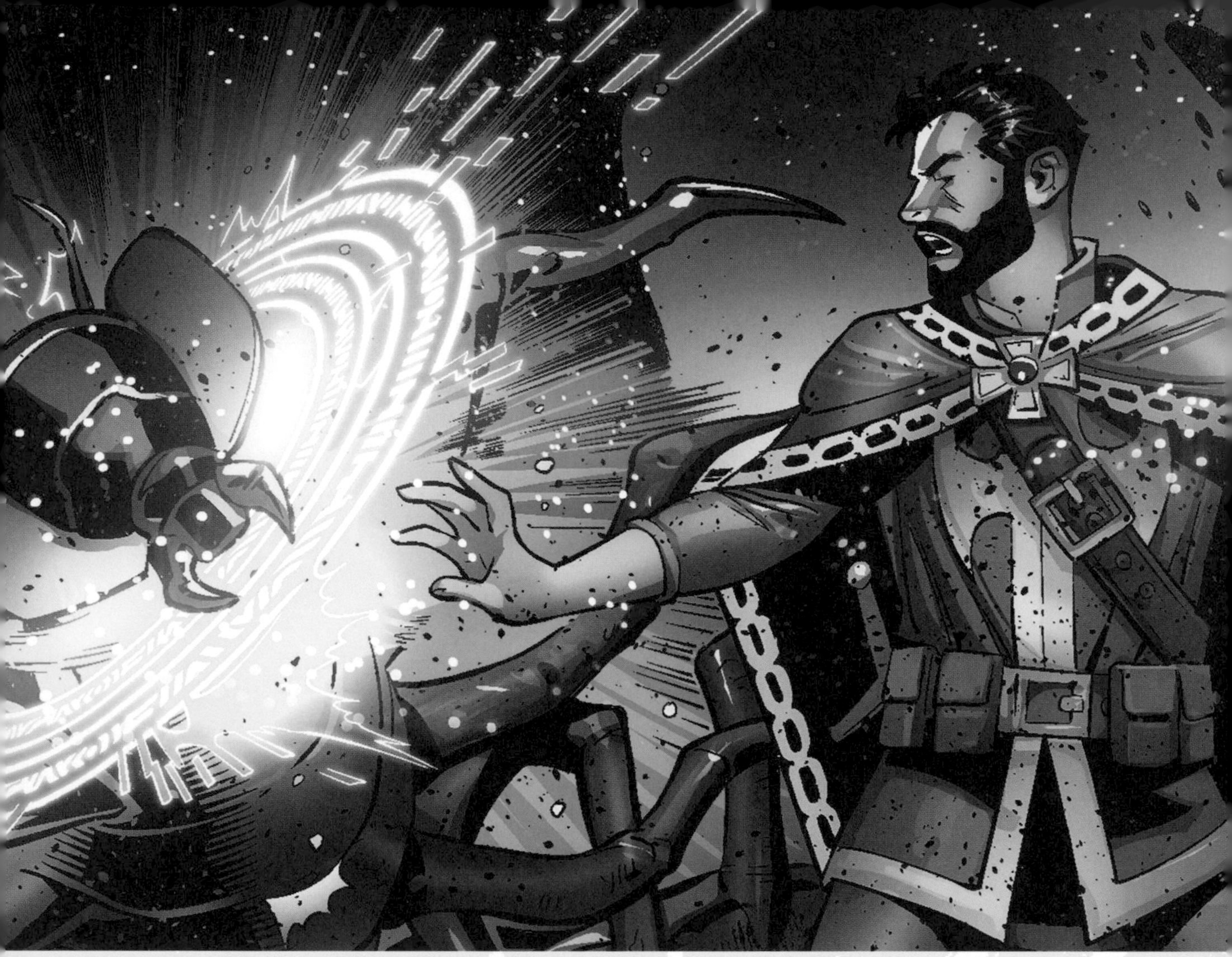

Meanwhile, in their cavernous abode, the Horde had been disturbed by the removal of Zgreb and had begun to tunnel their way to the surface of the planet. Earth, it seemed, was beset from both within and without. Alerted to the Horde threat, the Black Panther called on Doctor Strange to help turn back the terrifying tide. Although fully supportive of the mission, the Sorcerer Supreme cautioned that he was not yet back to full strength following the recent Empirikul attack. Magic was returning to Earth, but only very slowly. Some spells worked, while others were completely ineffective. In fact, it transpired that the depletion of magical energy had disrupted the mystical wards placed around Zgreb's tomb

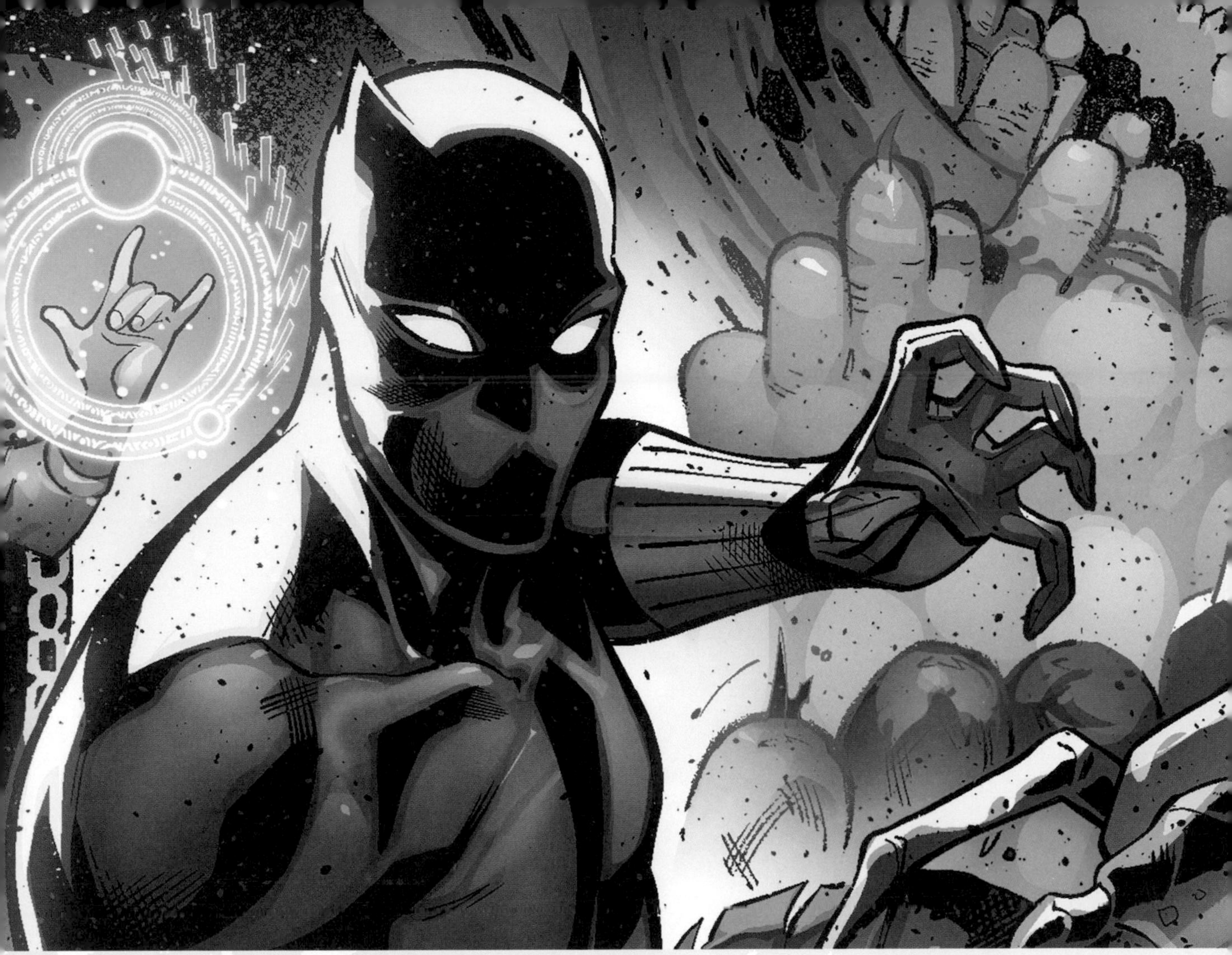

in ancient times by Agamotto, and this had contributed to the Horde's ability to roam more freely than in the past.

Doctor Strange and the Black Panther ventured below the Earth to fight the alien insects, but were soon overwhelmed by the multitudinous creatures. Far away in New York City, the Celestial Eson sensed the heroes' distress and used the last of his power to teleport the Savage She-Hulk from a nearby park to the site of the underground battle. She was joined by the supernatural hero Ghost Rider, who had been propelled into action following an encounter with the Horde. Together they saved the Sorcerer Supreme and the King of Wakanda from almost certain death.

Underground resistance
Investigating a disturbance from below ground, Black Panther and Doctor Strange encountered the insect-like Horde. They fought valiantly to hold back the swarm.
Avengers #3, Aug. 2018

The four heroes returned to New York City, where they joined the Avengers in a desperate quest to find some way to thwart the Dark Celestials. Iron Man and Doctor Strange flew to Olympus to consult with Ikaris and his immortal brethren. However, when they arrived, they found most of the Eternals dead. Ikaris still held on and, with his dying breath, he explained that his race had been consumed by a suicidal madness as a result of Loki's mass cull of the Celestials. He died in Iron Man's arms, suggesting cryptically that humanity's salvation lay in the power of the Uni-Mind.

Elsewhere, Thor and She-Hulk turned to Odin for assistance and were given access to the fabled Blood of Ymir. Odin warned that the life fluid of the legendary Frost Giant would not guarantee the Avengers victory over their foes, but it would make their inevitable death "far more spectacular."

"If we fall, we fall together." Thor (Odinson)

The Avengers reconvened and followed the Dark Celestials to Siberia. Iron Man donned a gigantic suit of armor, the Godkiller MK II, while Thor and She-Hulk imbibed the Blood of Ymir to grow to the same towering height as the Dark Celestials. Ghost Rider also received a significant power boost when he abandoned his muscle car ride to pilot the body of a dead Celestial into battle. The giant-sized Avengers were still hopelessly outmatched, however, especially when the Dark Celestials added to their ranks by reanimating the corpses of the fallen Celestials.

Avengers reassemble
A new line-up of Avengers came together to defend the world from the existential threat of the Dark Celestials.
Avengers #1, Jul. 2018

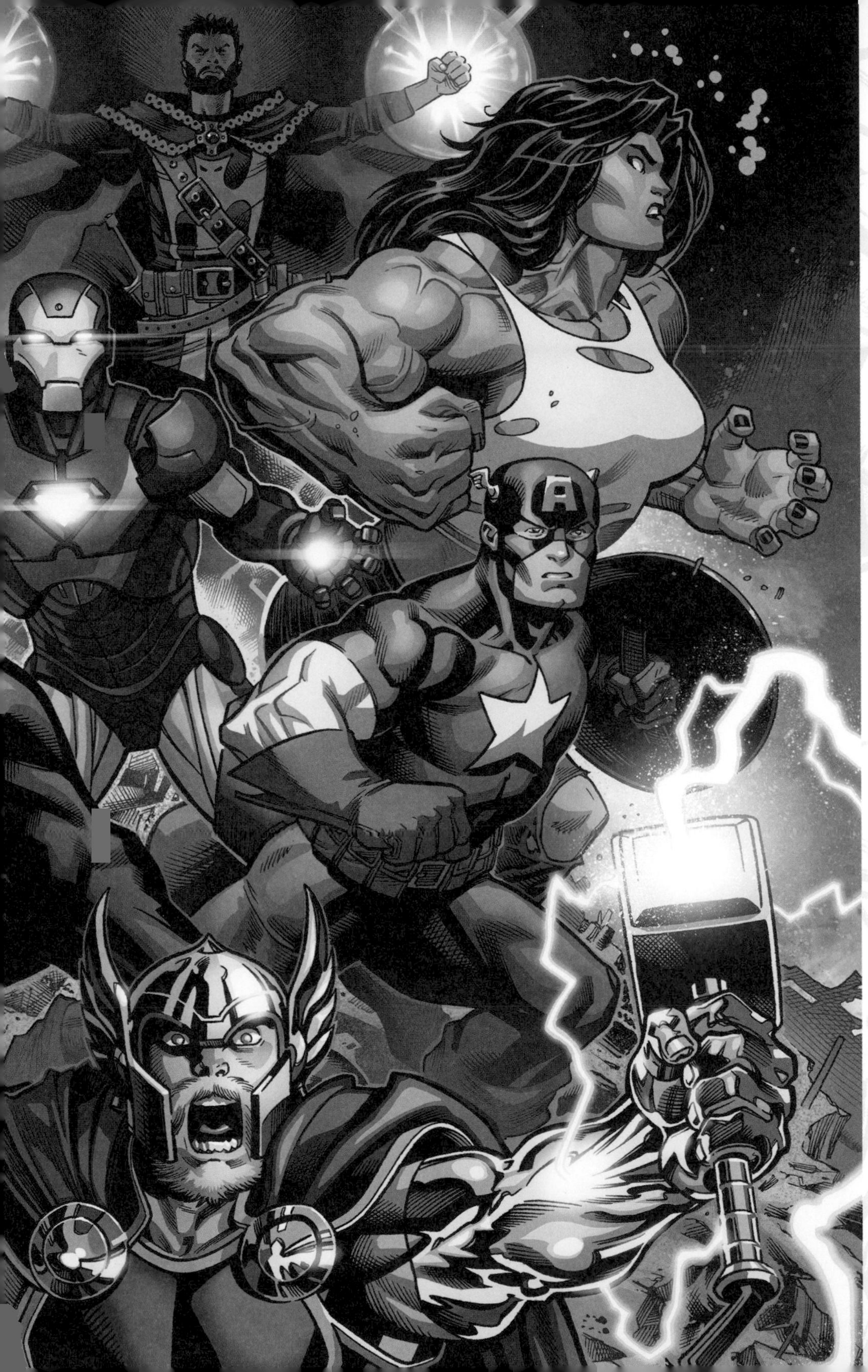

When all seemed lost, a post-hypnotic command placed in Iron Man's mind by the dying Ikaris, suddenly became active. The Armored Avenger had been granted temporary access to the power of the Uni-Mind, which he now used to bond telepathically with his teammates and channel their strength into the giant Ghost Rider. With an instruction from Captain America to "Save the world," Ghost Rider released the accumulated energy of his comrades in a single all-powerful blast. The resulting shock wave toppled the Dark Celestials and killed the Horde.

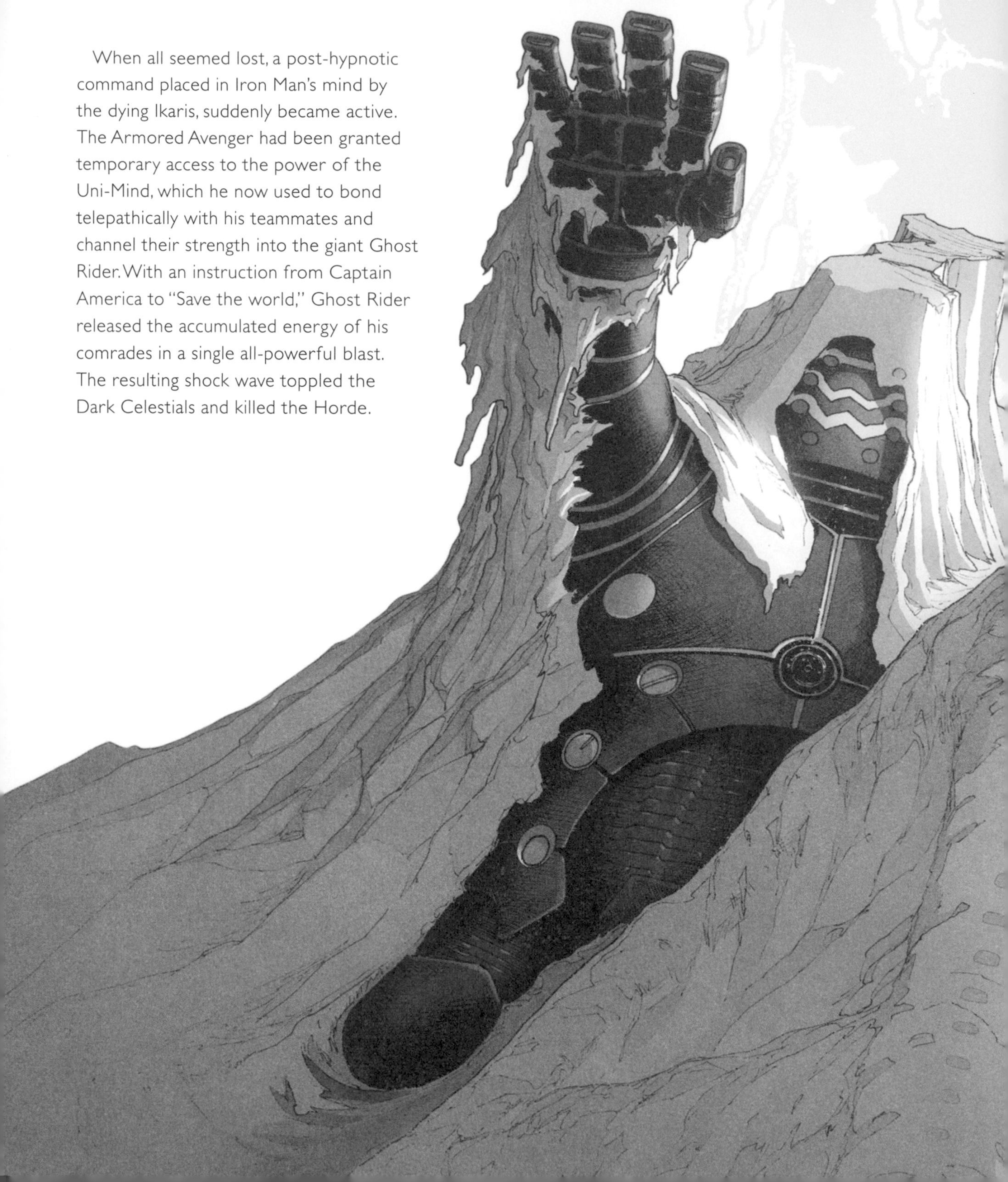

The fallen Celestials were restored to full life as a side-effect of the energy storm and, once again in control of their own destiny, joined forces with the Avengers to subdue the Dark Celestials and capture Loki. In the aftermath of victory, it was revealed that this had been the Celestials plan all along. Recognizing that the world had been infected by the Horde in ancient times, they had subsequently interfered in humanity's evolutionary path, nurturing the latent superhuman gene, so that one day the Earth would produce a unique strain of powerful individuals. The Avengers were the end product of that grand scheme, a band of women and men powerful enough to finally put a stop to the deadly scourge of the Horde.

"The Final Host is defeated." Captain America

The Celestials departed Earth with Loki and the Dark Celestials as their prisoners. Before they left, they gave the Avengers a gift. They raised the body of the Celestial Progenitor from beneath the North Pole where it had lain, undisturbed, since the formation of the planet. In a very real sense, the Progenitor's long-ago death had given rise to the modern age of Super Heroes, with the space god's cosmic energies making Earth a fertile breeding ground for superpowered beings. Now the Progenitor's armored shell would find fresh purpose as the Avengers' new headquarters—an empyrean relic from the mythic past contributing to the ongoing legend of Earth's Mightiest Heroes.

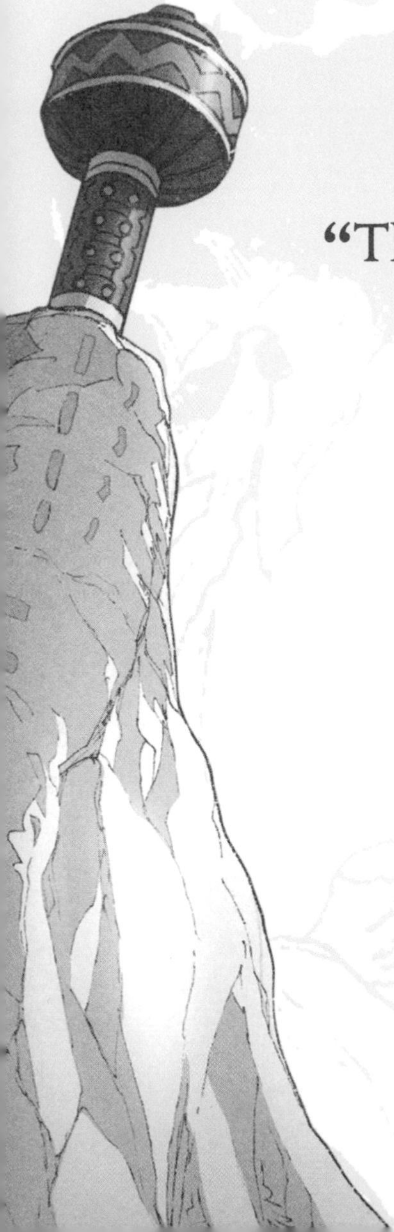

Mountain retreat
The shell of the long-dead Progenitor became the team's new headquarters —Avengers Mountain.
Avengers #8, Nov. 2018

INDEX

Page numbers in *italics* refer to illustrations

Senior Editor Cefn Ridout
Senior Art Editor Clive Savage
Designer Lisa Sodeau
Copy Editor Kathryn Hill
Production Editor Siu Yin Chan
Senior Production Controller Louise Minihane
Managing Editor Sarah Harland
Managing Art Editor Vicky Short
Publisher Julie Ferris
Art Director Lisa Lanzarini
Publishing Director Mark Searle

Cover artwork Tom Whalen

First American Edition, 2020
Published in the United States by DK Publishing
1450 Broadway, Suite 801, New York, NY 10018
20 21 22 23 24 10 9 8 7 6 5 4 3 2 1
001–318479–Dec/2020

© 2020 MARVEL

A catalog record for this book is available from the Library of Congress.
ISBN 978-1-4654-9775-8

DK books are available at special discounts when purchased in bulk
for sales promotions, premiums, fund-raising, or educational use.
For details, contact: DK Publishing Special Markets,
1450 Broadway, Suite 801, New York, NY 10018
SpecialSales@dk.com

Printed in China

ACKNOWLEDGMENTS
DK would like to thank James Hill for his text and expertise;
Brian Overton, Caitlin O'Connell, Jeff Youngquist, and Joe Hochstein at
Marvel for vital help and advice; Alastair Dougall for editorial assistance;
Jon Hall and David McDonald for design assistance; Julia March for proofreading;
and Vanessa Bird for creating the index.

For the curious

www.dk.com